FINDING THE WAY

RACHAEL C. DUNCAN

Finding the Way
by Rachael C. Duncan

Copyright © 2023 Rachael C. Duncan

Paperback Edition

Published in the United States by Wolfpack Publishing, Las Vegas

CKN Christian Publishing
An Imprint of Wolfpack Publishing
9850 S. Maryland Parkway, Suite A-5 #323
Las Vegas, Nevada 89183

cknchristianpublishing.com

Paperback ISBN: 978-1-63977-136-3
eBook ISBN: 978-1-63977-135-6
LCCN: 2023941236

NOTE FROM THE AUTHOR

When I began researching for my first novel, I was
blown away by the vast array of resources available
concerning anything and everything biblical! It was
thrilling to discover such a wealth of information
regarding topics that have always intrigued me.

Because I write Bible-based novels, please allow
me to state this simple disclaimer: The novels I write
are categorized as biblical fiction, which means I
have taken some literary license in instances where
the Bible story itself remains silent, unclear, or disputed. As you can imagine, a LOT of controversy
and differing opinions regarding certain biblical
characters, settings, dates, etc. As we dive into the
book of Acts in the *Crowning Crescendo: A New
Era*, exact dates pertaining to certain events remain
unclear, disputed, or unknown. I've also encountered tricky questions such as, *How do we know if
every story in Acts is listed in chronological order?*
Especially as the narrative passes back and forth
between multiple characters and settings, these
questions tend to surface. So just a reminder, while
based on the biblical narratives, this is indeed a
work of fiction.

So as I tackled this exciting new project, I sought
to honor the Word of God, and then I asked the Lord

to help me fill in the blanks in a way that will reach my readers, touch their hearts, draw them closer to Him, and bring these beautiful Bible stories to life, inspiring each reader to dive headfirst into the precious Word of God!

Thank you for purchasing this novel. I hope you are blessed page after page!

FINDING THE WAY

PRELUDE

Caiaphas

A.D. 31, Jerusalem

Donning the glorious white linen reserved for this sacred Day of Atonement, Joseph Caiaphas passed the glowing menorah in the Temple, plagued by a deep, abiding inner darkness that even the steadily burning seven-branched fixture could not dismiss. Perhaps it was the sin of this godless people weighing so heavily upon his shoulders. Today, he would cleanse the nation of unrighteousness. He, Joseph Caiaphas, high priest of Israel, possessed the power of life and death. He alone stood between these stiff-necked, rebellious people and a holy God. He was the bridge, the one to whom ultimate power had been given. He relished it, savoring the smell of fresh blood upon the altar.

Furrowing his brow in a futile attempt to suppress his fury, Caiaphas mentally dismissed the foolish dimwits who flocked about Jerusalem proclaiming that the pestilent Prophet, Jesus of Nazareth, had made atonement for the sins of all people by His death and alleged resurrection nearly six months ago. The strange happenings within the Temple compound simply fueled the high priest's desire to disprove the rapidly growing sect now called The Followers of the Way. Why, in recent months, the Temple doors often swung open of their own accord, as if beckoning anyone and everyone to enter into the presence of God. One erring priest had commented it was as if the invisible hands of angels flung open those massive doors, beckoning seekers toward the Most Holy Place. Even eerier than that were multiple occasions when the brightly burning candlesticks of the menorah—signifying the presence of God in the Temple—mysteriously blew out, leaving the holy chambers in utter darkness. Caiaphas was certain those cursed disciples of Jesus must be behind the bizarre happenings. Blasphemous fools! Joseph Caiaphas refused to relinquish his power to any man. Atonement was *his* to grant or deny.

And today, by his own pronouncement, the scapegoat had been led into the wilderness even as the second sacrificial animal was slaughtered. A scarlet ribbon, signifying the bloody sins of the people, was removed from the horn of the sacrificial animal and fastened to the Temple door. In the past, Caiaphas had savored the moment when that scarlet ribbon turned snowy white, indicating that God had accepted the sacrifice and thus cleansed the sins of the people. Moving calmly through the dimly lit chamber, Caiaphas stroked his beard thoughtfully as he considered this sacred act—an everlasting symbol of the power he wielded in his own two hands.

Emerging upon the Temple's graceful marble steps, Caiaphas paused before turning toward the towering, gilded doors. A chilly breeze swept through the Temple compound, and the telltale ribbon snapped smartly in response. Relishing the sharp sound, a brutal smile twisted the high priest's lips as his gray eyes traveled downward toward the frantically flapping ribbon. Reaching out, he drew forth as his cold eyes came to rest upon it.

Shockingly, *the ribbon remained the deepest shade of scarlet.* Scarlet—like the spilled blood of the saints. Scarlet—like the deathly stain of sin. Scarlet—like his own taut features, his color deepening in fierce, ungodly wrath. Gasping, Caiaphas withdrew a trembling hand as if a lethal cobra had sunk its venomous fangs deep into his flesh. Trembling in seething fury, a guttural growl escaped his throat as he recoiled in both fear and outrage.

For the very first time in the history of Temple sacrifice, the scarlet ribbon had failed to turn white as freshly fallen snow.

Balling his hands into white-knuckled fists, Caiaphas recalled the proclamation that had rung out upon Golgotha's bloody hill the moment before Jesus breathed His last: *It is finished.*

Caiaphas' gray eyes narrowed, forming two dangerously small slits. A low growl resonated deep within his throat as he tore the ribbon from the door in a fit of unrestrained rage, plunging headlong into the Temple. Pacing like a caged beast within the glorious Temple chamber, the high priest clutched the scarlet ribbon in an iron fist.

Instantly, without warning, the flickering candlelight of the seven-branched menorah ceased, encompassing the high priest in utter darkness.

Caiaphas knew only a moment of terror before his mouth hardened in defiance, forming a grim, uncompromising line. The followers of this blasphemous new sect would pay—with their lives and the lives of their wretched children. Blinded by his own fury as well as the inky blackness closing in on all sides, his hard mouth flattened, curving into a wicked, sardonic sneer.

It is finished? Not for him. In fact, it was only the beginning.

CHAPTER 1

Mary

Four years earlier...
Jerusalem

It was a lovely night for a moonlit stroll. Overhead, a dazzling canopy of glistening stars glittered like a vast sea of shimmering gems, bathing the age-old city below in glorious silver light. Strolling arm-in-arm with her beloved husband, Mark, Mary lifted her face heavenward, relishing the cool evening breezes that teased her sheer, scarlet head covering and tickled the elegant amphora earrings dangling from her ears.

"Jerusalem," Mary mused, her cultured voice laced with awe. "The beauty of this magnificent city never fails to steal my breath away."

"I feel the same way," Mark replied, pausing beside his wife and caressing her soft, bronzed cheekbone with the back of his knuckles. "About *you*."

Lifting observant gray eyes to her husband's,

Mary offered a mysterious smile. "I will never doubt the goodness of God," she said in her quiet yet straightforward manner. "How could He be anything but good when He gave me to you?"

"Truly Adonai has blessed us beyond measure," Mark agreed, taking Mary's hand as they resumed their leisurely stroll along a fashionably paved, torchlit avenue within Jerusalem's magnificent Upper City. Here, the streets were broad and well-kept, the surrounding landscapes neatly and meticulously manicured. The Upper City was home to the wealthiest and most famous residents of Jerusalem, including Joseph Caiaphas, the revered high priest. Even a luxury palace of the notorious tetrarch, Herod Antipas, graced the opulent region, in which the governor of Judea, Pontius Pilate, also resided during the rowdy festival seasons. Both the palace of Antipas and the house of Caiaphas was a mere stone's throw away from the magnificent, three-story Greco-Roman villa Mary shared with her husband near the Essene Quarter and the luxuriant ritual baths frequented by wealthy Upper City residents.

"Even so," Mark said quietly, drawing Mary from her silent musings and back to the present moment, "we must always remember that the Lord gives *and* takes away. Like our ancestor Job, we must choose to bless His name."

"I suppose we must always trust that His will is best, even if we feel bereaved," Mary observed, wondering if she possessed the faith and strength of Job. What if her husband were taken from her? What if they lost their laughing, teasing son, John Mark? What if her health failed her? What if the luxuries she had grown accustomed to were suddenly stripped from her, as they were from Job and his faithless wife? Would she stubbornly cling to her faith, or would she crumble beneath the weight of it all?

Sensing the direction of his wife's thoughts, Mark squeezed her hand, studying her lovely features in the soft moonlight. After ten years of marriage, Mary was still a stunning woman with waist-length, curly dark-brown hair she often pinned in elaborate Roman styles, a striking bronzed complexion, high cheekbones, full lips, and sharp, slender brows. Her delicate, aristocratic features were rather at odds with her fiery and sometimes dogged temperament, but Mark loved her passionate fire. Tall, slender, and dignified, she carried herself with the grace and bearing of a queen. Her elegantly clad form fairly resonated with an aura of intensity and unflinching determination, and yet she somehow possessed a feminine softness, a quietness about her, that he treasured.

Even more becoming than Mary's polished persona, however, was her unwavering commitment to Adonai, the God of her fathers. She was a strong, steadfast woman, full of faith and courage.

"We should head back," Mark sighed, noting the full moon rising in the night sky. "It's getting late."

"I treasure these evening walks with you," Mary said, her eyes confirming the truth of her words as she gazed up at her husband.

With a soft smile, Mark bent to kiss her gently before they turned to retrace their meandering steps.

An explosion of commotion interrupted their tender moment as the cries of a young girl pierced the night, followed by a man's angry shouts and the sound of a fierce scuffle.

Instantly, Mark swung into action, grasping his wife's delicate wrist and meeting her gaze. "Run home. Now! Don't stop until you are within the gates."

Mary's exotic gray eyes widened in horror. "I will not leave you."

Mark looked to her, exasperated. It was unlike her to defy him, but her concern for him was mirrored in her frightened expression. "Go! Now!"

At that moment, a young girl no older than eleven or twelve barreled around the corner of an elegant stone wall, weeping in terror—or was it rage—her dirty bare feet pounding against the paved stones like that of a galloping horse.

Her motherly instincts instantly engaged, Mary reached for the girl as she approached them, grasping her by the shoulders. "My child, are you hurt?"

"Let go of me!" the girl screamed, a flood of tears tracing slender lines down her filth-encrusted cheeks. "Let me go!"

Mary's heart nearly stopped as an ill-clad man swung around the corner, his face torn and bleeding as if he'd been attacked by a beast with vicious claws. Mary stared at the young girl before her with new respect. She hadn't a scratch on her.

Hearing her attacker's approach, the girl struggled violently against Mary's grasp. "He's after me! Let me go!"

Mary raised pleading eyes toward her husband, her message clear: *Get him, Mark.*

Protectively, Mark stepped in front of his wife and the trembling child, shielding them as the offender staggered up to him, clearly intoxicated. One look into the fierce eyes of Mary's husband, and the drunkard turned swiftly on his heels and ran for his life, retreating into the blackness of night.

"He's gone," Mary said, kneeling before the weeping child and taking her hands in her own. "You're safe now."

The young girl shook her head fiercely, her eyes afire. "I'm never safe!"

Mary exchanged one swift look with her husband, a silent message passing between them.

"Come with us," Mary said gently, squeezing the girl's hands. "We can help you."

"I don't need any help!"

"Have you a family? A home?" Mary asked, her heart breaking for the little girl.

Wary and distrusting, the girl shook free from Mary's grasp. "I have to go."

"But that man," Mary faltered, desperate to help her. "What if he returns?"

The homeless little fighter glanced in the direction by which her attacker had retreated, her eyes flashing angry fire. "I dare him to try again!"

Mary glanced at her husband. He hid a slight smile.

"Dear one, I am worried for you," Mary implored, rising, and stretching out her hand. "Come with us. A warm meal and a change of clothes would do you a world of good."

The little one faltered for the faintest moment, glancing anxiously between her powerful rescuer and the kind woman before her.

"I can't!" Turning on her heel, the girl took off with the speed and agility of an athlete in Herod's stadium, her tousled, honey-colored braid bouncing against a bony, ill-clad back.

For the briefest moment, Mary considered racing after her, swooping her off her feet, slinging her over her shoulder, and carrying her home. But it was quite clear that the child was frightened and untrusting. Perhaps that would only make matters worse.

"My name is Mary of Jerusalem," Mary shouted boldly after the girl's retreating back. "Please seek me out, dear one, when you are ready."

Shaking her head in dismay, Mary gazed into the somber face of her husband. Understanding her pain, he took her hand and held her gaze with sympathetic eyes. "Commit her to God, beloved. She is in His hands."

Heart pounding, Mary stared into the gathering darkness, beseeching her merciful God on behalf of the hurting child. *If it's Your will, Righteous Father, grant me the privilege of reaching that dear child.* Squaring her shoulders in righteous determination, Mary resumed her steps.

Thy will be done, Father.

CHAPTER 2

Mary

"You've scarcely touched a thing. Is the meal not unto your liking, beloved?"

Jarred from her anxious thoughts by her husband's concerned inquiry, Mary raised warm eyes toward Mark and tried for a convincing smile. "The meal is delectable, as always," she insisted, stopping herself from toying anxiously with the long golden stem of her elegant goblet. "Our chefs always prepare impeccable cuisine, my love."

"But you have no appetite this evening," Mark supplied with a knowing smile as his eyes traveled toward their eight-year-old son. "I daresay your mother's distress has failed to dim your own appetite, John Mark."

Having violently ripped the leg from a plump honey-glazed partridge, John Mark glanced sheepishly between his father and mother. As usual, his good humor overcame his sense of embarrassment as he pointed out with an impish grin, "I am, after all, a growing boy. Don't I require sustenance?"

Mark exchanged a humorous look with his wife, his dark eyes twinkling. "As long as you moderate your intake of so-called *sustenance* with discipline, my growing boy. After all, we wouldn't want you growing in the wrong direction."

Grinning, John Mark closed his teeth around the glazed partridge leg with boyish zeal.

Perched gracefully upon her own comfortable Roman couch called a *lectus*, Mary smiled at their son's ridiculous antics as she reached for a cluster of vine-ripened grapes, mostly to appease her husband. The family lounged about the large rectangular table in proper Greco-Roman style: three elegantly upholstered couches arranged about a low table. This allowed for the servants to deliver steaming entrees and replenish emptied goblets with ease, as one side of the table remained opened to them. As was expected, each family member reclined upon their left side on their own couch, their right hand extended toward the succulent feast gracing the decorated table. Mary had always enjoyed sharing intimate family meals in this dining hall, a smaller, cozier version of the magnificent *triclinium* where she and her husband often hosted lavish banquets to entertain wealthy neighbors or prestigious business associates.

Fondly observing the familiar surroundings within the impressive dining hall, Mary couldn't help but notice the beautifully painted, towering marble pillars supporting the monumental structure, the colorful frescoes splashed across the walls, the Grecian urns spilling over with fresh, seasonal flowers. Elegant Babylonian tapestries fluttered in the gentle evening breezes, revealing the breathtaking pastels of sunset beyond grand, arched windows gracing the outermost wall. A splendid chandelier overlaid in glistening gold hung high above the table, its festive oil lamps burning brightly and filling the chamber with a cheery glow. Beneath the gilded legs of the richly upholstered *lecti*, swirling mosaics meandered in dizzying geometric patterns across the cool marble floor.

The color in Mary's cheeks deepened as her thoughts were pulled—*once again*—toward the poor little homeless girl with the fire in her eyes and her rare honey-colored hair. Mary couldn't help but wonder why the Lord had blessed her own family with such good fortune when others hadn't a decent cloak to their name, nor their daily bread.

Delicately sampling a glistening grape, Mary's sharp brows furrowed, her thoughts troubling. Though Mark was extremely faithful in presenting their tithes and offerings at the Temple, she was certain that God had blessed them so that they, too, could bless others. Surely God expected more than an obligatory offering at the Temple, a tithe surrendered simply because it was required. Remembering the fear and desperation in the eyes of the homeless little one, Mary's heart broke anew. How could she possibly bless others when they refused to accept her charitable overtures?

"It's that poor child, isn't it? Her situation troubles you."

Yet again, Mary was drawn from her own brooding thoughts by her husband's gentle prodding.

"What poor child?" John Mark quipped, his brown eyes wide with interest as he reached for a sticky apple braised in fresh honey and cinnamon.

"We met a homeless girl on our evening stroll several nights ago," Mary explained, her eyes clouding with concern. "I've made several inquiries, but no one seems to know who she is."

"The Lord knows," Mark assured her, straightening to a sitting position and reaching for his wife's slender hand. "You must entrust the little one to Him, my love."

Mary smiled faintly, clearly wrestling against her own uncertainty.

"My lord!"

The entire family turned their heads at the unexpected address from the porticoed entryway.

Stationed within the vestibule leading into the smallest *triclinia* and peeking rather timidly through the entryway was the staid overseer, wringing his hands a bit nervously. "I apologize for this untimely intrusion, but—"

"Tobias!" Mark addressed the bearded overseer who also functioned as his own personal secretary with warmth. "You needn't hide in the vestibule. Come in!"

Hesitantly, Tobias slipped into the triclinium, his obsidian eyes darting about nervously as he addressed his master. "It's Zev, my lord."

The doorkeeper. Mark and Mary exchanged looks of concern.

"Apparently," Tobias continued nervously, "he's had a bit of trouble at the gate."

"What kind of trouble?" Mark asked, his eyes

narrowing in dismay.

"A filthy little street urchin appeared at the gate, not requesting but rather *demanding* entrance. She asked for Mary of Jerusalem, undoubtedly expecting a handout. Naturally, Zev sent her away."

Startling poor Tobias, Mary sprang to her feet, her face ashen.

The overseer's eyes darted nervously toward Mary's taut form, his neatly oiled mustache twitching in consternation. Clearly flustered, he plunged ahead with his explanation. "When Zev had no choice but to forcefully remove the beggar child, she clambered right up one of the tall palms near the gate, my lord, and she has stoutly refused to come down. She's quite a rascal, vehemently refusing to leave until she has spoken with Mary of Jerusalem."

"Praise God!" Mary's hand flew to her heart as the color began to return to her face. Relief flooded her entire being as she slipped past the floundering Tobias, the fabric of her trailing gown rustling softly as she disappeared swiftly beneath the elegant doorway in a flurry of joyous excitement.

At this unexpected turn of events, Tobias looked to his master, clearly lost. "My lord?"

"Thank you, Tobias," Mark said, acknowledging the overseer with a good-humored smile. "You may return to your duties."

The aging Tobias stared at Mark rather blankly, blinking several times before finding his tongue again. "Yes, my lord. As you wish."

Amused, Mark watched as the typically composed servant hurried from the room, certainly puzzling over the family's odd behavior. Exchanging a knowing grin with his young son, Mark lifted his goblet in triumph.

"It would seem your mother's prayers have been answered."

***

Heart pounding rapidly in her chest, Mary flew through the narrow vestibule, passed beneath another impressive doorway, and crossed the vast reception hall, attempting to compose herself as she reached the grand entrance of her palatial home. Elaborate bronze double doors groaned in protest as they bowed inward at Mary's insistent push. As the entire villa was encircled by impenetrable stone walls, Mary was required to cross a lavishly decorated stone courtyard to reach the outer gate where visitors often called. Passing under the large, arched stone entrance sheltering the iron gates, Mary held back a smile at the sight that met her eyes.

Just outside the grand entrance towered magnificent palms, standing guard like watchful sentries on both sides of the intricately patterned iron gate, lining the entire width of the stone wall. There, on the right, clinging with all her might to the sturdy trunk of one such palm, was the fiery little wraith, just beyond Zev's reach.

Zev, the doorkeeper, also functioned as captain of the household guard. Red-faced and furious, his fierce bearing indicated that he was clearly miffed, having been outsmarted by the little rascal.

"Zev!" Mary cried, rushing to his side, and gazing up at the determined intruder clinging stubbornly to the slanted trunk.

Zev wheeled around to face his mistress, his jaw clenched, one hand gripping the dagger strapped at his belt. "What would you have me do, my lady?" he snarled through gritted teeth.

Laughing musically, Mary motioned him aside. "It's all right, Zev. I asked her to come."

The swarthy doorkeeper arched his brows, incredulous. Clearly, he had no desire to grant his nemesis entrance. "*Her*?"

"Yes, *her*," Mary responded stoutly. "And why not? She is a brave and noble girl." Stretching her hand toward the rebellious climber, Mary offered her most convincing smile. "Come, my dear one. I am overjoyed at your presence."

Mary didn't miss the triumphant grin the girl cast in Zev's direction. Stifling another smile at Zev's obvious consternation, Mary watched as the young lady loosened her grip and slid down the tree as easily and nimbly as a monkey might swing from vine to vine.

"Thank you, Zev," Mary said politely, offering the zealous doorkeeper a pacifying smile. "I'll take it from here." Reaching for the girl's hand, Mary led her beneath the impressive stone entryway, pausing inside the luxurious courtyard. The girl's eyes grew wide as she surveyed her opulent surroundings: graceful marble benches were scattered about the lovely, enclosed patio, several encircling a magnificent marble fountain in the shape of a fierce, winged lion, his majestic head thrown proudly back, mid-roar. Glittering droplets of water sprayed forth from the lion's wide mouth, falling in silvery sheets upon the water gathered in the glistening pool below. Grecian urns spilled over with fragrant flowers, the fresh scent wafting pleasantly upon the cool evening breezes.

Mary noticed the girl appeared rather mesmerized by the lion-like fountain. Smiling softly, she asked, "Do you like it?"

"I thought graven images were forbidden."

Mary was taken aback by the girl's candid observation. She must have been reared in a religious household. Recovering, she quickly explained, "By God's standards, *worship* of graven images is strictly forbidden. And our religious leaders do, indeed, prohibit us from forging images of any creature in the heavens, on the earth, or in the sea. However, fantastical creatures—such as this winged lion—are permitted, as they are not to be found in the heavens, on the earth, or in the sea—or anywhere else, for that matter," Mary chuckled. "It's a silly little nuance, I know. But we often entertain prestigious religious leaders, and we must be careful not to cause offense."

"I shall get straight to the point, Mary of Jerusalem."

Mary did a double take, startled by the abrupt turn in conversation. Kneeling before the girl, she took both small hands in her own and smiled warmly. "I'm listening. But first, what is your name, dear one?"

The child's eyes darted nervously about, as if she were hesitant to disclose any more information than necessary. She must have trusted the compassion reflected in Mary's kind eyes, for she responded after a slight pause, "My name is Tabitha."

"Tabitha," Mary repeated the name fondly, taking a moment to observe the one who bore it. "A lovely name."

Despite Tabitha's shabby garment, dirt-streaked cheeks, and tousled hair, her vibrant eyes shone from her small face like two magnificent gems. Her thickly lashed, slanted eyes weren't necessarily green, nor hazel, but some unique shade in between the two. Her rare coloring, paired with her deeply tanned skin, created a truly exquisite combination. She was a little beauty, despite her fierce persona. Her features were lovely, bathed in the soft light of the gathering dusk.

"I made some inquiries about you," the small girl stated matter-of-factly, and Mary had to bite back a surprised chuckle, tickled by Tabitha's frank nature. "My sources assure me that you are a kind woman, worthy of trust."

Mary could barely contain her mirth at the little one's reference to her *sources*.

"Is it true that you own and operate the thriving oil press of Gethsemane?"

"My husband is indeed the owner and operator of the olive press, among other things. He owns another press in Cyprus, our homeland. Mark does love his business ventures," Mary admitted, studying the girl before her with great interest.

"Cyprus," Tabitha repeated, arching a brow in question. "I was told you are Jewish."

"I am," Mary amended, smiling faintly. "As I'm sure you know, our people are scattered all over the known world. I was born and raised in Cyprus. I met my husband there."

"You are Hellenists, then," Tabitha mused, referring to the Jews scattered across the vast Roman Empire—as well as those dwelling in Judea and

Galilee—who clung to the faith of their fathers even while adopting the language and customs of the Greeks.

"Your Greek is flawless for one reared in a traditional Jewish family," Mary observed.

"My father understood the importance of speaking the universal language of the empire along with our nation's native tongue, Aramaic."

"Your father was a wise man."

"Why did you leave Cyprus for the holy city?"

Mary smiled patiently. "We relocated to Jerusalem when my husband recognized the wisdom of operating an oil press supplying oil to one of the world's most dependable and worthy patrons."

"The Temple," Tabitha supplied knowingly.

"Yes," Mary responded, her eyes alight. "You are very astute, my daughter."

"I see you are a woman of business, as am I," Tabitha replied with the air of a practiced merchant. "And I have come to make you an offer."

Mary was intrigued. "An offer?"

"I don't expect to be coddled or pampered," Tabitha continued. "If you are looking for decent help, well, I'm a very hard worker, and I can earn my keep. I'm also a skilled seamstress, and I can sew or mend just about anything. In exchange for food and a roof over my head, I offer my services to you, Mary of Jerusalem. Will you accept this offer of mine?"

Blown away by the child's determination, drive, and diction, Mary rose to her feet, shaking her head in awe. "Tabitha, you are a brilliant girl and I see great potential in you. It is admirable that you wish to earn your daily bread. Of course, I accept your offer!"

A faint smile of satisfaction played about the corners of Tabitha's rosy lips.

"I must ask," Mary ventured, awed, "how you learned to speak and negotiate so?"

A look of deep sadness flickered across Tabitha's young face. Lowering her gaze, she said quietly, "My father was a successful merchant, my mother a gifted seamstress. I'm only twelve years old, but they taught me all they knew."

"What happened to them, beloved?"

Tabitha's eyes filled with the same familiar fire. "A break-in at my father's shop. Both were murdered in cold blood."

Mary's eyes filled with tears of genuine sympathy. "But you were spared."

"I shouldn't have been," Tabitha said forcefully, shaking her head. "My mother sent me to fetch a few supplies at the market. When I returned, I found them…" her voice trailed off, her eyes haunted.

Longing to gather the poor child in her arms, Mary tipped Tabitha's chin upward, looking directly into her eyes. "My precious girl, I'm so sorry. So very, very sorry."

Clearly struggling to dismiss her grief, Tabitha straightened and squared small shoulders. "My father taught me to make the most of what you've been given. That's the best I can do."

"You are a remarkable girl," Mary said with great conviction. "And I have no doubt that our faithful God will accomplish marvelous things through you."

Tabitha looked unconvinced.

Cupping the girl's dirt-stained cheek with a firm hand, Mary looked directly into her eyes. "Tabitha, our God never makes mistakes. You were indeed spared for a reason, even if that is difficult to believe right now. But someday—someday soon, perhaps—all the pieces shall fall into place. And you will look back on this difficult season of your life, fully recognizing that God has worked all things together for your ultimate good."

Tabitha spoke not a word, her emotions carefully tucked away.

Aching for her, Mary took her hand and held her gaze, her gray eyes burning with conviction. "Until that day comes, beloved, can you choose to believe it, to cling to the promises of our gracious God?"

The silence that followed was deafening. But after a thoughtful pause, Tabitha offered a faint nod, her eyes betraying the slightest flicker of emotion. "I will do as you say."

Warmed to her very core, Mary smiled. "Welcome to your new home, dear one."

CHAPTER 3

Mary

A.D. 30, Cyprus

Striding gracefully alongside her older brother, Joses, Mary breathed deeply of the salt sea air, lifting her face heavenward, savoring the warmth of the late afternoon sun. The bustling port city of Salamis was alive and humming with frenetic activity. Mary adored a leisurely stroll through the northernmost part of this city. Salamis boasted a rather showy display of Greco-Roman culture with paved, column-lined streets and breathtaking marble statues. Complete with bustling agoras catering to both Roman and Hellenistic clientele, a lavish theater, a massive stadium, an impressive gymnasium, luxuriant baths, and even public latrines, the city of Salamis thrived under Roman rule.

Joses turned to smile at his sister as they approached a bustling market square. Dressed in luxe, imported finery, her dark hair styled and elegantly covered, her gait strong and sure, Mary was the perfect picture of a confident, cosmopolitan woman. "No matter where your husband's business ventures take you," he observed, his eyes twinkling, "you look as though you belong."

"I love to travel," Mary responded, wishing she could lift her elegantly embroidered head covering and bask in the sun's gentle warmth. Cool sea breezes tugged at her long brown curls as she took her brother's arm affectionately. "When Mark asked me to review his business holdings here—specifically the olive press—I was thrilled you agreed to accompany me, Brother."

"How could I refuse my little sister? Plus, this trip presents the opportunity to visit relatives and review my own investments here."

"You've been so busy discipling, traveling from town to town."

"Sometimes I still cannot fathom the fact that He chose me to witness, to preach among the Seventy."

Mary needn't ask who *He* was. Joses spoke of little else these days. "Should I be honored that both my brothers were selected for such a worthy cause?" she asked, her tone tinged with a hint of sarcasm.

Joses halted mid-step, turning to grasp his sister's forearms. His dark eyes burned into her own with avid intensity. "Jesus is the Son of God, Mary. Mark my words."

"I do hope so, though I can't help but worry for you," Mary confessed, her delicate brow furrowing in dismay. "Surely you've heard about what happened to the Baptizer at Herod's fortress in Machaerus? Rome will not tolerate revolutionaries, Joses."

Joses arched a brow, his dark eyes teasing. "Do I

look like a revolutionary to you?"

"You are the kindest, gentlest, most compassionate and encouraging person I know," Mary affirmed, eyeing her brother with warmth. He was a tall, rather average-looking young man with a sturdy build, simply dressed. She adored the sea of abundant light brown curls atop his head and filling his beard. "I just hope the Romans know that."

"My message is a gospel of peace, Mary," Joses assured her. "You have no need to be concerned."

"I can't help but wonder," Mary said quietly as they resumed their walk, "why our people cry out for a Messiah to vanquish the Romans. Is Roman rule such a dreadful thing?" With a graceful sweep of her arm, she encompassed the decadent, marble-pillared walk by which they traveled. "Rome has brought culture and security to many nations. If our people would simply stop resisting—"

"But you are forgetting that we are among the privileged few," Joses interrupted gently, his soft eyes filled with sympathy. "We have richly benefited from the business and commerce of this great empire. But there are thousands, possibly millions, among our own people who have not been so fortunate."

"Sometimes I fear our people only make matters worse for themselves by opposing the Romans," she observed, shaking her head sadly. "The Romans will rule whether we like it or not. Perhaps our people should focus on making the best of their situation, rather than crying out against it."

"There are those among us who would rather die than submit to Roman bondage."

"Is that why your Messiah has come?" Mary asked, a smile teasing the corners of her full lips.

"No," Joses replied with great conviction, the sureness of his tone prompting Mary to pause beside him. "Jesus has come to free us from our *sin*, Mary, not from the Romans. His mission is to save us from *ourselves*."

"But the blood of the Temple sacrifices purges us from sin," Mary pointed out.

Joses only smiled. "In time, it will all make sense."

Entering a magnificent, open-air market, Mary blanched in dismay when the hawking cries of a slave trader assaulted her ears. Cilician pirates were notorious for bartering off the lives of human beings, and wealthy landholders were all too eager to support the wretched practice.

"Why must men enslave other men?" Mary said defiantly, shaking her head in disdain. She considered the servants under the employ of her husband. They were treated with decency and respect. Mark compensated them generously for their service. But to be enslaved by a fellow human being, completely at the mercy of the capricious whims of a cruel master? Mary couldn't fathom the horrid possibility. She was reminded of her brother's warning only moments earlier: *You are forgetting that we are among the privileged few.* Once again, she considered the sobering fact that she had been placed on this earth to make a difference, to bless others as Almighty God had blessed her.

But how?

Scanning the boisterous crowd gathered at the slave auction, Mary noted that many young boys and girls had already been purchased, their new masters or the trusted slaves of wealthy landowners leading them away by a rope. Ruthless slave traders often displayed their "merchandise" in shifts—today, captured children were on display. The following auction might be limited to able-bodied men, those skilled in the art of musical instruments, or highly educated captives. Such men and women were worth their weight in gold, in the eyes of the populace.

A well-dressed man wearing an impatient expression strolled past Mary and Joses, tugging the rope tied to a young boy with swollen, tear-stained eyes, traces of a merciless beating still visible.

Led away like mere animals, Mary thought, her heart breaking. Lifting keen eyes toward the front of the crowd, Mary saw that the bidding was about to commence for what appeared to be the final sell of the afternoon.

"Shall we go forth?" Joses asked, his strong jaw clenched in disgust as the crowd flung jeers and insults at a shivering little wraith forced to stand before the crowd.

"Wait," Mary said, her tone uncompromising. She watched as the rotating wheel upon which the girl stood was slowly turned, operated by personal slaves of the trader. The punitively clad little girl stood with trembling hands clasped before her, her cheeks afire with shame, her large brown eyes downcast. A wooden *titulus*, or placard, fastened by a rope around her neck touted her name, age, and gender, as well as a short list of her limited abilities. The humiliating cap, which the little girl bore in shame, was not lost on Mary. Only slaves of little promise or skill were forced to wear the cap, cautioning potential buyers that the slave trader was unable to guarantee any special gifts or abilities on the part of the slave in question.

"Six hundred sesterces!" an overweight man, donning ridiculous finery and reeking of incense, shouted, eyeing the pretty little girl with malicious intent.

Mary's own eyes narrowed in suspicion. "Now what would a fat old man like that want with an innocent little girl?"

Joses met her gaze, his own heavy with sadness. "Must you even ask, dear one?"

Brows drawing together fiercely, Mary crossed her arms in disgust, eyeing the proceedings with contempt. "Something must be done."

"Mary," Joses said softly, sensing the direction of his sister's thoughts. "You can't save all of them."

"No," Mary stated, her eyes flickering with her familiar fire. "But I can save that one." Startling her brother, Mary pushed her way toward the front of the crowd, ignoring the scathing looks and bitter threats of those she passed.

Up ahead, the trader teased the crowd, hoping for a higher price.

"Seven hundred sesterces!" another cried, receiving a scathing glare from the wealthy old man, who in turn snarled above the din, "Eight hundred sesterces."

The throng of onlookers went wild, savoring the hunt. "Eight hundred sesterces?" one scoffed. "That ugly little wench isn't worth a denarii!"

"A half-shekel, perhaps?" another quipped, eliciting raucous laughter from the wicked assembly.

Tears trickled down the cheeks of the helpless little girl.

Reaching the front of the crowd, Mary drew alongside the heavyset potential buyer, challenging him with a withering glare. Turning her head regally, she boldly addressed the slave trader. "One thousand sesterces."

Gasps of surprise rippled among the gathering crowd as Joses drew alongside his sister, breathing heavily. "What do you think you're doing?" he hissed.

Anxiously fumbling with the gaudy golden rings stacked upon fat fingers, the rich man rewarded Mary and her brother with a blistering stare. "Twelve hundred sesterces."

"Fifteen hundred!" Mary shouted, daring the man to defy her.

"Eighteen hundred!"

"Two thousand," Mary hissed, her eyes flickering dangerously.

"Twenty-five hundred," the fat man countered, dabbing at the beads of perspiration dotting his meaty brow. Clearly, he was reaching the end of his financial rope.

The turbaned slave trader, clearly relishing the competition, looked to Mary in gleeful anticipation.

Mary stood still as stone, her rigid spine magnifying her uncompromising stance. Tilting her head to one side, she ignored her brother's silent amusement as her eyes pinned the slave trader in place. "*Three thousand* sesterces, and the girl is mine."

Gasps of shock, followed by a hush of amazement, rippled through the blustering crowd. Clearly, they doubted Mary's sanity. What on earth was she thinking—offering over three times the annual income of the average Roman—for such a small, seemingly worthless mite?

Fluttering his excessive robes like an aggravated bird with ruffled feathers, the fat man turned to

Mary, his face inches from hers. "You'll regret this."

Unflinching, Mary returned his glare head on. "No, sir, but *you* most certainly will, if you continue to prey upon innocent children. Shall I send for my husband, Mark of Jerusalem, the famous keeper of many groves?"

The man's pallor deepened in consternation.

"I see you've heard of him," Mary said coolly, ignoring her brother's obvious chagrin. Clearly, her threats rendered him a bit uncomfortable. "And I daresay you will be hearing from him if you try this again. Do keep in mind that he has many sources throughout this city, as well as friends in high places."

Grunting in dismay, the corpulent Cypriot turned on his elegantly sandaled heels and stalked away through the tittering crowd.

Mary crossed her arms, turning to face the slave trader. Raising knowing eyes toward him, she lifted dark, slender brows. "Well?" she prompted coolly, her tone challenging.

Tickled by his good fortune, the shady slaver lifted a triumphant fist, his leathery face splitting to reveal a gap-toothed grin. "Sold!"

The crowd erupted with jeers and shouts of disapproval, but Mary was not disturbed by the fickle crowd. She refused to be cowed by evil men.

Joses studied his sister, clearly torn between admiration and concern. "Dear one, what will you do with the girl?"

"First, I shall grant her freedom. Then, if she wishes to serve at the estate in exchange for a generous wage, she may do so. If she so desires, I shall take her to Jerusalem when I return and entrust her to Tabitha's care." Mary couldn't help but smile at the thought of Tabitha. At fifteen years of age, the girl had blossomed into a beautiful, capable young woman. Her fire was still there, to be sure, but she had learned to conduct herself with grace and poise—at least, when necessary, Mary thought, hiding her smile. Tabitha was a worthy addition to the household, and Mary took great pride in her.

At that moment, the trembling little figure upon the wheel lifted frightened eyes toward Mary as one of the trader's men roughly removed the placard about her neck. At Mary's and Joses's approach, the trader's slave offered Mary the rough wooden placard.

Accepting it sadly, Mary took note of the little girl's name: *Rhoda*.

Meeting the little one's timid gaze, Mary offered a brave smile. Rhoda blinked in fear, her soft brown eyes far too large for her emaciated face.

Heart going out to the girl, Mary knew she had made the right decision. Turning toward her brother, she offered a knowing smile. "God does all things for a purpose, dear brother. It's no accident we stumbled upon this market square."

Joses returned her smile. "Jesus taught me that we honor God when we care for the *least of these*. It would seem, dear sister, you share more of His philosophies than you realize."

Lips tipping in good humor, Mary touched her brother's shoulder affectionately. "Are you trying to make a disciple out of me, Joses?"

Joses offered a cryptic smile. "I have no doubt it will happen, Mary. It's only a matter of time."

CHAPTER 4

Mary

A.D. 31, Jerusalem

Baffled, Mary gazed about the luxuriant banquet hall so lavishly prepared. Since she and her husband were expecting a huge gathering of many priestly families with whom they would partake of the Passover feast, they had spared no expense decorating the largest room on the third floor of their palatial villa. A massive, rectangular table, soon to be piled high with festive fare, crossed the expanse of the monumental Upper Room. Beautifully upholstered couches surrounded the triclinium-style setup, a smattering of plush pillows and cushions dusting each inviting seat. The magnificent chamber fairly glowed, bathed in the warm, flickering light of countless oil lamps. Decorative garlands graced the walls, complimented by overflowing urns of fresh spring flowers. The room was filled with the heady fragrance of the delicate blossoms. Everything was perfectly in order, exactly as it should be. Everything, that is, except for one small detail...

There were no guests to attend the banquet.

Shaking her head in dismay, Mary leafed through the mound of letters she had received throughout the late afternoon. The letters had been pouring in for hours, one right after the other. Each one had borne the seal of a powerful priestly family—along with each priest's deepest regrets that he and his family would be unable to attend the lavish banquet she hosted in honor of the sacred Passover. For nearly a decade, Mark and Mary had welcomed Mary's distant relatives into their home to celebrate the sacred feast, for she and her brothers were proud descendants of the Levitical priestly line. Why, they had always shared Passovers with those who served the God of their fathers, ministering in His magnificent Temple.

Until now. Something was amiss.

Gracefully exiting the breathtaking chamber, Mary descended a sweeping stone staircase, deep in thought.

It was the first day of Unleavened Bread, a holy and sacred day for any observant Jew. Why, to excuse oneself from partaking of the Passover feast was bordering blasphemy! She supposed one or two of the priestly families claimed a reasonable excuse for bowing out tonight. But *all of them*? What on earth could possibly be more important to a Levite than partaking of the feast God Himself had instituted centuries ago?

Descending yet another flight of steps, Mary emerged at the bottom of the sprawling staircase, pausing to survey several servants scurrying about the magnificent reception hall, tending to various tasks before the Passover officially commenced. Sighing sadly, Mary realized that the grand chamber would remain vacant this evening. She had greatly anticipated ushering her guests into this great room, making each one feel welcomed and valued.

The hall was truly an impressive affair. Elegant, straight-backed, gilded chairs lined the entirety of one frescoed wall. The marble floor boasted a dizzying array of brightly colored mosaics, corresponding with the marvelous frescoes splashed across all four walls. Even the ceiling was intricately patterned and decorated.

"You look distressed, my bride."

Drawn from her churning thoughts, Mary conjured up a warm smile and reached for her husband as he entered the reception hall with long, confident strides.

Taking her hand in his own and intertwining his fingers with her long, slender ones, Mark smiled down at her. "What troubles you?"

Holding up the disconcerting stack of regrets in one free hand, Mary's lips tipped in rueful amusement. "The Upper Room is lavishly decorated and beautifully furnished, the chefs have prepared a feast worthy to grace the table of a king, and yet—"

"And yet," Mark finished for her, "we find ourselves sorely in need of guests."

"What is happening, Mark?"

"The city is in turmoil," Mark mused, his eyes distant. "You can feel the tension hanging heavily in the air. It's nearly suffocating."

"But why?"

"Only God knows," Mark responded wryly. "But

I'm sure He has a plan. He always does."

"But what are we to do now? We have invested so much time and effort to make this the most spectacular Passover feast of which we have ever partaken, and now we have no one to share it with."

"Surely your brothers, Joses and Antigonus, will still be joining us."

"Antigonus' family is staying with his daughter, since her husband is with Jesus."

"And Joses?"

"He, too, will dine with Antigonus."

"God knows what He is doing, Mary," Mark reminded her, tucking a stray ringlet of dark-brown hair behind her ear. "We must trust that."

"I was so looking forward to this evening."

"And if the Lord has something better in store for us?"

Mary gazed into the face of her husband, somewhat exasperated. "Perhaps the Lord hadn't anything to do with this, Mark. Perhaps the conduct of our priests is simply shameful."

Mark laughed out loud. "Shameful?"

"Yes," Mary supplied rather vehemently. "The Passover is important, Mark. Why, Adonai commanded us to keep this feast even before the Law! Before the Prophets! When Almighty God delivered our ancestors from bondage, He commanded the blood of the sacrificial lamb be shed to atone for sin. The blood was to be spread upon the doorposts and lentils of our father's homes, as a covering. Those covered by the blood of the lamb were protected from the Destroyer. Of all the commands our God has given us, the very first was this: to *receive the lamb*, to accept it. To partake of it. The priests have snubbed their arrogant noses at God's everlasting statute."

Running a strong hand down the length of Mary's elegantly clad arm, Mark offered a calming smile. "But we needn't follow suit, dear one. Our family will honor the call of Adonai."

"We shall be honoring His call for months, I'm afraid," Mary said, maintaining her dignified, polished composure with great effort. "How on earth will the three of us consume a feast of such mammoth proportions?"

"My lady?"

Deep in their somewhat heated conversation, the couple had failed to notice Tabitha enter the reception hall from the ornate vestibule at the home's main entrance.

"Tabitha," Mary said, wearily drawing a hand to her forehead. "What is it, beloved?"

At sixteen years of age, Tabitha had blossomed into a lovely young woman. Dressed in practical, functional garb, she carried herself with both grace and strength. Despite the simple garments she donned, her presence was arresting, her face and form exquisite. Rather like her polished mistress, undulating, scarcely contained energy radiated from Tabitha's entire being despite her carefully maintained composure. Her hazel-green eyes, often flashing, were both observant and intelligent. Her golden hair still had a mind of its own, so she often tied it in a simple braid or secured a thick bun at the nape of her neck. Even so, wayward curls spilled out despite her best efforts, framing her face in the most becoming way.

Glancing innocently between her master and

mistress, Tabitha hid a knowing grin, sensing Mary's chagrin. "Zev is all worked up again," she informed them, her eyes sparkling with mischief.

"The cause?" Mark asked.

"There are two men at the gate," Tabitha continued, her eyes alight with suppressed interest. "Disciples of Jesus."

Mary's heart skipped a beat. Joses, Antigonus, and her niece's husband—one of the famous Twelve—had ultimately convinced her that Jesus was, in fact, the Messiah. Mark had believed even before she had accepted the truth. Though she was still a bit unsure about His mission, who other than God's Anointed One possessed the power to heal the sick, raise the dead, and restore sight to the blind?

"Go on, Tabitha," Mary prodded, her interest piqued. "Which disciples? Simon Peter?"

"I would have recognized your niece's husband, my lady. No, two others from the Twelve."

"Have they stated a request?" Mary shot back, her excitement rising steadily.

"The disciples followed a servant from your kitchen as he returned with a pitcher of water. Apparently, Jesus had instructed the disciples to do so. He told them to ask for the master of the house, and so they have. I believe they seek a quiet, private place to share the Passover meal," Tabitha finished in a rush. "Now what shall I tell Zev before he self-implodes?"

Exchanging a knowing look with his wife, Mark said without hesitation, "Send them in."

"Yes, my lord." Smiling jubilantly, Tabitha turned swiftly on sandaled heels and hastened to perform Mark's bidding.

Mark turned to face his wife, his eyes filling with warmth and tenderness. "It would seem," he said gently, brushing his knuckles against Mary's prominent cheekbone, "that the Lord had a plan, after all."

Mary shook her head in disbelief, her bright eyes alight with wonder. The feast fit for a king which she had so faithfully overseen would, in fact, grace the table of a King.

"Mark, do you see the wonder of it all?"

"Tell me, beloved."

"Jesus is coming. The Savior Himself shall dine in our home."

Mark smiled softly, sharing in her joy.

"We shall indeed keep our God's sacred command, my husband," Mary declared, basking in the unspeakable glory of her Father's will. "For tonight, we truly shall receive the Lamb."

The Lamb of God who takes away the sin of the world.

CHAPTER 5

Tabitha

Seven weeks later...

Tabitha's rare coloring of honey-toned tresses and vibrant hazel-green eyes paired with a smooth, bronzed complexion was certainly not the only unique thing about her. Rather like her beloved mistress, Mary, Tabitha was striking in many ways. Her entire being resonated with a restlessness that always lingered just beneath the surface, though she had learned to mask it well—almost as well as her poised mistress. As a child, Tabitha had adored Mary, her rescuer, determining to become *just like her*. As a result, Tabitha carried herself like Mary, with grace and confidence, though she was certain she would never quite possess the effortless, queen-ly and regal bearing of her lady. Full of impatient energy, the young maidservant attempted to curb her restlessness when necessary, which seemed to be most of the time, much to her great angst and chagrin. She recognized she was no longer a child, and as such she was expected to behave as a proper young woman rather than a laughing, teasing girl.

It wasn't easy. Tabitha was so full of passion she scarcely knew how to contain it. Bold like Mary, she agonized over her seeming inability to tame her wayward tongue. *He who has knowledge spares his words,* she often reminded herself—*after* regretting a thoughtless outburst, usually the resulting of her quick and fiery temper. *A man of understanding is of a calm spirit.* Ruefully, Tabitha had memorized these wise proverbs of Solomon, hoping to draw upon them in moments of fierce temptation. *Even a fool is counted wise when he holds his peace; when he shuts his lips, he is considered perceptive...*

Now, as Tabitha tidied the largest chamber of the third floor, known by Mary's family and staff—and now the disciples—as the Upper Room, her thoughts raced in a thousand different directions as she contemplated all she had learned in recent weeks.

For as long as she could remember, she had sought to follow in the footsteps of her mistress—the woman she admired more than anyone else on earth. And she admitted it was a worthy goal, for Mary was an impeccable woman. But, through the teachings of Jesus, Tabitha now recognized that merely attempting to emulate the character of a godly woman simply wasn't enough. Many areas of her life required a complete transformation, an eager readiness to submit to the Father's will.

Even in her greatest attempts, Tabitha realized that, by her own strength, she had failed in many ways. Though she possessed many similarities to her self-appointed role model, Tabitha still struggled in her walk. *Doesn't Mary ever struggle?* She often wondered. Had Mary moments of weakness, in which she succumbed to temptation like any other mortal? If so, Tabitha saw no evidence of such a struggle. Mary was determined and steady, whereas she, Tabitha, was simply headstrong. Mary was a capable woman who, with seemingly little effort, mirrored the exasperatingly *perfect* housewife described in the Proverbs of Solomon. Sighing, Tabitha acknowledged that she was easily distracted and prone to rushing haphazardly through her daily tasks. And even though no one would have dared to question Mary's unwavering capabilities, that woman firmly relied upon God for strength and guidance—not upon herself. Filled with regret, Tabitha realized that *she* tended to rely solely upon *herself* rather than God—a dangerous habit that had taken root during her time as an orphan battling for survival in the streets of Jerusalem. Tabitha's heart constricted as she considered these troubling things. Why was she tempted to doubt God's loving watchcare and provision? Didn't she believe He would always do what was best?

Tabitha had confided these doubts and frustrations to Mary only once, bemoaning her own weaknesses and feeling quite certain that she was the least faithful of all of God's children. But Mary had promptly assured her that every single one of them—herself included—was a work in progress.

"I am an unworthy role model," Mary had insisted. "Look to Jesus, Tabitha. Follow *His* example, not mine."

Now, days later, Tabitha reminded herself of Mary's practical remonstration: *Look to Jesus. Fol-*

low His example.

Oh, how Tabitha wished she had known Jesus even longer, loved Him even more! If only He was still here to guide her in the right direction.

Good heavens! Look at you—wallowing in your own self-pity! Once again, Tabitha checked her wayward thoughts. *Many never even met the Savior. I should be thankful for the precious moments I shared with Him! Focus on what He taught you!* Shaking her head, Tabitha's lips tipped in a rueful half-smile. *Father, forgive me for fretting. Help me abide in You. I know I cannot bear fruit unless I abide in You, for You alone are the true Vine. I am simply a branch. Without You, I can do nothing. But with You, Lord, nothing is impossible!*

Mary appeared in the doorway then, Tobias directly behind her. "Excellent work, as always, Tabitha," she said affirmingly. "I asked Tobias to join me in order to review a few important notes."

"Of course, my lady," Tabitha responded, reaching for the broom she'd propped against the wall.

"The number of followers joining the disciples here grows larger by the day," Mary mused, carefully evaluating the condition of the large Upper Room. "I must be certain we are prepared to host the meetings even as the numbers increase."

"I can scarcely wrap my mind around all that has transpired here in recent weeks," Tabitha declared to both Mary and Tobias, her fingers clutching the wooden handle of her broom as she vigorously swept the floor. Over forty days had transpired since that fateful night when Jesus had broken bread with His disciples there. No one among Mary's household could have possibly comprehended the dark forces at work that evening, as evil men plotted against the Lord's Anointed.

With a slight shiver, Tabitha recalled the sinister presence of Judas Iscariot that night. Overcome by curiosity, she and her little shadow, Rhoda, had tarried in the dark corridor just outside the Upper Room, soaking up Jesus' final words to His disciples. Jesus had spoken so quietly, Tabitha and Rhoda had missed more than they overheard.

But Tabitha was certain she would never forget the moment when Judas Iscariot had barreled out of the doorway like a raging animal, nearly plowing over them. Instinctively, Tabitha had reached for little Rhoda, shielding her from the disciple's seething rage. Casting them a look of utter disdain, Judas had stolen down the torchlit corridor like a hungry beast of prey, a dark, malevolent presence emanating from his very being. Tabitha's entire body had grown cold in his presence. At the time, she had wondered if she was merely imagining the presence of malignant demons trailing behind the troubled form of Judas Iscariot, like the eerie glowing trail of a fallen star. Tabitha shivered again, recalling Judas' bloody fate.

The morning after the Passover supper, Mary had received word from her brother, Joses: Jesus had been crucified. It was no small wonder that the earth had quaked and trembled, the sky had become dark as night, and the very elements were shaken! The earth itself cried out against the injustice committed against its Maker. Tabitha then understood why the priests had been unable to attend Mary's banquet—they were too busy plotting Jesus'—unlawful arrest, which eventually transpired in the Garden of Gethsemane. Tabitha wondered how Mark and

Mary must have felt, knowing that Jesus had been apprehended in their own tranquil grove. It was unthinkable!

At the time, Tabitha couldn't help but wonder—had she been mistaken about Jesus? Had the forces of darkness defeated the Light of the world? But her fears and doubts were shattered once and for all on the third day, when Jesus Christ accomplished the impossible—He had risen from the grave, conquering death, overcoming the wicked one! How anyone on earth could possibly question His divinity now was beyond her grasp, for it was just as the great prophet Isaiah foretold: *He will swallow up death forever, and the Lord God will wipe away tears from all faces.*

Swish, swish, swish. Tabitha's arms worked in graceful, fluid movements, unhindered by her distant thoughts. Her hazel-green eyes grew thoughtful as she considered the precious promises of God: Jesus Christ was the firstfruits of those who would be raised to life in Him. In time, she would be reunited with those she had dearly loved and lost. She could count on that, for her Savior had never broken a promise.

Mary spoke, drawing Tabitha from her silent reverie. "I was blown away when Jesus suggested His disciples continue meeting here, even after He returned to Heaven," she mused, standing calmly beside Tobias, the overseer. "It is a great honor to host the ones He dearly loved."

Tabitha smiled deeply in response, comforted by the soft, familiar *swish, swish, swish* of her busy broom as she pondered recent memories. "It makes sense, does it not?" she responded knowingly. "This is a safe place for Jesus' followers to assemble to pray, study, and strategize. It's the last place those blood-lusting priests would consider searching, after all. I'm sure they consider you an ally, my lady, since you are a descendant of Levi."

Mary nodded in acknowledgment of Tabitha's logical statement before turning toward her overseer. "These walls could use a fresh coat of paint, Tobias," she commented matter-of-factly, her observant eyes scanning the neatly ordered chamber. Very few adjustments had been made within the room since the night of Jesus' Last Supper. It was a splendid chamber, rivaling the extravagant *triclinium* on the first floor. Lamps burned brightly from their perches upon elegant hanging brass chandeliers, filling the room with warmth and light. Brightly frescoed walls matched the distinguished gold and crimson upholstered furniture scattered about the vast chamber. Every impressive fixture within the Upper Room was polished to perfection, gleaming beneath the amber glow of the burning lamps. "I shall speak with Simon Peter to see if he would like us to remove this large dining table," Mary murmured, deep in thought. "If so, it would provide even more space to move about. But until then, we'll need a new tablecloth, Tobias," Mary added quickly. "This one is rather worn and thin."

With the slightest twitch of his meticulously oiled mustache, Tobias nodded, hastily scratching notes with his stylus upon an oft-used clay tablet.

Tabitha hid a small smile, amused by her mistress's endless fussing over the Upper Room. There was absolutely nothing wrong with the elegant tablecloth draped over the long, rectangular table at which the disciples often supped. But to Mary, providing a haven for the disciples was an act of worship. Many times, she had reminded Tabitha of Jesus' famous teaching: *Inasmuch as you did it to one of the least of these My brethren, you did it to Me.* By providing nothing but the best for His followers, Mary was, in fact, ministering to her beloved Master, Jesus Christ. Tabitha was honored to participate in Mary's selfless act of love and service.

"That's all for now," Mary surmised, and Tobias' sharp eyes quickly reviewed the list she had dictated to him. It was his responsibility to oversee the household staff as they performed the mistress's bidding by tending to their respective tasks. She had no doubt he would see to it. "Thank you, Tobias. You may go."

"This will be handled immediately, my lady," the faithful overseer assured her as he slipped from the room.

Surveying her surroundings with hidden wonder, Mary shook her head and smiled. "You are correct when you say much has happened here, Tabitha," Mary agreed. "Not only did Jesus share His final Passover with the disciples in this room, He also appeared to them in bodily form after His resurrection! Every time I consider that, I'm nearly rendered speechless."

"And the disciples—along with Jesus' mother and the women who follow Him—spent hours in prayer here after Jesus returned to Heaven," Tabitha pointed out.

"Indeed," Mary agreed, her heart swelling as she considered the cloud of witnesses God had recently placed in her life. Already, she loved them—every single one of them. "And, here, Matthias was chosen to replace Judas Iscariot."

"I couldn't help but feel a bit sorry for Justus," Tabitha admitted. "Do you think he was embarrassed when the lot fell upon Matthias?"

"Justus is a strong and noble young man," Mary acknowledged sagely. "It was an honor for both Justus and Matthias to be chosen as candidates to replace the twelfth disciple. And Justus rejoiced with Matthias when the decision was made. He is full of faith, trusting God to use each one of us as He sees fit. I doubt he was the least bit embarrassed."

"I'm glad to hear that," Tabitha said wholeheartedly.

"Well," Mary sighed, rather hesitant to end their heartwarming discussion, "I suppose I must see to my other responsibilities."

"My lady," Tabitha dared, pausing her vehement sweeping, and leaning thoughtfully upon her broom.

Mary turned her head regally, halting just beneath the elegantly tiled doorframe, a question in her eyes.

"The night Jesus shared the Passover with His disciples, they sang a hymn, a Psalm of the *Hallel*. Do you remember?"

"Do I remember?" Mary repeated, her gaze clouding with both sorrow and joy. "How could I forget, dear one?"

"Sometimes," Tabitha confessed, a mysterious smile gracing her lips, "I lie awake at night, savoring that blessed memory, marveling anew at the beauty, the clarity, of Jesus' voice."

"I must confess, I've never heard anything quite so lovely," Mary agreed softly.

"I often ask myself, *How did He do it?*" Tabitha said quietly, shaking her head in awe. "He knew He was about to die, and yet His voice rang out, clear and steady as He praised His Father in Heaven."

For the briefest moment, both women were carried back to that fateful night. The melodic voice of the One who had spoken the universe into existence had filled the entire floor, wafting softly down the stairway, reaching even the secret recesses of the great house: *"I will praise You, for You have answered me, and have become my salvation. The stone which the builders rejected has become the chief cornerstone. This was the Lord's doing; it is marvelous in our eyes. This is the day the Lord has made; we will rejoice and be glad in it…"*

"The tortuous death of the cross awaited Him; even so, He chose to rejoice and be glad," Tabitha marveled.

"I must confess," Mary ventured, "I've sung that Psalm on the Passover my entire life. Not once did I realize it foretold the coming of Christ—until now."

Tabitha tipped her head in question. "How so?"

"My father told me a story years ago, when I was but a girl," Mary explained, her eyes soft, distant. "When King Solomon ordered the construction of the great Temple, the cornerstone was delivered in a timely manner. Somehow, the workers did not recognize the cornerstone for what it was. In sheer frustration, they sought a stone that would fit the proper criteria, little knowing the true cornerstone was right there among them, planted in the very midst of their efforts. Eventually, the cornerstone was brought to their attention—*after* they had pushed it over the side of the Temple Mount.

Imagine the great difficulty the workers must have experienced hauling that massive stone from the Kidron Valley and back up the Temple Mount! The men were infuriated when they realized the rock they'd been seeking had been right under their noses all along."

"*The stone which the builders rejected has become the chief cornerstone*!" Tabitha exclaimed, triumphant. "Jesus was rejected by men, but He is the true foundation of our faith!"

"*This was the Lord's doing*," Mary quoted flawlessly, a soft smile teasing the corners of her lips. "*It is marvelous in our eyes.*"

"It is, indeed," Tabitha declared, her tone bidding no argument.

"I have enjoyed our conversation, beloved," Mary confessed. "Now I must visit the kitchen and confer with our chefs."

"Ah, a busy woman," Tabitha teased, propping her broom against the wall.

"Busier now than ever," Mary laughed melodically, her eyes twinkling. "There is much to be done before the disciples arrive."

"Have they informed you of their plans?"

"Yes, indeed," Mary replied, her expression enigmatic. "I am expecting at least one hundred and twenty followers."

"One hundred and twenty! Have we space for so many?"

Once more, Mary performed a cursory scan of the vast chamber, her gray eyes betraying the slightest hint of concern. "For one hundred and twenty, yes. But by God's grace, the body of believers in Christ shall grow. In time, we may be required to make a few renovations."

Tabitha looked at her mistress in surprise. "You would alter this beautiful house?" she asked frankly.

Mary smiled. "This house isn't mine, Tabitha. It belongs to God. My husband and I have relinquished it entirely to Him. May He do with it as He sees fit."

"I believe He already has, my lady," Tabitha assured her with great feeling. "Even before you were called to host the disciples. I'll never forget all you have done for me, or for Rhoda, or for a dozen others. When shall your guests arrive?"

"They should arrive within the week, just in time for Pentecost."

"Well, then," Tabitha grinned, taking up her broom once more, "I imagine the great feast will prove exciting, indeed."

CHAPTER 6

Tabitha

"What is Shav… Shav… Shavoo—"

"*Shavuot?*" Tabitha supplied, her bright eyes crinkling with mirth as eight-year-old Rhoda struggled to pronounce a word completely foreign to her. "I suppose this must all seem very strange to you," she observed, fondly tweaking the little girl's dark shoulder-length braid. "You are a Cypriot, not a Jew."

"Is that bad?" Rhoda asked innocently, gazing up at her with soulful eyes.

"Of course not!" Tabitha declared vehemently, neatly arranging several steaming dishes upon a large tray in the bustling kitchen. "Our lady is also from Cyprus, although she has a Jewish heritage. Her ancestors were among those of the diaspora—Jews scattered across the vast Roman Empire."

"Our lady is Jewish *and* Cypriot?" Rhoda asked, puzzled.

"In a way, yes. Her Jewish ancestors intermarried with the Cypriots of that great island."

"Oh."

Setting aside her tray, Tabitha kneeled to take Rhoda's hands in hers. "You aren't any less important because you are not a Jew, little one. Some Jews of this city are rather pretentious, looking down their long noses at anyone who isn't Jewish by birth. But you needn't concern yourself about such things in this household, Rhoda. Here, you are safe."

"I am small," Rhoda confessed, chewing her bottom lip as though deep in thought.

Tabitha arched a sharp brow, straightening to her full height. "So?"

"The small ones are cheaper, less important."

"Did that nasty slave trader say that?" Tabitha fumed, turning Rhoda by the shoulders to face her. "Did you know that some traders claim children are even more valuable than grown men, selling them at a higher price?"

Rhoda's eyes clouded over, recalling the horror she had endured as the captive of a ruthless slave trader.

"Men are corrupt, Rhoda," Tabitha said firmly, holding her gaze. "They capture and sell other men for profit. But God is their Judge, and they will pay for their wicked deeds."

Lowering her gaze, Rhoda said softly, "I forgive them."

Cut to the quick, Tabitha blinked back tears. "You are a brave girl, Rhoda. Wicked men measure others by their race, their appearance, their abilities, their size. But never, ever forget this: *The Lord does not see as man sees; for man looks at the outward appearance, but the Lord looks at the heart.* God sees your heart, Rhoda. He loves you through and through."

Rhoda appeared to be contemplating Tabitha's words as she accepted a prepared tray from another servant. Rhoda balanced the heavy tray carefully, for it was piled high with glistening breakfast fruit. The large kitchen hummed with frantic energy, making the shy little girl nervous. In the bustling background, dishes clanked and clattered as servants shouted back and forth, feverishly performing the final touches on the festive fare to be served for Pentecost. Select dishes for the evening meal were already underway, despite the early morning hour.

Suppressing a shiver of excitement, Tabitha considered the Upper Room, overflowing with disciples and followers of Jesus. It was an honor to serve them, to participate in this sacred feast. She was glad Mary had possessed the foresight to provide a refreshing breakfast for the weary followers. Corralling her thoughts, Tabitha addressed Rhoda. "I still haven't answered your first question though, have I?" she chuckled, hoisting up her hefty tray and using her back to push open the kitchen's heavy double doors. "What is *Shavuot*, you ask?"

Quiet by nature, Rhoda simply shook her head and followed Tabitha out the door, bearing her own tray. She was a sweet, obedient child, eager to please. Delicate and fragile of frame, her soft brown eyes appeared even larger in her small, oval face. Her complexion was a creamy olive tone which suited her gentle features. Tabitha loved the child dearly, treasuring the moments they served together.

"*Shavuot*," Tabitha explained as she mounted a dimly lit, winding stairway—a shortcut the servants utilized to reach the home's upper floors—"is a Jewish festival signifying the end of the spring barley harvest and the beginning of the summer wheat harvest. By keeping this feast, we declare God's ownership of this land. It is by His grace that the land yields a bountiful harvest, and in keeping this feast, we praise Adonai for His goodness toward us."

"I heard my lady call it *Pennycost*," Rhoda observed, trailing happily behind Tabitha as she climbed the stairs.

"Yes," Tabitha laughed. "*Pentecost*. I suppose nowadays the holiday is better known by its Greek name, since that language is spoken universally."

"Pent-e-cost," Rhoda repeated with great effort, her dark brows furrowed in concentration.

"It has also been called the Day of Firstfruits or the Feast of Weeks," Tabitha went on patiently.

"Firstfruits, for harvest," Rhoda surmised wisely. "But why the Feast of Weeks?"

"According to Jewish tradition, the Israelites reached Mount Sinai fifty days after the first Passover," Tabitha explained, mounting a second flight of winding stairs. "So the Feast of Weeks not only commemorates the day the Law was given by God, it also marks a passage of time—the seven weeks between two holy days."

"The Passover and Pentecost."

"Exactly."

"Jesus died on Passover," Rhoda said quietly.

"Yes," Tabitha conceded sadly. "But then He rose on the third day, remember? While unknowing pilgrims and locals reveled amid the week of the great feast, God worked the most glorious miracle of all time!"

"What miracle, then, shall He perform on Pentecost?"

Tabitha froze just before emerging at the mouth of the second stairway, her spine tingling as she glanced over her shoulder, meeting the solemn gaze of the little girl. "What makes you think that Almighty God will work a miracle on *Shavuot*?"

Rhoda's brown eyes were large and innocent. "What makes you think that He will not?"

Heart pounding, Tabitha's mind raced with endless possibilities as she contemplated the child's faith-filled words. She had known this would be a special feast. How could it be anything but remarkable when those closest to the beloved Savior shared her home? But now, the practical confidence of a child bolstered her spirits, tickling her imagination and catapulting her sharpened senses into overdrive.

What wonders did the great God of Heaven have in store for them today?

"Come, Rhoda," Tabitha urged as the soft voices of those gathered within the Upper Room met her ears. Suddenly, she could hardly wait to join those assembled in the specially prepared chamber. "We should hurry. I'm sure our guests are plenty hungry."

Emerging at the top of the staircase, the maid-servants crossed a narrow corridor and entered the Upper Room, their faces flushed with excitement.

Despite the immense number of guests, the atmosphere was humbly quiet and serene. Men and women were grouped together in tight clusters, talking in hushed, respectful tones, while others lounged comfortably about the long, rectangular table at the room's center. Servants arranged trays of warm bread, sliced meat, rich cheeses, fresh fruit, olives, and candied figs, mindfully providing bowls of cool, scented water and plush hand towels for washing and drying. Tall, rectangular windows lined the outermost wall, filling the room with cheery morning sunlight. Tabitha knew the disciples—accustomed to sleeping outdoors in makeshift shelters—appreciated the luxurious hospitality of Mark and Mary.

Carrying their trays toward the table, Tabitha performed a cursory scan of the guests gathered within the Upper Room, a habit she had developed while living alone on the streets. There, where one careless moment could prove fatal, she had sensed the vital importance of being fully cognizant of her surroundings. Her observant eyes were always alert, her restless energy carefully concealed. She couldn't help but smile as her eyes fell upon various faces in the cheerful room, for she had already grown to love many of them.

Mary stood alongside her husband, Mark, near the main entryway, deeply immersed in conversation with another woman named Mary. Tabitha couldn't help but gaze at the older woman in awe, for she was the mother of the Lord Jesus. How that brave woman must miss her Son! Did her heart ache, knowing that He had returned to Heaven to be seated at the right hand of His Father? How Tabitha longed to sit at the woman's feet for days on end, absorbing every possible detail regarding the life of her Savior! It was then that Tabitha noticed a disciple hovering rather protectively near Mary's elbow. Suppressing a smile, she assumed he must be the one they called John. During His torment on the cross, Jesus had entrusted the care of his beloved mother to John, and clearly, the disciple took this responsibility seriously. John loudly pronounced himself *the disciple whom Jesus loved*—much to the chagrin and annoyance of Simon Peter, Tabitha noted with a twinkle of mischief in her hazel-green eyes. But she was far more intrigued by the nicknames Jesus had bestowed upon John and his brother, James: Sons of Thunder. She was certain there must be an interesting story there. Why else would John flush with frustration and embarrassment every time Simon Peter teasingly referenced the nickname? Simon Peter seemed to relish John's discomfort, much to Tabitha's amusement.

True, the disciples were an interesting lot. Some, like Simon Peter, his brother Andrew, and the Sons of Thunder, were fishermen from Galilee. Others were simple craftsmen or tradesmen. Surprisingly, a former Zealot and even a tax collector was counted among them. Some were bold and daring, others reserved and cautious. Though these men had deserted Jesus in His hour of need, their faith had been bolstered, strengthened like gold refined, following the miraculous resurrection of their Lord. Tabitha was certain that Jesus would complete the good work He had begun in this ragtag bunch of men. Clearly, He had a purpose for every single one of them.

Carefully depositing her tray on the table, Tabitha bent to help Rhoda lower her own tray. She was amazed by the large number filling the enormous chamber, for many followers had assembled along with the Lord's mother, the eleven disciples, and the newly appointed twelfth. Mary's brothers, Joses and Aristobulus, had joined them for the occasion as well, along with Aristobulus' daughter Anaia—Simon Peter's modest, soft-spoken wife. There were also several Marys present. It had proven rather challenging to keep track of the many Marys counted among Jesus' followers. There was her own mistress, Mary of Jerusalem, along with Mary, the mother of Jesus, Mary, the wife of Clopas, and Mary of Magdala, just to name a few. Also included among the vast number of those assembled were various members of the Seventy—traveling evangelists appointed by Jesus during His earthly ministry. Mary's brothers, Joses and Aristobulus, had been counted among them.

"Everyone in this room believes Jesus is Lord?"

Rhoda's question pulled Tabitha's attention back to her little helper. Taking her hand, Tabitha smiled down at her. "I would assume so, dear one."

Rhoda's dark brows drew together in confusion. "Even Tobias?"

Following Rhoda's gaze, Tabitha noticed two evangelists of the Seventy, Philip and Stephanos, had somehow managed to corral Tobias, backing him into a corner, talking and gesturing enthusiastically. The turbaned overseer wore a somewhat tolerant expression, resigned to the fact that he must endure the preaching of these zealous young men, at least temporarily. His dark eyes darted about the room, clearly seeking an escape route.

"Poor Tobias," Tabitha chuckled, shaking her head. She had to admire the brass of the two young men. Their personalities were completely opposed—which was perhaps the reason the Lord had paired them together. Philip was calm, humorous, and tenderhearted, a true peacemaker. Stephanos, a fiery Hellenist with a fearless disposition, stood in stark contrast with his closest friend.

"Does Tobias believe? He doesn't look happy like the others," Rhoda observed.

"Well, Tobias is a Jew through and through. He has served Adonai faithfully his entire life," Tabitha said honestly. Rigidly, Tobias clung to the traditions of his fathers. He hadn't approved of Jesus's teachings.

"But he doesn't believe Jesus is the Son of God?"

"He's a bit hazy on that point, I'm afraid."

Rhoda's brown eyes softened. "I am worried for Tobias."

"Why is that?"

"Jesus said, '*Whoever denies the Son does not have the Father either*', but '*he who acknowledges the Son has the Father also.*'"

Tabitha was sobered by the child's observation. "You are very wise, Rhoda. We must pray for Tobias."

Their conversation was cut short when Simon Peter stood, loudly clapping his hands to draw the others' attention. "Brothers and sisters," Simon Peter addressed the believers in the thickly accented voice of a Galilean. "May I have your attention, please? I have something important to say."

Instantly, every conversation ceased as all eyes turned to gaze upon Simon Peter.

CHAPTER 7

Tabitha

"I would like to be the first to thank our gracious hosts, Mark of Jerusalem and his lovely wife, Mary, for their hospitality," Simon Peter said officiously, nodding in their direction. "It is an honor to share your home."

"The honor is ours, my brother," Mark asserted graciously, and Mary, taking his arm, beamed in warm affirmation.

"As many of you know, before He returned to His Father in Heaven, Jesus commanded us not to depart from Jerusalem. He told us we must wait here for the promise of the Father."

Tabitha exchanged a knowing look with young Rhoda, hungrily absorbing the words of Simon Peter as other believers murmured quietly in acknowledgment.

"About this promise from the Father—we may not fully understand it now, but I believe we will all recognize it once we receive it. Jesus said we would be baptized with the Holy Spirit. Since this must happen before we can fulfill His great commission to preach His name unto the ends of the earth, I believe we should be seeking it earnestly, together, with one accord."

"Amen," echoed softly throughout the large chamber as the believers accepted the wisdom of Peter's admonition.

"We all long for Jesus' soothing presence, I know," Peter admitted, his voice growing thick with emotion. "Could we have possibly known what a privilege it was to walk with the Savior each day, basking in His healing presence? How differently might we have conducted ourselves had we known He would soon be taken from us?"

"Sometimes, I close my eyes and remember the sound of His voice, His hearty laughter, the gentleness of His eyes, His soothing touch," John, the beloved disciple, interrupted. Mary, the Lord's mother, gently touched John's shoulder as tears filled his eyes, slipping down his cheeks into his beard.

Lowering his head, Peter swallowed hard, struggling to compose himself. It was a moment before he spoke again, but every person present comprehended his inner struggle. "We do feel lost without Him here beside us," Peter acknowledged, blinking back tears as he examined the faces of those he loved. "Even so, we must press on. Let us pray in the manner which He taught us. Perhaps the Lord will grant us strength. We may not fully grasp His promise, but we can trust Him to fulfill it."

A respectful hush fell upon the occupants of the Upper Room. Tabitha's own heart constricted, for she, too, sensed the painful void among the followers. Jesus' presence had been like a soothing balm, refreshing the heart and spirit. Though she had met Him but a few times, she grieved His absence along with the others.

"Let us pray, as He instructed us long ago," Peter said as his wife, Anaia, drew alongside him, taking his hand. Other believers followed suit, rising to their feet and clasping hands. Noticing Rhoda's head come up, Tabitha followed her gaze and saw that John Mark had joined his parents, his countenance uncharacteristically solemn.

"*Our Father in Heaven,*" Peter's sturdy voice rang out, as over one hundred voices joined his, resonating with the power of the Living Word. The beautiful prayer resounded throughout the Upper Room with such force and power that Tabitha was certain the entire house shuddered beneath the awesome weight of their fervent prayer.

"*Hallowed be Your name,*" Tabitha joined in, taking Rhoda's hand and glorying in the power of God. "*Your kingdom come. Your will be done on earth as it is in Heaven...*" Her heart soared as she recited the prayer Jesus had bestowed upon His disciples. Somehow, in that sacred moment, she felt closer to the Lord. Like the faintest flicker of the candles upon the table, Tabitha sensed the slightest flicker of the Savior's presence. As if Jesus stood, unseen, somewhere in their midst, quietly watching, observing, guiding...

"*...do not lead us into temptation, but deliver us from evil,*" the believers prayed in unison, their voices steadily building in strength and power. "*For Yours is the kingdom and the power and the glory forever!*"

"Our Father," Peter's voice rang out, rising above the rest, "we ask in the name of Your precious Son, Jesus, fulfill Your promise, and show us what to do."

"Amen," Tabitha found herself murmuring softly along with the rest, tightly gripping Rhoda's hand, offering the little one strength and reassurance.

"We need You, Father," Peter prayed, his voice strained with emotion. "On this day, centuries ago, You spoke to Your chosen people upon Mount Sinai, saying, '*I bore you on eagles' wings and brought you to Myself. Now therefore, if you will indeed obey My voice and keep My covenant, then you shall be a special treasure to Me above all people; for the earth is Mine.*' During this sacred feast, Lord, we are reminded that the earth is Yours indeed. We thank You for Your goodness."

"Thank You, Father," others whispered softly. "Blessed be Your name."

"You also promised to make us a kingdom of priests, a holy nation. When You addressed our ancestors on the third day, fierce thunder and lightning shook the earth. Great balls of fire exploded in the heavenlies, striking our fathers' hearts with terror. The mount was encompassed in roiling clouds and thick smoke. We know it was Your Shekinah Glory, Lord, resting upon that holy hill. For on that sacred day, You entrusted our people with the Law of Moses, the holy covenant. Later, Your glory filled the Most Holy Place—first, in the tabernacle; next, in the Temple. And now, Father, anoint us and fill *us* with Your glory, that we may be Your ambassadors, a kingdom of priests proclaiming the way, the truth, and the life."

"*Jesus* is the way, the truth, and the life," many

believers breathed softly, gripped by an unseen yet powerful presence. Something was happening.

A gentle wind whispered its way through fluttering curtains.

Slowly, Tabitha raised her head. Her skin tingled, every nerve ending strangely alive, as an unearthly sensation filled the air, crackling with tension like the telltale stillness before a lightning storm. Did the others sense it, too?

As Simon Peter's strong voice filled the Upper Room, beseeching Almighty God, a gentle gust—like the faintest breath of life—puffed through the open windows. The candles upon the table were mysteriously extinguished, one by one. As if in confusion, the oil lamps flickered from their stands.

Peter froze, his dark eyes warily scanning their surroundings. At his side, Anaia's large brown eyes grew wider, her body tensed like a reluctant doe just before taking flight. The room grew instantly silent. Tabitha held her breath, watchful, still.

In that silent moment, the gentle caressing breezes wafting through the windows exploded into a mighty gust of wind, whistling and whirling its way through the massive chamber. Gasps of awe rippled through the great hall as women reached for their head coverings, their garments whipped about like palm fronds in a mighty gale. The believers huddled together in amazement as the very breath of God swirled about their trembling bodies, filling them with something remarkable, something new.

Kneeling to wrap her arm protectively about the trembling child beside her, Tabitha's heart pounded heavily in her chest as the sound of the mighty, rushing wind tore through the entire house. Shutters slammed back and forth as dishes, trays, and utensils clattered off the table onto the floor. Several women cried out even as most were stunned to silence.

"God hears us!" Peter shouted jubilantly, his voice nearly drowned in the mighty din, and the men joined his cry of victory.

The sound of the rushing wind grew deafening. Tabitha had never heard anything like it and doubted that she ever would again. Fleetingly, she wondered if the entire city could hear it! Suddenly, flaming balls of fire exploded in the air high above their heads, coming to rest upon those gathered in the Upper Room and filling the chamber with crackling heat.

Tabitha's eyes grew wide as she dared a glance heavenward. There, directly above her head, a flaming tongue of fire sputtered and hissed, bathing her entire being in warmth and light. Forcing herself to tear her gaze away from the steadily burning flame, she looked to Rhoda, for the poor child must be terrified! But rather than fear, Rhoda's eyes reflected a wondrous joy unlike anything Tabitha had ever seen.

And in that awesome moment, Tabitha was stunned by a shocking, impossible realization: she sensed the presence of Jesus Christ as keenly as if He stood beside her, taking her by the hand. His presence was so close it was nearly tangible. But no, Jesus was not *beside* her, as she might have guessed. Instead, He dwelled *within* her, His powerful presence filling her heart.

Was *this* the Spirit He had promised? Had her own heart become the home of her precious Savior? Faintly, she recalled the Lord speaking about

His body as the Temple of God. For the very first time, Tabitha understood. Their bodies had become the temples of the Holy Spirit, who dwelled within each of them! What an unspeakable, sacred honor to house the presence of Jesus Christ within her heart! It was almost too much to fathom.

Eyes filling with tears, she lifted her gaze toward that of her mistress, an unspoken question passing between them: *Do You sense it? His presence is here among us!* Tabitha nodded her response, tears slipping down her cheeks. Flames of fire rested upon Mary, Mark, and even their young son! In fact, it would seem all the believers were being baptized by—dare she even think it?—the *Holy Spirit*! His presence was indeed among them! Surely the believers would miss His physical, bodily presence on earth, but His Spirit now rested upon them to lead, to comfort, to guide. The gaping hole in their hearts had been filled by the unchanging, everlasting power of God through the presence of the Holy Spirit!

Gazing upon the faces of those gathered around her, Tabitha knew in an instant that every single one of them was experiencing the presence of Jesus even as she was.

But wait! Had the skeptical, practical Tobias witnessed this shocking miracle? If so, how was he responding? Surely he would accept the believers' testimony now! Tabitha's gaze traveled toward the two young evangelists near the overseer and saw that they, too, bore flames of fire above their heads. Philip shook his head in wonder, laughing joyously, while Stephanos pumped a fist heavenward and shouted impassioned praises to his God.

Tabitha was relieved to see that Tobias was still

with them, his bearded face bathed in tears. But her heart constricted, for she realized that no flame rested upon him. Stephanos, always the evangelist, turned to the overseer then, placing a sturdy hand upon the man's shoulder. Tabitha couldn't hear their dialogue above the din, but Tobias willingly bowed his head along with Stephanos.

Instantly, a flaming tongue of fire exploded and came to rest above Tobias, a steadily burning flame. Glancing cautiously upward, Tobias' eyes grew wide, reflecting the ball of flames hovering above his turbaned head. Clearly stunned, the overseer dropped to his knees, raising his hands heavenward in worshipful submission.

Grinning broadly, Tabitha's heart nearly burst within her. *Thank You, gracious Father!* Their beloved Tobias had finally accepted the Lord Jesus!

Sensing Tabitha's joyous gaze, Stephanos and Philip flashed jubilant smiles in her direction. She shook her head in amazement, dashing away her tears.

And then, just as swiftly and unexpectedly as it had descended, the dynamic maelstrom abruptly ceased. The villa grew strangely, eerily silent.

Reminded of the disciples' story about their Maker calming a storm, Tabitha could only shake her head in wonder. Here, too, there was a great calm. Only Jesus held the power to calm the raging elements in an instant. Truly, His presence was among them once again!

"Yes!" Pumping a triumphant fist into the air, Simon Peter shouted victoriously, shattering the newfound stillness. "Praise be to God! The Shekinah Glory has returned!"

CHAPTER 8

Mary

Peter's joyous announcement was followed by a shrill, unearthly cacophony that sent cold shivers up and down Mary's spine. Heart pounding furiously in her chest, she looked to her husband and then to the mother of her Lord. "Where is that uproar coming from?"

Bolting toward the large, rectangular windows, Peter's eyes grew wide. "Mark, Mary. It would seem you have a few more visitors."

Ignoring his obvious chagrin, Mary took her son's hand and dragged him toward the window, her husband close behind them. Peering out, her heart sprang into her throat. Overwhelmingly thankful she had possessed the foresight to double the guard, her eyes absorbed the endless sea of people pressing about all sides of the house. "They must have overheard the commotion," she told her husband, fighting to maintain her composure. Clustered tightly about their home, the group was boisterous and rambunctious. *Busybodies and thrill seekers,* she supposed. Men and women shouted, attempting to persuade the guards to grant them entrance. Were the believers still safe in her home?

"We should go to them," Mark said evenly, turning from the window.

Are you out of your mind? Mary wished to argue. Instead, she said tactfully, "But is it safe?"

"They have come to hear the Good News."

Mary doubted that was the reason the rowdy mob was closing in on their beautiful home.

"Brethren," Mark said boldly, his tone and stance sure as he addressed the believers in his home, "shall we present the gospel to these hungry people? The time has come to fulfill our Savior's great commission."

"What are we waiting for?" Simon Peter declared, despite the doubtful look his wife cast him. "What?" Peter argued, defensive. "Have we not just witnessed a miracle? The Holy Spirit will protect us!"

Mary, the mother of the Lord Jesus, drew alongside Mary of Jerusalem, peering intently out the window. "There are Jews from many nations gathered below. They have come to Jerusalem for the feast, but it is doubtful that all of them speak Aramaic or even Greek. Most appear to be foreigners."

"How many nationalities are counted among the crowd?" Peter asked, clearly put off by her logic.

"By their looks, I would say Parthians, Medes, Elamites, Mesopotamians, Egyptians, and Libyans, among others."

"Have we a translator among us?" Peter demanded impatiently, eager to reach the crowds.

"After all we have witnessed this day, you would

seek a translator?" All eyes turned toward Stephanos, the bold Hellenist who radiated both faith and charisma. "Shall we place limits upon the Almighty, even after this miraculous display of His unrivaled power?"

Mary, the mother of the Lord, looked steadily at the young man, her slim brows lifting in delight. "Stephanos, I didn't realize you spoke the Egyptian tongue."

Stephanos stared at her rather blankly. "Actually, I do. My father sent me to Alexandria as a boy, where I was schooled under the supervision of the brilliant scholar, Philo. But how is it that you are familiar with the foreign tongue?"

"My husband Joseph and I took refuge in Egypt during the reign of Herod the Great and his massacre of the innocents. Jesus was a mere infant then."

"Amazing," Stephanos admitted, shaking his head. "How did you know I spoke Egyptian, Mary?"

"Why, you were speaking it just now."

The confusion that passed over the faces of everyone present was somewhat comical.

"Respectfully," Stephanos explained, slightly uncertain, "I wasn't speaking Egyptian. I was speaking in Greek...wasn't I?"

"I heard Egyptian," Jesus' mother observed, tilting her head in confusion.

"I heard him speaking in Greek," Philip supplied, his curiosity piqued.

"Aramaic," Peter inserted abruptly. "My mother tongue."

Murmurs of agreement rippled through the group of followers, along with whispers of dissension.

"I heard you in my own native tongue, and I

must confess, it brought tears to my eyes." All eyes turned toward Nicolas, a committed proselyte from Antioch. "I have not heard the Syriac tongue spoken since I left the land of my fathers."

"I heard him, too," said a very small voice, and the believers were stunned when shy Rhoda stepped forward, her cheeks aflame with embarrassment. Timidly, her eyes sought her mistress's for approval.

"Go on, my dear Rhoda," Mary encouraged her maidservant gently. "Tell us what you heard."

"The Greek of my country differs a bit from yours," Rhoda said shyly, her gaze fastened on her own small, sandaled feet. She seemed to draw strength from the lovely young woman beside her, for she added quietly, "I heard Master Stephanos speak just like they do."

"And I heard the same," Mary confirmed, her heart hammering in her chest. "The Cypriot dialect varies slightly." It was incomprehensible, really. Too much to even fathom!

Mary, the mother of the Lord Jesus, looked to the other believers, her careworn features filled with light and wonder. "The Holy Spirit has granted us the gift of tongues! Not only can we reach those gathered outside of this home—we can truly fulfill my Son's great commission, carrying the Good News unto the ends of the earth."

"Praise God!" Stephanos declared, his dashing frame already hastening for the door. Philip followed closely behind him as Tobias watched them, astounded.

Peter released a low whistle. "I've never seen—or should I say, *heard*—anything like this."

"Peter," Mary said, sensing her husband's approving eyes upon her, "you may address the crowds from the balcony overlooking the outer courtyard. Mark and I will speak to the guards. We will allow as many as possible into the gates. But you will have to raise your voice to be heard above the walls enclosing our home."

"He's very good at that," Anaia said teasingly, squeezing her husband's arm. "I think the entire city will hear him."

Peter rolled his eyes, an easy grin splitting his rugged features.

"Everyone else," Mark said, addressing the body of believers gathered in his home. "Let's weave our way through the crowd—especially those unable to fit inside the gates. By God's grace, we shall use this gift of tongues to reach as many as possible."

***

Tabitha

The sound of the mighty whirlwind had attracted a crowd unlike anything Tabitha had ever seen.

Bravely, Mary supported her husband in his desire to share the gospel from their home. Now Tabitha, gripping Rhoda's small hand protectively, watched, spellbound, as a swollen sea of people flooded Mary's stone courtyard, standing shoulder to shoulder and filling every available nook and cranny. The uproarious din created by the monstrous gathering was truly deafening. Amazed by the diversity of the crowd, Tabitha vigilantly tracked every possible detail from her vantage point below the open doorway. Local Jews, along with those of far-flung Roman provinces, clustered tightly about the house, spilling out of the spacious courtyard and huddling close to the magnificent structure. Still, throngs of men and women spilled into the neatly paved streets, their necks craned and their eyes lifted as they struggled to see above the towering walls sheltering the elegant villa. Babies fussed and children teased while men and women, both young and old, rich and poor, believing and skeptical, animatedly conversed in over a dozen diverse languages. Tabitha spotted merchants and craftsmen, elders and scribes, common laborers and slaves, widows and housewives.

Her slender brows lifted at the unwelcome approach of severely clad Pharisees and Sadducees. Their sharp eyes scanned their surroundings with unveiled displeasure as they stood aloofly amidst the crowd, their dark garments fluttering in the gentle morning breezes. Instantly on guard, Tabitha hoped the glistening spears and uncompromising expressions of the household guards would serve their purpose. The religious leaders abhorred the teachings of Jesus, and they were powerful men, capable of causing a dangerous stir. She imagined they falsely assumed that Jesus' controversial message had been extinguished the moment His body had been sealed in the tomb of Joseph of Arimathea. How very wrong they were! In their attempt to extinguish the Light of the world, they had unknowingly fanned the flames of a raging wildfire. Who could deny the power of the resurrected Lord?

Suppressing a grin, Tabitha imagined the religious leaders would have something to say about Simon Peter's impending address! Sobering slightly, she prayed for the safety of the disciples, the followers, and her master's household. Once Simon Peter addressed this vast crowd, there would be no turning back. The private convictions of Mark and Mary would be laid bare before the eyes of brutal men intent on crushing the message of the gospel.

CHAPTER 9

Mary

"Brothers and sisters," Simon Peter's powerful voice boomed over the vast expanse, stilling the active tongues of the curiosity-drenched crowd. "Today we are honored to share the Good News of our Lord and Savior, Jesus Christ!"

An eerie hush fell over the multitude as everyone waited with bated breath.

Standing resolutely beside her husband, her hands resting protectively on the shoulders of her young son, Mary dismissed her rising concerns and attempted to focus on the present moment. Her mind was awhirl with a dozen conflicting emotions and concerns. Even as she gloried in this blessed opportunity to host one of the greatest events in history, her unbending logic reminded her that there would surely be consequences for this faith she had embraced with reckless abandon.

Simon Peter, along with several other disciples, stood on the highest balcony of the third floor, overlooking the entire courtyard and beyond. From his lofty position, he could be seen by nearly everyone assembled, including those gathered beyond the uncompromising stone walls enclosing the villa. The remaining disciples and many of the followers stood among the crowd, ready to be of service if needed.

Her observant eyes mindfully scanning Simon Peter's rapt audience, Mary was amused by the confusion passing over the faces of the multitude. Amazingly, all understood the guttural tongue of the Galilean fisherman. And clearly, that revelation was shocking to every single one of them. She marveled at this gift of the newfound Holy Spirit, equipping the followers to reach men and women from the farthest reaches of the empire.

Gracious Father, may Your Holy Spirit move among this crowd today, Mary prayed silently, her heart pounding in fierce anticipation. *Move in mighty ways. Draw the hearts and minds of these hungry souls to You.*

"How is it that you speak and we *all* understand?"

Drawn from her quiet prayer by the shrill cry of a bystander near the front of the crowd, Mary's slender brows drew together in dismay. Peter hadn't even begun his speech, and the people were already disturbed by what they could not comprehend.

"Allow us to explain," John interrupted, standing near Peter's elbow on the balcony.

The multitude buzzed with sharp questions as men and women argued amongst themselves.

"Him, too? We can understand him as well!"

"How can this be?"

"Look, are not all these who speak simple Galileans?" A swarthy man near the front scoffed loudly, drawing the attention of the crowd. "So how is it that we hear our own languages spoken?"

"This is an act of God," Peter boomed over the large gathering, his voice plainly authoritative. "Clearly, our God desires to reach every single one of you today. Why else would we be granted this extraordinary gift of tongues?"

"Many nationalities are represented here," another in the crowd cried out, consumed with excitement. "Parthians and Medes and Elamites, those dwelling in Mesopotamia, Judea and Cappadocia, Pontus and Asia, Phrygia and Pamphylia, Egypt and the parts of Libya adjoining Cyrene, visitors from Rome, both Jews and proselytes, Cretans and Arabs..." Pointing ecstatically toward the disciples on the balcony, he exclaimed, "We hear them speaking in our own tongues the wonderful works of God!"

Mary suppressed a smile. The bystander had summed it up quite nicely. Perhaps now the people would be more inclined to listen quietly and respectfully.

"Whatever could this mean?" another shouted in obvious confusion.

"God must be moving through these men."

"We are witnessing a miracle!"

Releasing a frustrated sigh, Mary shook her head. How was Peter to present the gospel to this rowdy bunch? They were behaving like a mob of unruly children!

It was then that the crowd's excitement took a turn for the worst. A zealous young Pharisee in severe black garments pointed a critical finger toward the balcony, his features tightening in rage. "These men are but clever magicians and tricksters! Do not be deceived!"

"Perhaps they are simply drunk, full of *new wine*!" The Pharisee's companion mocked, his tone full of venom as his lip curled in derision.

Mary's countenance paled as she attempted to curb her rising anger. Possessing ties to many priestly families, her husband's firm disapproval of alcoholic beverages was no secret to the elders and chief priests. New wine—unfermented grape juice—was his beverage of preference, even if it was expensive and difficult to obtain. Clearly, the young Pharisees sought to shame Mark's family with their snide comments.

Chancing a glance at Mark, Mary was surprised. His strong features were etched with calm amusement rather than angst. What a pillar he was! Silently, she resolved to become more like her steadfast husband. Here she was, stewing over the insult of a careless bystander, while Mark probably chose to accept the slight as a compliment! He was a powerful, intelligent businessman. Everyone respected him, and his shining success would have proven impossible had he been given to strong drink.

"Men of Judea and all who dwell in Jerusalem," Peter shouted above the din, drawing Mary from her own silent thoughts. His bearing exuding both confidence and authority, the disciple stood high above the people, clutching the tall stone ledge encircling the large balcony. "Let this be known to you and heed my words."

The crowd grew silent, stunned by the power and persuasion of Peter's uncompromising tone and bearing.

Mary couldn't help but feel a bit smug when the

two young Pharisees squirmed uncomfortably beneath Peter's steely gaze.

"These are not drunk, as you suppose, since it is only the third hour of the day!"

At this unexpected bit of humor, the crowd rippled with nervous chuckles. He had their attention now.

"No, but this is what was spoken long ago by the prophet, Joel: *And it shall come to pass in the last days, says God, that I will pour out My Spirit on all flesh; Your sons and your daughters shall prophesy, your young men shall see visions, your old men shall dream dreams. And on My menservants and on My maidservants I will pour out My Spirit in those days; and they shall prophesy.*"

Mary's skin prickled as a gentle breeze whispered its way through the crowded courtyard, tickling the leaves of the tall palm fronds beyond the gate. A cool mist from the central fountain gently grazed her cheek, carried by the soft wind.

The multitude listened, spellbound, as Peter explained the impossible, backing his argument with the irrefutable Word of God.

"This is truly remarkable, sister. How mysterious the ways of our God!"

Mary murmured in gentle agreement as her brother, Joses, drew alongside her small family.

"Mark," Joses said, humbly addressing his sister's husband, "your courage is inspiring. I imagine this is how God intends for us to utilize the resources He graciously bestows upon us. You have given me much to ponder."

Mark squeezed Joses' shoulder in appreciation as Peter's voice continued to carry over the crowd.

"*I will show wonders in heaven above,*" Peter declared, the words of an ancient prophet rolling easily from his tongue, "*and signs in the earth beneath: blood and fire and vapor of smoke. The sun shall be turned to darkness, and the moon into blood, before the coming of the great and awesome day of the Lord.*"

The courtyard fairly shook with resounding *amens*. Apparently, these Jews and proselytes were familiar with the Scriptures.

"*And it shall come to pass,*" Peter shouted, his voice rising in both strength and intensity, "*that whoever calls on the name of the Lord shall be saved!*"

The crowd erupted with resounding cheers of approval. Even the sullen-faced Pharisees and skeptical Sadducees scattered among the commoners appeared somewhat subdued, mesmerized by the power of the ancient words.

"Now men of Israel," Peter cried out, his face alight with the joy and confidence of the Holy Spirit, "hear these words, for I want to tell you about a man named Jesus - Jesus of Nazareth. You witnessed the miracles, wonders, and signs which God did through Him in your midst." Skillfully, Peter testified about the lawlessness of Christ's trial, His impending crucifixion, and the power of His resurrection. "You are Jews, no?" Peter ascertained, his dark eyes scanning the sea of people gathered below Him. "You are familiar with Torah. These sacred Scriptures pointed toward Christ, our Messiah, all along. Even the mighty King David knew the Savior would come, writing about Him for our benefit. For David said concerning Him: *I foresaw the Lord always before my face, for He is at my right hand, that*

I may not be shaken. Therefore my heart rejoiced, and my tongue was glad; moreover my flesh will rest in hope. For You will not leave my soul in Hades, nor will You allow Your Holy One to see corruption. You have made known to me the ways of life; You will make me full of joy in Your presence."

"You cannot prove that David spoke of your Christ," the young Pharisee argued, even as his eyes flickered with doubt.

"Ah, allow me to speak freely to you about the great patriarch David. He was a mighty king, yes?"

Murmurs of agreements rippled through the crowd.

"David was a valiant warrior and a hero of Israel, yes?" Peter's question was followed by emphatic nods and more muttered concessions. "But where is David now?" Peter demanded, and men and women exchanged nervous looks. "Is he sitting upon a throne, reigning over a kingdom of everlasting peace?"

The eyes of the young Pharisees near the front narrowed in indignation. Several other religious students had joined them, their eyes widening beneath the oversized phylacteries strapped to their foreheads. Entertained by their obvious chagrin, Mary couldn't help but liken their appearance to that of crows with ruffled feathers as their trailing prayer shawls fluttered in the cool morning breezes.

"Obviously, he is not," Peter expounded, a wry smile tipping the corners of his lips. "Even the mighty David was laid to rest, and his tomb is with us to this day. His kingdom was magnificent, yes. But his was not the everlasting kingdom of Heaven. And David had plenty to say about our Christ in his famous Psalms. For example, of Jesus he said, *I will open My mouth in a parable.* Didn't our Savior teach in parables? Not only that, but David prophesied about the Messiah's death. Heed this Psalm of David: *All those who see Me ridicule Me; they shoot out the lip, they shake the head, saying, 'He trusted in the Lord, let Him rescue Him; Let Him deliver Him, since He delights in Him!' ... They gape at Me with their mouths, like a raging and roaring lion. I am poured out like water, and all My bones are out of joint. My heart is like wax; it has melted within Me. My strength is dried up like potsherd, and My tongue clings to My jaws; You have brought Me to the dust of death. For dogs have surrounded Me; the congregation of the wicked has enclosed Me. They pierced My hands and My feet; I can count all My bones. They look and stare at Me. They divide My garments among them, and for My clothing they cast lots.* Now tell me," Peter declared, his eyes sweeping over the vast crowd hanging upon his every word. "Does any of this sound familiar to you?"

Many among the crowd exchanged nervous glances, having witnessed or even participated in the bloody persecution of Jesus Christ. The truth in David's passage was undeniable, far too close for comfort.

"So clearly, David was not referencing himself in his passage," Peter went on to explain, expounding upon the sacred text. "But being a prophet, he knew that his faithful God had sworn an oath to him that by the fruit of his body, according to the flesh, God would raise up the Christ to sit on his throne. Foreseeing this, David spoke concerning the resurrection of Jesus Christ—that His soul was not left in Hades, nor did His flesh see corruption, you see? This Jesus of whom I speak God has raised up from the dead, and we are all witnesses. And being exalted to the right hand of God and having received from the Father the promise of the Holy Spirit, He poured out this miracle of the Spirit by which you now see and hear! Jesus is among us even now, made manifest in the form of the Holy Spirit. Can any of you deny His presence here?"

The crowd became strangely silent, gazing upon Simon Peter with rapt attention.

"Therefore," Peter cried out, his eyes burning with fiery intensity, "let all the house of Israel know that God has made this Jesus, *whom you crucified*, both Lord and Christ!"

Oh Father, Mary prayed, *open their hearts and minds to Your truth.* Would this sea of diverse, opinionated people be offended by Peter's honest accusation? Or would they recognize the call to repentance and turn from their wickedness? Frozen in place, Mary beheld the faces of those assembled at her home. Her heart pounded so fiercely in her chest she was certain everyone could hear it in the gathering silence. Hesitant to draw a single breath, she beseeched her risen Lord in silent prayer. *Father, pierce their hearts with contrition rather than offense.*

***

Tabitha

Astonishingly, expressions of pained remorse and genuine repentance passed over the faces of those in the multitude. Tabitha watched, amazed, as one by one, men and women dropped to their knees, tears streaming down their faces. Shoulders shuddered as many covered their faces and wept, cut to the very heart.

"What is happening?" a small voice inquired, and Tabitha's gaze shifted toward Rhoda, standing innocently at her elbow. The shy little girl continued to clutch her hand like a lifeline.

"The Spirit of God is moving among these people," Tabitha explained, her voice tinged with excitement. "They have chosen to repent rather than harden their hearts."

Rhoda nodded, satisfied with the simple explanation.

From their post in the main doorway, Tabitha and Rhoda possessed a bird's-eye view of those assembled within the courtyard, although those gathered outside the gates were beyond their line of sight. Observant as always, Tabitha's bright eyes absorbed every detail of the miraculous scene before her. She was overwhelmed by the humility mirrored in the eyes of most of the listeners. Stunned, Tabitha noticed several scribes, priests, Pharisees, and Sadducees kneeling with the rest, despite the dark looks cast upon them by their companions. For the very first time, the weight of their dark deeds and their rejection of the long-awaited Savior had crushed their apathy and pride.

Thank You, God! Tabitha's heart soared with joy and adulation. Lives were being utterly changed, transformed before her eyes!

Much to her surprise, it was the pompous young Pharisee at the front of the crowd who spoke first, lifting a tear-streaked face toward the disciples on the balcony. "Men and brethren, what shall we do? Our thoughts and our deeds cry out against us."

Tabitha marveled at the sudden change in the young man's demeanor. How awesome the ways of her God!

It was then that Peter spoke, his dark eyes uncharacteristically tender, washed in the grace and mercy of God. "Repent, and let every one of you be baptized in the name of Jesus Christ for the remission of sins." His eyes glittered knowingly as he added with a broad smile, "And then you, too, shall receive the gift of the Holy Spirit."

CHAPTER 10

Mary

Peter spoke for several hours with the crowd hanging upon his every word. James and John joined in occasionally, expounding upon the teaching of their fellow disciple. Amazingly, the multitude continued to comprehend the words spoken by the Galilean fishermen. As some left the assembly with full hearts, others joined the fray, curious about the massive gathering. The disciples weaved their way through the crowd, leading new converts in heartfelt prayers of repentance.

Surrounded by her husband, her brothers, and beloved, like-minded followers, Mary's heart overflowed with gratitude. Draping a slender arm casually across young John Mark's shoulders, she shook her regal head in awe, overcome by the goodness and the grace of her God. How could she have possibly comprehended the mighty works He had in store for them? Heart bursting with thanksgiving, Mary returned her attention toward her niece's husband as he continued to address the sea of listeners below.

"You will recall," Peter declared, his eyes afire as he recounted tales of old, "the day Almighty God spoke to our ancestors in the wilderness. His Shekinah Glory rested upon Mount Sinai, and every person present heard God's Law delivered in their own tongue. Today, as we observe *Shavuot*, we celebrate the day He entrusted us with the Law of Moses. Is it any wonder Adonai has now confirmed His covenant on *Shavuot*, granting us the Holy Spirit? For by the Holy Spirit, our ancestors received the Law. And now, by the Holy Spirit, we are enabled to walk in obedience by His grace!"

Murmurs of consent flittered through the vast crowd as every eye remained locked on Simon Peter, every ear absorbing his remarkable words.

"Remember this great day, my brothers," Peter cried out, his eyes scanning the sea of eager hearers. "For on it, both the old and the new covenant has been confirmed. And how fitting it is—for as we observe this feast commemorating the completion of the grain harvest, Jesus, the *bread* of life, has gifted us the Holy Spirit, signifying the fulfillment of His earthly mission. Though He is now seated at the right hand of the Father in the heavenly places, we can be sure of this, my brothers: He will come again!"

The crowd erupted in shouts of heartfelt celebration, thrilling Mary with their faith and exuberance. How many had been saved on this joyous occasion? How many had turned from their depravity to embrace the Savior?

"In the meantime," Peter said, his tone growing serious, "let us remember that Jesus conquered death! The grave could not keep Him captive. And now He has become the firstfruits of those who will be raised in glory. Those who taste death or bury loved ones before Jesus returns needn't fear, for His own will be raised to everlasting life! For the believer, death is the ultimate victory. Our God has defeated death. It is swallowed up in victory! *O Death, where is your sting? O Hades, where is your victory?* The victory is ours, my friends, for by God's grace we have triumphed over death through Jesus Christ our Lord!"

More resounding cheers, followed by shouts of jubilee.

As the sun rose higher and higher in the sky, the crowds began to dwindle, little by little. There was now plenty of space in the elegant courtyard for the few who remained, thirstily absorbing the disciple's words. Mary accepted the strength Mark offered as he wrapped a solid arm around her shoulders, drawing her close to him. Peter's sweet wife, Anaia, had joined them shortly after Joses led John Mark and several other children into the coolness of the villa for a refreshing snack.

"Never forget," Peter cried, "our God is greater than the enemy! Jesus Christ is the way, the truth, and the life. When there seems to be no way, we must always remember HE IS THE WAY! And we, as followers of that Way, must stand firm in our faith, no matter the cost!" Peter declared, his voice ringing out over the crowd.

"Hmmm. Followers of the Way..." Mary mused, savoring the sound of it.

"The Way," Anaia repeated softly, trying it out. "I like it."

"It would seem your husband has unwittingly provided a worthy title for the movement of Christ," Mark surmised, his eyes twinkling in his amusement.

"Your husband is remarkable," Mary told Anaia. "Look at him. He is a born leader."

Anaia smiled sweetly. "The Lord has done a mighty work in him. But we are all still works in progress."

Don't I know it, Mary thought, considering her steadily mounting concerns. She thought she had understood God's plan for her family—to offer their lovely home as a secret haven for the followers of Christ. Dangerous men were determined to uproot and choke out the growing seedlings before they were given the chance to take root. Here, she had hoped the believers could gather for worship and prayer, untouched by the Sanhedrin's wrath.

But now? It would seem all the world was aware of her unwavering allegiance. She thought of her husband and his successful businesses. He had so much to lose. And their young son? How was she to protect him now?

"Brothers and sisters," Peter's voice projected over the crowd, momentarily distracting Mary from her turbulent thoughts. "I must warn you that there will be opposition. The enemy of our souls will come against us, but we must stand firm. From the beginning of time, wicked men have sought to crush the truth. If they crucified our Lord, why then, should they welcome us? Again, I must remind you: Stand firm."

As if confirming Peter's strong warning, men donning trailing black robes, prominent phylacteries, and prayer shawls floated beneath the arched entryway, their expressions even more severe than their garments. With grave expressions, their dark eyes swept across the courtyard, absorbing the crowd of sincere men and women with keen displeasure.

Mary felt Anaia stiffen beside her, no doubt concerned for the safety of her husband. Though these were certainly not the first religious leaders to make an appearance, there was something inexplicably dark and oppressive about this particular procession.

Alarmed, Mary skillfully masked her unease, standing staunchly beside her husband. She noticed that the young Pharisee at the front of the procession looked vaguely familiar. Sensing her perusal, he turned to reward her with an icy glare.

Saul of Tarsus.

A promising student of the celebrated, highly esteemed rabbi, Gamaliel, Saul had schooled alongside her brothers, Joses and Antigonus. Though slight in stature, Saul possessed the broad shoulders and muscled form of a brawler. His very being exuded powerful energy, a daring restlessness, a burning zeal. He carried himself with an air of dangerous brutality, daring anyone he encountered to defy him. His dark eyes, full of venom, locked upon Mary, his message clear: *I'm coming for you.*

Heart pounding a battle rhythm in her chest, Mary returned his glare with an air of challenge: *Best of luck to you, sir.* Standing staunchly between her husband and Peter's wife, she held Saul's gaze unflinchingly until, reluctantly, he shifted his attention to the bold disciple on the balcony.

In that moment, Mary knew there would be no turning back. God had blessed her family with an unspeakable privilege: the founding of the faith, finding the Way, and leading as many as possible down that sacred path of repentance and restoration.

Well, so much for a secret haven, she thought, bemused. Clearly, God had His own plans for their home. And, by His grace, she would stand firm, holding her ground now that her cherished secret was known, despite the enemy's endless advances. Despite relentless persecution. And despite the dark stares and scathing threats of wicked men—men like Saul of Tarsus—determined to crush the truth, hinder the way, and extinguish the faintest, flickering hope of life.

CHAPTER 11

Mary

He seemed so young, so vital. How could she have known something was wrong? Could she have possibly guessed that his strong, seemingly healthy body was ailing? Only yesterday, Mary had strolled along Jerusalem's elegantly paved streets with him, hand in hand, basking in the glory of the bright, sun-soaked morning, delighting in the security of his company and the assurance of his love.

And now, a few short hours later, he was gone.

Oh, Mark, Mary's heart cried. *Mark, why did you go? Why did you leave me?*

She had sent for a physician the moment her husband had collapsed. Locating a doctor at that late hour, amidst a festival week, had proven challenging indeed. Dispatching a dozen servants to comb Jerusalem's swollen streets for a practicing physician, Mary had prayed unlike she'd ever prayed in her life, cradling her husband's still body in her arms.

It had been the perseverant Tabitha, relentless by nature, who returned first, practically dragging a confused young doctor through the massive entryway.

But despite Tabitha's dogged efforts, it was too late. Mark had slipped away from them.

Now, Mary sat woodenly in a straight-backed chair, unaware of her own surroundings in the vast reception hall, her heart throbbing in pain, her body numb. Her mind, muddled in shock and confusion, could scarcely piece together a decent thought. She was faintly aware of her young son's presence in the chair beside her. He sat ramrod straight, his face drained of color, his body tense, clenching and unclenching his fists in agitated grief.

How on earth was she to comfort her bereaved child when her own heart was ripped to shreds, devastated beyond repair? *Oh, God, grant me strength...*

"My lady?"

Simply lifting her head felt like a monumental task.

Tabitha stood at the foot of a winding staircase, her hazel-green eyes welling with sympathy. "The doctor has examined your husband's body," she said quietly, her voice low. "He has requested permission to speak with you."

Mary wondered if she possessed the strength and presence of mind to carry a conversation. "Send him in."

"Yes, my lady."

Tabitha disappeared. She returned a moment later, the young doctor following closely behind her. Descending the elegant stairs, he approached the grieving widow, his expression solemn, his kind eyes filled with pity.

Mary rose stiffly, turning to face the doctor in the flickering lamplight. Noting his bearing, his clean-shaven face, and his elaborate Greco-Roman apparel, alarm coursed through her. This man was a Gentile.

"My lady," he said, his voice unexpectedly comforting. "I am terribly sorry for your loss."

His genuine sympathy struck a chord in her heart, but Mary stoutly refused the comfort of tears. "What happened to him?" her voice sounded odd in her own ears, reverberating off the cold, frescoed walls.

"Based on his sudden, unexpected departure, we can safely assume his heart was the cause of death."

"But...but how?" Mary asked, her tone hollow.

"Some people are born with structural heart abnormalities which later become life-threatening. In most cases, there is little to no warning that something is amiss."

"Mark was born with a heart condition?"

"Most likely." The young man's dark eyes filled with empathy. "I beg you, my lady: Do not blame yourself for this shocking incident. Even if your maidservant had reached me before his passing, there is no treatment, no cure, for this condition. I could not have saved him."

Only God could have saved him, Mary thought, her mind clouded with confusion. Why hadn't He done so? How on earth was she, a lone widow, to carry on the Lord's work without her husband's protection and reassuring presence?

Clasping her hands before her, Mary maintained her composure before the Gentile physician. "You may see Tobias, our overseer, now. He will see to it that you are properly recompensed for your services—"

The physician lifted a hand of protest, halting her mid-sentence. "That will not be necessary, my lady. I was unable to help your husband."

"No," Mary sighed, a dull ache wrenching her heart. "But you were dragged from your bed in the middle of the night—"

"I hadn't yet bedded down for the evening," the doctor insisted, a hint of a smile lighting gentle, kindly features. "I often lose track of time when buried in my medical studies and research."

Mary gazed upon the physician with new respect. It was obvious the young man who stood before her was studious, intelligent, and ambitious. Most Gentiles avoided the holy city like the plague amidst the crowded festival weeks. She wondered what possible business this successful young foreigner had in Jerusalem during *Shavuot.*

"Thank you," Mary whispered, touched by this stranger's warmth and kindness. "May God be with you, sir."

"And you as well," the Gentile responded warmly.

"*Shalom*, my lady."

Shalom? Mary was surprised. This Gentile was familiar with Hebrew sayings and customs. With a pang to her heart, she watched as Tabitha led the young doctor away.

Shalom. Peace. Reaching for her grieving child, Mary wondered if she would ever know peace again.

***

Tabitha

"You're either a very brave man, Doctor," Tabitha observed, leading the curious young man beneath an elegant archway, and passing into the narrow vestibule beyond, "or you're insane. Which, I suppose, is yet to be determined."

Intrigued by the lovely maidservant's frank manner, the physician paused within the ornate vestibule, his mild features soft in the flickering lamplight. "May I ask how you reached that conclusion, miss?"

"You are Greek, yes?" Tabitha asked forthrightly.

"I am. Has my presence defiled the house of your mistress?" It was an honest question, free of offense.

Tabitha appreciated his humility. After all, it was rare. "Of course not. My lady values the lives of all men, both Jews and Greeks."

"Your lady is a strong woman."

"The strongest I know."

"She will get through this."

"You are very insightful, Doctor," Tabitha remarked, her innate curiosity piqued by this mysterious Gentile.

"Observing the conditions and responses of my patients is required in order to administer proper care and ascertain accurate diagnoses," the physician explained. "But I must point out that you still have not answered my initial question."

Tabitha waited, her expression enigmatic.

"You stated I must be courageous or insane. Why is that?"

"A Gentile, braving the streets of Jerusalem amidst a festival week?" Tabitha responded, her eyes betraying a hint of mischief. "Most foreigners head for the hills during the feasts and festival seasons— those who value their lives, anyway."

The doctor chuckled in amusement. "I've always been intrigued by the customs of your people. I must confess, I study your sacred texts most evenings."

A *Greek* interested in Jewish customs? "Are you a proselyte?"

The young man smiled wryly. "Not yet."

For the first time that evening, Tabitha allowed herself a moment to observe this unusual guest. Wondering at his earnest disclosure, she estimated him to be in his late thirties. There was nothing particularly striking about his features, and yet his humble bearing and endearing manner rendered him extremely attractive. Clearly, he was a quiet man, but she sensed a sound determination and a will of steel beneath his gentle demeanor. Earnest, patient, and compassionate, in her opinion, he was a worthy candidate for the Kingdom of God.

Reaching for the ponderous double doors just beyond the narrow vestibule, Tabitha pushed them open with great effort. As the bronze doors bowed inward, her senses were instantly filled with the soothing sounds of another peaceful night. Crickets chirped their merry dirge, filling the darkness with a mysterious song. Mounted torches cast writhing shadows upon the stone courtyard beyond, as gentle breezes whistled through verdant greenery, teasing the torches' flickering flames. Even the pleasant splashing of the great stone fountain filled the air with a peaceful, soothing calm. Fleetingly, Tabitha wondered at creation's moonlit serenity. How could the universe possibly carry on so, when her beloved mistress's entire world was in shambles? Battling against helplessness, Tabitha forced herself to dismiss the waves of uncertainty sweeping over her. Though many years had passed since the loss of her own father and mother, Tabitha knew she would never forget the raw agony of bereavement. It tore at her heart to consider the great suffering of Mary and her young son, John Mark. She knew exactly what they were going through.

Oh, how swiftly life could change! In one fateful instant, one's entire world could be turned inside out, upside down. How was one to cope with the blows of this sinful, fallen world? Tabitha knew the future must loom before her mistress, filled with dreadful forebodings. In one awful moment, everything had changed.

But Jesus Christ is the same yesterday, today, and forever. The promise surfaced in Tabitha's mind with even greater clarity than the night song, and her troubled heart was quieted. Despite these present troubles, Jesus remained the same. He was still in charge. He could still be trusted.

Oh, God, may my lady be comforted by these

precious promises of Yours!

Entrusting her cares to God, Tabitha drew her thoughts back to the present. The doctor stood before her, one hand resting lightly on the strap of his leather satchel, watching her intently. His brown eyes were so full of understanding she couldn't help but wonder if he sensed the direction of her anguished thoughts.

Gesturing toward the stone courtyard beyond, Tabitha said with great feeling, "Thank you for your assistance, doctor. I know your kind words were a comfort for my lady."

"I can only hope so," the doctor replied earnestly, his dark eyes tinged with sorrow. "I wish I could have saved him."

"He is in God's hands," Tabitha assured him, attempting to convince herself as well. And then the words of Simon Peter on Pentecost returned to her full force, filling her entire being with hopeful expectation: *Those who taste death or bury loved ones before Jesus returns needn't fear, for His own will be raised to everlasting life! For the believer, death is the ultimate victory. Our God has defeated death. It is swallowed up in victory! O Death, where is your sting? O Hades, where is your victory? The victory is ours, my friends, for by God's grace we have triumphed over death through Jesus Christ our Lord.*

Amen, Father, Tabitha prayed silently, observing the physician's retreating back as he crossed the stone courtyard. *Thy will be done.*

Sighing, Tabitha prepared to close the gilded doors. Zev would open the gate for the physician. She was disappointed to see him go, imagining it would be difficult for anyone *not* to be drawn to the benevolent young doctor. And then she felt the faintest stirring in her spirit, a gentle prompting...

This was an entirely new and exciting experience, recognizing the gentle whispers of the Holy Spirit, communing with God and experiencing His presence as profoundly as if she stood before Him in the Most Holy Place. Tabitha was reminded of that sacred moment when Jesus had given up His Spirit on the cross. Once Jesus had breathed His last, the enormous curtain barring the people from the presence of God had rent from top to bottom, inviting all believers to approach their God with faith and confidence.

Before Christ's finished work on the cross, only the high priest was permitted entrance in the Temple's Most Holy Place, and that only once a year on the sacred Day of Atonement. But now, the Holy Spirit dwelled in the hearts of believers, guiding them in the way of truth. A priest was no longer required to bridge the gap between God and men, for Christ Himself had become that bridge. Tabitha was awed and thrilled by this unspeakable privilege—to freely commune with her Savior, the King of the universe!

Glorying at this gentle stirring in her spirit, Tabitha knew what she must do: *Go therefore and make disciples of all the nations.*

"Doctor?"

Pausing mid-stride, the physician turned toward the attractive young woman, his dark eyes inquisitive.

"You said you study the sacred texts?"

"Extensively."

"Have you heard of Jesus of Nazareth?"

The physician's eyes sparkled with a hint of mischief. "Who hasn't?"

"Then you've heard about His selfless mission, His sacrificial death, and the power of His resurrection."

"His resurrection?" the doctor repeated dubiously. "I've heard rumors about an alleged resurrection, but that's clearly impossible. As exciting as it sounds, a resurrection is completely unfeasible both medically and scientifically."

"But doesn't that make it even more glorious?" Tabitha dared.

The doctor's expression grew troubled. "*If* it was possible...but surely, miss, you don't expect me to believe—"

"Jesus is alive. I saw Him with my own eyes, in this very house."

"I beg your pardon?"

"Ask around. I'm not the only one. Over five hundred witnesses have seen the resurrected Lord."

The young man stared at her with wide brown eyes.

"What do they call you, good Doctor?" Tabitha pressed, sensing his mounting alarm.

"I am Luke, the physician," he responded, obviously questioning her sanity at this point.

"Then perhaps it is time to ask yourself a crucial question, Master Luke."

The doctor studied her with a veiled expression.

"Do you believe in a God of miracles? Are you ready to embrace the impossible?"

"I'm afraid I'm a bit confused," Luke admitted, clearing his throat and shifting rather uncomfortably. "What does this dead Rabbi have to do with the sacred texts?"

"Everything," Tabitha responded without missing a beat. "And He isn't dead, Master Luke. He's alive and seated at the right hand of His Father in Heaven. Truly, Jesus is the long-awaited Messiah. The Scriptures prophesied His coming. Jesus fulfilled hundreds of Messianic prophecies during His time on this earth."

"How so?"

"You are familiar with the prophet Isaiah?"

"Of course."

"Then you will remember this: *He was wounded for our transgressions, He was bruised for our iniquities; the chastisement for our peace was upon Him, and by His stripes we are healed.*"

"Surely the great prophet spoke not of the crucifixion of a rebel!"

"Jesus Christ was no rebel, Doctor. He was sinless—the perfect, spotless Lamb who bore our punishment for us. *We like sheep have gone astray; we have turned, every one, to his own way; and the Lord has laid on Him the iniquity of us all.*"

"A woman reciting Torah," Luke mused, fascinated.

"Like you, I, too, study the sacred texts."

"You can *read*?"

"In Hebrew, Aramaic, and Greek."

"Remarkable!"

"Please, Doctor, ask God to grant you wisdom and understanding when you study the sacred texts. He will reveal the Messiah to you if you search for Him with all your heart."

"But will a Jewish Messiah be interested in a Gentile doctor? That is the question."

"Not only is Jesus the glory of His people, Israel," Tabitha explained. "He is the Light to bring revelation to the Gentiles."

"These are dangerous and controversial teachings. Your own priests cry out against them!"

"They cried out against the Messiah, too. That's why we must earnestly seek after God's truth, not the traditions of men."

"Is everything all right here?" a gruff voice interrupted the intense conversation.

Tabitha cast a look of exasperation toward Zev as the burly guard drew alongside the confused doctor.

Avoiding Tabitha's penetrating gaze, Luke turned to face the guard. "All is well," he quickly stated, noting Zev's glistening spear.

Biting back her frustration at the interruption, Tabitha wondered if Luke thought she had gone mad. At this point, he was clearly eager to escape. Would he even take the time to ponder her words, or would he simply dismiss them as the fanciful exaggerations of a silly young woman?

"I suppose I must bid you all goodnight," Luke said rather abruptly, his expression deeply troubled. "*Shalom.*"

"*Shalom,*" Tabitha replied softly, watching in dismay as Zev shut the iron gate behind Luke with an unfriendly *thud* of finality.

Silently, Tabitha committed the earnest physician into the hands of his Creator.

CHAPTER 12

Mary

Slowly, Mary rose from her position on the edge of her canopy bed, careful not to awaken her slumbering son. Torn with grief, the typically independent child hadn't argued when she suggested he share her room that night. Instead, he had cried himself to sleep while Mary stroked his quaking back.

Quietly crossing the room, Mary lowered herself onto the gilded chair before her vanity. When she gazed into the shimmering glass, she was startled by the haunting image of a pale, bleary-eyed, and somewhat unkempt woman staring back at her. Catching her breath, she turned sharply from her own reflection, her red-rimmed eyes sweeping across the dimly lit suite. The enormous canopy bed crouched like a slumbering beast in the shadows, its lush Babylonian curtains fluttering gently as evening breezes wafted through open windows. Silver moonlight cast slanted beams across the vast chamber, revealing a room richly furnished with elegantly upholstered couches, tall brass lamps, and a smattering of tables and stands overlaid in both silver and gold. Fresh summer flowers spilled over Grecian urns and elegant vases, supplying the staid chamber with unexpected bursts of vibrant color. Decorative oil lamps flickered dimly from their mounts upon vividly frescoed walls, casting a somewhat cheery glow upon the otherwise dismal scene. Underfoot, plush Persian rugs were scattered becomingly about the swirling mosaic floor. With his cherished wife in mind, Mark had spared no expense preparing this extravagant bedchamber—a suite fit for a queen.

Gripping the arms of her straight-backed chair, Mary closed her eyes tightly, attempting to dismiss a dreadful sense of foreboding. She could scarcely believe that Mark was gone. What on earth was she to do now? Mark had established booming business ventures from the ground up, expertly maintaining them and delegating worthy men to oversee each venture's daily operations. But if those businesses collapsed, hundreds if not thousands of men would lose their only source of income. What of those faithful workmen? How would they provide bread for their families if Mark's businesses imploded? The dreadful responsibility weighed heavily upon Mary's conscience. But how was *she*—a grieving widow—to fulfill her husband's impossible commercial obligations! Where to even begin?

And this great house, Lord! Mary lamented, her lovely eyes sweeping across the lavish surroundings. *I was so certain You had a plan for this beautiful house—a plan for us. But now? What now, Lord?*

I do have a plan for you, beloved. Plans of peace and not of evil.

Mary's eyes snapped open. Perched upon her throne-like chair, she raised her head, the goose-flesh prickling upon her cool skin. By the power of the Holy Spirit, she could indeed pour her heart out to God amidst great pain and uncertainty. But should she dare commune with her Creator now, revealing her raw inner struggle, her doubts and her misgivings?

Plans of peace? her heart cried as warm tears trickled down her cheeks. *I sense no peace in this, Father. Mark wasn't supposed to die. Didn't You know that? Why didn't You intervene? He was too young to die, too precious to me. He had his whole life ahead of him. What am I to do? What of my little son? Our hope, our future, perished along with my darling husband.*

My plans for you are good, dear one, plans to give you a future and a hope.

Where is the hope in this, Father? What kind of future can we expect now?

I AM your hope, beloved. I AM your future.

Covering her mouth with a trembling hand, Mary's shoulders shook as she suppressed her own racking sobs. She mustn't awaken her sleeping child. *Oh, God, I want to believe You, but my spirit is weak. How can I face the future without my husband? How can I carry on Your work without him? Violent men seek to crush this movement, and I'm an easy mark.*

Trust Me.

But I cannot do this without my husband, Lord. I cannot press on without Mark.

Through Me, you can do all things. I will give you strength.

I can't do it, Lord, Mary protested, her heart throbbing.

My grace is sufficient for you.

But, Father...Oh Father, I am so weak.

Fear not, beloved, for My strength is made perfect in weakness. When you are weak, then I AM strong.

Troubled, Mary rose shakily upon elegantly sandaled feet. Crossing the room, she paused before an open window. Drawing aside the fluttering tapestry, Mary gazed upon the holy city slumbering beneath a storybook moon, millions of dazzling stars glittering like tiny, brilliant gems in the heavenlies. Wispy clouds drifted lazily across the night sky, obscuring stars here and there, buffering the moon's bright light. And then a promise from the Word of God whispered its way into her heart with such tender clarity Mary nearly wept: *The Lord God will help me; therefore I will not be disgraced; therefore I have set my face like a flint, and I know that I will not be ashamed.*

Wrapping slender arms around her body to ward off the unwelcome evening chill, Mary raised shining eyes toward Heaven, her heart communing with the Creator of those dazzling midnight stars. "So be it," she whispered, her uncompromising tone boding no argument. "I choose to trust You even if I don't understand. No power on earth can keep me from Your will. No force of darkness can separate me from Your love. I am Your servant, Father, and I won't back down now."

As if in response, brilliant beams of silver moonlight burst through the wispy clouds, bathing the entire city—and Mary's tear-stained face—in brilliant, heavenly light.

"I, too, have set my face like a flint," Mary resolved, drawing a steady breath, "and I know that I will not be ashamed."

CHAPTER 13

Tabitha

The remainder of *Shavuot* culminated in a dizzying whirl of dreaded, though necessary, affairs. There was little time left for celebrating the festival week, but Tabitha doubted the recently bereaved, nor the household staff, had the heart for celebration, anyway.

After Mark's body had been washed and prepared for burial, Mary gathered the entire staff, along with family members and fellow believers, at the same quaint garden tombs where their Savior had been laid to rest. As the land readily welcomed the warm summer season, the garden respite exploded with fragrant blooms and breathtaking summer blossoms, bursting with vibrant color. Tabitha was awed by the beauty and serenity of the beautiful yet somber site.

Even as the body of Mary's beloved husband was committed to the tomb, a spirit of hope abounded within the gathering. For here, in this quiet place of death, Jesus Christ had gained the ultimate victory over it. Mary stood tall, resolute, as Simon Peter spoke a few words of encouragement and offered an earnest prayer on behalf of the entire gathering. Mary did not shed a single tear that morning, for she had already poured out her griefs to God, both finding solace and taking refuge in Him.

Sadly, Tabitha watched John Mark standing woodenly beside his stalwart mother, numb with both shock and confusion. Her heart ached for him. Young Rhoda stood beside Tabitha, clasping her hand. Tabitha noted Rhoda's gaze pinned upon her young master, John Mark. Sympathetic tears coursed down both cheeks. Tabitha knew Rhoda's tender heart was breaking for those she loved.

It was a blessed relief to return home, although Tabitha knew their troubles were far from over.

A quiet, solemn procession entered the somber villa, each servant quickly returning to his or her respective task. Accepting Mary's proffered shawl, Tabitha draped it over one arm and stood at her mistress's elbow, ready to be of assistance. "How may I best serve you, my lady?" she asked gently, concerned for the young widow.

Mary scarcely seemed to comprehend the helpful inquiry, for her eyes roved about the vast reception hall, a thousand different responsibilities begging for her attention. "I'm sure John Mark would appreciate some refreshment," she said distractedly. "Please speak with the chefs and see if something can be done about that."

"John Mark is still walking home with his little friend, Simeon," Tabitha reminded her, grateful the grieving twelve-year-old was at least momentarily distracted from his loss in the company of his good friend.

"I'm sure both boys will be hungry," Mary responded, briskly crossing the vast hall. "Refreshments are certainly in order." Pausing at the staircase, she said quietly, "I shall change into something more practical before reviewing the business accounts. If anyone asks for me, I will be working in the *bibliotheca*."

"Perhaps you should rest a bit first, my lady," Tabitha dared, concerned for her.

"Thank you for your concern, Tabitha, but I prefer to keep my hands busy and my thoughts occupied. After all, Mark's ventures won't run themselves, and I have no intention of letting them fall apart, one by one."

"I understand, my lady. Will you take any refreshments?"

"None for me, thank you."

"But you must keep up your strength—"

"I'll be fine. Truly."

"As you wish, my lady." Feeling helpless, Tabitha watched as Mary mounted the winding staircase, each step betraying her weariness.

I'm quite certain I've never seen a woman more tenacious than Mary, Tabitha thought after speaking with the kitchen help. Amused, she watched as her lady—now dressed in uncharacteristically simple, practical garb, her dark, lush curls pinned beneath a modest covering—descended the grand stairway, summoned Tobias, and marched straight for her former husband's office library, eager to settle the business accounts.

With a heavy heart, Tabitha went about her daily

tasks, praying for Mary and John Mark even as she worked.

***

The sun hung low upon the hilly western horizon, bathing the magnificent city of Jerusalem in dusky golden hues.

Despite the lateness of the hour, Mary remained sequestered within the opulent *bibliotheca*, immersed in piles of maps, charts, and ledgers.

Reluctantly, Tabitha approached Mark's grand office library, tucked snugly in a quiet corner of the first floor, overlooking another peaceful, open-air courtyard nestled at the heart of the exquisite home. Pausing in a dim, lamplit corridor, Tabitha shifted the heavy tray she bore in tired hands, hoping the tantalizing supper lovingly prepared by the head chef would trigger Mary's seemingly dormant appetite. Taking a deep breath, she passed beneath the library's grand entrance upheld by painted marble pillars, praying that Mary would listen to reason. After all, the hour was late and the bereaved woman hadn't had anything to eat or drink since very early that morning, long before her husband's funeral. Tabitha knew Mary possessed the drive and determination of a battering ram, but surely even the strongest and the best required rest and sustenance!

"My lady?" Tabitha ventured gently, hoping she hadn't startled her distracted mistress.

Standing behind an imposing desk near the back of the large library, Mary was bent over a large mound of open scrolls and ledgers, her dark brows furrowed in concentration, one slender finger tracing the long, numbered columns on a page.

Shaking her head to clear the fog of deep concentration, Mary acknowledged Tabitha's presence with a tired smile.

"It is late," Tabitha ventured, raising the tray of steaming food, "and we're all concerned for your welfare. Will you take supper, my lady, and retire for the evening?"

Tiredly massaging her temples with delicate fingertips, Mary straightened slowly and closed her eyes. "Is it getting late?"

Tabitha's eyes drifted toward the open courtyard just beyond a row of marble pillars. The sun's rays had nearly vanished as dark shadows slanted across the cool stones. "The sun has nearly set."

"Oh my! And still so much to be done," Mary mused, meticulously rolling several open scrolls and setting them aside. "But I suppose I should retire for the evening."

Tabitha was relieved. "Where will you take your supper?"

"In the family *triclinium* with John Mark," Mary supplied, cringing inwardly. Mark's painful absence would be blatantly conspicuous, his vacant *lectus* looming across the banquet table. Would these gut-wrenching reminders ever cease?

"John Mark has asked if Simeon may stay the night," Tabitha informed Mary, her tone slightly hesitant. "Shall I prepare a third setting at the table?"

"Of course he may stay," Mary responded with a tired smile. "I daresay his presence is a helpful distraction. Simeon is a kind, thoughtful child. He takes after his grandfather."

Nodding, Tabitha couldn't help but wonder if

Mary would remain in the good graces of Simeon's grandfather, Gamaliel, despite his amiable disposition.

Recently succeeding the famous Shimon ben Hillel, Gamaliel bore the power-charged title of *Nasi*, meaning prince, *or Rabban,* master. Presiding as president of the great Sanhedrin in Jerusalem, only Joseph Caiaphas, the high priest, surpassed Gamaliel in power and influence. The great-grandson of the powerful teacher, Hillel the Elder, Gamaliel remained the leading authority in Jerusalem, favoring his great-grandfather's liberal interpretation of Jewish law. Tabitha couldn't imagine Gamaliel, a highly esteemed and celebrated teacher of the Law, would favor the followers of the Way.

"Can I help you close up shop here before I ready the small *triclinium*?" Tabitha asked with a hint of a smile, dismissing her concerns about the *Nasi*. "You look rather at home behind that massive desk."

Chuckling softly, Mary lifted several heavy scrolls, carrying them toward the imposing floor-to-ceiling shelves lining the entire wall behind the desk. Each wooden shelf was divided into uniform squares with neatly ordered cubby holes for the scrolls. Tabitha had always marveled at the orderliness of Mark's library and his efficient filing system. It would seem Mary had resumed her husband's work with very little difficulty.

"After reviewing these ledgers, I am even more amazed by my husband's efficiency and generosity," Mary said, a slight tremor in her voice. Slipping scrolls into the proper cubby holes, the stoic woman turned her back to the golden-haired maidservant, and Tabitha suspected Mary had turned to shield her misty eyes and turbulent emotions rather than replace the documents.

"Have you accomplished your purpose this evening?" Tabitha asked, setting the tray upon a marble-topped table to help Mary organize the remaining scrolls.

"I believe so," Mary said, forcing a smile she was far from feeling. "Mark runs multiple businesses, all of them booming. I have two options: sell them off, one by one, or resume Mark's responsibilities myself."

"And what have you decided?"

"Honestly, it would be far simpler to sell his holdings, but I'm concerned for his workers and their families. Should I choose to sell, there's a huge possibility those hard-working men would lose their jobs or suffer at the hands of harsh employers."

"You've decided to run the businesses yourself?" Tabitha dared, her tone tinged with admiration. Why, a *woman*—and a *widow*, no less—overseeing the operation of multiple business ventures? It was practically unheard of!

"It sounds reckless, I know," Mary conceded, filing the last of the scrolls. "But after spending an entire night in earnest prayer, I'm more at peace than ever. There's still pain, yes, but the peace triumphs over it."

Tabitha shook her head in awe. "If anyone can do it, my lady, *you* can!"

"Not by my own strength," Mary admitted, touching Tabitha's shoulder as a mother might. "Apart from Christ, I can do nothing. But with Him, all things are possible—even this."

"Have you a plan?"

"Mark outlined his business plans for each of his ventures, and I intend to follow them. He is—*was*—" she amended, her voice catching, "a brilliant man. But I will need an assistant—someone with special knowledge and training—to walk beside me as I learn the ropes."

Tabitha's brows lifted in surprise. "Where will you find such a person?"

"Initially, I considered asking Tobias," Mary replied, "but he has more than enough on his plate, as he is already my personal assistant and busily managing this enormous estate."

"Who, then?"

Mary's luminous gray eyes sparked slightly, and Tabitha knew the tenacious young widow had already made up her mind. "I plan to hire Stephanos."

Tabitha's jaw dropped. "Stephanos?"

"He's a brilliant man, and he's studied under the tutelage of the most exceptional scholars of our time," Mary rushed to explain, sensing Tabitha's shock. "He has a keen mind for numbers and mathematics, and he speaks multiple languages. He is also schooled in the art of business. These skills are essential to oversee multiple ventures scattered across several regions."

"But will he accept your proposition?" Tabitha protested, attempting to curb her own surprise. "Stephanos is an *evangelist*!"

"Even evangelists need to make a living," Mary pointed out, a hint of a smile teasing her features. "I'll pay him well, although I imagine most of his earnings will be invested to help the poor. He is passionate about reaching the lost."

Tabitha was well aware of that. She often ministered to the orphans and widows at the Synagogue of the Freedmen, distributing handmade garments and blankets to the many poor. There, where Gamaliel presided over the popular synagogue, Stephanos' fiery preaching often drew the attention of those to whom she ministered. Sometimes, his interruptions were rather untimely. Annoying, even. She had to remind herself that his impassioned speech was the vessel by which the gospel was being preached, even if his style was a bit brash for her liking.

The thought of sharing the same quarters with the fiery Hellenist—even for just a few hours a day—was a bit daunting.

"It's all so overwhelming," Mary admitted, drawing Tabitha's rebellious thoughts back to the present moment. "I can't help but wonder, *Why Mark?* Why was his life taken when mine was spared? Wouldn't *he* be a far better candidate to run these operations? Wouldn't he be far more capable of furthering the growth of the Way—using this house for God's glory—than I? It's all in God's hands, I know, and I trust Him. But I must confess, I am perplexed."

Going to her mistress, Tabitha took her hands and met her gaze, her own hazel-green eyes shining with promise. "In my darkest moment, a very wise woman encouraged me with these words, an admonition I will never forget: '*Our God never makes mistakes. You were indeed spared for a reason, even if that is difficult to believe right now.*'"

Mary's eyes widened as poignant recollection swept across her entire being. Closing her eyes, she allowed her tears to fall freely, tracing slender lines down both cheeks.

"'*But someday—someday soon, perhaps—all the*

pieces shall fall into place,'" Tabitha reminded her, exhorting her lady with the very words by which she had been encouraged in her hour of need. *"'And you will look back on this difficult season of your life, fully recognizing that God has worked all things together for your ultimate good.'* Carry these words with you, my lady, as I have," Tabitha urged, her eyes brightening with confident hope. "They were meant for you, too."

Mary's eyes filled at the great irony of her own words of wisdom, the foreknowledge of her omnipotent God. She remembered standing in the stone courtyard with a much younger Tabitha, the pain of bereavement shining in the orphan's eyes. And she marveled at the fact that God had allowed her to comfort that little girl, already knowing, years later, she herself would find solace in her own promise.

CHAPTER 14

Tabitha

Tabitha was becoming extremely familiar with the *bibliotheca*, the chamber she seldom entered before the untimely death of her master. But as Mary dedicated more time to business affairs, Tabitha often found herself serving at her lady's elbow in the imperious office library. Fleetingly, she wondered if Mary felt closer to her beloved husband when sequestered within the workspace dearest to his heart.

"My lady," Tabitha announced cheerfully, passing beneath the pillared entrance. "Are you ready to partake of the midday meal?" she asked, lifting a heavy tray and nodding toward Rhoda as the little girl drew alongside her, bearing her own tray heavy laden with fresh fruit, wild olives, and flatbread.

Glancing up from the scrolls strewn about her desk, Mary smiled warmly. "That sounds lovely. Thank you, Tabitha. You may serve Stephanos first."

Biting back her own sharp protest, Tabitha crossed the room toward Stephanos' workstation—a modest wooden desk overlooking the lovely, flow-er-strewn courtyard just beyond a pillared, red-tiled portico. She often found herself repenting about her attitude toward this aggravating young man. After all, it certainly wasn't his intent to plant himself right in the midst of her own happy world, hinder-ing both her time and conversation with Mary. In fact, his business knowledge and unwavering work ethic was a great help to Mary, and Tabitha knew she should be grateful for that.

Not only was Stephanos a brilliant man and ca-pable associate, but he was also a powerhouse for the furtherance of the gospel. Daily, he visited idealistic locations where crowds were sure to gather, such as Solomon's Porch and the Synagogue of the Freed-men, to share the Good News with anyone willing to listen. The religious leaders both loathed and envied his dynamic preaching and uncanny ability to reach any audience, while observant Jews scoffed that he was wasting his limitless talent and potential—not to mention his expensive education—by becoming a simple street preacher. Stephanos' wealthy and affluent father clearly agreed with his Hellenized brethren, for he had disinherited his son the moment he learned of Stephanos' "defection" to the "bizarre new sect" called the Way. But when the believers asked Stephanos if he planned to return to Athens to change his father's mind and thus procure his in-heritance, Stephanos merely insisted he counted his loss as gain, reminding them of the Savior's gentle admonition: *If the world hates you, you know that it hated Me before it hated you...if they persecuted Me, they will also persecute you.* Stephanos deemed it a great privilege to suffer for the sake of Christ.

In addition to his great faith and powerful, eloquent speech, Stephanos was handsome and charismatic. A tall man of medium build, his olive skin, intense brown eyes, and jet-black hair suited his bold disposition. When he smiled—which he did quite often—the deep-set dimples framing his broad smile matched the one on his clean-shaven chin, emphasizing his firm jawline and chiseled facial features. Tabitha had noticed numerous young women watching him in open admiration, yet Stephanos seemed completely oblivious to their rapt attention, so intent was he upon his gospel work. Tabitha was secretly amused when doe-eyed young maidens vied for Stephanos' attention. A bit snidely, she assumed the fiery Hellenist, already in his early thirties, was far too busy changing the world to settle down and find himself a wife.

Setting aside his stylus with a bit of dramatic flair, Stephanos shook his head in amazement as Tabitha reluctantly approached his desk, bearing a tray piled high with refreshments. "Mary, you already pay me well! This is an incredibly kind but unnecessary gesture—providing the midday meal. You must reserve your funds for the Lord's work, not to fill my own stomach!"

"This *is* the Lord's work, Stephanos," Mary smiled, graciously accepting the tray Rhoda placed before her. "These are the Lord's resources. This is His house. We must be good stewards, blessing others less fortunate than we. Without your help and management, I fear everything would fall apart."

"Highly unlikely," Stephanos responded, a smile teasing his handsome features.

Tabitha approached his desk, the tray growing

heavier by the minute. Setting it before him, she prepared to retreat in silence.

It was almost as if Stephanos sensed her chagrin. *Perhaps he's a prophet, along with his many other talents,* Tabitha thought snidely, avoiding his penetrating gaze. It wouldn't surprise her in the least. Why not include yet another noble distinction in addition to his impressive repertoire of spiritual and educational achievements?

"Good afternoon, dear sister," Stephanos greeted her warmly, and Tabitha resisted the urge to be drawn by his attractive charisma. "Thank you for providing this delectable feast."

"I only bore the tray," she replied a bit stiffly. "The chefs prepared your meal."

"I imagine you prepare fine cuisine, as well," Stephanos responded without missing a beat. "Mary says you are a woman of many talents."

Clearly, not as many as you, she wished to retort, though she held her tongue. Even as the unlovely thought crossed her mind, Tabitha was doused with an unwanted helping of guilt, sensing the unwelcome heat of those dreaded burning coals referenced by the sagacious King Solomon. After all, her dislike toward Stephanos was unfounded. He had been nothing but kind to her, and—what's more—he had led their beloved Tobias in his prayer of repentance and restoration. Stephanos was a powerful speaker, zealous for Christ, full of life and purpose. Surely it was no fault of his that the entire world—including Mary and the entirety of the household staff—was naturally drawn to him! Was it his fault that he possessed seemingly every possible skill or talent known to man?

In frustration, Tabitha recognized her own dislike for what it was—envy, plain and simple, rearing its ugly head. *Stephanos* dominated Mary's time and attention these days, though Mary hardly seemed to mind. *Stephanos* "stole" the attention of Tabitha's own small following every time she spoke to the widows and orphans at the synagogue—never mind the fact that they were not *her* widows and orphans in the first place. And *Stephanos* was one of the few people who—unwittingly, no doubt—made her feel dull and uneducated. After all, the believers were always impressed by her knowledge, practicality, and unrivaled skills in many varying arenas—until Stephanos entered the stage, snatching the limelight with little to no effort.

God, forgive me, Tabitha sighed inwardly, acknowledging Stephanos' sincere compliment with a forced smile. *Help me behave myself. Heaven knows I can't do it myself!*

"Thank you, Stephanos, for delivering our tithe to the Temple this morning," Mary said sincerely, and Tabitha was relieved when Stephanos' intense gaze flickered to Mary rather than resting enigmatically upon *her*.

"It was no trouble at all," Stephanos replied easily, setting aside some paperwork to make more space for his tray. "I had a speaking engagement at Solomon's Porch, anyway."

Of course you did, Tabitha thought rather glibly, silently chastising herself once again for her lack of self-control. Preparing to leave, she motioned for Rhoda to join her.

"Tabitha, Rhoda, please stay and fellowship with us," Mary invited warmly, beckoning toward two elegant, straight-backed chairs across from her massive desk. "I can't possibly consume this entire tray of food myself."

Tabitha never could resist her lady's kindness. Mary was unconventional in many ways, for most women of aristocratic breeding wouldn't be caught dead sharing a meal with the household help. But the love of Christ had torn down the barriers between the rich and poor, master and servant. In Mary's eyes, those who worked for her were every bit as valuable as the wealthiest of her patrons.

As if seeking permission, Rhoda gazed up at Tabitha with large brown eyes. Smiling at her, Tabitha nodded and crossed the room once more, seating herself across from the large desk and accepting the plump bunch of glistening grapes Mary offered her. "Thank you, my lady. You spoil us." Tearing off a smaller cluster, Tabitha offered it to Rhoda. Taking the seat beside Tabitha, the little girl accepted the glistening fruit with eager hands.

"Stephanos, will you bless this meal, please?" Mary requested, bowing her head.

Somehow, Tabitha managed to tame her unruly thoughts as Stephanos uttered a remarkably eloquent prayer of thanks.

"Thank you, Stephanos," Mary said, dipping a piece of flatbread in fresh oil manufactured at her own olive press. Her resolute posture and purposeful expression indicated that she intended to work through the midday meal. Tabitha smiled to herself. Something was clearly on Mary's mind.

"As I've continued to review Mark's ledgers," Mary said thoughtfully, confirming Tabitha's suspicion, "I've realized he not only paid faithful tithes, but also set aside large funds each month to further the Lord's work. He called them *love offerings*—probably because *offerings* refer to gifts our fathers devoted to the Lord apart from their obligatory tithe. I would like to continue that practice," Mary explained, her eyes searching Stephanos' for counsel.

Glumly, Tabitha popped a grape into her mouth. In the past, Mary would have asked *her* opinion. Apparently, Stephanos' advice was more highly regarded.

"I love it," Stephanos responded, his dark eyes dancing. " *'Bring all the tithes into My storehouse, that there may be food in My house, and try Me now in this,' says the Lord of hosts, 'If I will not open for you the windows of Heaven—'*"

" '—*and pour out for you such blessing that there will not be room enough to receive it,'*" Mary finished, her expression thoughtful. "The prophet Malachi."

"It's God's promise to those bold enough to embrace it," Stephanos affirmed, his dark eyes betraying his excitement. "Did your husband specify how the funds for the offering were to be distributed this month?"

"I haven't found anything yet, but the Lord has placed something on my heart."

Three pairs of eyes fastened upon Mary, curiosities piqued. Momentarily, Tabitha's envy was forgotten.

"At night, I am plagued by the terror I experienced the night Mark died, when I was waiting for a doctor to save him," Mary confessed, her eyes glistening with unshed tears. "But the world is filled with sick, dying people. When I think of those with sick husbands, wives, children, parents…how they must be hurting, the fear they must be experiencing…" Mary shook her head, leafing through the ledger nearest her tray. "There must be some way to help them."

"Have you prayed about this?" Stephanos asked, his gaze penetrating.

"Without ceasing."

"My lady?"

Three heads swiveled toward Rhoda in surprise, for the shy little mite scarcely spoke a word.

"Yes, my dear Rhoda?" Mary asked, her warm smile dismissing Rhoda's timidity.

"I think you may have dropped this," the child said shyly, lifting a rather tattered slip with hurriedly scratched markings on it.

"Why, thank you, Rhoda," Mary said gratefully, accepting the slip of papyrus.

Tabitha leaned forward in her seat, ever curious. "What is it, my lady?"

Mary's face whitened as her eyes scanned the ink on the page. "Oh, my," she exclaimed, her hand fluttering to her heart.

Tabitha and Stephanos were on their feet in an instant, both rushing to Mary's side.

"My lady!" Tabitha exclaimed, taking Mary's arm.

"Mary! Are you all right?" The typically confident Stephanos looked nearly frantic.

Laughing, Mary waved them aside. "Good heavens, I'm fine!" she chuckled. "Just a bit surprised, that's all."

Stephanos and Tabitha exchanged looks of sheer relief, and Tabitha couldn't help but appreciate his genuine concern for Mary. Warmed by his affection for the person dearest to her own heart, Tabitha was plagued by yet another wave of guilt. *Oh, Lord,* she prayed silently. *Stephanos is a godly man. Empty me of myself and fill me with your Holy Spirit instead, so I can receive this man as a faithful brother. My heart isn't in the right place.*

"May I ask what gave you such a start, Mary?" Stephanos asked a bit teasingly, drawing Tabitha's attention as he returned to his desk.

"I should know better than to doubt the Holy Spirit's prompting," Mary chuckled, shaking her head in awe. "Mark must have scribbled this reminder for himself while working on the ledgers."

"What does it say?" Tabitha asked before she could stop herself.

Mary's eyes glistened with determination as she read the note aloud: "*This month's offering: provide relief for the sick and the dying.*"

Stephanos shook his head in amazement. "It looks like you're on the right track, Mary. The Holy Spirit is at work."

"It would seem the Lord spoke to you *and* your husband," Tabitha observed, returning to her chair and offering Rhoda a piece of flatbread. The little girl ate in silence, her bright eyes alert as she absorbed the conversation swirling around her.

Setting aside the note, Mary intertwined delicate fingers, resting her chin upon them. "Now how to go about fulfilling this commission?" she mused.

A thought occurred to Tabitha with such force she knew it must be from the Holy Spirit. "Perhaps you should consult Master Luke," she exclaimed, her excitement rising. "He would know exactly where assistance was needed."

"Master Luke?" Mary repeated, her brows lifting. "I'm not familiar with the name."

"The young physician who spoke with you the night your husband passed, my lady."

Mary's brows lifted in consideration. "The Gentile doctor," she murmured, her gaze distant as painful memories resurfaced in her mind. "He was remarkably kind."

"Indeed," Tabitha agreed. "Wouldn't he know all about those in need, considering his profession?"

"Ah, the good doctor," Stephanos mused, stroking his dimpled chin. "I know of him."

Of course you do, Tabitha thought with a bit less animosity this time, a small smile playing about the corners of her lips. Stephanos knew *everyone,* and anyone privileged to meet the daring Hellenist seldom forgot him.

"Is he a local?" Mary asked.

"He's Greek, and I believe he currently resides in Antioch. He's well-traveled, so keeping up with him proves rather difficult at times."

"Syrian or Pisidian Antioch?" Mary inquired.

"Syrian."

"Hmm...I wonder why he was in Jerusalem for the festival week," Mary thought aloud.

"He said he is intrigued by our customs and festivals," Tabitha explained knowingly. "He even studies Torah. I think he may become a proselyte."

"Perhaps," Mary mused. "It's likely he's already returned to Antioch. The festival ended weeks ago."

"Not necessarily," Stephanos supplied, his dark eyes twinkling. "Luke's a benevolent soul. He won't leave a sick patient behind. If he happens to be treating a patient here, he won't return to Antioch until they've made a full recovery."

Tabitha's respect for the young doctor increased even more.

"What else do you know about this physician, Stephanos?" Mary asked, and Tabitha could almost hear the wheels turning in her lady's head. The food upon Mary's tray remained virtually untouched, so intent was she upon fulfilling this mission instigated by the Holy Spirit.

"He's long desired to set up his own practice, but doctoring is a costly business. Medical instruments, expensive herbs and medicinal remedies, not to mention a permanent location conducive to treating patients, are all costly expenses. Unfortunately, it just hasn't happened for him yet."

"And why is that?" Mary asked, tapping a slender stylus thoughtfully against her cheekbone.

Tabitha turned in her chair, her eyes resting expectantly upon the young evangelist. Her burning curiosity was stoked by the young physician's unusual story.

"Luke is a rare breed," Stephanos expounded, his tone colored with admiration. "He's notorious for treating *anyone* seeking medical attention—whether they can afford it or not."

"Does he institute payment programs for those unable to compensate him for his service up front?" Mary inquired in a businesslike fashion.

"He does," Stephanos responded slowly. "But Luke refuses to turn anyone away. He doctors even the poorest and the destitute, knowing they can't pay him back."

"Hence his inability to set up his own practice," Mary surmised softly. "He loses money treating those who cannot pay."

"Had Luke met our Savior when He walked the earth, I think the good doctor would have discovered they have much in common," Stephanos said quietly. "Both are passionate about ministering to the sick, the maimed, the outcasts."

"He is an exceptional young man," Mary stated, her tone decisive. "Had he chosen to follow our Savior, Tabitha," she declared stoutly, drawing the maidservant's surprised attention, "I would arrange a betrothal for you this instant."

"But, my lady!" Realizing her mouth was hanging open, Tabitha promptly closed it. "I'm not seeking a betrothal! Heavens, no."

Stephanos chuckled heartily, amused by the feisty young maidservant's sudden discomfiture.

"It's true," Mary declared unapologetically. "Perhaps someday the physician will accept Christ. A man of his character comprises a worthy husband."

"But, my lady, I cannot marry," Tabitha argued vehemently, sensing both Rhoda's and Stephanos' gazes resting upon her in merry amusement. "I am but a servant!"

"Oh, nonsense," Mary laughed, tickled by Tabitha's reaction. "Servants marry. Half the servants in this household are married, or have you so swiftly forgotten?"

"Well, perhaps it's fine for *them* to marry," Tabitha protested, her color deepening in her chagrin. "But I haven't a father to arrange a marriage nor provide the dowry."

"I am more than capable of making such arrangements," Mary persisted vehemently. "And if the Lord sends the right man along, you can be sure I will do so!"

Tabitha's heart pounded so heavily in her chest she was certain everyone in the room could hear it. As her entire face flushed with the heat of embarrassment, she could have gleefully wiped the broad grin right off Stephanos' face.

"You are a lovely young woman who adores our Savior," Stephanos countered, shocking Tabitha to her very core. "And someone is bound to notice you," he added cryptically. "Best not deny nor reject the inevitable, dear sister."

"No man in his right mind would consider such a thing," Tabitha insisted stoutly, crossing slender arms before her chest. "I'm far too headstrong to please a man."

"Well," Stephanos mused, flashing her an impish grin, "I won't argue with that."

Perturbed, Tabitha considered smacking Stephanos upside the head, but quickly decided against it since it wouldn't be very Christlike.

"Now, now, *children*," Mary teased, easing the mounting tension in the office library. "Back to the matter at hand. Stephanos, I want you to locate this physician named Luke."

"Consider it done," Stephanos responded, exuding confidence. "And what, dear lady, shall I tell him?"

Turning around in her straight-backed chair, Tabitha looked toward her mistress then, relieved the conversation had finally shifted its course.

"You may tell the good doctor," Mary responded, her dark eyes dancing with joyful mischief, "that the Lord has decided to fund his practice. He'd best prepare himself for action."

CHAPTER 15

Mary

"Thank you for joining me this evening," Mary said sincerely, reclining upon her elegant *lectus* in the family *triclinium* and addressing the familiar guests at her table. "I'm so thankful you have continued meeting here to strategize and regroup, but I believe the Lord has even greater plans than this for the house."

Lounging somewhat uncomfortably upon his own *lectus*, Simon Peter lifted his goblet and took a thoughtful sip of the cool, scented water Mary had graciously provided. It was comically obvious that the rough-and-tumble fisherman felt a bit out of place reclining at the fine table like a wealthy patron. A bit self-conscience about his is tousled hair and travel-stained tunic in the presence of his dignified aunt by marriage, he asked a bit hesitantly, "What exactly did you have in mind?"

Mary's soft eyes swept across the lavishly furnished room, where several apostles had gathered at her request. She was still getting used to the term, *apostle*. In fact, several new terms had developed in recent weeks as the Messiah's movement spread like wildfire. The collective group of those who followed Jesus Christ had been dubbed *ekklesia*, the church. This Greek term, meaning *called out*, was quite fitting, in Mary's opinion; for the body of believers had been called, set apart, by the Savior Himself to go forth, making disciples of all the nations. This privilege, this sacred trust, was the true mission of the church. And Mary intended to embrace it with her entire being, offering all that she was, all that she had, for the blessed work of her beloved Savior.

"As the church continues to grow, the believers must be instructed in the Way," Mary explained earnestly, studying the attentive faces of the four men gathered about her table. "As you all know far better than I, this is a daily process rather than a one-time lesson or tutorial. To grow in our faith, we must study the Word and learn to apply it in our daily lives."

"We certainly agree with you, dear sister," John, the beloved, responded easily, leaning forward upon the *lectus* he shared with his brother, James. The burly brothers had adjusted to a relaxed sitting position, their elbows resting casually upon weathered knees.

"We have continued to meet with the believers outdoors," James, the Lord's brother, clarified. "But at times, the weather is not conducive. Other times, those farthest from the speakers struggle to hear the instruction."

"And we meet in a few small homes scattered about Jerusalem, as well," the brother of John added. "But the homes are small, and few can assemble within."

"Even so, God is working mightily," the Lord's brother confessed.

"That's exactly what I wish to discuss, my dear brother," Mary said, warmed by the presence of her Savior's brother, James. Previously, she'd found it incredibly difficult to believe that this humble man of God had rejected his own Brother until the morning of His miraculous resurrection, for James was now among the most zealous of Christ's followers. He seldom spoke, but when he did, his speech was both powerful and profound. When asked the secret of his great wisdom, he quietly responded, "My Brother taught me to *be swift to hear, slow to speak, and slow to wrath*. Only now have I begun to abide by His Word, putting it into practice. If only I had done so sooner."

"By God's grace, the gospel is reaching thousands," Mary surmised, studying the men before her.

"True, followers are joining the Way at a rapid pace," Peter admitted, leaning conspiratorially across the table, his features cast in flickering lamplight. "We've baptized thousands. The problem is, we don't have adequate space to instruct them all."

"The animosity of the religious leaders increases by the day," James, the brother of John, spoke up. "I fear that, in time, we will be banned from hosting gatherings on public grounds. Then what?"

"When that time comes, we will obey God rather than men," Peter put in vehemently, his dark eyes flashing. "They cannot forbid us to preach the gospel!"

"Speaking in public locations is a sure way to win

the hearts of new converts," Mary said, her soothing tone easing the mounting tension in the *triclinium*. "But we also need a place to gather with our brothers and sisters, to worship and study the Word without fear of the Romans or the religious leaders."

"But where to find such a place?" John's brother, James, asked frankly. "Already there are thousands counted among us."

"We would need a building the size of Herod Antipas' palace," John scoffed. "And I doubt the man who murdered John the Baptizer will throw his doors wide open for our gatherings."

"Miracles do happen," Peter jested, giving his fellow apostle a playful shove.

"Here's what I propose."

Stilling, the men shifted their gazes to rest upon the quiet, dignified woman before them.

"My husband believed that God had a plan for this house. And God's purpose was not buried with my precious husband. The believers can gather here for prayer and instruction. The doors are open to you anytime, day or night."

"Mary," Peter's dark eyes betrayed his great surprise, "it is a generous offer, truly. But even this enormous home isn't large enough to house several thousand believers."

Mary had already considered that. Her eyes grazed each of the dear men resting at her table, for she knew that God had assigned them the sacred responsibility of building His church. The leadership rested squarely upon their shoulders, and she had no desire to overstep her bounds by assuming the leadership role belonging to them. Instead, she would offer all that she had, serving in any capacity the Lord supplied. Rather than addressing Peter's concern by offering her own opinion, she waited quietly, allowing the men to converse.

"What if we met in shifts, so to speak?" Surprisingly, it was James, the Lord's brother, who spoke first. "The apostles could address gatherings throughout the day, taking turns."

Peter raised dark brows, deep in thought. "It's not a bad idea."

"This, too, would allow each of the apostles a turn to address the believers; also granting them time to rest and prepare while others gave the instruction," John's brother remarked in his typically solemn way.

"It could work!" James' more excitable brother, John, declared enthusiastically.

"But what of those already hosting gatherings in their homes?" John's brother persisted, reluctant to cause unnecessary dissension.

"We can continue to meet with them as well, if they desire to keep their doors open," John pronounced, as if the answer was glaringly obvious. "And, of course, they can join us here as well!"

Mary smiled, pleased. "I have already spoken with Tobias, my overseer. We can tear down all the walls on the third floor, creating a wide-open space for the followers to meet. This would allow for larger groups to assemble, which in turn would require fewer gatherings."

"Whoa, whoa, just a minute," Peter interrupted, going to his wife's aunt, and kneeling beside her *lectus*. "Mary, you can't just tear this place apart. It's your home!"

"I thought we already addressed this," Mary teased, roughing Peter's wild hair. "It's *God's* home, and I believe this is what He wants me to do."

"I must address the fact that there are many valuables in this home," John's brother, James, said reluctantly. "The believers can be trusted, I'm sure. But there will also be walk-ins and seekers joining us to hear the Word. It's possible things could go missing, Mary."

"I've already considered that," Mary replied. "And I have plans for many of those valuables, anyway. They are no longer of use to me. But even if something does go missing, I believe that this mission is far more important."

"It might be necessary to double your guard for your own safety," Peter said, always protective. "Certain men aren't going to like what you're doing, Mary."

"I've alerted Zev, the captain of the guard, about such possibilities," Mary readily responded. "And I'm already recruiting new men. By God's grace, everything seems to be in order."

The room grew very quiet, very still, as four apostles contemplated the decision laid before them. Finally, Peter spoke.

"If you truly believe this is what God wants you to do, Mary, then we cannot thank you enough."

"It is," Mary responded wholeheartedly, her exotic features shining with joy.

"Praise God," John exclaimed, pumping a fist in jubilation. His excitement was contagious, for the other apostles responded with broad grins of their own.

"It's settled then," Mary declared, rising gracefully from her *lectus*. "We will begin construction first thing in the morning."

CHAPTER 16

Tabitha

Cringing inwardly when Zev admitted Sapphira, a ridiculously wealthy, middle-aged heiress, past the gate, Tabitha attempted to dismiss her inner turmoil. Something about this haughty woman's bearing unsettled her spirit. Though Sapphira's background and appearance was drastically unlike that of the other women counted among the Way, Tabitha doubted it was anything quite so superficial that prompted her own keen dislike of the patrician.

Sapphira was a tall, angular woman with sharp features and an even sharper tongue. Expertly applied cosmetics did little to soften her façade. Donning extravagant, imported finery, her ears, neck, and arms glistened with bulky layers of expensive jewelry.

Rather like her dress and presentation, Sapphira's speech was ridiculously overdone, in Tabitha's humble opinion. She "deared" and "darlinged" everyone within twenty cubits of her person but demonstrated very little charity in action. Even her compliments were often shrouded in a layer of biting sarcasm.

Stealing down the now familiar corridor leading to the *bibliotheca*, Tabitha hoped Mary would be too busy to welcome a guest today. Even so, she knew that was unlikely. Mary was far too gracious to turn anyone away.

"My lady," Tabitha said upon entrance, "Sapphira, wife of Ananias, wishes to see you."

Setting aside a long stylus, Mary's calm expression reflected her amusement. Sapphira seldom called without purpose. Most likely, the nosy heiress was simply curious—and possibly envious—about the new affairs centering around Mary's home.

"She says she has come to pay her respects and offer her condolences," Tabitha supplied, her tone tinged with a hint of satire. The woman was a tad bit late, as Mark had been laid to rest several months ago.

"Send her in," Mary said with a tired smile, rising gracefully. "We will take refreshments in the inner courtyard," she added, almost as an afterthought. Sapphira would not welcome the idea of sitting across from Mary's desk as they conversed. Most likely, the lofty woman would be terribly offended by such a suggestion.

"As you wish, my lady," Tabitha responded dutifully, dreading the whole affair.

Soon, Sapphira was situated comfortably across from Mary upon an elegant marble bench, a low table piled with tempting refreshments between them. This courtyard was much smaller than the grand plaza at the home's entrance, but Mary preferred the intimate setting. With autumn's swift approach,

Mary relished these balmy summer days beneath the courtyard's colorful awnings, providing deliciously cool shade for those beneath. Even in the heat of the day, the courtyard was a pleasant respite.

"This is a lovely setting, dear," Sapphira purred, taking a slow sip of cool, fruit scented water. "It's rather small, but...quaint."

Tabitha, who—along with Rhoda—stood ready to be of assistance, bit back a sharp retort, carefully guarding her expression. It would seem the insults had already begun!

But Mary simply smiled, her eyes grazing her familiar surroundings with warmth. "This used to be one of my favorite places," she said fondly. "Here, my husband often found respite after hours of dull paperwork. I would join him, and we would talk, delighting in each other's company. That's why he wished to build the *bibliotheca* overlooking this delightful escape."

Unlike Sapphira, Tabitha agreed with Mary's assessment of the quiet courtyard. Underfoot, smooth, polished stone was laid in perfectly symmetrical rows, reminding her of the dazzling, perfectly fitted stones of the Temple Mount. Sophisticated Grecian urns boasted stunning bouquets of fresh wildflowers, providing brilliant pops of color in the stone courtyard. Elegant ivy tendrils climbed beautiful trellises, spilling over the graceful walls and stonework. Curved marble benches invited weary guests to rest beneath the canopy's inviting shade.

Noting Sapphira's dwindling goblet, Tabitha reached for a nearby pitcher and hastened to refill it. Sapphira didn't offer her so much as a second glance, so involved was she in her own conversation. The heiress's strident voice grated on Tabitha's nerves as she boasted about her most recent vacation on the sandy beaches of Cumae, a gorgeous Greco-Roman city abounding with opulent pagan temples.

"I suppose I shouldn't be raving to you about such luxuries," Sapphira sighed coyly, reaching for a sticky candied fig. "After all, what with your husband's passing, I imagine you must soon begin downsizing. Oh, Mary, I do hope you won't have to sell this magnificent house and all your husband's assets!"

Tabitha's lips formed a thin line, grim disapproval seething just below the surface. Evidently, Sapphira's not-so-subtle fishing expedition had begun.

Mary acknowledged Sapphira's feigned sympathy with a confident smile. "Thankfully, Mark's businesses are still in operation, and I intend to keep them that way."

"Oh my!" Sapphira gasped, a bejeweled hand fluttering to her heart. "How...how *unorthodox*. Now I'm sure you've considered all the details, darling, but how on earth do *you*—a helpless widow—intend to keep Mark's operations in order?"

"The same way your husband, Ananias, keeps *his* in order," Mary responded with an easy smile, dismissing Sapphira's irksome label of *helpless widow*.

Sapphira's wide eyes registered shock. "But you're a *woman*!" she protested.

"Yes, indeed," Mary laughed, amused by her reaction. "For many years, I was exceedingly blessed and privileged to be a wife and mother, fully reliant upon my dear husband's provision. But my beloved Mark has departed from this life, and now I must provide for my son and continue to nurture the growing church here. I'm sure you understand."

Doubtful, Tabitha thought, passing a bowl of scented water to Rhoda and retrieving one for herself. The ladies had partaken of their refreshments and would need to cleanse their sticky hands. Draping a plush towel over her forearm, Tabitha approached Sapphira, allowing Rhoda the privilege of serving Mary rather than her nosy guest.

"So tell me," Sapphira gushed, leaning forward conspiratorially. "Is it true you plan to house the growing church here, opening your doors for services throughout the day?"

"It is," Mary replied without missing a beat. "In fact, services have already begun. John plans to instruct the followers this evening. You are welcome to join us, along with your husband."

"We have an important business engagement tonight," Sapphira was quick to inform her. It hadn't taken Tabitha long to notice Sapphira chafing beneath the apostles' lengthy, Scripture-filled instruction, remaining restless and uneasy through the long services. Already, her attendance was dwindling.

Acknowledging Sapphira's dismissal with a brief nod, Mary turned to Rhoda. Smiling at the little girl, she dipped delicate fingers in the cool water, then dried her hands on the soft, proffered towel. "Thank you, dear Rhoda."

Sapphira followed suit, intentionally keeping her eyes averted from the lovely maidservant at her elbow. Swishing her fingers a bit noisily in the bowl of scented water, she then dabbed her hands roughly against the towel, not bothering to remove it from Tabitha's forearm. Dirty water seeped through Tabitha's sleeve, causing her even further chagrin.

"It is wondrous to behold the growing church," Mary said, aware of Sapphira's disdain toward the maidservants. "We are learning so much about the Way. Tabitha, how would you describe James' instruction last night? When he taught about the consequences of partiality and favoring the rich at the expense of the poor?"

Sapphira's slender brows shot up in alarm. "Good heavens, dear! You converse freely with your slaves?"

Tabitha's heart skipped a beat, her simmering temper skyrocketing. She reached for Rhoda's small hand, aware of the girl's sensitivity and tender heart.

"I own no *slaves*," Mary stated firmly, her gray eyes flashing. Rising regally from her curved marble bench, she calmly explained, "Each member of my staff has hired out his or her services, and I'm thankful for every single one of them. Their hard work and dedication keep this estate running smoothly."

Sapphira's countenance paled, her kohl-rimmed eyes widening with mortification as if caught in a terrible faux pas. "I meant no disrespect, my dear. I simply—"

"I do hope you and your husband will join us in worship soon, Sapphira," Mary said sincerely, gracious to the last despite her visitor's lack of sensitivity. "Unfortunately, I have some business I must attend to, and I'm sure you're on a very tight schedule, as well."

Sensing that her interrogation had drawn to an abrupt close, Sapphira rose rather reluctantly, nervously toying with her ostentatious, beaded headdress.

Instantly, the serenity of the peaceful garden courtyard was shattered as Anaia, Peter's pretty, young wife, burst beneath a porticoed entrance, tears tracing slender lines down her dusty cheeks. "Oh, Mary! Thank God, you're here!"

"Anaia!" Mary exclaimed, her tone laced with concern. Hastening toward her troubled niece, Mary placed firm hands upon her shoulders. "What has happened, dear one?"

Sapphira stared blankly between the two women, intrigued.

Instinctively, Tabitha stiffened, her grip tightening upon Rhoda's hand. Her heart pounded violently within her chest, for she sensed that terrible circumstances had transpired. One glance at Anaia's huffing chest, dust-stained features, and tousled braid told her everything she needed to know. Clearly distraught, the poor woman had run a great distance.

"It's my husband, my Simon," Anaia gasped, dragging air into her burning lungs with great difficulty. "And John," she added, an afterthought.

"Oh no," Mary breathed, silently beseeching the Holy Spirit for strength, for wisdom. "Anaia, you must tell us what's happened."

A fresh stream of tears spilled over Anaia's cheeks as she struggled to regain her composure. Covering her mouth with a trembling hand, she cried out, heartbroken, "They've been arrested!"

"We must act quickly," Mary instructed without hesitation, adjusting her niece's disheveled head covering and swinging into action. "Tabitha, come with me. Rhoda, you must stay here. Tell John Mark he is not to leave this house for any reason. Do you understand?"

Eyes widening with fear, Rhoda nodded as she

hastened to perform her mistress's bidding.

"Sapphira," Mary said, her tone commanding, "I trust you can see yourself out?"

"Of course," Sapphira responded, eager to be off and clearly relishing the thought of sharing this interesting piece of news.

"We must be on our way," Mary told Anaia and Tabitha as they followed her into the house. "Please, pray without ceasing."

Tabitha nodded, already immersed in silent prayer. *Oh, God, spare our brothers. Deliver them from the hands of wicked men.*

They'd all known it was coming, just not quite so soon. Taking a deep breath, Tabitha steeled herself for the inevitable, drawing upon God for strength.

Already, the persecution had begun.

CHAPTER 17

Mary

"It happened this afternoon, when Simon Peter and John went to the Temple for the hour of prayer," Anaia explained breathlessly as the three women hastened across the enormous, stone-paved bridge spanning the gap between the great Temple and Jerusalem's elite Upper City located on the city's western hill. The impressive structure also transported water from Solomon's Pools to the Temple Mount via aqueduct, providing a panoramic view of the bustling city. "I wasn't there when it all started, since I had arranged to meet them later."

"But why were they arrested?" Tabitha demanded, chafing at Anaia's slower pace. Her own nimble legs ached to explode into action, spanning the lengthy bridge with the speed and agility of a racehorse in Herod's magnificently pillared hippodrome.

"Do you recall the poor old man who begs at the gate called Beautiful? The lame man called Lazarus?"

"Indeed," Mary replied, her tone laced with sadness. Though she had filled his coffer upon many occasions, she knew all the money in the world wouldn't cure his painful condition. Born with crippled legs, the lame beggar would never know what it was like to stand upon his own two feet. Daily, faithful friends carried him to the famous Temple gate to beg for coin.

"Well, the Holy Spirit moved mightily today," Anaia plunged ahead, her delicate features beaded with perspiration. "My husband commanded Lazarus to rise up and walk...and he did."

Both Mary and Tabitha halted abruptly, turning to face the anxious young woman in utter astonishment.

"Peter *healed* him?" Tabitha exclaimed incredulously.

"Of course not," Anaia declared vehemently. "*Jesus* healed him—*through* my husband, *by faith*. When I arrived with the other women, Lazarus was bounding upon two strong legs like a wild gazelle, laughing and weeping tears of joy, giving glory to God. You can imagine the stir it created. I'd scarcely arrived when we were swarmed by priests, Pharisees, Sadducees, temple guards, curious bystanders, and the like. Sensing a great opportunity, my husband addressed the crowd."

Mary's slender brows drew together as she pondered Anaia's anxious explanation, weighing their options. "I imagine the religious leaders weren't particularly thrilled by your husband's speech."

"Worse than that," Anaia admitted, her large brown eyes betraying her steadily mounting fear. "They were *enraged*. My Simon tried to tell them that *Jesus* had healed Lazarus, through faith and the power of the Holy Spirit. Boldly, he proclaimed Jesus to be the Christ, the long-awaited Messiah. Then he urged the crowd to repent, to be converted. He reminded them that Jesus came to turn us from our iniquities, so that times of refreshing might come from the Lord. But the moment he began preaching about the resurrection, the Sadducees became incensed."

"Of course they did," Mary sighed, resuming their walk at an even brisker pace. "The Sadducees refuse to accept the resurrection of the dead or the existence of angels. Even Joseph Caiaphas, a Sadducee himself, refuses to embrace these Scriptural concepts."

"And how exactly does the venerable high priest intend to lead the people spiritually when he denies the hope of glory, the promise of eternity?" Tabitha quipped, annoyed.

"I suppose it's easier for Caiaphas to dismiss these biblical principles since the Sadducees only accept the Books of Moses as the inspired Word of God," Anaia mused, always merciful. "Imagine all they have lost by rejecting the sacred Scriptures penned after Moses' death."

"It's no small wonder the Sadducees are in such a snit," Tabitha smirked, her hazel-green eyes flashing in indignation. "I'd be cranky, too, if I believed there was no hope beyond this life."

Mary suppressed a small smile, always amused by her maidservant's blunt practicality and fiery nature.

"Already, good has come from this trying situation," Anaia admitted, changing the subject. "As a result of Lazarus' healing, many have believed," she continued, her delicate features lighting with hope. "Many promised to join us for prayer services this evening." Lowering her gaze, she added quietly, "But I suppose that's impossible now."

"Nothing is impossible with God," Mary stoutly assured her, her stride resonating with unbending determination.

"It was John's turn to provide the instruction this evening, but he is imprisoned with my husband," Anaia pointed out, her eyes filling with tears.

"Our prayer service will commence as planned," Mary stoutly assured her, her gait betraying her firm resolve, "regardless of the religious leaders' threats and this unexpected turn of events."

Pausing mid-stride, Anaia turned a tear-streaked face toward her aunt. "Oh, Mary, pray that God will strengthen my faith. If anything happens to Simon—"

Taking Anaia by the shoulders, Mary met her gaze, stating firmly, "God will see you through this." If only she could promise her trembling, young niece that Simon Peter would be released, unscathed. Even as her heart longed to assure the tearful bride of the apostle's safety, she knew she could not promise Peter's release. After all, the Lord worked in mysterious ways. He had allowed her own husband, Mark, to pass from this life. She might never fully understand why God had allowed her husband to slip away from her—at least not before she walked side by side with her Savior in paradise. Even so, she knew with unwavering clarity and unbending faith that God's will could be *trusted*.

As if sensing the direction of Mary's private

thoughts, Anaia whispered brokenly, "How did you ever bear it, Mary? The loss of your husband?"

"God is faithful."

"Thank God *He* is, because *I* am not—" the apostle's wife wept softly.

"When *you* are weak, *He* is strong," Tabitha cut in, touching her shoulder in gentle admonition. "Remember that."

"Amen," Mary replied, drawing on the strength her Lord provided.

Anaia forced a tearful smile, recognizing that both Mary and Tabitha had known the dreadful sting of loss, yet by God's grace had remained faithful to His work. She, too, would go bravely forth, clinging to God for faith and guidance.

Turning her head to survey the scene stretching before them, Mary offered another silent prayer to her God. *Grant us wisdom, Lord. Grant us strength.* Her bronzed features glowed in the sun's retreating, dusky rays as her large gray eyes, luminescent and observant, absorbed the magnificent scene ahead.

Before them, the Temple compound loomed upon the eastern horizon, in all its glorious, gold-crowned splendor. The sun hung lazily upon the opposing western hills like a blazing sphere of flames, washing the entire Temple complex in radiant, russet-colored, sunset hues. Just beyond the great eastern wall rose the gentle slopes of the Mount of Olives and Gethsemane, Mark's treasured olive press. It was truly a magnificent sight, worthy of stealing one's breath away.

But now, for the first time in her entire life, Mary's whole being was filled with a fearsome sense of dread and foreboding as she approached the Temple compound, once a place of refuge, now the house of fierce opposition. At the compound's highest level, a resplendent, marble façade, crowned with shimmering gold adornments, towered into the heavenlies like an impenetrable stone castle floating in the sky. Rather like the Herodian tyrant responsible for its construction, the Temple compound undulated raw, unrestrained power—the power of life and death, blessing or condemnation. Unrivaled in both beauty and magnificence, the holy house, once a beacon of light to all the world, loomed before Mary like a slumbering beast—every bit as unyielding and uncompromising as the massive, monumental stones that composed it.

Mary tilted her head, intently studying the house of worship. *Something has changed.* Once, the mighty Spirit of God had dwelt here, bathing sincere worshipers in glory, light, and peace. But now? The magnificent marble Temple towered heavenward, cold and empty, like a vacant tomb. Where had the Spirit fled?

As if in response, words penned by the worthy prophet, Moses, surfaced at the forefront of her mind, reminding her that the Spirit of God now dwelled *within her*. Her *body* was now the Temple of the Holy Spirit. *But the Word is very near you... in your heart...*

Fleetingly, her thoughts returned to a recent memory shared with Simon Peter. The apostle had been with Jesus before His arrest, when the Savior mourned the hardened state of His holy city. With tears in his eyes, Peter had relayed to her the words of their heartbroken Savior. "*O Jerusalem, Jerusalem, the one who kills the prophets and stones those who are sent to her! How often I wanted to gather your children together, as a hen gathers her brood under her wings, but you were not willing! See! Your house is left to you desolate..."*

Your house is left to you desolate.

Your house.

For the first time since His public ministry had begun, Jesus spoke as if the Temple belonged to man, not God. No longer did He consider this gleaming Temple of Jerusalem, this crowning jewel of an entire nation, *His Father's house.* Wicked, grasping men had stormed the citadel, taking firm hold of the place of worship, refusing to relinquish their prize.

Your *house is left to you desolate.* God's house was meant to be a house of prayer for all the nations, but arrogant, willful men had reduced it to little more than a den of thieves.

Shuddering slightly at these disturbing recollections, Mary hastened her pace. "Let's be on our way."

CHAPTER 18

Saul of Tarsus

Passing endless rows of magnificent marble columns, Saul of Tarsus strode purposefully down an exquisite portico called the Royal Stoa—a resplendent, red-roofed Roman-style basilica gracing the entirety of the Temple compound's southern wall. Famous for its breathtaking rows of uniform Corinthian pillars—precisely one hundred and sixty-two of them, in fact—the impressive, partially open-air structure boasted three lengthy, parallel marble halls housed beneath its elegantly red-tiled roof, along with an elaborate domed central apse in which the Great Sanhedrin now convened.

Someday, his own destiny would be fulfilled. He, Saul, would take his rightful place among the dignified members of the Sanhedrin. He had no doubt he would rise above the rest, surpassing all in wisdom and intelligence. How long must he simply sit at the feet of the great sages, a mere student enduring endless hours of instruction? He was ready to take the reins. As Gamaliel's star pupil, the possibilities for his own advancement were endless. He could easily envision himself bearing the title of *Av Bet Din*, Master of the Court, second only to the *Nasi* presiding over the Great Sanhedrin. The *Av Bet Din* was considered the most learned member of the religious order, and, in his humble opinion, he possessed every qualification to rightly assume the exalted role. That aside, it was entirely possible he might even ascend to the loftiest of all positions, claiming the coveted title of which his own mentor now boasted.

Saul of Tarsus, Prince of the Great Sanhedrin. He liked the sound of that. He deserved it, after all. He had worked longer and harder than any of the rest, memorizing entire books of Scripture and studying the Law and the traditions of the elders until he could recite each and every clause by heart. His intelligence far surpassed that of his peers. His perseverance was unrivaled. He excelled in every subject, having displayed unprecedented promise from a very young age. Not only had he disciplined his mind, but he had conditioned his body with hours of stringent exercise. His diet was impeccable. He, Saul, refused to surrender his destiny into the hands of anyone else. He refused to be overlooked, exploited, or stepped on. No, he had taken his own future by the horns, refusing to surrender the outcome to anyone or anything but himself. He would rise above the rest like a bright ascending star. His name would become famous in the glowing annals of human history.

Pausing in the middle of the grand walkway overlooking the stunning Temple complex, the relentless young Pharisee froze, his body tense. Gripping the stone ledge before him, his sharp eyes swept over the tumult below. Even as the sun retreated rapidly beyond the western hills, unruly crowds overwhelmed the Temple courts, clearly demanding the release of two worthless insurgents.

Eyes narrowing, Saul's piercing gaze revealed his keen displeasure. The dimwitted fools! The swelling throngs pervading the courts and porticoes below had worked themselves into a state of frenzy, mere steps away from revolt. And for what? They sought the release of two worthless necromancers, deceived by the trickery of uneducated, uncouth Galilean fishermen! The rowdy imbeciles would have none but themselves to blame for their own miserable demise should the Romans choose to crush their pathetic little uprising beneath merciless, steel-toed boots.

Did these brainless fools wish destruction upon the entire nation? Hadn't they any sense at all?

Dark eyes narrowing, Saul noted a purposeful figure emerging atop a sprawling marble staircase at the western gate, crossing the bustling Court of the Gentiles with an uncompromising stride. Two women, humbly dressed, trailed behind the arresting form of the elegantly clad woman, one clearly frustrated, the other frantic.

Even though the women's forms appeared shadowed and miniscule from his lofty vantage point, Saul instinctively recognized Mary of Jerusalem leading the way toward Solomon's Porch, an ancient, pillared colonnade bordering the eastern side of the complex, just opposite the daunting Temple façade.

Clenching his fists to check his rising fury, Saul's

dark eyes formed two narrow slits as Mary joined the fray of followers assembled beneath the sprawling portico, assuming a calm, controlled stance as other members of her bizarre sect swarmed about her, undoubtedly divulging details and bombarding her with questions.

Resentment flooded the rigid young Pharisee's entire being as the heat of rage coursed through his veins. Of every sacrilegious gathering, of every questionable religious encounter, this deplorable woman was the common denominator. Already, she had begun hosting "prayer meetings" in her palatial manor. Swallowing the bile rising in his throat, Saul shook his head at the unremitted gall of that cursed woman. To call her gatherings *prayer meetings* was downright blasphemy! The lowlife assembled in her home sought not the one, true God of their fathers—instead, they offered prayers to a dead Man, fantasizing about a fictitious, fabricated resurrection. Not only did they offer prayers to a deceased Revolutionary, but they sought the guidance of some ethereal, mystical Being, fondly referenced as the Holy Spirit. Their falsified religion reeked of idolatry, bordering blasphemy. And that wretched woman was at the very heart of it all! She was utterly intolerable—a pain in his side, a stench in his nostrils. Why, she was no better than a modern Jezebel or a crafty Delilah, wooing the people into a state of apathetic sin! There was something decidedly unsettling about her person, for her very presence rendered him uncomfortable, filling him with wrath and indignation.

But this time—*this time!*—she would not have her way! An unexpected smile tipped the corners of Saul's hard mouth. It would seem that Mary of Jerusalem had finally met her match. She was but one hapless widow against the beastly might of the Great Sanhedrin—a worthy opponent, indeed.

This time, Mary of Jerusalem would suffer the bitter sting of defeat. And he, the indomitable Saul, would savor every moment of her ruinous downfall.

"Saul, my zealous student. What dark portents have transpired to render your countenance so?" Lost in his own vengeful thoughts, Saul hadn't noticed the distinguished, older Pharisee draw alongside him, his trailing black robes swishing in a dignified manner.

"Rabbi," Saul said, acknowledging his mentor, the venerable *Nasi* of the Great Sanhedrin. Surely Gamaliel needn't question his obvious chagrin!

"The Sanhedrin will reconvene upon the morrow," Gamaliel indulged sagely, grasping the stone ledge with worn, weathered hands.

"And the prisoners?" Saul demanded, thrown by Gamaliel's unperturbed calm.

"Will be tried at dawn."

"*Tried?*" Saul spat, the veins in his wide forehead bulging beneath an oversized, gilded phylactery. "Those heretics should rot in a cold stone cell!"

"Since when has the Sanhedrin convicted untried men?"

Saul could have easily listed several examples, namely Jesus of Nazareth, the Sanhedrin's most recent victim of convenience. Instead, he held his tongue.

"You needn't fret, Saul. Justice always prevails."

Perturbed by his teacher's placid amusement, Saul adjusted his fringed *tallith* and drew a calming breath. "I'm sure you will recall, this Jesus of Nazareth—the one these mindless halfwits affirm without question—garnered quite an impressive following before His execution. But rather than accepting defeat, this delusional sect is spreading like wildfire, polluting the hearts and minds of our people at an alarming pace."

Gamaliel studied his favored student with a calm, practiced eye. "And this troubles you?"

"As it should!" Saul declared, instantly defensive. Startled by Saul's abrupt outburst, several dark-robed Pharisees huddled nearby glanced their direction. Others looked their way as they filed from the stoa's large hall in a leisurely, dignified manner.

Lowering his tone, Saul leaned in, mere inches away from the bearded face of his instructor. "This sect claims that the blood of their so-called *Christ* is the ultimate atonement for all sin. By their standards and godless teachings, the sacrificial system upon which our entire religion stands has been *absolved*! They profane our Temple and the traditions of our fathers."

"Hmm," Gamaliel mused, thoughtfully stroking his well-kept gray beard, his practiced eye traveling over the restless throngs assembled in the compound below, now cast in writhing shadows as faithful Levites lit thousands of mounted torches. The sun had disappeared upon the bleak western horizon, cloaking the entire city in shadow and mystery.

Standing rigidly beside his mentor, Saul waited impatiently, his muscled body tense, chafing beneath the unspoken protocols between teacher and student. Hadn't the man eyes in his head? Was Gamaliel simply too naïve, too trusting, to recognize a blasphemous threat staring him right in the bearded face?

"Have you weighed the grand claims of this new sect against the Law and the Prophets, as you've been trained to do?" Gamaliel suggested, sensing Saul's keen agitation.

Saul stared at his instructor in disbelief. "As if there's any need to do so!"

"Have you?"

"I'm not in the habit of wasting precious time," Saul seethed, his fists clenching violently at his sides.

"I see." Gamaliel offered a beatific smile, his grandfatherly features both soft and majestic in the gathering darkness. Judiciously, his old eyes swept over the tightening form of his star pupil. Rage seethed just beneath the surface in the passionate young man standing beside him. It was like an ever-present, malefic being emanating from Saul's staunch form. "You are concerned this new sect might prove denigrating or disparaging to all that we hold dear."

"Exactly," Saul affirmed, somewhat appeased. Gamaliel was beginning to see reason.

"And what is it, my young disciple, that we hold dear?"

The honest question was like a punch in the gut. Wrath blazing, Saul gazed levelly upon his staid instructor, his jaw stiffening in outrage. What exactly was his teacher implying?

"I appreciate your zeal, Saul. I always have," the elder Pharisee assured him, his wise eyes betraying a hint of sympathy. "Rest assured, for the Sanhedrin is taking this matter under consideration."

Gamaliel's sympathetic expression and casual

attitude further infuriated the zealous young Pharisee. Dark eyes flashing angry fire, Saul nearly spat, "But we must do more than merely *consider*, Rabbi! Something must be done about this blasphemous new sect! They must answer for their misdeeds and their deception!" he declared, turning to pace the long, paved walkway in an agitated fashion, his dark robes trailing behind him like the plumage of a large, pompous bird. "Who knows what devilish methods of sorcery or black magic those crude fishermen employed to deceive our people with a false healing!"

"That's what makes this matter all the more confounding," Gamaliel admitted, thoughtfully stroking his manicured beard. "Did the healing of the man called Lazarus appear *false* to you? Even now, the man bounds about the Temple upon two sturdy feet."

"I cannot accept it. I *will not* accept it!" Saul argued vehemently. "Something is amiss, and diabolically so."

"Perhaps," Gamaliel conceded, watching as throngs of worshippers began to funnel out of various Temple gates, eager to return home to their families. "Had any other source been restored, I could have questioned the validity of such a healing. But Lazarus? I've known the poor man from the time of his birth. His father and mother mourned his crippled state. For decades, he has groveled at the Temple gate, seeking alms."

Saul halted mid-pace, facing the venerable *Nasi* head-on. "What exactly are you saying, Rabbi?"

"I'm saying that only God could have wrought such a profound miracle...and that is exactly what troubles me."

Saul's entire body went cold as an unwelcome shiver skittered down his rigid spine. "It is a clever deception, an evil ploy. And we will get to the bottom of this," Saul insisted, unwilling to concede defeat. "Are you aware that crowds have begun assembling in an Upper City mansion belonging to one Mary of Jerusalem?"

"Ah, yes," Gamaliel replied, his expression thoughtful. "Mary, recently widowed."

Saul refused the woman any form of sympathy. "Her husband's death has not deterred her from her mad course."

"My grandson studies with her son, John Mark. A delightful child."

Marvelous, Saul grimaced, further chagrined. A family connection.

"She is a charming woman, a pillar of this community. Perhaps those flocking to her home are simply friends offering their condolences."

"By the thousands?" Saul remarked drolly, arching a derisive brow.

Gamaliel released a low chuckle.

"Rabbi, this woman welcomes blasphemers and sinners into her home!"

"Ah, yes. Her Lord was reputed to do the same."

"And this does not concern you?" Saul marveled, attempting to curb his wrath. "That reckless woman is setting a very dangerous precedent!"

"Saul, Saul," Gamaliel mused, shaking his head in gentle admonition. "Mary of Jerusalem is but one insignificant woman."

Futilely, Saul had been reminding himself of that fact all afternoon. But if Gamaliel's assumption held any merit, then why was his own spirit so disturbed?

"And if this movement Mary has embraced with such fervor proves to be nothing more than a frivolous fancy—"

"*If?*" Saul demanded in angry disbelief.

"—then nothing will come of it," Gamaliel concluded sagely, returning his staid attention to the emptying Temple courts. Clearly, the matter was settled.

Attempting to curb his rising temper, Saul drew alongside the irritatingly reasonable *Nasi*, gripping the stone ledge with such force he wondered if it would snap. Gamaliel was old and tired, clearly lacking the fire and drive that he, Saul, possessed. So be it. Saul refused to lose hope, to succumb to a spirit of apathy.

Tonight, he would fast and pray, readying himself for the trial at dawn. For tomorrow, the wretched apostles would be forever silenced.

Tomorrow, they would get what they deserved.

CHAPTER 19

Mary

"Joses!" Mary was delighted when her older brother emerged from the crowd of believers at Solomon's Porch, wrapping his arms about her in a warm, brotherly embrace. "I hadn't realized you were back from Cyprus."

"Just in time, apparently," Joses responded with a wan smile. "I trust Anaia filled you in?"

"She did," Mary affirmed, taking her niece's arm as Tabitha drew alongside the two of them. "What else do we know?"

"We know those men worked a miracle by the power of God, only to suffer for their kindly deed." Tears sprang to Mary's eyes as Lazarus stepped forward, standing before her, whole and restored for the first time in his entire life. "I am responsible for their arrest."

"No," Anaia said, shaking her head firmly.

"My healing drew the attention of the guards and religious leaders."

"The religious leaders are at fault, Lazarus. Not you," Anaia insisted. "They are responsible for their own misdeeds."

Lowering his head, Lazarus fought to maintain his composure. Judging by his unrecognizably clean appearance, he must have visited the ritual baths on the premises after gaining the use of his legs.

Worried conversation buzzed all around her as Mary scanned the body of believers. She noted the stormy presence of John's brother, James, as he stood among the throng with Philip and Stephanos.

"It's too late for the Sanhedrin to conduct a trial," Mary observed as James, Philip, and Stephanos drew alongside Joses. "Might they be released?"

"According to the Sanhedrin's ruling, the trial will commence at dawn," Stephanos said grimly, exchanging looks of concern with Philip.

Anaia blinked back tears. "Where are they?"

"Antonia Fortress?" Mary asked, considering the imposing Roman citadel abutting the northwest corner of the Temple Mount.

"Doubtful, since they were arrested by the Temple guards rather than the Romans," Stephanos assured her, his eyes resting apologetically upon Peter's troubled wife. "As of now, they haven't been classified as political prisoners."

"Remember, the Sanhedrin has been stripped of its power to administer capital punishment," Philip reminded them gently, mostly for the sake of Anaia and James, John's protective older brother. "So we needn't fear a capital trial."

"And since when has the Sanhedrin played by the rules?" James snarled, shaking his fist in anger. "Have you already forgotten our Lord's crucifixion?

What if my brother is next?"

"James, please," Anaia pleaded, her eyes spilling over with tears. "We mustn't assume the worst."

"No, we needn't *assume* the worst," James declared vehemently, struggling to contain his righteous anger, "since we can most certainly *expect* it from Caiaphas and his pack of wolves in priestly robes."

Tucking a protective arm about her niece's shuddering shoulders, Mary sought her brother's gaze beseechingly.

"James," Joses said gently, dropping a hand upon the fisherman's powerful shoulder, "your fear is understandable, my brother, and we are here for you. But even more than that, *God* is here. He can be trusted. You know that."

Looking as if he'd like to argue, the distressed brother of John held his peace for the sake of Peter's frightened wife.

"It's likely Peter and John were taken to the house of Caiaphas," Stephanos observed quietly.

"Why the house of Caiaphas?" Tabitha challenged, unable to still her tongue any longer. "The apostles aren't exactly what you'd call *cozy* with the high priest, at the moment."

Folding frail arms across his chest, Lazarus lifted wizened brows and nodded his agreement.

"I've heard there's a holding cell on the priestly premises intended for those accused of religious violations," Stephanos explained.

"I've heard the same," Philip agreed.

Reluctantly, Tabitha accepted the explanation.

Quietly mulling over the possibilities as harried conversations continued to swirl about her, Mary raised her head and addressed the believers with confidence. "Brothers and sisters, we have a change in plans," she announced, her eyes grazing the troubled assembly. "Our prayer service shall commence as planned, only at a slightly unexpected location." Mary sensed hundreds of eyes upon her as a beatific smile illuminated her exotic features. "Many of you must return to your homes now, and that's perfectly understandable. But those of you who are free tonight—please meet me outside the gates of the house of Caiaphas. There, we will seek the Lord on behalf of our brothers in chains."

A cheer erupted from the gathered throng, even as Mary sensed the questioning eyes of her brother, the apostles, Lazarus, Anaia, and Tabitha upon her.

"Are you sure that's a wise decision?" Philip, always cautious, ventured quietly.

"The priest's house is off limits, obviously," Stephanos interrupted, already afire with excitement. "But the public roadways are fair game. As long as we don't start a riot, we shouldn't have any trouble with the Romans."

"Hear that, everyone?" Joses called good-naturedly, his soft brown eyes sweeping over the crowd. "No riots tonight."

"They never let us have any fun," Tabitha teased, playfully tweaking Anaia's shoulder and receiving a genuine smile from the tearful bride, along with a look of amusement from Stephanos.

Turning to face the apostles, Mary said calmly, "James, will you lead the prayer service in your brother's stead?"

James' features clouded as he sought to corral fragile emotions. Nodding, he said rather tremulously, "It would be my honor."

"Brothers and sisters, we have a plan," Stephanos declared, clapping his hands in readiness. "We will spend the night in earnest prayer at the mansion of Joseph Caiaphas. Then we shall return here, to the Temple, at dawn, when the Sanhedrin reconvenes, and the trial commences." Turning toward his plucky employer, Stephanos offered Mary, Tabitha, and Anaia a winning smile. "We've seen God work miracles before, and this man right here—" he proclaimed, slapping Lazarus on the shoulder, "—is living proof."

Lazarus smiled weakly, still agonizing about the apostles' arrest.

"All right, then. Let us be on our way," Mary declared, nodding her head in finality. "We shall pray without ceasing until our brothers are released."

***

The priestly mansion was a ridiculously overdone, but impressive, affair. Perched upon the lavish Upper City's eastern slope like a watchful bird of prey, the sprawling manor was a mere stone's throw away from the Royal Bridge, a breathtaking structure adjoining the Temple compound, providing a convenient entrance for the wealthy priests residing in the prestigious neighborhood. As the Upper City was already topographically higher than the rest of Jerusalem, Caiaphas' hillside mansion provided a marvelous bird's-eye view of the Temple and its goings-on. With bubbling fountains, towering palms, magnificent marble pillars, and elegant terraces, even the exterior of the priestly home was exquisite, enclosed by imposing stone walls and heavily guarded gates.

Gathered before the magnificent home, the body of believers attempted to ignore the grim row of armed guards encircling the priestly residence, the tips of their deadly spears glistening in the burning torchlight.

John's brother, James, stood confidently before the assembly, his dark head bowed as he prayed fervently on behalf of the imprisoned apostles.

Standing among the crowd with Anaia, Tabitha, and her brother, Joses, Mary clasped her hands and bowed her head, her own silent petitions in agreement with James' spoken prayer. Though she rejoiced over the many new faces among them, her anxious heart was soothed by the presence of many she knew and loved, although she couldn't possibly locate all of them in the massive throng. She knew most of the Twelve had arrived, along with Mary of Magdala and Zebedee and Salome, the anxious parents of James and John. The Lord's brother, James, and His mother, Mary, were also counted among them, along with devout members of the original Seventy, including her brother, Antigonus—Anaia's father—and Philip, Stephanos' dearest friend. Lazarus was also there, proudly standing on his own two feet, eager to support his champions.

"Almighty God," James said, his deep voice tremulous as he interceded on behalf of Peter and John, "please hear our plea, our cry for help. Jesus taught us to ask in His name, Father, and so we shall. Jesus also told us that times of weeping and lamenting would come. Jesus warned us that, during those times, the world would rejoice—as Caiaphas and his lackeys, shrouded in a cloak of false religion, are undoubtedly rejoicing at our brothers' downfall. But Jesus also promised that our sorrow would be turned to joy. In this we trust, gracious Father." Lifting his head, James addressed the believers, his dark eyes burning with zeal. "When He was still with us, Jesus said, '*Whatever you ask the Father in My name He will give you…ask, and you will receive, that your joy may be full.*'"

Reaching for Anaia's arm, Mary gave it a gentle squeeze. Her heart responded to the remembered words of her Savior as powerfully as if He stood before her now, speaking the precious promises directly to her heart.

"Therefore," James continued, his voice rising in both power and conviction, "we will beseech our holy God in the name of His precious Son, Jesus! We will not cease to pray until we see the fulfillment of His perfect will. Some of you will remember what Jesus told us shortly before His arrest: *In Me you may have peace. In the world you will have tribulation; but be of good cheer—*"

"*I have overcome the world!*" Mary cried along with James, Anaia, Tabitha, Joses, and a hundred other believers who cherished their Savior's promise. The declaration resounded loudly in the otherwise quiet, fashionably paved, palm-lined street of the priestly neighborhood, filling the believers with hope and joy amidst their trial.

"Jesus has already overcome the world!" James cried out triumphantly, raising a large fist in glorious jubilation. "As the psalmist declared, '*The Lord is on my side; I will not fear. What can man do to me?*'"

"Amen," Mary murmured softly, as a hundred other voices lifted in tearful, yet joy-filled, agreement.

"And never forget," James remonstrated, his tall form cast in flickering shadows before the faithful body of believers, "even amidst great persecution, we are blessed. Didn't Jesus say, '*Blessed are you when they revile and persecute you, and say all kinds of evil against you falsely for My sake?*' What, then, did He instruct us to do in these times?"

"Rejoice," Mary said softly, her own voice joined by a hundred others.

"Yes!" James declared, his excitement rising as the Holy Spirit of God covered him with mercy. "*Rejoice and be exceedingly glad, for great is your reward in Heaven!*"

"What in the name of all the gods in the universe do you think you're doing?"

Mary's heart sank as a Roman soldier, flanked by two others, roughly approached James, their ominous armor glistening in the firelight. She felt both Anaia and Tabitha stiffen beside her; Anaia in fright, Tabitha in defiance.

"I recognize him," Anaia whispered softly, leaning in toward Mary and Tabitha.

"How are you familiar with that Roman mongrel?" Tabitha protested curtly, dismayed.

"God loves him too, Tabitha," Mary reminded her gently.

Anaia's eyes widened in fear. "He was one of the soldiers assigned to guard Jesus' tomb. I would know those cold eyes anywhere."

Turning to survey the rigid soldier, Mary agreed with Anaia's assessment. He had the coldest eyes she'd ever seen.

The Roman halted before James, circling him like a predator evaluating its prey. "I am Lucius, captain of the priestly guard. By whose authority do you address this gathering?"

James stood, unflinching, before the crisply uniformed soldier, his gaze flickering in resistance. "You wouldn't like it if I told you," he said coolly.

"Do I look like I have time for games?" Lucius spat, one hand resting casually on the hilt of his gladius, the other waving a flaming torch before James' face. "I suggest you speak forthrightly, unless you'd prefer to join your wretched brothers in chains!"

"All right, then," James said staunchly, levelly eyeing the sturdy mercenary. "Tonight, I address this gathering by the authority of Jesus Christ, the Messiah, the Son of the Most High God."

Catching her breath, Mary waited, silent prayers ascending to God a mile a minute. Vaguely, she felt Anaia's cold, trembling fingers close around her wrist. Beside her, Tabitha's breath came out in short, angry puffs. She felt Joses' steady hand upon her shoulder as he stood behind her, willing her his strength and support.

Lucius studied the solid fisherman standing before him, his cold eyes narrowing in suspicion. Mary noticed that James towered several inches above the armed soldier. But despite Lucius' lack of stature, there was something significantly unsettling about the Roman, apart from his glistening weapons. There was a ruthlessness about his person, a disturbing presence that lingered and emanated from his staunch form. Her heart pounded heavily in her chest as the soldier's features split into a wicked grin, for she sensed this was a man who'd willingly sold his soul for the sake of worldly gain. Already, rumors were circulating: the high priest had bribed the soldiers guarding Jesus' garden tomb, instructing them to say the disciples had stolen the Savior's body in the dark of night. If this rumor concerning the high priest was true, then Lucius had no excuse for his denial of the Way, for he had seen the truth with his own eyes, witnessing the spectacular and miraculous resurrection of Christ! No, it was not blind unbelief that stilled his tongue. Like the stubborn Pharaoh of old, this man had willfully hardened his heart against the Savior, intentionally rejecting His Messiahship, throwing the door of his heart wide open for the devil, the enemy of his soul, to take up residence.

Shuddering, Mary forced herself to watch the exchange between Lucius and James, fervently praying all the while, subconsciously knowing that the entire body of believers was praying, too.

"You and your pathetic little band of fools had best vacate the area unless you want to be treated like the scum you are," Lucius hissed, inches away from James' unbending form.

"Rome permits peaceful public gatherings, soldier!" Startled by the emboldened outburst, all eyes turned toward Stephanos as he emerged from the crowd, pausing calmly before the surprised legionnaire.

Eyes narrowing, Lucius directed his wrath toward the charismatic young man, his rigid form exuding venom. "Not when you're blocking the road."

Shrugging his shoulders, Stephanos nodded in humble concession. "My apologies."

Lucius stared at him coldly, distrustful of the fiery speaker's easy capitulation.

Turning to face the believers, Stephanos lifted his hands, offering one swift gesture of instruction.

As one mighty unit, Mary and the entire body of believers stepped back, fanning out to line the entirety of the stone-paved road, over one hundred persons in all. The road was now wide open as followers of the Way lined the entire palm-dotted street, paved white stones glistening like the walls of marble palaces in the silver moonlight. Knowingly, Mary grasped Anaia's hand on her left and Tabitha's on her right, as each believer took the hand of the person beside them, standing firmly together like an unbreakable chain, united in both prayer and purpose.

Stephanos turned to Lucius then, a wizened smile teasing the corners of his mouth. "Problem solved."

Despite his stony façade, Lucius and his henchmen appeared somewhat alarmed by the uncanny sense of unity pervading the bold gathering. Lifting his torch, Lucius glared at Stephanos and James in disgust. "Why are you here?"

"We stand united in our desire to procure the release of our brothers."

"Don't hold your breath," the soldier snarled, toying with the hilt of his gladius. "They've brought this trouble upon themselves."

"How so?" Stephanos demanded.

Exasperated, Lucius shook his head. "You have no right to question me! *I* conduct the interrogations! Not *you*, you worthless dog."

"I suppose you meant that to be derogatory," Stephanos remarked, a hint of mischief upon his handsome features. "Personally, I favor the happy little creatures."

"Go back to whatever hole you crawled out of and beseech your God *there*," Lucius growled, his tone threatening. "You have no business here."

"Indeed, we do. Our innocent brethren are imprisoned here."

"What makes you so sure they're here?"

"An educated guess, I suppose," Stephanos mused, stroking his clean-shaven chin. "Plus, you doubled the priestly guard."

Annoyed, Lucius ignored the telltale sea of guards outlining the entire premises.

Stephanos grinned, unperturbed.

"Your brothers are fools," Lucius said darkly. "They will pay for their misdeeds."

"As you can see," Stephanos replied, waving an outstretched arm to encompass the vast sea of followers lining the entire street, "we have a rather large cloud of witnesses prepared to attest to the apostles' innocence."

Lucius turned on Stephanos then, his rage seething just beneath the surface. "If you or any one of your worthless followers place so much as a toe on this street, I'll have you all beaten, flogged, and thrown into a miserable stone cell."

"No toes on the road," Stephanos grinned, offering a crisp salute. "You have my word, soldier."

Eyes narrowing in derision, Lucius turned sharply on his heels, his hobnailed sandals pounding a foreboding rhythm upon the stone pavement as he stole toward the gates of the priestly mansion, the two younger soldiers close behind him.

Stephanos turned then, surveying the crowd of

believers before him with an air of triumph. "Praise God!" he shouted in jubilation, raising both hands heavenward. James clapped him on the back, his eyes moist as his heart overflowed with thanksgiving.

Still grasping the hands of her lovely maidservant and her grieving niece, Mary smiled through her tears. Together, they would continue to pray for Peter and John's release.

Together, they were stronger. For Mary's practical mind, the pieces were beginning to fall into place, one by one. Soon, the watching world would behold the church of God and its sacred calling—to bear the gospel, to offer healing, to unite in prayer, to encourage the growing body of Christ. By the grace, strength, and power of God, this small, fledgling church would stand strong in the Way, lighting the path of salvation for all who were hungry, thirsty, weary, or heavy laden—for all who longed to embrace it.

CHAPTER 20

Mary

The sun lingered lazily upon the eastern hills, washing the slumbering city in soft pastel hues as Jerusalem's occupants reluctantly left their beds, preparing for another day. Approaching the Temple, along with Tabitha, Anaia, and Joses, by crossing the graceful viaduct spanning the peaceful Tyropoeon Valley, Mary marveled at the beauty of her city.

"When do you think the trial will commence, Mary?" Anaia asked quietly, deeply shadowed eyes betraying her great anxiety and her night-long prayer vigil.

"It could begin any moment," Mary said honestly. "James, Philip, and Stephanos are already waiting for us. We should hurry."

"I agree," Tabitha said, hastening her steps. "If only we needn't mill aimlessly about the Temple courts awaiting a verdict. Oh, what I wouldn't give to witness this trial!"

Mary smiled knowingly, sympathizing with her

maidservant's restless curiosity.

"Why shouldn't you witness the trial?" Joses asked casually, strolling a few paces behind the three persistent women.

"Obviously, we won't be permitted within the Chamber of Hewn Stone, where the apostles will undoubtedly be tried," Tabitha flung over her shoulder, further quickening her pace.

Joses halted abruptly in the middle of the road, surprised. "You hadn't heard?"

"Heard what, Joses?" Mary asked, turning to face her brother.

"The Sanhedrin no longer assembles in the Chamber of Hewn Stone."

Mary's slender brows lifted in surprise. "Since when?"

"Since the day Christ's body was committed to the tomb. The Sanhedrin gathers in the Royal Stoa now, in the large alcove at the eastern end."

Mary stared at her brother, puzzled. "The Sanhedrin relocated from a sacred and holy space within the inner courts, to a secular, commercialized area on the outskirts of the Temple compound?"

"Indeed."

"But why?" Anaia asked, astonished.

"The priests have remained very secretive about the whole affair," Joses admitted. "But I've heard rumors, bits and pieces. The moment Jesus relinquished His spirit upon the cross, the veil in the Temple was torn in half, rent from top to bottom. You'll remember hearing about that."

"Yes," Mary replied, still amazed. "As if the hand of God Himself rent the mighty tapestry, ushering us into His holy presence."

"That wasn't all. The earth shook, ravaged by a quake unlike any we've ever seen. Buildings collapsed, tombs burst open, streams were redirected in their watery courses. While serving my time at the compound, I learned that an enormous stone lentil within the Holy Place split and collapsed, causing considerable damage. Repairs have been underway. As the Chamber of Hewn Stone is located within one hundred and twenty feet of the Holy Place—which seemed to be the epicenter of destruction—I suspect the incredibly elaborate hall was so damaged in that quake it has since been deemed structurally unsafe. Why else would the Sanhedrin agree to relinquish their cherished hall in exchange for a common market seat among the money changers?"

"And you say all of this took place at the time of Christ's death and resurrection?" Mary repeated, amazed.

"Indeed."

"Incredible," Tabitha breathed, picking up her pace again.

Contemplating all that her brother had revealed, Mary marveled. As a Levite, Joses would certainly be privy to the happenings involving the Temple. He didn't function in the Temple performing Levitical duties like many of their brethren, since he had been born and raised in Cyprus, far removed from the Temple in Jerusalem. But he was a respected member of the Levitical community, having been sent to Jerusalem at the age of twelve to study under the tutelage of Gamaliel. Once his studies had ended, Joses had returned to Cyprus, only to relocate to the holy city shortly after, when his sister and brother-in-law chose to reside there. Joses had learned to love Jerusalem, desiring to reach the lost people within her borders.

"And that's not all," Joses divulged, a beatific smile lighting his comely features. "Bizarre happenings have been occurring in the Temple compound since the time of Christ's resurrection, driving the priests utterly mad—especially Caiaphas."

"What kind of bizarre happenings?" Mary pried, intrigued.

"The eternal flame of the golden seven-branched menorah within the Holy Place goes instantly dark, without explanation."

"Doesn't the light of the menorah represent the presence of the Spirit of God within the Temple?" Anaia asked.

"It does," Joses replied.

"That can't be a coincidence," Tabitha put in stoutly, her excitement rising. "We know the Holy Spirit of God now resides in the hearts of His children—no longer in a Temple forged by the hands of men."

"Exactly," Joses agreed. "Not only that, but Temple gates and doors have been swinging open of their own accord, as if inviting anyone who so desires to enter and partake of the presence of God. You are all familiar with the magnificent Eastern Gate?"

"Of course," Mary supplied for the rest.

"Then you know it is fashioned of brass, and it's unbelievably heavy. With great difficulty, twenty strong men working together can shut it. But recently, that mammoth gate has been bursting open of its own accord, often in the middle of the night."

"No!" Tabitha breathed, as Mary and Anaia halted mid-stride.

"Now, the captain of the Temple guard is a ruthless man, certainly one to be reckoned with," Joses explained, his eyes dancing at the implications of such awesome miracles. "Not once have I seen him back down from a fight or shy away from a challenge. But when informed about the Eastern Gate standing open of its own accord, I'm told his entire countenance paled, his swarthy complexion growing chalkier than a freshly whitewashed tomb."

Mary shook her head in utter amazement as Anaia dared, "But what does all of this mean?"

"I think it means that the presence of God has forsaken the Temple, grand as it may be, to reside in the hearts and minds of His faithful children," Joses explained humbly. "Even now, our merciful Father demonstrates His power to those who refuse to believe, working marvelous signs and wonders that point to His finished work upon the cross. If the priests would but open their eyes, they would clearly see what the Lord is trying to show them."

"Good heavens," Tabitha declared, disgusted. "What will it take for those pompous windbags to humble themselves and submit to God?"

"Only God knows," Joses said grimly. "And God will never *force* a man to accept His mercy and forgiveness."

"But wouldn't the priests prefer the Holy Spirit of God residing *in them*, rather than in a remote, distant Temple?" Anaia asked.

"Not necessarily," Joses said slowly, choosing his words carefully. "You see, the power of the chief priests depends solely upon the sacrificial system. If the blood of a sacrifice is no longer required for atonement, then the priests no longer stand as the bridge between God and men, offering that atonement upon the altar. When Jesus shed His blood upon the cross, He took our sins upon Himself. *He* became the bridge. If we accept His mercy, then we are forgiven."

"But shouldn't the priests be thankful that God has fulfilled His covenant, making us *all* a kingdom of priests in His name?" Anaia asked innocently.

Joses smiled wistfully. "If we are *all* members of God's sacred and holy priesthood, then what is to set *us* apart from the religious leaders? Christ's sacrificial death, resulting in our atonement, abolished the need for the continuance of animal sacrifices. How, then, will the religious leaders wield their power and influence over us like a sword? If they accept the blood of Christ as a once-for-all atonement for sin, then they must accept the fact that daily blood sacrifices are no longer required for our cleansing, resulting in the loss of their own advantage over us. The priests won't allow it. The religious leaders refuse to place themselves on equal footing with the common people."

"I see," Anaia said, grieved. "If only they could see that their need for power and recognition will ultimately cost them their souls."

"Sadly, the religious leaders guard their priesthood as zealously as the emperor guards his throne," Joses observed. "Their motives are the same."

"I suppose," Mary said slowly, mounting the wide marble steps which passed beneath a grand portico, opening into the Court of the Gentiles, "if men measure their worth apart from the fact that they are created in the image of God, deeply loved and treasured by Him, then they will always seek fulfillment and self-worth in other areas."

"Such as the priesthood," Joses finished solemnly, his soft eyes betraying his deep sadness on behalf of his Levitical brothers. "Perhaps, if we can better understand their weaknesses and insecurities, then we will have a better chance of reaching them with the gospel."

"*Reaching them*?" Tabitha declared, incredulous. "They want to wipe us off the face of the earth!"

"But how do we overcome evil, beloved?" Joses asked, a knowing smile upon his gentle face.

Emerging from the portico into the bustling Court of the Gentiles, Tabitha crossed her arms and huffed, "I can think of a few ways."

"Always remember," Joses said, his kind eyes shining with warmth, "we overcome evil with good, dear one."

Sighing wistfully, Tabitha muttered, "I'm not sure I'll ever be *that* good."

Amused by the conversation of her dear companions, Mary smiled as they stood within the gleaming outer court of the Temple. "There are thousands gathered here already," she observed, astounded. "I knew those who prayed with us planned to attend, but I never expected an outcome like this. They must have come to witness the trial."

Anaia shook her head in awe. "I hope they will stand in favor of my husband and John."

"You needn't worry about that."

Relieved, the group acknowledged Philip and Stephanos as they approached, grinning broadly.

"We've been making our rounds throughout the Temple courts," Stephanos continued, his dark eyes shining with merriment. "These people have gathered in support of Peter and John. They wish to make a statement to the high priest and the Sanhedrin."

"God is so gracious," Anaia breathed, her eyes filling with tears. Covering her face with trembling hands, she wept quietly.

Mary touched her niece's shoulder in a gesture of comfort and support, both touched and exceedingly grateful to see God's hand at work among His followers.

"Daily, the Lord is showing us what He desires," Philip remarked, his eyes sparkling, a serene smile upon his bearded face. "God is raising up a massive army of believers willing to walk in His steps and accomplish His work."

Once again, Mary was reminded of their calling. Taking the hands of her teary niece and her high-spirited maid, Mary smiled warmly upon the brethren standing before her, this time speaking her thoughts aloud. "Together, we are stronger."

"Amen, dear sister," Stephanos declared exuberantly, turning to gaze upon the elevated Royal Stoa stretching across the southernmost wall, its flaming red tiles glistening in the morning sunlight. "And by the grace of God, we shall overcome."

***

Saul of Tarsus

Scowling, Saul stood upon the upper level of the Royal Stoa, surveying the cacophony in the raging Temple courts below. The scene was disturbingly reminiscent of another trial, another time and place.

Clenching his fists, Saul dismissed the troubling recollection of a bloodied Figure standing upon Pilate's platform, donning a bloodstained royal cape and a twisted crown of thorns upon His head. Loathing the unwelcome prick of conscience, Saul folded powerful arms across his broad chest, his scowl deepening. This time, the fickle mob clearly stood in favor of the accused. The cursed fools.

As thousands poured into the Temple gates, Saul's growing unease heightened sharply. Men and women from all walks of life flooded the Temple courts—rich and poor, distinguished and lowly. Masters, servants, and slaves. Scribes, Pharisees, and Sadducees. The highly educated and common day laborers. Creating a vast, swelling tide of humanity which completely permeated the Temple Courts, spilling over into Solomon's Porch and the covered pavilions beyond the gates, the restless crowd undulated like the churning waves of a troubled sea.

Unsettled by the people's unexpected reaction and their uncharacteristic display of loyalty toward the accused, Saul shut his eyes tightly and forced himself to focus upon the matter at hand.

The Great Sanhedrin was a powerful religious body responsible for supervising and legislating nearly all aspects of Jewish life, both religious and political, excepting unwelcome Roman interference. Consisting of seventy-one distinguished, high-ranking members—all former high priests, illustrious family relations of the current and former high priests, or the most acclaimed and learned among the scribes, chief priests, and elders—the mere possibility of a trial before the Sanhedrin was enough to strike fear in the hearts of the most daring rebels.

Mentally reviewing each member of the Council, weighing their preferences, prejudices, and predictable tendencies, Saul's stormy countenance relaxed ever so slightly. Surely the tide of this trial would swell in his favor, establishing his own will—as long as Gamaliel, the most important member of the Sanhedrin, didn't sway his comrades with one of his famous "have mercy upon the outcasts" speeches. Furrowing his brow in frustration, Saul clenched the parapet before him and considered more favorable allies. Annas, the revered former high priest and father-in-law of Joseph Caiaphas, the current high priest, remained the most powerful and influential member of the Sanhedrin, and Saul knew he needn't concern himself with Annas' vote. The man was relentless, as cold and unbending as steel. Annas loathed heretics with a single-minded determination, possibly even surpassing the hatred his son-in-law bore toward those who bucked the tradition of the elders and threatened his own prestige. Surely Annas' opinion would overshadow Gamaliel's, despite his esteemed title of *Nasi*. There was also the *Av Bet Din* to consider, but his vote was in the bag. The toady bowed and scraped before Annas' and Caiaphas' every move, ensuring the security of his coveted title. Of course, Caiaphas' vote against the apostles was guaranteed. And Annas' son, John, would certainly condemn the apostles, along with his close companion, Alexander, a striking and powerful figure possessing the commanding voice of an orator.

Clenching his jaw, Saul considered the liabilities presented by defectors among the Council, men such as Nicodemus and Joseph of Arimathea. The two prominent men had openly endorsed that pestilent Prophet—the One ultimately responsible for this blasphemous dilemma—when they obtained permission from Pontius Pilate to remove the dead rebel's disfigured body from the cross, burying Him in Joseph's pristine new tomb. Why, it was highly possible that Joseph was involved in the suspicious disappearance of the body, being intimately familiar with the tomb in which the Nazarene was laid! And now *he* was to judge that dead Man's overzealous disciples? The thought was maddingly absurd!

Drawing a calming breath, Saul turned from his study of the chaos below, his dark eyes narrowing as richly clad members of the Council trickled into the elaborately columned stoa. True, weak-willed men like Nicodemus and Joseph of Arimathea did indeed pose a serious problem. Even so, Saul was certain that the influence of two infidels would pale in comparison with the vehement outrage of sixty-nine others.

Meticulously adjusting his regal garments, Saul prepared to enter the stoa's pillar-lined marble halls. Very soon, the trial would commence. Scarcely aware of the predatory smile tipping his mouth, Saul savored the apostles' impending doom.

CHAPTER 21

Mary

The Royal Stoa was a stunning work of Herodian architecture with its endless rows of towering marble columns, each breathtaking Corinthian pillar topped with a gleaming golden crown. Though Jerusalem boasted its fair share of both Greek and Roman architecture, the awesome structure, sometimes called the Trading Place, had been brilliantly engineered and meticulously fashioned to combine the impressive features of a Greek stoa and a Roman basilica, resulting in a truly stunning work of art.

Despite the grandness of the great hall, Mary doubted the lofty members of the Sanhedrin appreciated the undignified relegation from the renowned Chamber of Hewn Stone. The sprawling marble hall buzzed with frenetic activity as Mary, Tabitha and Anaia approached the enormous, dome-shaped, semi-circular apse at the far eastern end of the stoa, where the Council met. Regal members of the Sanhedrin sat in elegant, straight-backed chairs overlaid in both silver and gold, forming a massive semi-circle consisting of over seventy chairs. The gilded, throne-like chair of the high priest occupied the place of honor at the very center of the semi-circle, elevated upon a raised golden platform, graced by velvety scarlet tapestries on either side. Situated directly beneath a gold-framed, elegantly latticed window, early morning sunlight streamed through the circular opening upon the elevated dais like a strange, unearthly beacon, doing little to soften the severe features of the stony-faced high priest. Seated upon his "throne," Caiaphas gripped the golden armrests with white-knuckled, jewel-studded fingers, clearly impatient to begin.

"I've never seen a man with such a stormy countenance," Anaia breathed, troubled by the severity of the high priest's expression.

Sighing, Mary acknowledged her niece's observation. The man was everything one would expect of someone bearing his venerable title—he was tall, prestigious, powerful, calculating, and, somehow, typically one step ahead of everyone else. Meticulously groomed, his flowing robes and carefully styled beard presented a rather regal, aristocratic bearing. His opaque gray eyes were both cunning and intelligent, a dangerous combination. "Caiaphas is relentless," Mary admitted slowly, "but he is no match against his Maker."

"Perhaps God will strike him dead, putting an end to this ridiculous trial," Tabitha muttered, folding slender arms in agitation. She hated injustice with every breath she drew, and the pompous high priest reeked of it.

"Or perhaps, someday, Caiaphas will see the truth," Mary countered, gently touching Tabitha's shoulder. "God loves him, too. Salvation is for all men, Tabitha."

"*If* they will accept it," Tabitha argued, rattled by the possibility of mercy bestowed upon the treacherous priest. "Caiaphas considers *himself* the savior of our people. He's far too proud to consider himself in need of one."

"Jesus told us to love our enemies, Tabitha," Mary said quietly, comprehending her inner struggle. "I know it isn't easy."

"Especially when your enemies have tortured your Savior and arrested your husband," Anaia admitted, somewhat chastised by Mary's reminder. "Oh, Mary. My thoughts have not been kind toward the high priest, God help me. The man's salvation is the last thing on my mind."

Mary understood and sympathized. At times, she, too, found herself harboring rancid thoughts toward those who persecuted the Way. It was only natural to dislike those who hated you. But Jesus had taught an entirely new way: *Love your enemies, bless those who curse you, do good to those who hate you, and pray for those who spitefully use you and persecute you.* It was a tall order—one Mary knew she was incapable of meeting herself. Thank God for the gift of the Holy Spirit! How else was she to fulfill these impossible commands apart from the Helper sent by God to comfort, to aid, to guide, and sustain her?

Turning her attention back to the matter at hand, Mary watched as the final, straggling members of the Sanhedrin took their assigned seats in the central apse. Onlookers continued to pour into the Royal Stoa, pressing so tightly about Mary and the others that she wondered if they would be smothered. Mary knew she was surrounded by a great cloud of witnesses, all of them praying fervently for God to intervene. Somewhere amidst the enormous gathering was Philip and Stephanos, and her brother, Joses, along with the apostles, an overwhelming number of followers, and many members of the Seventy. Hundreds, if not thousands, of new converts had also rallied in support of Peter and John. The assembly spilled out beneath the massive, covered portico, crowding the stoa's entire pillar-lined balcony overlooking the Temple compound, even filling Solomon's Porch and the walled layers of Temple courts below. The turnout was truly staggering, and Mary couldn't help but wonder if Caiaphas and his lackeys were somewhat daunted by this shocking display of unwavering loyalty and devotion.

Noting concerning members of the Sanhedrin, Mary thanked God for the presence of both Nicodemus, a quiet Pharisee with a generous spirit, and Joseph of Arimathea, a fearless nobleman possessing a fiery temperament—both her brothers in Christ. She was also somewhat relieved by the presence of the *Nasi*, seated at Caiaphas' right hand. Even though Gamaliel had not embraced the Way, he was a gentle, fair-minded ruler, grieved by the hardness of heart so prevalent among his peers—unlike the pretentious *Av Bet Din* seated at Caiaphas' left hand. Touched by Gamaliel's humble bearing, Mary made a mental note to include the reverent *Nasi* in her daily prayers. How she longed to count him among the children of God!

As a pair of simply dressed yet sophisticated-looking stenographers took their seats at the assigned wooden desks placed at either end of the sprawling semi-circle of Council members, three rows of twenty-three dark-robed, intellectual scholars were seated upon the cold, mosaic floor before the Sanhedrin, tablets and writing instruments in hand.

Mary immediately spotted Saul, his magnificent robes trailing behind him in a dignified manner, as he seated himself among the privileged scholars, taking a prominent place at the center of the first row. Casting a glance over his shoulder, Saul's cold eyes scanned the crowd of eager observers.

Supposing she should look away, Mary met the gaze of the aloof young Pharisee instead. A teasing smile tipping the corners of full lips, her eyes danced a subtle challenge: *We meet again.*

The look of rage and consternation tightening Saul's neatly groomed, bearded features was not lost on Mary. Grinning triumphantly, she watched as he angrily adjusted an expensively embroidered, heavily tasseled outer tunic, sharply turning his attention to the Sanhedrin seated before him.

Well, it would seem I have been quite easily dismissed, Mary thought with a flicker of humor, amused by the young Pharisee's petty reaction.

Pray for him, beloved.

Startled by the sudden, shocking revelation, Mary lifted questioning eyes heavenward. Was the Holy Spirit *truly* prompting her to pray for Saul, the most heartless and arrogant of Gamaliel's students?

Pray for those who spitefully use you and persecute you.

I can't imagine how my prayers could possibly impact that *one, Lord,* Mary mused silently, *but I will do as You say.*

Mary's ponderous reverie was shattered when Anaia cried out, both disturbed and relieved at the sight of her husband. "Look! It's my Simon!" she gasped, her soft eyes filling with tears as a slew of temple guards sporting deadly looking spears, brown leather outer tunics, and strange triangular shaped caps, shoved Simon Peter and John into the open space between the Sanhedrin and the scholars. With their hands tied behind their backs, Peter and John briefly scanned their surroundings, no doubt stunned by the significant turn out.

At the sight of the two bound apostles, their tunics torn and soiled, their faces and bodies streaked with dirt, a resounding cheer went up from the enormous crowd assembled within the stoa, fairly shaking the towering pillars and resounding off the basilica's marble walls and vaulted ceiling. But unlike the trial of Jesus, which was seared into the hearts and minds of many followers present, the cry of the people was *for* the apostles rather than against them.

"Be strong in the Lord, brothers!" a man standing near the front shouted, clearly ignoring the unspoken protocol observed before the Sanhedrin.

"Yes! Trust in the Lord!" another shouted. "Stand firm!"

"The Lord is with you!"

Mary looked to Anaia and Tabitha, shaking her

head in wonder. "If Caiaphas condemns Peter and John today, he will be answering to Rome for a riot instigated by his own hand."

"Then they are saved!" Tabitha exulted, appearing even more beautiful as her exotic features shone with hope. "Surely even Caiaphas possesses a healthy fear of Rome. I doubt he's so easily forgotten how swiftly the priesthood was stripped from his father-in-law."

"Praise God," Anaia breathed, tears coursing down both cheeks.

The excited crowd of onlookers continued exhorting Peter and John, swaying and waving their hands, giving glory to God...which only further infuriated the high priest.

"Enough of this! I said, *enough*!" Springing to his feet, Caiaphas glared at the crowd gathered before him, his cold gray eyes reflecting the tumult of a vast, tempestuous, and stormy sea. "You will show restraint before my Council, or you shall be beaten, flogged, and punished!"

The crowd quieted slightly, amused rather than daunted by the high priest's impatient outburst.

Ah, Caiaphas. Gracious to the last, Mary thought, repenting afterward for the rebellious course of her own thoughts.

"*My* council?" Tabitha echoed, bemused. "Silly me. I thought this was supposed to be the *Lord's* assembly. Apparently not."

Mary hid a small smile as Caiaphas addressed the Sanhedrin, dramatically pronouncing the court to be in session. Realizing that she was holding her breath in stark anticipation, she released it, offering silent prayers to God even as her lovely eyes remained fixed upon the two bound, bedraggled apostles standing before the Sanhedrin.

"Do you think he knows we're here?" Anaia whispered, a small catch in her voice as tear-filled eyes bore into the back of her husband.

"He would if he'd turn around," Tabitha remarked, receiving a reprimanding look from her mistress.

"They are showing respect by facing the Sanhedrin," Mary explained quietly. Taking Anaia's hand, she gave it a gentle squeeze. "Of course, he knows we're here, dear one."

Taking his seat upon the throne-like chair once again, Caiaphas' gray eyes bore into the humble, yet confident, forms of Peter and John. "You have been charged with disrupting the peace by performing a false healing in the sight of all the people," he began, his eyes flashing venom even as he spoke. "And now I shall ask each of you a very simple question, and you'd do well to carefully consider your response. *By what power or by what name have you done this?*"

Breathless, Mary awaited the apostles' reply. She knew the question lurking within the mind of every Council member: Where had these simple, uneducated, and singularly unimpressive fishermen received such great power and authority? Clearly, they had received no warrant on the part of the Sanhedrin! Even so, Caiaphas' question was a loaded one. For centuries, Jewish exorcists insisted certain names possessed the power to invoke wonders and cast out demons. Even the religious leaders had been blinded by this common practice, placing their faith in "sacred" names or titles, like an omen or good luck charm. Perhaps Caiaphas intended to distract the masses from the apostles' gospel message by insinuating the healing had been invoked by the strange art of incantation rather than the power of Christ.

Regardless of Caiaphas' twisted motives, Mary possessed a sneaking suspicion that the Sanhedrin wasn't going to appreciate Peter and John's rebuttal. Catching her breath, she immersed herself in silent prayer, awaiting the apostles' response.

CHAPTER 22

Mary

By what power or by what name have you done this?

Caiaphas' terse demand seemed to linger in the air, now crackling with tension, as the crowd waited with bated breath, their eyes glued upon two common fishermen emanating the very power of God.

Sensing Anaia trembling violently beside her, Mary pulled her close. "God is here. He is working."

"I am a selfish woman," Anaia trembled, swiping at her tears. "I cannot bear to lose him, Mary."

Tabitha gazed solemnly between the two women, aching for Anaia, longing to comfort her. Having never been married, she hadn't the slightest idea what it was like to love a man with one's entire being, only to have him violently ripped from your life, tearing your heart in half. In fact, she'd convinced herself that she hadn't the slightest desire for a man. The chances of losing a husband were great in the days in which they were now living, for a follower bearing the mark of Christ became a wanted man.

For Tabitha, this trial was proof enough. She didn't wish to experience the joy of falling in love, only to lose her beloved shortly thereafter. Though she felt unable to fully empathize with Anaia's concern, she knew one thing: Mary knew Anaia's fear, having experienced it herself. And Tabitha prayed that God would supply her mistress with the proper words to comfort her frightened niece.

"I just found myself desperately hoping for Simon to remain silent, to hold his tongue," Anaia confessed softly. "But then I remembered the agony he endured after denying the Lord the night of Jesus' trial. How could I wish that upon him again? My thoughts dishonor the Lord."

"But the Holy Spirit is convicting you even now, Anaia, gently reminding you to conform your thoughts to the will of God," Mary reminded her. "Lean on Him, and He will uphold you."

The whispered dialogue between them was cut short when Caiaphas propelled himself to elegantly sandaled feet once more, glaring menacingly down upon Peter and John. "I will ask you again," he bellowed, his taut features transformed by raging hatred, his threatening demand echoing and bouncing off the marble walls in a bizarre, unearthly manner. "*By what power or by what name have you done this?*"

With one arm draped around her niece's shuddering shoulders, Mary leaned forward, her lips moving rapidly as she petitioned her God in silent prayer. A gentle murmur rose from the gathering, so soft one might have missed it if they hadn't been looking for it. Instinctively, Mary knew what it was, and her heart was lifted in response. It was the quiet murmur of a thousand saints, beseeching Almighty God on Peter and John's behalf—the prayers of a mighty army, ascending to the very Throne Room of God like a sweet-smelling incense, an offering of faith and praise.

A gentle wind fluttered ever so subtly through the marble hall, tickling the scarlet curtains shrouding Caiaphas' throne. Feeling a familiar pricking sensation, Mary recognized the power of the Holy Spirit—a gentle whisper possessing the force of a violent, mighty whirlwind.

Turning her head to study the two apostles, Mary saw their backs straighten, their shoulders rise. Peter lifted his head, levelly meeting the gaze of a hostile high priest. And Mary's entire being exulted, for she knew in that moment that Peter and John sensed it, too. Bathed in the Holy Spirit, they were now ready to answer their accusers.

*But when they deliver you up, do not worry about how or what you should speak...*the gentle instruction of Jesus whispered its way into Mary's heart, exhorting, edifying, uplifting.

Peter spoke first. "I am privileged to speak before the rulers of the people and the elders of Israel," he declared, addressing the Sanhedrin with deep respect.

Having seated himself again, Caiaphas leaned forward in his chair. The looks of confusion that passed over the faces of the Council members wasn't lost on Mary. Peter had their attention.

*...For it will be given to you in that hour what you should speak...*Jesus once promised. And the Holy Spirit reminded.

"Today, we are judged for a good deed, for ministering to a helpless man," Peter said evenly, his dark eyes traveling over the faces of his accusers.

...for it is not you who speak, but the Spirit of your Father who speaks in you.

"And if you wish to know by what means Lazarus has been made well," Peter continued slowly, the tension steadily mounting as the Sanhedrin shifted nervously in their seats. "I will tell you—"

"By which that man *appears* to have been made well," Caiaphas interrupted coldly, his eyes boring into Peter with startling hatred. "Whether or not you invoked power by incantation or performed a false miracle with malintent is yet to be determined."

"*Yet to be determined?*" a familiar, gravelly voice shouted above the din. And then Lazarus bounded onto the judgment floor, his eyes blazing, standing staunchly, protectively, before Peter and John.

Mary drew in a sharp breath as gasps of surprise and trepidation rippled through the crowd. It would seem Peter and John now had an unlikely champion!

"Let me ask you, priest," Lazarus demanded, standing firmly upon two sturdy legs, "does this healing still look *false* to you?"

The crowd erupted with shouts of triumph and encouragement, even as Caiaphas' features became mottled with rage. He exchanged an infuriated glance with Annas, his stoic father-in-law, seated near the *Nasi*'s elbow.

Tabitha groaned, covering her face with one hand. "What is he doing? He's going to get himself killed!"

Anaia stared, openmouthed, as the former beggar guarded Peter and John with flashing eyes and a daring stance.

The Apostle John looked to Lazarus, a broad smile crossing his boyish face. Then he looked to Peter and nodded. It was time.

Understanding, Peter addressed the Sanhedrin, emboldened by the Spirit of God. "It is by *the name of Jesus Christ of Nazareth*, whom you crucified and whom God raised from the dead, that this man stands before you whole!"

A shout of victory arose from the crowd, mingled with gasps of shock from the scholars seated before the Council, as Caiaphas and several members of the Sanhedrin sprang to their feet, outraged. With little success, Caiaphas attempted to stifle the cheers, shouts, and applause from the crowd. "Silence! Enough of this! *Enough*!"

"Don't you see it?" John cried out, draping an arm across Lazarus' gaunt shoulders. "There is power in the name of Jesus!"

"Nor is there salvation in any other name!" Peter shouted, pumping a jubilant fist in the air. "For there is no other name under Heaven by which we must be saved!"

"There is no other name!" John affirmed, smiling broadly, even as Caiaphas shouted for silence. "This earth is not our home. It is a broken world, filled with pain and injustice. Eternity in paradise with our loving, heavenly Father—that's our destination, and Jesus is *the Way*! Put your hope in Christ!"

"Don't you see it?" Peter cried, impassioned by unwavering belief. "Salvation cannot be obtained by our own works or merit—it's a gift from God."

"And *Jesus* is the way, the truth, and the life," John added emphatically, tightening his grip on Lazarus' shoulders. "No one comes to the Father except *through Him*!"

"We have created our own religion in which prideful man parades about, claiming the power to reconcile God and men," Peter stated boldly, his eyes resting upon the many faces among the Sanhedrin before finally settling on the seething high priest. "But we needn't a *human* priest to go before the Throne Room of God, interceding on our behalf. *Jesus* cleansed us once for all when He shed His blood on the cross, rising on the third day. Jesus is our High Priest, and He alone can seal the gap between sinful man and holy God! When we claim that power for ourselves, we strip the Son of God of His priestly garments, claiming them as our own. That, dear friends, is blasphemy—not a kindly deed performed toward a suffering man."

"And *that*," Lazarus stated, taking several dramatic steps toward the Sanhedrin, "is precisely why I stand before you now, a changed man!"

"Insolent mendicant!" Caiaphas said, his voice a low growl resonating deep within his throat. "Your newfound freedom has emboldened your tongue, and I daresay you've yet to consider how easily your freedom, your very life, can end."

"You want my life, priest?" Lazarus challenged, lifting wizened brows. "You can have it. I've discovered life everlasting, and no power on earth can touch the eternity I'll share with my Father in Heaven." The stoa resounded with cheers as believers and seekers alike applauded the old man, admiring his courage before the most powerful religious body in the nation.

"Enough!" Caiaphas nearly spat. "This Council is adjourned for the time being. The prisoners will remain under guard until summoned, when judgment is rendered. Everyone else, you are dismissed and forbidden to reenter this court."

***

"You're going to wear out these lovely stones, dear sister," Stephanos remarked as Tabitha paced back and forth like a watchful tigress, her tension mounting as the trial dragged late into the afternoon.

"I can't simply stand here waiting," Tabitha countered, lifting her head. A sea of golden ringlets spilled beneath her simple head covering, framing her lovely face. "I'll go mad if I do."

"At least you're getting some exercise," Stephanos teased, his swarthy features bathed in sunlight.

Tabitha paused midstride, eyeing Stephanos suspiciously. What was he implying? That she needed to shed a few pounds?

Already sensing the direction of her maidservant's thoughts, Mary laughed out loud, thankful to be in the presence of fellow believers during this trying time. "Be at ease, Tabitha," she soothed. "You're in better shape than all the rest of us combined." Mary would never forget how nimbly Tabitha had clambered up that towering palm as a young girl, and she hadn't lost her touch. The young woman was still a swift runner and a gifted climber, agile and athletic in many ways.

The others chuckled their agreement, but Mary couldn't help but notice Stephanos' fond smile as Tabitha resumed her restless pacing. The two worked closely together in her home, for Stephanos was her right-hand man, and Tabitha, her chief maid. They would make a handsome couple, if not for the vast age difference between them. After all, Tabitha was diligent and hard-working, with a heart for the needy and distraught. Weekly, she visited various synagogues throughout the city, distributing handmade clothing to widows, young mothers, and children in desperate situations. She was also fiercely loyal, faithful to the last. Mary had no doubt that Tabitha would stand beside a husband with unwavering commitment and devotion, encouraging him in the Lord's work. Though she was yet to realize it, Tabitha possessed the makings of a worthy helpmate. Absent-mindedly, Mary reviewed various young men of the Way, wondering if any were worthy of her Tabitha. It was a sobering question, indeed.

Forcing her thoughts back to the present moment, Mary smiled kindly at James. "How are you holding up, my brother?"

Biting his lower lip, the apostle looked away. "The best I can."

"By the grace of God, my brother," Philip smiled, touching James' shoulder. They all remembered a time when the quick-tempered apostle—dubbed a Son of Thunder, along with his brother, John—would have erupted in frustration amidst minor provocations, much less during a crisis like this. The Holy Spirit was truly at work in him.

After Caiaphas' terse dismissal at the Royal Stoa, throngs of believers had relocated to the various Temple courts, tensely awaiting a verdict. The compound still buzzed with activity as thousands of believers and thrill seekers milled about the complex, praying for the apostles' release. Now Mary stood with Anaia, Tabitha, Joses, Philip, Stephanos, and James in the Court of the Gentiles. The largest of the Temple courts, the Court of the Gentiles was a sprawling, stone-paved platform flanking all four sides of the grand Temple proper. A low wall no more than four and a half feet high encircled the Court of the Women, forbidding foreigners to pass beyond the outer court. Anyone disregarding this dire warning received a swift reward: the pain of death. Grim-faced Temple guards patrolled thirteen entrances within the dividing wall, the tips of sharpened, deadly looking spears glistening in the sunlight.

This barricade had always troubled Mary. After all, hadn't God created *all* men, Jews and Gentiles alike? Didn't it stand to reason that He should wish to commune with His creation? Sighing quietly, Mary was shaken from her silent reverie when Anaia released a sharp gasp of surprise. All heads turned when the young bride cried out, rushing forward with arms outstretched, tears coursing down her face. "Simon! It's Simon!"

Mary's heart constricted in utter relief when Peter and John, bearing broad smiles upon shining faces, jogged toward them. Lifting her face heavenward, she thanked her gracious Father. *You are so good, righteous Father. So very, very good!*

"Praise God! They've been released!" Stephanos declared, as Philip slapped him heartily on the back. Tabitha shook her head in awe, her hazel-green eyes shining in triumph. And Joses could only smile, warmed by the unabashed tears of relief James shed for his beloved little brother.

"Praise be to God," Mary breathed, smiling

through her own tears as Anaia rushed her husband, falling into his arms and weeping tears of joy. Bending down, Peter kissed the top of her modestly covered head, whispering tender words of consolation.

Yet again, God had worked mightily on their behalf!

CHAPTER 23

Saul of Tarsus

The southern side of the Royal Stoa boasted a pillar-lined, open-air section overlooking the entire length of the sprawling Temple compound below. Standing between two colossal Corinthian columns, Saul crossed burly arms before his chest, sternly observing the mayhem below. No doubt, word of the apostles' release had reached the masses by now, and he was sorely tempted to throw back his head and bellow out the rage which now consumed him.

For the love of all that was holy and good, why hadn't the Sanhedrin put an end to the wretched heretics, setting a chilling precedent for any future insurgents who dared disrupt the fragile peace they now enjoyed? For the first time in his career, Saul detested Joseph Caiaphas. The indecisive high priest was no better than Gamaliel, sorely incapable of producing much-needed results. Clearly, Caiaphas was far more concerned about appeasing a fickle mob than upholding their holy religion!

Saul understood Caiaphas' concerns—to a degree. After all, the masses had rallied in favor of Peter and John. A guilty conviction could have easily resulted in a riot or stampede, eliciting Rome's attention. Caiaphas would then, without a doubt, be deposed, only to be replaced by another priest appointed by the Roman prefect—someone considered capable of keeping peace and order within the realm. Caiaphas, a shrewd politico, had maintained his position longer than any formerly appointed high priest precisely because he had mastered the art of manipulating the populace even while appeasing the Roman regime. Perhaps Caiaphas knew what he was doing, but Saul was certain the only way to crush any rebellion was to destroy the tiny seedlings before they were given the chance to take root. Gritting his teeth, Saul's dark eyes swept over the throngs of men and women in the Temple courts, now rejoicing over the apostles' unexpected release. The Sanhedrin should have made an example of Peter and John! The wretches should have been beaten within an inch of their miserable lives—or better yet, flung into a pit and stoned. His was a stubborn and headstrong nation, and submission must be forced, not requested!

Closing his eyes, Saul drew a ragged breath, recalling the events which transpired after the ill-bred Galileans had been summoned before the Sanhedrin a second time. Gravely, Caiaphas had forbidden them to speak or teach in the name of Jesus. The apostles' bold response had resonated through the marble hall like a power-packed punch, raising Saul's hackles even now as he considered the brass of two insignificant, plebian fishermen: *"Whether it is right for us to listen to you rather than Almighty God, you judge!"*

Caiaphas had propelled himself to his feet then, towering over the staunch prisoners standing, undaunted, before his pedestal. "*I am* God's representative on this earth, whom all men must heed," he hissed, his gray eyes narrowing dangerously. "Supreme and universal power over the souls of men rests solely in my hands. I stand as God upon this earth. Fools! You don't know what you are saying, or to whom you now speak!"

Now, hours later, Saul's own spirit was strangely disturbed by Caiaphas' shocking outburst. In Saul's strictly religious mind, the high priest's claim tottered dangerously upon the brink of blasphemy. A *man* standing as God upon the earth? It was an appalling claim, indeed.

Dismissing his initial unease, Saul focused his attention upon the problem at hand, instead. Two dangerous heretics had been released. And even as Caiaphas threatened them within an inch of their wretched lives, Saul suspected that Peter and John had already returned to their mad course, crediting their bloody Christ for their miraculous release! Surely it was that vile serpent, the devil—not some whimsical, fanciful Messiah—by whom those worthless Galileans received their mystical power!

"*By the ruler of the demons He casts out demons!*" Saul straightened, alarmed by the sudden recollection of a conversation Gamaliel had relayed to him regarding the apostles' famed Jesus of Nazareth. After the Teacher had allegedly cast out many demons, restoring the sanity of countless demoniacs, a band of scribes and scholars cornered Him, demanding to know if He obtained His power from Beelzebub, the prince of demons. Jesus' response rankled, for deep in his spirit, Saul sensed that it shattered his own assumptions about the apostles, as well: *How can Satan cast out Satan? If a kingdom is divided against itself, that kingdom cannot stand. And if a house is divided against itself, that house cannot stand. And if Satan has risen up against himself, and is divided, he cannot stand...*

Gritting his teeth in consternation, Saul struggled to dismiss the maddeningly annoying logic of a departed Rabbi. The Nazarene was dead and buried, even if His body was unaccounted for. Why, then, did the words of a deceased, self-proclaimed Prophet haunt his nights and plague his days?

Taking several measured steps forward, Saul peered over the stone ledge, observing the ensuing madness within the Temple courts. While the majority clapped and cheered and danced and praised, those who had relished the apostles' demise fumed and seethed. Arguments erupted as the people discussed the apostles' situation and the Sanhedrin's response. Unbelievers plagued and tormented followers of the Way. Pharisees argued with Sadducees. Scholars and scribes vied for attention and recognition, each attempting to outdo the other. Temple guards sneered, threatening dissenters with menacing expressions and even more menacing spears. Heated conversation wafted upon the late afternoon's stifling breezes, filling Saul's entire being with the deepest sense of dread and foreboding, for this Temple, the house of God, had indeed become a house divided. Jew against Gentile. Pharisee against Sadducee. Student against fellow student. Radical converts against religious traditionalists...

Gazing upon the swirling madness within the gleaming courts of the glorious Temple complex, Saul's mouth hardened, forming a thin, grim line. He could not argue with the truth, for it stared him boldly in the face. The Temple of God had indeed become a house divided.

How much longer could it stand?

CHAPTER 24

Tabitha

Life resumed a somewhat familiar pace shortly after the apostles' release, and Tabitha was immensely grateful. Balancing a delicate basket heavy laden with fresh produce upon one arm, the lovely young maidservant strolled alongside her mistress, intrigued by the bustling activity of Jerusalem's famous Upper Agora, also known as the Upper Market. Situated directly before the imposing palace fortress of Herod Antipas, the Upper Market consisted of a massive, rectangular stone court surrounded by three impressive Roman arcades, both stories of the enormous, red-tiled structure upheld by countless rows of perfectly symmetrical marble pillars. Within the stone court, a multitude of merchants had set up shop, all of them eagerly hawking expensive wares beneath colorful, makeshift canopies and over-crowded booths. Hundreds upon hundreds of bored customers milled about the shops, surveying merchandise, and ignoring the shrill cries of sellers advertising overpriced goods. Within mere seconds of their arrival, Tabitha had spotted multiple jewelers, perfumers, weavers, gold and silversmiths, grocers, bakers, and tailors. Swarthy, turbaned shopkeepers dangled expensive baubles and bangles before avaricious eyes, and Tabitha noticed several heavyset, richly clad women, their necks, fingers, ears, and wrists stacked with bulky layers of glittering jewelry, arguing over a gaudy pendant at a jeweler's stall. Wealthy, well-dressed patrons examined merchandise with a practiced air, while nervous, poorly clad slaves scurried about the stone court, no doubt running errands for impatient masters. Uniformed Roman soldiers patrolled the bustling court as well, their glistening armor *clank-clank-clanking* a disturbing rhythm as hobnailed sandals pounded upon the stone tiles. Ever watchful, Tabitha observed that most of the shoppers appeared entirely oblivious to the soldiers' presence, having grown quite accustomed to the Roman occupation. Others, resigned to their unfortunate fate, merely tolerated the Romans, while still others eyed the unwelcome legionnaires with open animosity, their eyes flashing, their stances hostile.

A pair of young soldiers sporting glistening bronze armor and scarlet-plumed helmets loitered near a gated entrance, and Tabitha's stomach twisted in a series of unpleasant knots when one of them—a fair-skinned Briton with piercing blue eyes—flashed her a leering, roguish grin. Annoyed, she swept the end of her pale, beige-colored veil over one shoulder, covering the lower half of her face and sending the soldier a plain, clear message. Smirking, the handsome young Briton muttered something to his companion, clearly unperturbed by Tabitha's cold statement.

The exchange wasn't lost on Mary as she turned from pressing several coins into the sweaty palm of an eager merchant. Noting Tabitha's indignation and flashing eyes, she thanked God that her lovely maid-servant guarded her own modesty and chastity. It was a rare trait, for Rome was fast becoming amoral and licentious, seducing her citizens with alluring promises of fleeting, fleshly pleasures. Once again, Mary was reminded of yet another heavy responsibility that had fallen squarely upon her own slender shoulders. Since her beloved Mark had passed, she was now entrusted with the unbelievably daunting task of arranging her lovely maidservant's future.

But no, she reminded herself firmly. *Tabitha's future is in* Your *hands, Father, not mine. Show Me what You desire for her, Lord. Help me to walk in accordance with Your will.*

Sighing, Mary tucked several packets of aromatic spices within the folds of her own heavy basket, flashing a look of warning toward the bold young soldier who continued to study the shapely young maid. Tabitha was a stunning, spirited young woman. Even now, while donning modest, earthy-colored garments falling in loose, graceful folds, her lovely shape, exquisite eyes, and rich cascade of golden curls was rather difficult to obscure. Clearly, men noticed her. And Mary was certain she would breathe easier once the young woman was betrothed to a suitable, God-fearing man. In this dangerous age, the protection and security of a husband was desirable, indeed. But would Tabitha accept the proposition of marriage? Up to this point, she had displayed little to no interest in matrimony.

As if confirming Mary's secret doubts, Tabitha shook her head in exasperation, declaring, "Men can be such arrogant louts!"

Hiding her smile, Mary said soberly, "The soldier, you mean?"

"Yes! I detest feeling as if I'm under inspection. Haven't they the slightest sense of honor, of decency?"

"We are privileged to know many good men, Tabitha," Mary reminded her gently, sorely tempted to stomp over to the arrogant soldier and demand that he behave like a mature human being.

Sensing the subtle reprimand, Tabitha sobered. Above all else, she hated to disappoint her mistress. "Yes, we do know many godly men," she admitted, tightening her shawl about her shoulders. "And I suppose I've been a bit spoiled by our fellow brethren. I go to a secular marketplace and expect Roman mercenaries to conduct themselves like the apostles who received three and a half years of instruction from Christ Himself."

Chuckling, Mary squeezed her arm in sympathy. "It's a good reminder, isn't it? Some women, desirous of a husband, frequent all the wrong places. They expect to find a godly man in the most godless of places, only to be swept away by the wrong suitor. Oftentimes, they realize their mistake far too late."

Sobered by her mistress's tragic observation, Tabitha shook her head in dismay. "Women would do far better to trust their fathers to arrange a godly union. A girl's father always desires her very best, after all."

Mary smiled, touched by Tabitha's faith and

practicality. "Have I told you that you're a very wise young woman?"

"On occasion," Tabitha teased, a hint of mischief glistening in her thickly lashed, hazel-green eyes, "but I certainly won't object to hearing it again."

Pausing before a jeweler's booth, Mary's gaze traveled over the exquisite pieces on display. With a hint of sadness, she said, "Tabitha, there's something I need you to do for me once we return home."

"Anything," Tabitha said wholeheartedly.

"I'd like you to compile a detailed inventory of all my fine jewelry. For several months now, I've intended to have it appraised."

Tabitha halted, surprised. "But...but why?"

"For the same reason we have visited the market today," Mary explained, lifting her basket brimming with fresh bread and aromatic spices. "As the church grows, we welcome more and more people in need. It is our responsibility to help meet those needs."

Tabitha studied her mistress, a bit confused. She wasn't quite following her train of thought. "But what does your jewelry have to do with all that?"

"I haven't any use for it now," Mary laughed, resuming her stroll. "*As a ring of gold in a swine's snout, so is a lovely woman who lacks discretion*," Mary continued, quoting the sagacious Solomon with a bemused smile. "Jewelry is lovely to behold, but since it is incapable of increasing godly wisdom or accomplishing any lasting purpose, I've decided to sell mine to donate the proceeds to meet the needs of the poor."

Fleetingly, Tabitha recalled a recent conversation in which she'd overheard Mary ask Tobias to designate servants to gather the valuables from each magnificent chamber in the grand villa, to have them all appraised. Concerned for her mistress's reputation, Tabitha ventured cautiously, "My lady, if you do this, rumors will abound. People will think you've fallen on hard times."

"People may think whatever they wish, and they will anyway," Mary teased as they passed the last few booths at the southwestern end of the monumental court. "I might as well give them something to talk about!"

Tabitha considered her mistress's stunning collection of fine jewelry comprised of both gold and silver, delicate amphora earrings, jewel-studded bracelets and pendants, dazzling brooches adorned with myriad precious stones, and even elegant strings of rare pearls, particularly prized by the Roman elite. The sale of such luxurious merchandise would surely result in a small fortune—probably a sum larger than most garnered over the course of a lifetime. Tabitha could scarcely comprehend her mistress's poignant sacrifice, especially since most of her jewels were gifts from her beloved late husband. But with the proceeds of such a large sale, hundreds of needy children would soon be clothed and fed, and Jesus had promised it was far more blessed to give than to receive. Tabitha knew He was worthy of their trust. Even so, she was amazed by Mary's devotion. Would she, Tabitha, possess the strength of will to make such a sacrifice?

Having purchased what was needed from the Upper Market, Mary and Tabitha left the bustling stone court brimming with harried shoppers. Embarking on the broad avenue which would take them to Mary's opulent neighborhood, Tabitha was relieved to leave the tumultuous marketplace—and the Roman's bold stare—far behind them. Removing her simple veil from the lower portion of her face, Tabitha lifted her head and drank in the cool autumn air. The seasons were passing so very quickly, and with them, the clear memory of her Lord's tender features. At times, Tabitha gloried as the months sped by, for it meant that Jesus' imminent return drew nearer. No one knew exactly when He would return, but He had promised, and they believed. Still, a nagging thought continued to plague her, one she attempted to dismiss with little success. When Jesus returned for His followers, would she be ready? Could she truly be counted among the children of God? True, she had accepted the Savior's incomprehensible sacrifice. She had borne the fiery flame of the Holy Spirit upon the day of Pentecost. And yet, she felt…unworthy.

Gazing up at the clear blue sky, Tabitha basked in the early morning sunshine, observing the fluffy white clouds drifting lazily across an open sky. Soon, autumn would slip by, ushering in the cooler winter months. And then spring would be upon them once again—a full year after Jesus' death and resurrection, and the advent of the Holy Spirit.

"You're rather quiet this morning," Mary observed, concerned that the Roman's brazen behavior had upset the young woman more than she cared to admit.

"Just lost in thought, I suppose," Tabitha mused, swinging her basket upon one arm, her expression clouded with concerns.

"What kind of thoughts?" Mary pressed, smiling gently as they passed several towering arcades lining the beautifully paved street. Towering palms graced either side of the fashionable avenue, providing a delicious canopy of shade for weary pedestrians.

"Do you remember the afternoon the apostles were released, my lady?" Tabitha asked earnestly. "When everyone returned to the Upper Room, Simon Peter led that incredible prayer in which he asked the Holy Spirit to empower us to speak the Word with boldness," Tabitha explained, her slender brows furrowed as she mentally traveled back in time. "It was a truly wondrous experience, for the entire place was shaken in response. Poor Rhoda was petrified, her eyes round as saucers!"

"The Holy Spirit is indeed working in mighty ways," Mary agreed, sensing that Tabitha had even more to say. "The quake was powerful confirmation that our prayers were heard and received."

Pausing amidst the quiet street, Tabitha raised concerned eyes toward her mistress. "My lady, at the time, I couldn't help but wonder if perhaps I was praying for the wrong thing. When Peter prayed for boldness, the thought that crossed my mind was this—it isn't *boldness* that I lack, it's *discretion*. I want to serve God mightily. I want to walk in His will. But it seems my own stubborn will is constantly in the way, barring the path of righteousness. *Sharing* the gospel is easy—but *living* it? That's the hard part."

Mary chuckled her understanding, fully sympathizing with Tabitha's dilemma.

"The Lord's brother, James, says we should be quick to listen and slow to speak, but I'm quick to speak and even slower to listen. And Jesus said we should love our enemies, but I'd like nothing more than to witness their swift demise. Jesus also said that vengeance belongs to God, and yet, at times, all I can think about is getting even with the people who prey upon the ones I love. Sometimes," she admitted, her eyes sparkling with a soft sheen of tears, "I can't help but wonder if I'm even saved."

Mary halted beside her maidservant, her heart going out to the young woman. Touching her shoulder gently, she said, "Tabitha, do you remember the story of Jacob?"

Tabitha glanced sideways at her mistress, perplexed. "Of course. He was the son of Isaac, the grandson of our father, Abraham. Jacob later begot twelve sons—twelve sons who became the pillars of our nation."

"Then you remember that Jacob was given a new name."

"Yes," Tabitha nodded slowly, squinting in recollection. "Jacob's entire life loomed before him, frightening and uncertain." *Somewhat like my own,* Tabitha thought, troubled by her own restlessness. Did the Lord have a plan in store for her, or was she simply drifting aimlessly about, at the sheer mercy of chance? Breaking free from her troubled thoughts, she returned her attention to Mary. "Jacob had spent the entire night wrestling with God, clinging relentlessly, refusing to release Him. Jacob refused to let go until God had blessed him."

"Precisely. And then God said, *'Your name shall no longer be called Jacob, but Israel; for you have struggled with God and with men, and have prevailed.'* You see, the people of God were raised up through enormous struggle, through intense wrestling. And any man who has engaged in the sport can tell you that wrestling is a painful exercise, requiring every ounce of strength that one can muster. It is an exhausting, consuming feat, requiring one's entire being and unfaltering concentration. And so it is concerning our walk with God." Mary resumed her stride at a much slower pace, and Tabitha joined her, her expression both thoughtful and troubled.

"It is no mere coincidence that God's chosen people bear the name of *Israel*, signifying a deep, inner struggle, a constant wrestling," Mary continued. "Every child of God is at war within himself—will he live by the power of the Holy Spirit, or by his own willful flesh? The enemy of our souls would like nothing better than to crush us beneath the burden of our weaknesses, inadequacies, and shortcomings. He is, after all, the great accuser of men. But that's precisely why we must always remember that we can do nothing of ourselves. It is by the Spirit's power that we gain victory over our flesh."

Tabitha nodded slowly, comprehending Mary's wisdom.

"Unfortunately," Mary explained with a wry smile, "our struggle against the flesh will not cease until we are perfected with Christ Jesus in paradise. But rather than being discouraged by it, we must recognize that our wrestling is a blessed sign—an indicator of the Holy Spirit *at work in us*, convicting us of sin and leading us down the path of righteousness for His name's sake. So your wrestling, my dear Tabitha, is *proof* of the Holy Spirit at work in your life, and certainly not a lack of salvation on your part."

Tabitha stared at her mistress in awe, pausing as they reached the enormous gated entrance of Mary's palatial villa. "I'd never thought of it like that," she admitted, somewhat relieved.

"The fact that you recognize your faults and desire to remedy them is a trustworthy indicator that the Holy Spirit is at work in you, Tabitha," Mary said warmly. "Now it's up to you to heed His gentle nudging."

"Just the other night," Tabitha said as Zev opened the gate for them, wearing a bored expression, "John preached about the words of Christ, reminding us that a tree is known by its fruit. But I don't like some of the fruit that I'm producing."

"You have borne much good fruit, Tabitha," Mary said firmly. "You have a heart for the Lord and a huge desire to share the gospel and reach those in need. Daily, you retire to your chamber after your work is done, weaving beautiful garments for the widows and needy children of this city. You also seek to obey the Lord by keeping His commandments. If that isn't worthy fruit, then I don't know what is."

Tabitha longed to accept Mary's exhortation. But was it really that simple?

"Remember," Mary remonstrated, pausing before the great stone fountain at the center of the elegant courtyard, "John said it was those who make a *practice* of sinning who produce bad fruit. Such people disregard the commandments of God, living as they please, quenching the Holy Spirit, and gratifying the desires of their flesh. But you, Tabitha, practice righteousness. And when you *do* sin—which we all do, on occasion—your repentance is both heartfelt and genuine."

"I *do* want to turn from my sin," Tabitha said

emphatically, crossing the large stone courtyard, opening heavy double doors, and ushering her mistress into the narrow, frescoed vestibule. "But *how*? No matter how hard I seem to try, I find myself falling into the same petty sins."

Entering the vast reception hall, Mary removed her pale blue shawl, draping it delicately over one arm. "It's only by the grace of God, Tabitha, that we are transformed. You will frustrate yourself until Kingdom come if you attempt to attain righteousness by your own strength. Instead, lean on God. Pray without ceasing, asking Him to transform you from the inside out. The moment temptations arise, turn to God in fervent prayer. Live by the Holy Spirit, immersing yourself in the Word of God. The more time you spend in prayer, in the Word, and actively denying the carnal flesh to live by the Holy Spirit, the more you shall be conformed into the image of Christ by His grace, through faith. Do you understand?"

Taking Mary's delicate shawl and folding it carefully, Tabitha nodded, her previously careworn features lighting with recognition. "Perhaps I should spend a bit more time praying and a little less time worrying," she smiled.

Mary laughed, the melodic sound echoing pleasantly throughout the vast marble hall. "That's the idea, dear one."

Taking a deep breath, Tabitha watched as Mary mounted the broad staircase, her entire being radiating with joy and peace. Though she had lost her beloved Mark, the dearest person in her life, Mary had embraced the Way with her entire being. By God's grace, she was happy, content. Mary's life shone as a powerful beacon, an undeniable testimony, to anyone she happened to encounter.

A small smile teased the corners of Tabitha's lips. She, too, longed to bear the Light of the world in her own life and actions. It wouldn't be easy, but she was now ready to embrace the transforming power the Holy Spirit offered to all the saints. And now it was time to move forward, trusting God with her future, depending on the power of the Holy Spirit to transform her from the inside out. Tabitha had never run from a challenge, and this was one she now embraced with zeal. It was time to fight the good fight, to finish the race. She intended to keep the faith, to kneel before the throne of God someday and hear Him say, "Well done, good and faithful servant."

That journey had begun with a single step, one she had taken many months ago when she accepted Jesus Christ as the Son of God, the atonement for all mankind. Surely, God would complete the good work He had begun in her, seeing it through to the very end.

CHAPTER 25

Mary

A.D. 32

Mary was utterly delighted when her brother, Joses, paid an unexpected visit. Having been delayed in Cyprus the previous autumn and winter, Joses had recently returned to Jerusalem, hopefully to remain for quite some time. Overjoyed, Mary fluttered about the villa, instructing the servants to prepare refreshments and ready the family *triclinium*.

An hour later, as Mary lounged comfortably upon an elegant *lectus*, a dainty goblet in hand, she smiled fondly, watching her dear brother converse with John Mark, each of them occupying their own plush couch across the table. At thirteen, her son was fast becoming a handsome young man. This was a jarring revelation, one Mary both celebrated and lamented. His shoulders had broadened considerably in the last year or so as his gangly, boyish form had begun to fill out. Closing her eyes, Mary attempted to soothe the sharp pang in her heart, for John Mark's intuitive dark eyes, broad smile, and sturdy build were becoming poignantly reminiscent of the husband she had adored. Opening her eyes, Mary watched John Mark's interaction with her brother, gratified. Joses' great love for the boy was evident as he leaned forward on his couch, patiently absorbing his nephew's every word.

As Mary's thoughts returned to her silent evaluation, her mouth tipped ruefully, another thought dawning rather unexpectedly. Apparently, John Mark had inherited a few of his mother's attributes, as well—noticeably her beautifully bronzed skin tone, dark hair, and direct, straightforward manner. And despite his mischievous, teasing nature, the boy possessed a stubborn streak that was nearly impossible to budge—a stubborn streak very much like hers. She was abundantly thankful that the Lord was faithful to refine such qualities, using them to advance his Kingdom rather than hinder it, transforming human stubbornness into godly determination. John Mark was also adventurous and innately curious, driving her to near distraction as an infant, constantly getting into absolutely *everything*. Amused, Mary hid a subtle smile. Not much had changed since then.

Tuning in to her relatives' lively conversation, Mary realized John Mark was updating his uncle about the church-related activities he had missed while tending to business matters in Cyprus.

Joses looked at her then, his soft brown eyes filled with warmth. "What you've done here, Mary—offering your home for the sake of Christ's growing church, selling your earthly goods to feed and clothe

the poor, it's truly remarkable."

Humbled, Mary met her older brother's warm gaze with a genuine smile. She was convinced he had the kindest face in the world.

"Mark would be so proud of you, dear sister."

Completely unprepared for the hot tears that burned her eyes, Mary was touched by her brother's genuine sentiment. Reaching across the table, she grasped his large, weathered hand. "I seek the will of God, Joses," she tried to explain. "But I do it so imperfectly. Only the grace of God keeps the church afloat."

"Amen," Joses agreed softly. "Praise God for His grace and unmerited favor."

Mary nodded, warmed to the core by her brother's edifying presence. He was a gentle man with a mild spirit, always ready to exhort and encourage. Joses saw the best in everyone, and he was remarkably gifted at nurturing the positive qualities he glimpsed in others. She admired him greatly.

At that moment, young Rhoda entered the elegant triclinium, bearing a bowl of scented water, a plush towel draped over one arm, as it was customary to wash after partaking of a meal. Allowing her mistress to wash her smooth, delicate hands first, Rhoda then waited upon Joses, and last, John Mark.

"My, how you've grown, dear Rhoda!" Joses smiled at the young Cypriot his sister had rescued from ruthless slavers. "It is good to see you, little one."

Shyly acknowledging Joses, Rhoda offered a timid smile. "And you as well, Master Joses." Her voice was so small, so delicate, one had to lean forward to catch the quiet greeting.

Mary watched, bemused, as Rhoda redirected her attention toward John Mark. With a bit of a splash, John Mark dipped stained fingers into the bowl of scented water Rhoda offered him, then dried his hands upon the proffered towel. The small maid-servant lowered her gaze, her fair cheeks stained with deep, rosy color.

"Thank you, Rhoda," John Mark quipped, flashing the nine-year-old little girl a winning smile.

Flustered, Rhoda lifted large brown eyes, shyly meeting his gaze.

"Thank you, my dear Rhoda," Mary interrupted, dissolving the spell her handsome son had unwittingly cast upon the innocent serving girl. "You may go."

"Yes, my lady," Rhoda managed, her voice little more than a whisper. Hastening from the room, she cast one last, soulful glance over her slender shoulder before disappearing beneath the pillared entryway.

Exchanging a knowing look with his sister, Joses chuckled and clapped his nephew on the back. "It would seem you have yourself a sweet little admirer, John Mark."

Mary shot her brother a disapproving glance, along with a silent reprimand. John Mark was a very handsome young man. Already, girls were beginning to notice him—far too soon, in her opinion. And she was quite certain that her charismatic son needn't any encouragement from his uncle or anyone else. She certainly didn't want the attention going to his head, rendering him useless and conceited.

Joses merely grinned, sensing his sister's line of thought. Smiling, he held his tongue, though it was obvious he had even more to say.

Sensing his mother's obvious discomfort, John Mark flashed a boyish grin. "May I be dismissed? Simeon is waiting for me outside."

"Of course, you may be dismissed," Mary responded, relieved that her son appeared unaffected by her brother's casual observation.

Rising, Joses drew his nephew close, trapping him within the confines of an inescapable bear hug. Ruffling the boy's dark hair, Joses released him. "It was wonderful to see you again, my son."

"And you as well, Uncle."

Once John Mark had vacated the *triclinium* with the grace of a charging bull, Joses returned to his *lectus*. Settling comfortably, he smiled fondly at his younger sister. "You are doing so well with him, Mary."

Mary smiled, gratified. "When my husband was taken from us, I couldn't imagine raising John Mark without him. Instantly, I was to become the breadwinner, as well as the doting mother. And then there were the responsibilities God had bestowed upon me regarding the church. I was so afraid there wouldn't be sufficient time to invest in my son. But God is so faithful. He has graciously supplied the time I was so certain I would lack. John Mark and I begin each day together in the Word. We study and grow. And we end each night in the same fashion. I cherish my time with him, and I will always treasure our relationship."

"How you accomplish all that you do is beyond me," Joses commented, taking a swig of his fruit scented water.

"Only by the grace of God," Mary laughed.

"And with an immense amount of help from my hard-working staff!"

"But do you ever sleep?"

"Occasionally," she chuckled, her dark eyes twinkling. "I've noticed that Simon Peter has established a particularly strong bond with John Mark. They need each other, in a sense, as Peter lacks children, and John Mark, a father. It is precious to behold their flourishing friendship."

"And it appears that sweet young lady you rescued in Cyprus is doing well?"

"Rhoda is wonderful," Mary said wholeheartedly. "And a bit smitten with my son, I suppose," she chuckled in amusement. "But I know the Lord directed us to her for a reason, Joses."

"God does *everything* for a reason," Joses agreed. "Now tell me more about this growing church."

Propped up on one elbow, Mary pondered Joses' question. Where to even begin? "We've all learned so much in recent months," she explained, recognizing anew the enormity of God's calling upon each of His children. "God has established a flourishing church here in Jerusalem. Those who join the Way are sincere in their faith, seeking to honor God in all they do. Our purpose is to fulfill the commission Jesus entrusted to us—to share the gospel."

"Clearly, the church's efforts have borne much fruit."

"Our numbers increase daily," Mary affirmed, somewhat overwhelmed by all that God was doing. "And some things have become perfectly clear. God is establishing His church, His people, upon the earth to share the Good News with unbelievers. Our mission is to teach the Word, resulting in the conviction and conversion of the unbelieving. By doing this, we fulfill His call to make disciples of all the nations. However, Jesus' great commission doesn't end there. Jesus said, '*Make disciples of all the nations, baptizing them in the name of the Father and of the Son and of the Holy Spirit.*' But then He went on to say, '*teaching them to observe all things that I have commanded them.*'"

Joses nodded his understanding, intrigued as he mulled over the command once more. "So not only are we to share the gospel, but we are then to *instruct* and *establish* believers in the ways and commandments of God."

"Yes!" Mary said, her shining eyes betraying her excitement. "In our great zeal to see the lost embrace the Way, it's easy to forget the second part of this command—to firmly establish those who have already embraced the truth by teaching them how to obey God's commandments."

"And this we do through prayer and study of the Word," Joses mused, thoughtfully stroking his neatly groomed, curly beard.

"Exactly," Mary agreed. "Which is yet another reason why our times of prayer, study, and fellowship are so important. We must always remember to pray for each other and hold each other accountable. Something I've learned beyond any shadow of doubt, Joses, is this—together, we are stronger."

"Amen to that," Joses smiled, setting aside his goblet with a soft *thud*.

"It's exciting to watch the followers banding together, working tirelessly to meet needs. As the church continues to expand, we gather here, as well as in other houses scattered throughout the city, preaching and ministering to those in need. The believers share everything they have with reckless abandon, so the number of poor among us is greatly dwindling. It's incredible to see what the Lord can do when His children care for their own."

"Is it true the great merchant prince of Jerusalem, Simon, and his fair wife, Iskah, have become patrons of the church?"

"It is," Mary affirmed. "In fact, they attend our meetings often, along with their lovely daughter's family and various members of their staff."

"Incredible."

"I am amazed by influential men and women who desire to use the resources God has given them for the furtherance of the gospel," Mary mused.

"The Lord has granted the church a measure of peace, for a time," Joses observed.

"We savor every moment of it," Mary said with great feeling. "And yet, one thing is certain—the persecution will increase. We know this because Jesus said it would."

Rising soberly from his *lectus*, Joses crossed the room, pausing before a row of elegantly framed windows. Leaning calmly against the ledge, he crossed his arms over his chest, his gaze resting cryptically upon Mary. "I'm afraid such events are taking shape, even now. A great drama is unfolding upon the world's grand stage, and the repercussions may prove unfavorable toward followers of the Way."

Drawing herself up to a sitting position, Mary eyed her brother in dismay. "What do you mean, Joses?"

"The emperor of Rome has retreated to his pleasure gardens in Capri. Rumor has it he's become rather paranoid."

"Emperor Tiberius has been a just ruler in the past. Why the change?"

"Who knows? Perhaps he simply wearied of having his life threatened."

"And now?"

"He's an old man in poor health," Joses said resignedly. "The empire has fallen into the hands of a bureaucracy established by Tiberius' predecessor, Augustus. To make matters worse, Caligula has joined Tiberius in Capri."

"Caligula?"

"The son of the famed Roman war hero, Germanicus, not to mention the great-grandson of the legendary Marc Antony. No doubt, Caligula harbors great political ambitions. Many are speculating that he plans to murder the emperor and assume his throne."

"That's terrible, truly," Mary said, shaking her head in dismay. "But how will these developments in far-away Rome impact followers of the Way?"

"The leadership of this empire is crucial," Joses explained. "For now, Jews are permitted certain rights—the right to worship our God, the right to conduct business and earn a fair wage, the right to abstain from labor on the Sabbath Day, and so on and so forth. But the emperor possesses the power to strip us of our freedoms with the mere snap of his finger."

"And if this Caligula assumes the throne, you believe he would do that?"

"I certainly hope not, but I don't like what I'm hearing."

Mary furrowed her brow, deep in thought.

Sensing his sister's unease, Joses offered a soothing smile. Straightening, he said cheerfully, "But enough of this dismal topic. Let's discuss more pleasant subjects."

"All right," Mary consented, her manner frank. "When were you going to tell me about your selfless act of unrivaled generosity?"

"Didn't Jesus say, '*When you do a charitable deed, do not let your left hand know what your right hand is doing?*'"

"The apostles frequent this home many times a day, Joses. You can't keep secrets from me."

"A man would be hard-pressed keeping *anything* from you. Tell me, dear sister, is it your matchless intelligence, or do you simply possess a deeper connection with the Holy Spirit than the rest of us?" Joses grinned, his brown eyes sparkling with mischief.

Laughing at her brother's absurdity, Mary rose from the table and joined him at the window. "You can't distract me from the topic at hand, Joses. Is it true you sold your magnificent grove in Paphos, Cyprus, bestowing all your earnings to the apostles for the Lord's work?"

"The grove produced oil for the sanctuary of Aphrodite," Joses shrugged. "I wearied of supplying oil for the promiscuous pagan goddess, and I realized those funds could be put to far better use."

"I'm glad you're not superstitious," Mary teased. "The Romans insist their deities are terribly petty and vengeful."

"Thank God they are but cold, stone idols, then!" Joses chuckled. "Besides, Aphrodite still gets her oil," he grinned. "Another is simply overseeing its production now. I've washed my hands of that entire ordeal."

"Joses, you amaze me."

"Because I dislike pagan goddesses?" Another teasing grin.

"Because you are kind, encouraging, and selfless. I can't think of another soul who would even consider laying that huge sum of money at the apostles' feet."

Joses turned to gaze out the window, observing the light afternoon traffic on the neatly paved streets. "The Lord has far better use for it than I do. He knows where the funds are needed better than I."

"And is it true the apostles have given you a new name?" Mary pressed, knowing she'd have to pry the information from her modest brother.

Joses looked at her then, clearly humbled. "They have."

"May I ask what it is they now call you?"

Joses chuckled, his bearded cheeks coloring slightly in embarrassment. "They have decided to call me *Barnabas*."

"Barnabas! I love it, Joses." Mary smiled to herself, pleased. Barnabas, *son of encouragement*.

It was a perfect fit.

CHAPTER 26

Tabitha

Located at the lower end of the famed City of David, near the colossal Hippodrome, the Synagogue of the Freedmen was an ultra-orthodox Jewish community comprised of Cyrenian, Alexandrian, Cilician, and Asian Jews of the Hellenistic Diaspora. Founded as a religious establishment for both Jewish freedmen and converted proselytes, the synagogue, boasting a modest guesthouse and its very own ritual baths, was a rather plain stone building fashioned after those scattered across Capernaum of Galilee. Within, the large stone structure housed an open, square-shaped floor plan upheld by tall pillars on all four sides. This inner court, lined with spartan stone benches, also consisted of a single raised platform by which the speaker addressed the attendees, proclaiming lengthy passages from the Torah. As a small child, Tabitha had delighted in climbing the stone steps with her father and emerging at the top of the synagogue's second floor—an open, wrap-around balcony enclosed by a crude wooden railing, overlooking the goings-on in the austere stone court below.

It was here, in the modest district of the common people, that Gamaliel himself, the venerable *Nasi* of the great Sanhedrin, presided over the synagogue, freely mingling with the many poor and common-ers in attendance. Here, the esteemed, elderly rabbi often instructed avid pupils like Saul of Tarsus, a Cilician himself and a zealous attendee of the Hellenistic synagogue. Over various decades, the Synagogue of the Freedmen had become a gathering place for citizens of the Lower City to study Torah, worship Adonai, pray, debate, and fellowship—not only on the Sabbath Day, but throughout the course of the busy week, as well.

The constant flow of traffic provided an excellent channel by which one might share the gospel message, and Tabitha had long since established the Synagogue of the Freedmen as her home base, a place where she was permitted to distribute lovely handmade garments to tired, elderly widows, anxious young mothers, and ill-clad children. Often-times, after distributing the much-needed clothing, Tabitha would be seated on the broad stone steps outside the synagogue, sharing parables of Jesus as a sea of children gathered around her, utterly delighted and transfixed, while their parents studied, prayed, or fellowshipped within the large stone building after a busy workday.

Now, as Tabitha sat upon the broad stone steps before the synagogue and its adjoining guesthouse, a sea of children clustered tightly around her, she raised her hands in animated gestures, delighting the little ones with tales of her Savior, silently praying that, in time, their hearts would be opened to their Messiah.

"Now when evening came," Tabitha said, her eyes expressive, her tone laced with intrigue, "the disciples boarded the boat of my friend, Andrew, and his brother, Simon Peter. And as they were gliding across the water, they noticed the sky growing darker, darker, darker...billowing black clouds filled the sky, and the lightning flashed brilliantly overhead like this—*swoosh, swoosh*!" Grinning, Tabitha traced invisible beams of lightning near the faces of the children closest to her, eliciting giggles of delight. "And then great claps of thunder burst through the air, filling the men in the boat with fear and dread! The storm was very great, and the waves rocked the boat to and fro, like this!" At this, Tabitha rocked her upper body back and forth, reaching for the bright-eyed little girl at her elbow and drawing her into her lap. Imprisoning the little girl in her arms, Tabitha rocked her back and forth, gaining delighted squeals from the small child and her rapt audience.

"Were they scared?" A little boy demanded, his cheeks flushed with excitement. A sea of eager voices joined his, enthralled by Tabitha's storytelling.

"The men were terrified! They thought their situation couldn't possibly get any worse! And then, they saw something even *scarier* than the maelstrom— the faint form of a Man walking upon the crashing waves, coming directly toward them!"

"What was it?" asked the little girl in her lap, turning around to get a better look at Tabitha's expressive face.

"Was it a ghost?" a chorus of small voices demanded. "Maybe it was an angel," one child argued, while another interrupted, "Or maybe it was an evil spirit!"

"My friends in the boat were filled with panic," Tabitha plunged ahead, and the children quieted, unwilling to miss any of the interesting details. "They thought it was a ghost. But then, a familiar voice closed the chasm between them, saying, '*Be of good cheer! It is I; do not be afraid.*'"

"But who was it?" This from the dark-haired little girl in her lap.

"It was a Man named Jesus. You see, Jesus could walk on the water because He created it! The laws of nature binding mere humans don't apply to Him."

"Maybe He was a ghost," the little girl suggested, dissatisfied with Tabitha's grand explanation.

"No, He was their Teacher. Jesus lived on this earth for thirty-three years before returning to God in Heaven."

"Is He in Heaven now?"

"He is, seated at the right hand of God, His Father. But He will return, and when He does, those who believe in Him will get to spend eternity with Him in paradise," Tabitha finished with a warm smile.

"Did your friends know it was Him?"

"Not at first," Tabitha admitted, smiling faintly. "My friend, Peter, decided to test Him—which is never a good idea, by the way. Peter said, '*Lord, if it is You, command me to come to You on the water.*' So Jesus did. Those in the boat gasped, shocked and frightened, when Peter climbed right over the side, his sandaled feet resting eerily upon the water even as the waves crashed furiously about him. Instantly,

Peter knew it had to be Jesus on the water. Who other than the God of Creation could enable him to defy the laws of nature? And as long as Peter fixed his eyes upon Jesus, he remained above the crashing waves. But then Peter became unsettled. The wind was boisterous, and the waves crashed furiously against him. Panicked, he took his eyes off Jesus, focusing instead upon the stormy sea. It was then that he began to sink."

"Did he die?" a little boy shouted, fascinated.

"No. Peter cried out to Jesus, saying, '*Lord, save me!*' Immediately, Jesus stretched out His hand and caught hold of him. '*You of little faith,*' Jesus said sadly. '*Why did you doubt?*' Once Peter fixed his eyes upon Jesus rather than the waves, his foundation was sure again."

"What happened next?" the children demanded, their wide eyes sparkling with interest.

"Jesus helped a very drenched—and very embarrassed—Peter into the boat, and instantly, the wind ceased."

"You are a remarkable storyteller, dear sister."

Startled by the unexpected comment, Tabitha chanced a glance over her shoulder. Stephanos stood upon the step above her, a mysterious smile crossing his handsome features. Cheeks flushing prettily in her embarrassment, Tabitha wondered how much of her animated dialogue Stephanos had overheard.

"Master Stephanos! Master Stephanos!" the children squealed, delighted by his appearance.

Annoyed, Tabitha closed her eyes and offered a silent prayer of repentance. She knew she should be pleased, not irked, by the arrival of her brother in Christ. But why was it that Stephanos always turned up when she least desired his presence? She'd had the children's rapt attention before his unwanted intrusion, planting seeds of faith that she hoped and prayed would take root in their hearts. Couldn't Stephanos see that? Why had he interrupted that sacred moment, shattering the spell and stealing the children's attention away?

Unexpectedly, Stephanos lowered himself upon the step beside Tabitha, his broad shoulders brushing slightly against hers. Instantly, her senses were filled with the heady fragrance of the scented oil upon his skin. He looked at her then, gently meeting her gaze, a question in his dark eyes.

Discomfited by his closeness, Tabitha shifted her position slightly, tightening her grasp upon the little girl in her lap. Clearly, Stephanos silently sought her permission to join their discussion. Tabitha knew she should say something, especially as the children watched her every move with rapt attention. Instead, she pursed her lips and remained silent.

Forgive Me, Lord, but he's so exasperating! Help me to receive him as You would.

"What do you think of Tabitha's story, children?" Stephanos asked enthusiastically, characteristically smoothing over the awkward moment with maddening skill and poise.

The children erupted with shouts of approval and excitement, begging for another story.

"Before we move on to another story," Stephanos said, "shall we discuss the theme of this one?"

Tabitha resisted the urge to point out that these children were far too young to recognize the *theme* of any story.

"Tell me," Stephanos clarified, as if sensing the

direction of Tabitha's rebellious thoughts, "what can we learn from this incredible account our dear sister has kindly shared with us today?"

To Tabitha's great angst, the eager little girl wriggled off her lap and climbed into Stephanos', placing two chubby hands upon his broad shoulders. "This is what we learned, Master Stephanos—don't be like Simon Peter!"

A small gasp escaped Tabitha's lips as her eyes widened in horror. Instinctively, she glanced around just in case Peter or Anaia happened to be within earshot. That hadn't been the point of her lesson at all! Thankfully, she was certain the young couple hadn't joined the meeting today.

Laughing, Stephanos said, "And what was Peter's mistake, dear one?"

"He took his eyes off Jesus."

Stephanos exchanged looks with Tabitha then, surprised by the child's insight. "Exactly. When we focus on the storm, we lose sight of the only One who can calm the storm. Simon Peter is a good, courageous man, but in that moment, he focused on the fearsome waves, rather than trusting Jesus to guide him safely through them. We must always remember to keep our eyes fixed upon Jesus, even amidst our darkest storms." Gently lifting the little girl from his lap, Stephanos rose and smiled down at Tabitha. "I must be going now. But, Lord willing, I will see you this evening at Mary's house, dear one."

Unsettled by the intensity of his gaze, Tabitha merely nodded, wondering where her voice had gone.

"I can see why the children are delighted by your stories." Flashing her a final smile, Stephanos turned and jogged down the enormous flight of stairs. Retreating down the neatly paved walkway below, his gait was markedly purposeful, as usual.

Tabitha watched his retreating back, amused. Though Stephanos had the absolute worst timing of anyone in the world, she recognized that the Lord was softening her heart toward the powerful evangelist. Perhaps even a bit more than she desired.

Her thoughts were disrupted when the synagogue's heavy wooden doors burst open, releasing a flood of simply dressed men and women and severely clad Pharisees donning fluttering black and white garments and tasseled prayer shawls. Spotting their parents amidst the large gathering streaming from the synagogue, the children sprang up on dirty, bare feet, chattering excitedly as they rushed toward their waiting families.

Noting the particularly grim expressions upon the faces of the Pharisees, along with the flushed features of the common men and women, Tabitha sensed that something was strangely amiss.

"Good afternoon, my lovely sister."

Warmed by the pleasant greeting, Tabitha rose from the stone steps. A beautiful African woman with soft, feminine features, expressive brown eyes, and a graceful smile approached her, balancing her youngest son, Rufus, upon one curved hip. "My boys will be disappointed they missed your stories today. I didn't see you arrive."

"I was a bit late today, Candace," Tabitha admitted, leaning forward to kiss Rufus' plump, baby-soft cheek. The toddler studied her soberly, and she chuckled heartily in response. "My, that's a somber expression for such a small little boy!"

"I imagine he's a bit dazed after witnessing that distasteful ordeal," the exotic young woman sighed, her deep brown eyes downcast.

Tabitha was confused. "An ordeal?"

"Stephanos didn't say anything when he left?"

"Only that he would see me this evening."

Candace bit her lower lip, glancing nervously about as if gauging who was within earshot. She was a lovely woman, the true embodiment of feminine grace, peace, and serenity. Soft-spoken and compassionate, Tabitha had been drawn to Candace the moment they had met, shortly after Jesus' resurrection. Candace and her husband, Simon of Cyrene, had embraced the Way shortly after the bloody crucifixion. Commanded by the Romans, Simon had shouldered the Savior's bloodstained cross, carrying it up Golgotha's dreadful hill. Overcome by Jesus' great sacrifice, Simon had remained near the cross until Nicodemus and Joseph of Arimathea arrived to wash and bury Jesus' lifeless body. But when Jesus accomplished the impossible, rising from the grave, Simon and his lovely young wife had determined to follow Him, no matter the cost. "On the darkest day of earth's history, the Lord showed my Simon what it truly means to deny oneself, to take up one's cross, and to follow Him," Candace had testified softly on many occasions. "The way was narrow, and mockers jeered, pressing in on all sides, as my husband dutifully followed the Savior all the way to Calvary's hill. The enemy sought to destroy him, to demoralize him. The cross grew heavier with every step, tearing the flesh upon his back, drawing beads of sweat upon his brow. But Simon persisted, his eyes fixed upon the bloodied back of his Savior. In that moment, my Simon knew there would be no turning back."

"Candace?" Tabitha persisted, forcing her memories aside to better focus on the present moment. "What happened?"

"Stephanos addressed the crowd again," Candace said, leaning in and lowering her voice. "The Pharisees didn't like it."

"The Pharisees never like it," Tabitha reminded her, a small smile playing about the corners of her lips.

"This time, they descended upon Stephanos like vultures. I've never seen anything like it. Saul challenged him in front of everyone."

Tabitha shook her head in frustration. "What happened?"

"Saul could not refute Stephanos' arguments. The debate grew heated."

"How heated?"

"Saul threatened to 'silence' Stephanos 'once and for all.' Tabitha," Candace said, her expression troubled, "I think he really meant it."

Disturbed by the tight knot forming in her stomach, Tabitha wondered at the intensity of her own emotions. "Saul is a dangerous man, and he has the ear of Gamaliel and even Caiaphas," Tabitha declared, her tone laced with anger. "Stephanos is reckless. He's going to get himself killed."

"Greetings, dear Tabitha." Simon of Cyrene drew alongside his wife, their older son, Alexander, in tow. A dark-skinned man of both African and Jewish descent, he bore himself with both confidence and quiet humility. Turning toward Candace, he asked, "Shall we return home before this evening's prayer service, beloved?"

"Of course," Candace responded, her slanted brown eyes betraying her deep concern. "I was just telling Tabitha about how Saul threatened our Stephanos."

"Saul has a frightful temper," Simon sighed, shaking his head grimly. "We must pray for him."

Tabitha stared incredulously at Simon, battling her own stubborn will. *Pray* for him? That was the *last* thing she wished to do for Saul of Tarsus! She considered *praying* him right off the nearest cliff! Groaning inwardly, she recognized her own rebellion and silently begged the Lord to help her resist the temptation to despise her enemies. After all, Jesus had called her to love them.

Sighing dismally, Tabitha studied her friends' troubled expressions. Sensing the tense undercurrents swirling about the synagogue, their two young sons appeared anxious as well. "Was Saul chastised for his inappropriate behavior?" Tabitha asked, teasingly ruffling Alexander's unruly dark hair. Forcing a smile, she hoped to set the children's minds at ease. "Did anyone stand in Stephanos' defense?"

"Only my Simon," Candace said sadly, shifting her son's weight with one arm and taking her husband's hand. "I believe Gamaliel would have, had he been present."

"Most likely, his absence is what emboldened Saul to speak as he did," Simon observed, dismayed. "But Gamaliel will hear of Saul's brashness. Perhaps the rabbi will talk some sense into his zealous young pupil."

Tabitha crossed her arms over her chest. "Stephanos testifies of Jesus nearly every day. Surely a few here have opened their hearts to the truth by now!"

"This synagogue was founded *by* freedmen *for* freedmen," Candace said, her eyes glistening with unshed tears. "And though our ancestors were freed from human bonds, their descendants are now enslaved by something far more dangerous—their own stubborn unbelief."

Tabitha nodded slowly, disturbed by Candace's powerful assessment. As hostility toward the followers increased, she couldn't help but wonder what the future held for those she loved.

CHAPTER 27

Mary

Smiling deeply, Mary watched as believers milled comfortably about the Upper Room, enjoying the laughter, chatter, and fellowship following John's evening prayer service. The upper floor had undergone quite a transformation since that fateful evening when Jesus had partaken of the Passover feast with His disciples. The faithful Tobias had overseen the construction project as the walls were demolished to create a wide-open floor plan large enough to house the growing body of believers in various shifts. A raised platform had been constructed at the front of the massive chamber, where the apostles stood to address the church body seated upon neat rows of low wooden benches. Even now, as the first glistening stars began dotting the dusky evening sky, the gathering place boasted a cheery glow, fueled by the flickering light of dozens of mounted oil lamps and hanging candelabras. After much prayer, careful consideration, and the grueling labor of numerous hirelings, Mary was immensely pleased with the outcome. Every inch of space was meticulously and practically utilized, even while the atmosphere remained warm and welcoming.

"My, my. You've been quite the busy little bee, have you not?"

Mary forced what she hoped appeared to be a sincere smile as the incorrigible Sapphira joined her near an elegant row of windows, the intricate latticework painted in warm shades of emerald, yellow, gold, and crimson. "Good evening, Sapphira."

"All these renovations must have cost a fortune," the heiress remarked rather tactlessly, her long, painted nails *tap-tap-tapping* the goblet she balanced between soft, tapered fingers. "It's a pity, truly, that such drastic reconstruction was required. In the past, this was such a lovely space."

"Actually, I'm very pleased with the results," Mary assured her, ignoring the slight. "These renovations were essential to house such a large assembly."

Inspecting her surroundings with a critical eye, Sapphira shrugged. "It's a bit drab, but I suppose a meeting house must be functional rather than aesthetically pleasing."

"I'd like to think this space offers both functionality and charm," Mary replied cheerfully.

"There's no need to become defensive, darling," Sapphira chided a bit too loudly, drawing the attention of several women chatting nearby.

Maintaining her customary graciousness, Mary resisted the urge to point out that her reaction hadn't been the least bit defensive. She couldn't help but wonder why some women of Sapphira's breeding and affluence assuaged their own insecurities by belittling others in public.

"Did you and your husband enjoy the prayer service?" Mary asked politely, tactfully changing the subject.

"I must ask you, dear, are the services always this long?"

"The length of the prayer service depends on the number of prayer requests we take before the Lord," Mary replied, striving for patience. "As hostility increases toward followers of the Way, there's much to pray about."

"Is it really as dreadful as the apostles say?" Sapphira plunged ahead, clearly miffed. "Ananias and I haven't suffered a speck of persecution since joining the Way."

Perhaps that's because, up to this point, you've posed no threat whatsoever to those on the outside, Mary wished to retort. Instead, she said graciously, "The religious leaders become increasingly hostile by the day. It's important to pray for our brothers as they proclaim the gospel before dangerous men."

"Speaking of the apostles," Sapphira pried, "is it true Simon Peter asked to house the church treasury here in your home?"

Suppressing her mounting annoyance, Mary replied, "It is. As the Holy Spirit moves upon the hearts of believers, many of them are selling their homes, properties, or possessions, designating the proceeds for the Lord's work. The apostles have decided to set up a system to manage such funds responsibly." Reluctantly, Mary had capitulated to Peter's request, allowing the apostles to store church funds within the cool storage vaults beneath her sprawling mansion. There, donations were carefully chronicled, stored, sorted, prayed over, and distributed at the Holy Spirit's leading.

"It would seem the believers have been inspired by your brother's shining example, selling their belongings to increase the church's treasury," Sapphira crooned. Somehow, even the compliment was tinged with contempt. "Tell me, did he really donate the entirety of his grove's profits?"

"Barnabas is a generous man," Mary responded, warmed by voicing her brother's new name. She was still getting used to it, even though it was perfect for him. "He was just happy to have something to offer."

"It was a heroic gesture, even if he was misguided," Sapphira quipped, taking a long, somewhat noisy sip from her goblet.

"What do you mean, misguided?" Mary inquired, irritated that the woman was already downplaying her brother's sacrifice.

"His was a profitable grove, producing a reliable and passive source of income, was it not? Barnabas would have done much better to sell a vacant field or a piece of land—something that wasn't garnering profits month after month. I'm sure the church would have held him in high esteem, even had his donation been a bit less substantial."

"Barnabas sold his grove at the Holy Spirit's leading, not to garner esteem," Mary said, carefully guarding her tone. She didn't wish to sound defensive, for Sapphira would certainly point it out—loudly—if she did. "Sometimes, God requires sacrifices that don't make any sense at all by man's standards. This was certainly one of those times."

"Of course it was, my dear," Sapphira crooned, patting Mary's arm in a patronizing manner. "You needn't defend your brother's contribution. After all, not everyone possesses the business acumen required for financial success."

Piqued, Mary ached to point out that Barnabas was far more "successful" than Ananias and Sapphira on both a spiritual *and* financial level, but she held her tongue. Such displays of pride were not pleasing to the Lord. Instead, she offered a cordial smile. "I'm delighted you could join us this evening, Sapphira."

Sensing the subtle dismissal, Sapphira tilted her head back and emptied her goblet. Thrusting the empty vessel toward Mary—an obvious slight, as there were many servants nearby attending the guests—she chidingly clicked her tongue. "Your brother has certainly caused quite a stir, hasn't he? And to think—his hefty, little donation ensured his instant elevation to an apostle's status. How nice for him."

Having delivered her final slight for the evening, Sapphira flashed a pearly smile before moseying away to fetch her husband, Ananias.

Quietly, Mary watched her go, her own amusement overriding her exasperation. After all, Sapphira needed prayer, not condemnation. Only God could change the wealthy woman's heart, providing opportunities in which she might surrender her pride, humble herself, and submit to His gentle leading.

***

Silver moonlight streamed through Mary's open window, bathing the entire bedchamber in a soft sheen of pale, otherworldly light. After several hours of miserable tossing and turning, Mary lifted herself to a sitting position and thrust aside her plush covering.

Something was amiss.

Gently swinging her legs over the side of the bed, Mary rose gracefully, reaching for the soft robe she'd shed several hours earlier. Slipping slender arms into the sleeves, Mary shrugged into the warm outer garment, somewhat comforted by the feel of the lush fabric against her cool, clammy skin.

Crossing the spacious bedchamber, Mary knelt beside the open window, gazing quietly upon the sleeping city. Ever since the arrival of the Holy Spirit last spring, Mary had been plagued by nights like this, when sleep utterly eluded her despite extreme exhaustion. Now, she recognized this bizarre restlessness for what it was—the prompting of the Holy Spirit. Many a night, the Spirit of the Lord had awakened her, urging her to intercede in fervent prayer.

"Lord," Mary whispered, tucking a stray ringlet of dark-brown hair behind a delicate ear, "I desire to be obedient to Your will. For whom or for what shall I pray?"

Sapphira. Pray for Sapphira.

Startled, Mary drew her warm robe tightly about her slender body, considering the wealthy woman's plight. Mary worried for Sapphira. Though the heiress relished the thrill of signs and wonders associated with the Way, she detested the rigorous disciplines required of the faithful. Sapphira loathed spending time in quiet prayer or study. Clearly, she envied those in leadership, craving attention and acclamation. Having known nothing but luxury and self-indulgence her entire life, Sapphira refused to relinquish her own will, her own ideas. Mary had no doubt the woman wished to follow Christ, but she refused to take up her cross unless it was a padded one, devoid of pain, suffering, or discomfort.

Despite the woman's intense struggle against the flesh, Mary knew that Jesus loved Sapphira fiercely. He desired her salvation above all else. And He would stop at nothing to open doors for Sapphira—*if* she was willing to enter and partake of His saving presence.

Folding her hands upon the window's cool ledge, Mary bowed her head, praying fervently on behalf of the woman who'd gained the entire world, and yet risked losing her very soul.

CHAPTER 28

Sapphira

"You are suggesting we sell our plot near Akeldama?"

Seated behind the large desk in his study, Ananias stared at his wife, clearly puzzled. "It's a rocky, infertile plot, virtually useless. We'll make little more than a few scrappy shillings—*if* we can procure a buyer, in the first place!"

Leaning forward in the straight-backed chair opposite her husband's desk, Sapphira's sharpened features glowed in the flickering light cast by the elegant lamp between them. "I've already made the arrangements."

"Without my knowledge or consent?" Running a hand over his balding head, Ananias released a short sigh of frustration. He supposed he shouldn't be surprised by his wife's peremptory behavior. Accustomed to having her own way, she seldom consulted him about *anything*. She snapped her pretty, little fingers, and he performed. *Like a trained dog,* he thought, frowning, as he laid aside his stylus.

"The land is doing us little to no good," Sapphira plunged ahead, ignoring her husband's initial protest. "In fact, we're losing money maintaining that worthless tract. It doesn't produce a single mite, and yet we pay taxes on it year after year."

Ananias folded his hands, resting his chin upon them. "I'm listening."

"I propose we sell the parcel and donate the proceeds to the church."

Ah, so there it was. Sapphira couldn't bear to be upstaged or eclipsed by anyone or anything. Though Barnabas had intended to keep his generous donation anonymous, word had spread like wildfire. And Barnabas' popularity had skyrocketed within the church, virtually overnight. Characteristically, Sapphira coveted the newly appointed apostle's fame, desiring the same acclaim for herself.

"Why not simply bestow a donation? Why sell the parcel?" Ananias muttered, annoyed. It was the middle of the night, and he hadn't the time nor the inclination to deal with his wife's petty jealousy right now. His desk was stacked with important documents, all of them begging for his attention.

"Our finances will undoubtedly suffer should we present a sizable donation without making a substantial sale to supplement the loss."

Ananias' lips thinned, forming a narrow, disapproving line. He was a wealthy man, and yet their accounts increasingly dwindled as Sapphira squandered nearly every shilling he produced. Should she spend a bit less times browsing the high-end markets or frequenting exclusive, upscale baths, their coffers might remain full! "And you think that useless plot of land will produce a substantial fee?"

"I know it will," Sapphira purred, her dark eyes gleaming. "You may have forgotten that our field shares a border with Akeldama. As you know, the Field of Blood now functions as a common grave-yard for the wretched poor."

Ananias waited, his expression betraying his impatience.

"My buyer wishes to expand the Field of Blood," Sapphira said in exasperation, speaking as if instructing a particularly slow child. "The plot is lousy for farming, but it's perfect for dumping corpses. Our client plans to carve out common graves, selling them to the masses at affordable prices."

"How much has he offered?"

Sapphira told him, her red-stained lips tipping in an arrogant smile.

Ananias fell back in his chair, taken aback.

"You can sign the paperwork first thing in the morning," Sapphira announced a bit too smugly. "There's no need to keep our buyer waiting now, is there?"

"No," Ananias mused, wishing he'd made the move before Sapphira. "No, there certainly isn't."

"Excellent. We will meet with him at sunup."

Ananias glanced at the heavy hourglass perched atop his desk. The night was nearly spent. He'd best begin drawing up the paperwork now.

Rising from her chair, Sapphira crossed the large office, pausing in the doorway. "Once the transaction is complete, we shall deliver the funds to Simon Peter."

Leaning back in his plush chair, Ananias crossed his arms and studied his wife pensively. "That's an exorbitant amount of money."

"Even more than Barnabas contributed," Sapphira purred, her dark eyes glowing avariciously.

"Will we donate all of it?"

Sapphira's mouth dropped open. "*All of it*? Are you mad? That's an enormous sum!"

Ananias released his breath, relieved. "How much, then?"

"Just enough to level out the playing field. The church has fallen into the hands of common day laborers and fishermen. Those people are in desperate need of leadership—the kind of leadership *we* can provide, my husband."

"And what makes you so certain the apostles will turn to us for direction?"

"Did they not do so with Barnabas? And we shall bestow a far grander sum than he! They'll have no choice but to elevate our status above the rest."

Reaching for his stylus, Ananias tapped it thoughtfully upon his desk. He wasn't nearly as convinced as his wife. "Barnabas sacrificed his *entire* earnings," he pointed out.

Sapphira rolled her eyes, peeved. Leaning against the doorpost, she said coolly, "They'll never know we didn't relinquish the entire sum."

"And if they discover our little secret?"

"They won't," Sapphira hissed, her expression daring Ananias to defy her. "They may work miracles, but they can't read minds! And I certainly don't intend to tell them. *Do you*?"

"Of course not."

"Good."

Ananias looked away, strangely unsettled. Odd that his conscience should disturb him now. Sapphira was the "religious" one in this marriage, not him. She insisted upon attending the services and prayer meetings, "praising God" and "thanking Jesus" with every other word she spoke. Quite frankly, he was tiring of it. And as the authorities grew more and more hostile toward their growing sect, he became increasingly uncomfortable associating with it.

Crossing her arms before her chest, Sapphira's lip tipped in a mocking half-smile. "Only God will ever know," she said, lifting a jewel-studded finger to her lips, "and He can't tell, now, can He? After all, He'd have to get off His throne to do that, and frankly, I don't see that happening." Turning sharply, she passed through the doorway, her faint footsteps echoing strangely as she padded down the marble hall.

Was it simply his imagination, or had the chamber visibly darkened, as if a disturbing presence now lingered in the air, watching, waiting, biding its time? Frowning, Ananias returned his attention to his paperwork.

The woman whom You gave to be with me, she gave me of the tree, and I ate. Ananias froze, stylus in hand. One of the apostles had recently expounded upon the tragic tale of Adam and Eve. Adam had indulged his wife's sinful desire, even participating in it with her, rather than putting a stop to it. In so doing, he had relinquished the sacred role God had bestowed upon him as the spiritual leader of their home. And as a result, both the man and the woman ultimately perished.

When the apostle had delivered the unsettling sermon, Ananias had fidgeted in his seat, wondering if perhaps the account was simply the whimsical product of an overimaginative writer. But now, the strange tale returned to him full force, bowling him over, nearly knocking him out of his chair.

There was still time, he realized, inexplicably disturbed—still time to broach the subject with his wife, still time to change his mind. And yet, the prospect of a heated debate with a stubborn and demanding woman was the last thing he desired. Sapphira would get her way, after all. She *always* did. What was the point in arguing, anyway? Hadn't he been down that path a thousand times before?

Sighing, Ananias returned his attention to the blank parchment spread upon his desk. After selling the field, he'd walk away with a hefty sum in his pocket, even if Sapphira was determined to donate part of it. It would be worth it, in the end.

Lifting his gaze, Ananias' attention fell upon the golden hourglass situated at the corner of his desk. Snowy white sand poured through the narrow opening, emptying into the glistening dune below. He couldn't help but notice that the hourglass had nearly emptied. Somehow, that observation unsettled him. Like a dark omen, staring him in the face.

Like he was running out of time.

***

Mary

Soon, the sun would rise above the sleepy eastern hills, bathing the holy city in warmth and glorious light. Exhausted from her lengthy prayer vigil, Mary rose, stiffly and painstakingly, to her feet, reluctantly returning to her bed. She couldn't shake the feeling that this balmy, predawn hour held a dreadful sense of dark foreboding.

Spiritual forces were at work. She sensed it with every fiber of her being. Shivering slightly, Mary leaned against plush pillows, drawing her blanket over her lap. She supposed she should try to squeeze in a few short hours of sleep before starting the day, and yet Sapphira weighed so heavily upon her heart that she knew the prospect of rest was entirely futile.

The enemy is at work, Father. He has come against us from the start, but I fear the war has only just begun. And the devil is at work, even now, Father, eager to wage war against Your saints. Help us, Lord—every single one of us. Lead us not into temptation. Deliver us from evil. Tossing aside her blanket, Mary rose from her bed. Squaring her shoulders, she lifted her face heavenward, her eyes shimmering with a sheen of unshed tears.

We don't stand a chance without You.

CHAPTER 29

Tabitha

Crossing the central courtyard, Tabitha peered over the pile of freshly laundered linens she balanced carefully in her arms, fully expecting to glimpse her mistress in the *bibliotheca* straight ahead, most likely bent over the massive desk, sorting through stacks of tedious documents and ledgers. Instead, Tabitha heard heavy footfalls approaching on her left-hand side, traveling laboriously up the steep stone staircase which sharply descended into the cool depths of the vaulted storage rooms beneath the mansion.

Baffled, Tabitha glanced toward the narrow opening at the left corner of the courtyard, where one began the cool, steep descent into the storage vaults below. Peter, James, and John had sequestered themselves within the dark, lower chamber earlier that morning, cataloging recent donations and discussing the distribution of the funds. There were many widows and orphans among them, and resources were utilized daily to meet the needs of such. It was a time-consuming, taxing responsibility—this distribution of food, clothing, and funds—and Tabitha had noticed the worry lines creasing the young faces of the apostles in recent weeks. Caring for the destitute of their city had become a full-time affair, and the apostles were hard-pressed to meet all the needs, in addition to teaching, preaching, and instructing new converts.

Tabitha's attention returned to the doorframe when a young man presented a rigid back as he emerged from the staircase backward. Muscled calves tensed as he navigated the narrow staircase, clearly bearing a heavy load. Recognizing him as one of several young men who assisted the apostles, Tabitha blanched when a second man emerged from the stairway, bearing the other half of the assistant's load.

Recognizing the large burden for what it was, Tabitha's stomach lurched, and for the briefest moment, she felt faint. Dropping the freshly laundered linens in her alarm, Tabitha wanted to rush the men, but her feet felt nailed in place. Staring dumbly, her eyes traveled the length of the heavy corpse borne by the two men, wrapped snugly in fresh white grave clothes. Two additional young men jogged up the staircase, joining them, reaching out to ease their companions' heavy load, just as James and John emerged from the stairway behind them. Heart racing, Tabitha looked pleadingly back and forth between the two somber-faced apostles.

John, always sensitive toward others, placed a brotherly hand upon her shoulder. "Fear not, dear sister," he said gently. "It's over now."

"What...what happened?" Tabitha stammered, her stomach tightening in knots of dread. "Who... who is it? I mean, who *was* it?"

James and John exchanged sorrowful expressions as the four younger men carefully navigated the corpse around the elegant furniture in the courtyard, disappearing beneath a pillared entryway.

"James? John?" Tabitha demanded, her voice thick with concern. *Oh, God, not Mary. Please. Or Barnabas. Or Tobias.*

"It was Ananias," James responded, his voice low. "Regrettably, he has passed from this life."

Ananias? Tabitha's brow furrowed as she attempted to place the name with a familiar face. It hit her like a ton of bricks, and her stomach twisted in further discomfiting contortions. "The husband of the wealthy heiress, Sapphira?"

"One and the same," James confirmed.

Plagued by a hint of remorse, Tabitha realized she was somewhat relieved. She scarcely knew Ananias. He held himself pointedly aloof from anyone he considered beneath him, including Mary's household staff. But praise God, her mistress and her closest friends were alive and well! Shuddering, Tabitha doubted herself capable of bearing the death of yet another loved one after the immeasurable loss of her father, her mother, and then her beloved master, Mark. As guilt overrode her insurmountable relief, Tabitha recognized that Ananias' wife, Sapphira, must be notified about her husband's death.

The poor woman. Though Tabitha had never cared for the condescending woman, she wouldn't wish this fate upon her worst enemy. Having experienced devastating losses herself, Tabitha knew there was nothing quite like the debilitating pain of bereavement.

Sighing sympathetically, John squeezed Tabitha's shoulder once more before lifting his hand. "Our assistants have left to bury Ananias, but they will need direction in carrying out the gruesome task. James and I must go."

Tabitha nodded woodenly, numb. "Where is Mary?"

"Down below, in the vault with Simon Peter," James supplied, his dark eyes flashing angry fire. "You should go to her. She witnessed the whole ordeal, and I imagine she's a bit shaken."

The whole ordeal? Wondering what dreadful circumstances could have possibly transpired in the underground vault, Tabitha nodded, rushing for the swiftly descending stairway, deeply concerned for Mary.

"My lady? My lady!" Taking the stone steps two at a time, Tabitha hurried down the first flight of steps, reaching a rectangular stone landing before taking a sharp left and hastening down the final flight of steps which emptied into a narrow underground vestibule. From this point, one could take one of two simple stone entrances leading into two distinct storage spaces, or rather pass beneath an elegantly tiled entryway leading to the luxurious *mikveh*, or ritual bath.

"Tabitha. We're in here, beloved."

Tabitha's heart leaped at the sound of her mistress's voice. Passing beneath the arched entrance leading to the largest storeroom, Tabitha's entire being flooded with relief when she spotted Mary seated upon a wooden chest, white-knuckled hands clutching her knees. Peter stood solemnly beside his wife's aunt, his heavy hand resting protectively upon her shoulder. Even the deeply tanned fisherman appeared rather pale, his features taut, his stance defensive.

Swiftly kneeling before Mary, Tabitha grasped both her hands, searching her face intently. "My lady, you're so pale!"

Mary lifted her head slowly, as if that one simple move required great effort. Her shawl fell about her shoulders in graceful folds, further shadowing her lovely features.

"What has happened?" Tabitha demanded, her eyes darting back and forth between her lady and the agitated apostle. "I saw the young men removing the corpse. Are you both all right?"

"I'm fine," Peter said gruffly, crossing his arms before his chest.

"My lady?"

Mary met her maidservant's anxious hazel-green eyes, her own slightly dazed.

Clasping her mistress's cold hands, Tabitha realized, stunned, that the woman was trembling. "My lady, please speak to me. Are you all right?"

Shaking her head as if to clear the fog of confusion, Mary managed tonelessly, "I don't know what to make of this, Tabitha."

"Please, tell me what happened."

"Ananias arrived earlier, claiming he had sold a piece of land," Mary explained, clearly attempting to make sense of what she had witnessed. "He brought a very generous donation. He said the Holy Spirit had led him and his wife, Sapphira, to lay the entire proceeds of the sale at the apostles' feet."

Tabitha was surprised. The couple had never struck her as particularly generous.

"Instantly, the Holy Spirit hit me with a shocking revelation," Peter cut in, picking up where Mary had left off. "Ananias was *lying*—not to me, but to the Holy Spirit of God. First, Ananias claimed to be led by the Holy Spirit, when instead, he was guided by the spirit of the devil, the spirit of antichrist. From the beginning, the enemy has masqueraded as an angel of light, and in this case, Ananias aided the spirit of darkness in his sick impersonation of the Spirit of light."

Nodding slowly, Tabitha reluctantly released Mary's hands. She remained kneeling at her feet, cautiously gauging her lady's reaction as Peter recounted the dreadful affair.

"Then," Peter continued, troubled, "Ananias claimed he was donating the entirety of the sum resulting from the sale of his property. And yet, he was holding back a large portion of the proceeds. He wished to appear more generous than he actually was, seeking the elevation and the praise of men rather than the approval of God."

Tabitha looked to her mistress, attempting to follow Peter's shocking explanation. "How did you know this?"

"Only by the Holy Spirit," Peter declared, shaking his head in awe. "It was as if the Teacher stood beside me once again, speaking directly into my ear, revealing details I couldn't have possibly known on my own. Remember, Jesus said, '*He who is not with Me is against Me.*' So any man, teaching, or doctrine that contradicts the Holy Spirit is propagated by the spirit of wickedness. There is no middle ground.

Ananias presumed he could serve two masters, and it cost him his life."

"But what happened to him? How did he die?" Tabitha demanded, perplexed. Had Simon Peter struck the man in a fit of righteous anger? Surely not! Or perhaps, in a moment of unbearable shame and remorse, the businessman had ended his own life.

"I rebuked him," Peter admitted, his dark eyes haunted. "I demanded to know why he chose to heed the temptation of Satan, reminding him that the money was his to employ as he saw fit. Instead, he chose to lie about his contribution, attempting to exalt himself above the others, nursing his fatal pride."

"And then?" Tabitha was growing impatient.

Sensing her maid's agitation, Mary reached for her arm, the color slowly returning to her face. "He dropped dead, Tabitha. Instantly. Without explanation."

"I've never seen anything like it," Peter breathed. "And that's saying something, because I've seen a *lot*."

Tabitha looked between them, bewildered. "I don't understand."

"Neither do we, and we witnessed the appalling event," Mary admitted, shaking her head in dismay. "It was truly dreadful, Tabitha."

"Ananias dropped dead, and yet no one laid a hand on him?" Tabitha pressed, somewhat skeptical.

"Ananias was struck down by the hand of God," Peter said grimly, clearly reliving the horrid scene. "There's simply no other explanation."

Inexplicably troubled, Tabitha's practical mind

filled with dark portends. Ananias had been a powerful man, no doubt possessing dangerous connections. Exactly how would those allies react to Ananias' sudden, suspicious demise? She seriously doubted they would simply accept Peter's shocking, supernatural explanation. And she couldn't help but wonder what dangerous retaliation the church might face at the hands of vengeful, unbelieving men.

Shutting her eyes tightly, Tabitha forced herself to draw a calming breath. Right now, Mary certainly didn't need her to point out the vast array of potential dangers they now faced. No, her mistress needed her support.

"What on earth will we tell Sapphira?" Tabitha finally asked, dreading the unavoidable confrontation.

"We will tell her the truth," Mary sighed, straightening her shoulders as she resumed her characteristically flawless posture.

"She'll never believe it," Peter mused, stroking his bearded chin. "But what else can we say? We cannot lie."

"No, we can't," Mary agreed firmly, her strength returning as she recovered from the shocking ordeal.

"Who will tell her?" Tabitha dared, thankful that her resilient mistress appeared to be recovering well.

"I will," Peter said, his tone allowing no argument. "Sapphira should hear it from me."

"I will stand beside you, Peter," Mary assured him staunchly.

"When shall we inform her?" Peter asked his aunt, clearly dreading the whole ordeal.

Mary's glance rested sympathetically upon her niece's husband before flickering over to her loyal maidservant. "I shall send for her now. We needn't delay the inevitable." Rising from the wooden chest, Mary drew a deep, steadying breath. "May God be with us all."

CHAPTER 30

Mary

Nearly three hours had passed before a doorkeeper reluctantly ushered a gushing Sapphira within the reception hall of Mary's quiet villa. Having enjoyed a luxurious afternoon of pampering at an exclusive bathhouse which served the upper classes, the heiress was in high spirits, raving about a classy new eating establishment she'd spotted on the same upscale avenue as the baths.

"I do apologize for the delay, darling," Sapphira laughed, her expensive garments fluttering about her like the plumage of some strange, colorful bird. "My doorkeeper did, in fact, receive your messenger, delivering his summons earlier this afternoon. I employed a litter, hurrying over as soon as convenience allowed." Nearly giddy in her enthusiasm, Sapphira failed to notice the grave atmosphere within the staid reception hall, the solemn expression upon the face of Simon Peter, or the clouding concern in Mary's soft eyes.

"Sapphira," Mary said gently, taking the woman's elbow and guiding her toward one of the elegant, straight-backed chairs lining one frescoed wall. "Please, be seated."

Sapphira did so, chattering blithely as Mary took the seat beside her. "The eatery caters to the upper class," Sapphira was saying, waving a hand dismissively, "so one needn't worry about dining amongst riff-raff."

Exchanging a sober look with Mary, Peter crossed muscled arms before his chest, standing before the seated heiress like a solemn sentry. "Sapphira," Peter said, "we summoned you because we must inform you about—"

"Ah, I already know what this is about." Sapphira smiled, imperiously waving aside his comment. "You received our gift and you wish to express your deepest gratitude, yes? I confess, I anticipated an audience with you, though not quite so soon—"

"It *is* about the donation," Peter conceded grimly, clearly curbing his impatience with the woman's conceited chatter. After all, he was about to inform the poor lady that she was now a widow! Surely compassion was required.

"Well, truly, it's the least we can do," Sapphira purred, stretching out a heavily bejeweled hand to survey her long, manicured fingernails. "I certainly hope our generosity hasn't overshadowed the mere *pittance* others have contributed—"

"You needn't worry about that," Peter interrupted somewhat gruffly. "We are most grateful for any gift—however small—when surrendered joyfully from a pure, honest heart. As you may recall, our Lord often recounted the story of the widow's two mites. Her gift was acceptable to God because she willingly surrendered all that she had for the sake of His kingdom."

Sensing Peter's tension for the first time since her arrival, Sapphira glanced at the apostle askance.

Quietly, Mary watched the exchange, her stomach clenching in the most unpleasant way. Gracefully, she folded her hands in her lap, praying silently as she sensed spiritual forces at work—cold, dark, oppressive.

Something wasn't right.

"I detect a hidden implication in your tone," Sapphira observed coldly, her eyes narrowing in suspicion. Rising from her chair, she met Peter's gaze head-on. "Though I recognize you're but a provincial fisherman with little experience in any field of true value, this conversation is *not* a fishing expedition, so you'd best speak frankly, sir, without subterfuge."

It was then that a dreadful realization hit Mary like a ton of bricks. Contrary to her initial impression, Sapphira was not ignorant about her husband's deception. In fact, Mary was now certain that Sapphira herself had conceived the wicked scheme. Like Adam and Eve in that paradisal garden, Ananias had relinquished his spiritual authority, gratifying his wife's duplicity.

Clenching her fists in her lap, another dreadful thought hit Mary full force. Both Adam and Eve were cast from paradise, the fatal cost of their shared sin. And it seemed quite likely that Ananias and Sapphira might suffer that same awful fate, perishing in their rebellion, cast from the sweet fellowship and communion of the Holy Spirit.

Daring a glance toward Simon Peter, Mary saw his eyes hardening in realization. Clearly, the pieces were falling into place for him, too.

"All right, then," Peter said, his deep voice dangerously low. "You wish for me to speak frankly, Sapphira? Then so be it. I shall do so."

Sapphira stared him down, an icy challenge in her cold, dark eyes.

"Your husband claimed he donated the entire price you received for the sale of your land bordering the field of Akeldama. Tell me, Sapphira, can your husband's word be trusted?"

"How dare you," Sapphira hissed, her dark eyes glowing in her steadily rising fury.

It was then that Tabitha emerged beneath an arched entry, bearing a tray of refreshments as previously instructed. Inhaling sharply, Mary caught Tabitha's gaze, conveying a silent message that all was not well. *Be on guard, Tabitha.*

Instantly alert, Tabitha crossed the vast marble hall, dipping her tray before the disgruntled visitor. Without so much as a second glance toward the lovely maid, Sapphira snatched a goblet brimming with cool, fruit-flavored water. Taking a short sip, she turned more fully toward Simon Peter, her eyes flashing. "In answer to your outrageous question, *yes*! *Yes*, my husband can be trusted. *Yes*, we donated the entire sum, not that it's any of your business. And I've a mind to take it all back, if *this* is how you repay those who—"

"How is it that you dared to test the Spirit of the Lord, Sapphira, plotting this deception with your husband?" Rising in both volume and intensity, Peter's voice shook in his fierce emotion. So imposing was his taut form that the lofty heiress appeared to check herself momentarily.

Praying in earnest, Mary watched the dangerous undercurrents swirling between Simon Peter, an apostle of God, and Sapphira, the woman who had sold her soul in exchange for the world's empty promises. Tabitha, too, watched tentatively, standing rigidly near the exit, clearly prepared to escort the irate guest out, if necessary.

"You should be groveling at my feet, Simon Peter," Sapphira snapped, her ridiculous garments fluttering with her angry gestures. "We gave more than *you* could possibly accumulate in your entire lifetime! Your insolence is truly appalling!"

"It's not about the money, Sapphira," Peter said, his voice low.

"It's always about the money," the woman countered, her sharp brows lifting in challenge.

"Perhaps for some," Peter said sadly, "but not here, not now. That money was yours, Sapphira, to employ as you saw fit. You could have given some of it, all of it, or even none at all. That was your decision to make."

"Indeed it was," Sapphira hissed, crossing her arms in disdain. "*You* certainly haven't the right to tell me what to do with my earnings. God help us should we choose to listen to you! You haven't the slightest trace of business sense."

Lowering her head, Mary continued to pray fervently for the arrogant woman. Sapphira hadn't a clue what she was up against. She was deceived by a cruel master, drawn away and enticed by deadly lusts of the flesh, little knowing it was her soul the enemy sought to claim. And she had all but handed it over to him on a silver platter, in exchange for what? Hadn't the Savior warned them about laying up treasure on earth, where moth and rust destroy, where thieves break in and steal? Lifting her gaze, Mary glanced across the room and saw that Tabitha, too, was bowing her golden head in silent prayer.

"You're right to say I'm ignorant in matters of business," Peter conceded humbly.

"Amen to that, brother." Placing a hand upon her hip, Sapphira arched a sarcastic brow.

"But I *am* in tune with the Holy Spirit," Peter amended, his dark eyes burning like two fiery coals, the intensity of his gaze pinning the haughty heiress in place. "Let me reemphasize that this is not about your money—it's about your *intentions*, the motives of your heart. Do you realize the trouble you could have caused? Your deception, your hypocrisy, could have taken root, choking the tiny, sprouting seedlings of this infant church. A little yeast leavens the entire batch of dough, and hypocrisy and deceit often spread like wildfire."

"You have no right to judge or accuse me, you miserable ingrate!"

"It isn't I who accuse you, Sapphira," Peter said, inexplicably grieved. "It is the *Holy Spirit*. For you pretended to be led by the Holy Spirit of God, when instead you were guided by the lying spirit of the antichrist, the spirit of deception. How dare you and your husband masquerade as agents of light while being led by the spirit of darkness!"

A chill breeze swept through the marble hall, raising the gooseflesh upon Mary's cold, clammy skin. The oppression hanging heavily in the air was eerily reminiscent of that ominous night when

Judas Iscariot slammed out the door, intent upon the Savior's demise, consumed by the spirit of darkness. Those dark forces were working even now, seeking to claim the souls of men.

Rising from her chair, Mary lifted her face heavenward, praying unlike she ever had. But she was jarred from her fervent, silent pleas when Sapphira lunged toward Peter, her teeth bared in feral rage. "Pompous, ignorant fool!" she screamed in untamed fury, her face contorting grotesquely. "This church will never succeed, and if you think otherwise, you are a mindless imbecile! A word of advice? *Give up now*, before you find yourself nailed to a bloody cross or stoned at the bottom of a rocky pit!"

Mary looked to Peter, then to Tabitha, stunned to her very core.

"You are worthless and stupid—every last one of you—utterly incapable of success," the woman raged, waving her fists at Peter. "And you will *never* accomplish anything of lasting importance! Your efforts are entirely futile." By now, Sapphira's entire countenance had changed, transformed by the evil one. Even her voice had lowered several decibels, taking on a strange, guttural growl. Stunned and sickened, Mary's heart pounded violently in her chest, recognizing Sapphira's threat for what it truly was. The woman had handed herself over to the evil one, and now, the great accuser spoke *through her*, cursing the church and its mission, attempting to utterly crush and demoralize it. Steeling herself, Mary exchanged a knowing look with Peter, then Tabitha, their boldness bolstered by the mighty Spirit within them as they acknowledged Sapphira's curse for what it was—an attack from the pit of hell.

With one slow nod, Mary conveyed a silent message to Simon Peter: *Be strong and courageous, dear one. The Holy Spirit is on our side. He fights for us. Stand firm.*

Turning toward the feral woman, Peter stood his ground. Resuming a confident stance, he met Sapphira's flaming gaze, fully aware that the eyes of demons peered back at him, seething, challenging, threatening. "I begged my God it wouldn't come to this," Peter said, his voice low, his gaze steady. "But you have taken your stand, and I regret it's with the evil one."

Sapphira smirked, her eyes blazing, daring him to continue.

"The feet of those who have buried your husband are at the door," Peter said, his voice choked with inexplicable sorrow. "And they will carry you out, as well."

Mary's hand flew to her heart at Peter's unexpected pronouncement, as a small gasp escaped from Tabitha's parted lips.

Sapphira's dark eyes widened, registering shock, then horror. Releasing a shrill, hair-raising scream, the woman was clearly dead before her lifeless body hit the marble floor with a sickening *thud*, her goblet clattering noisily to the ground.

Gasping, Mary drew both hands over her mouth, her entire body gripped with violent trembling. Thrusting aside her tray, Tabitha rushed to her mistress, throwing her arms protectively around her. Shuddering, the women clung to one another, sickened by the dreadful scene.

Simon Peter looked at them then, his dark eyes filled with sorrow and righteous anger. The young men of whom he had spoken returned within seconds, and Sapphira's corpse was carried away in silence.

Ananias and Sapphira, the most prestigious of Jerusalem's citizens, were laid to rest within a common grave, buried in the same rocky plot of land which they had sold that very day.

CHAPTER 31

Stephanos

Pausing beneath an elegant stone arch, Stephanos crossed his arms, thoughtfully tilting his head to one side. Studying the lovely, yet restless, young woman seated on a marble bench several paces before him, he allowed himself an amused half-smile. Tabitha was a fiery one, brimming with zeal for life and her Lord. This past year, he had witnessed her flourishing faith as she learned to live by the Spirit rather than her own strength. True, it was a lengthy process, and transformation seldom occurred overnight. But Stephanos couldn't help but imagine that Tabitha's beloved mistress, Mary, had been very much like her at seventeen—bursting with vibrant life, innately curious, and strong-willed, yet seeking to surrender her own stubborn will in obedience to her Maker. If Tabitha continued in faithful obedience, he had no doubt the Lord would also continue to mold and shape her into a strong, godly woman, fully surrendered to Him. It was a beautiful process to behold!

Breathing deeply of the scent of fresh garden flowers, Stephanos beheld yet another lovely sight. Though her head was modestly covered with a simple, auburn colored veil, honey-gold curls spilled from beneath Tabitha's covering, catching the sunlight and fairly shining. Her head was slightly bent, her hands folded in her lap, as she sat before the massive fountain in the garden courtyard, while gently falling sheets of clear water cast dancing, rainbow-colored hues in the scattered early morning breezes. Though he glimpsed only her slight profile, Stephanos sensed that Tabitha was deeply troubled. Otherwise, the observant maidservant would have sensed his presence far before he'd set foot upon the cool flagstones. Not only that, but this was the first time he could recall finding the maiden seated, quiet and still, longer than a mere thirty seconds at best. Like Mary, Tabitha was a woman of action. Seldom did she sit still for very long!

I shouldn't be standing here, watching her, Stephanos admitted, a hint of guilt creeping into his mind. Somewhat nonplussed, he realized he could have gladly watched her the remainder of the morning. She was so lovely, and yet, he knew his growing attraction had little to do with her outward appearance. Having resided in Alexandria and other opulent cities throughout his life, Stephanos had met many, many beautiful women—most of them unapologetically forward, shamelessly bold. And yet, none of them had piqued his curiosity nor roused his interest as this one had. There was something about Tabitha—her fire, her passion for life, her burning desire to be used by God—that thrilled him. Though he'd always assumed God had called him to serve as a single man, unhindered by wife and children, he couldn't help but wonder what it might be like to share his calling with a woman who would embrace it with her entire being.

A woman like Tabitha.

Even so, Stephanos refused to act upon his desire until perfectly convinced His Lord would bless such a union, and that sort of confirmation often required both time and prayer.

But hopefully not too much time, Stephanos mused with a hint of mischief, a secret smile tipping the corners of his mouth. He was no stranger to waiting on the Lord, though this time, he had to admit the delay surely tried his patience!

***

Tabitha

"You look troubled, dear sister."

Stiffening slightly at Stephanos' unexpected approach, Tabitha turned her head to face him, unaccustomed to being caught off guard. "Stephanos. You startled me."

"In a good way, I should hope." His expression slightly veiled, Tabitha wondered what he was thinking. She couldn't have possibly known he was savoring the sound of his name upon her lips. Unexpectedly, he sat down beside her, his broad shoulders brushing against hers as he did so.

Aware of his closeness on the bench, Tabitha shifted ever so slightly. Sensing her quiet withdrawal, Stephanos cleared his throat uncomfortably, confusing her even further. After all, Stephanos was the most confident man she'd ever met. Brimming with personality and charisma, absolutely nothing appeared capable of throwing him. But lately, he'd seemed…unsure of himself. Distracted, somehow. As if her very presence rendered him clumsy and slow of tongue. Tabitha was completely stupefied by the matter. Had she done something to offend him or make him feel uncomfortable? If so, wouldn't he be retreating at the mere sight of her? But instead, he seemed to seek her out, initiating somewhat stilted and awkward conversations again and again.

Regardless of how often Tabitha turned the matter around in her mind, she just couldn't figure it out. All she knew for certain was this—something had changed dramatically between them. For better or for worse, she hadn't yet determined.

"May I ask," Stephanos began, gently lifting his gaze to meet hers, "what troubles you, dear one?"

Dear one. For some reason unbeknownst to her, the endearing address sent a strange little shiver up her rigid spine, a sensation completely foreign to her. Silently chiding herself, she wondered at her own reaction. Why should Stephanos' address affect her so? He was her brother in Christ, a dear friend just like Simon Peter, James and John, and all the rest. Besides, Stephanos greeted every believer in the same loving manner!

Even so, she couldn't help but wonder if she was merely imagining it, or if his tone was slightly different when he addressed her, if his gaze lingered just a bit longer, if his smile was just a bit warmer.

"I'm sorry," Stephanos apologized, preparing to rise. "We won't speak of it. I shouldn't have pried."

"No," Tabitha exclaimed, touching his arm. "I wasn't ignoring you, Stephanos. I was merely lost in thought."

"So I noticed." Stephanos grinned wryly, his dark eyes traveling toward her hand resting lightly upon his forearm.

Cheeks flaming with color, Tabitha swiftly withdrew her hand.

"What is it that troubles you?"

Gazing into his eyes, Tabitha wondered if Stephanos would condemn her for asking questions. After all, shouldn't her steadfast faith demolish all doubts? But she answered honestly, "What happened yesterday—it troubles me."

"Ah." Folding tanned, well-shaped hands in his lap, Stephanos nodded his consent. "I thought as much."

"How so?"

"Everyone is talking about it. The apostles and church leaders were briefed about it this morning."

"I was there when it happened, and I've never seen anything like it. I didn't sleep at all last night."

"I can't even imagine," Stephanos said, shaking his head in sympathy. "Tabitha, I'm so sorry you had to see that."

"I've seen worse," Tabitha murmured, recalling the grisly scene she'd stumbled upon after the senseless murder of her father and mother. Why did death of any kind arouse those dreadful memories, memories she longed to erase? "But yesterday... well, it was different, somehow. First Ananias, then Sapphira, simply dropped dead, struck down by the hand of God Himself. And I can't help but wonder... *why*? Why such drastic measures, such devastating punishment?"

"I'm sure we're all asking ourselves the very same questions," Stephanos admitted, relieving Tabitha of her fear of condemnation. "But we must always remember—we serve a God of mercy *and* judgment. Though God is merciful, He is also just. And until now, the church has been privileged to witness nothing but miracles of His tender mercy. Isn't it only logical to assume we will witness miracles of judgment as well?"

Surprised by the practicality of Stephanos' assessment, Tabitha nodded slowly. "Even so, I can't help but wonder why Ananias and Sapphira weren't granted more time to repent."

Stephanos smiled sadly, his gaze drifting over the lovely garden courtyard they shared. "God needn't explain Himself to us, *ever*. We know and trust that His will is always best. However, something to keep in mind is *this*: God is *omnipotent*, all-knowing, meaning He already knows who will repent, and who will not. He knows the entire story of a man or a woman's life, Tabitha, from beginning to end. Knowing this, perhaps God's seeming judgment against Ananias and Sapphira was actually an act of mercy toward the church. If God knew their pride and hypocrisy would take root, destroying this infant church, was it not merciful to crush it now? Already knowing the husband and wife would not repent, would God allow that root of bitterness and pride to flourish, permeating this entire body of believers? Surely, knowing all this, God dealt severely with Ananias and Sapphira, demonstrating the true danger of hypocrisy within the church."

"I hadn't thought of it like that," Tabitha admitted, impressed by Stephanos' wisdom and spiritual insight.

"It's just a thought," Stephanos replied humbly. "But I imagine their example will encourage all of us to think twice before succumbing to our own innate hypocrisy and pride."

"I imagine so," Tabitha agreed sadly, shuddering slightly, recalling the horrid scene.

"Ultimately, Ananias and Sapphira became a very real example of what happens when a man or a woman spends their life resisting the Holy Spirit. The result is always death, which deeply sorrows the Spirit of God. We know the Father desires for everyone to be saved, but He will never force us to accept His gift of grace, nor will He condone our sins, allowing an unrighteous person to enter the gates of Heaven. If He did, how would Heaven be any different than this mess we have here on earth, brimming with greed, violence, and injustice?"

"Thank God, Heaven will be entirely different, unlike anything we can possibly imagine," Tabitha said dreamily, imagining the glorious day when she would be reunited with her loved ones. To hear her father's hearty laughter once again, to listen to her mother sing an ancient psalm in her clear, lilting voice, to witness her beloved mistress, Mary, running into the open arms of her husband, Mark, and to never fear losing them again...truly, Heaven's splendor was far more glorious than she dared to imagine!

"I think it's crucial we recognize that the enemy has now come against us from within and from without," Stephanos said grimly, drawing Tabitha from her blissful reverie. "First, he attacked the growing church from without by provoking the religious leaders, fanning the flames of their hatred against us. But God's people rallied against the injustice, and righteousness prevailed."

Tabitha studied the handsome young man thoughtfully, her attention captured by the gravity of his expression.

"But when the enemy recognized the church could not be undone from without, he attacked us from within, on the *inside*, by planting insurgents directly within our midst," Stephanos continued solemnly. "In the future, we must be cautiously aware of both deadly tactics. Clearly, the enemy knows how to utilize them well."

Tabitha studied Stephanos with new respect. She'd always known of his reputation, for he was known to be a man full of faith and the power of the Holy Spirit. But in recent months, she had been amazed by the wisdom and insight he possessed. Revitalized and refreshed by their conversation, Tabitha squared her shoulders, feeling prepared to take on the day.

"Thank you, Stephanos," she said sincerely, blushing slightly when he turned his full attention upon her. The intensity of his gaze was rather unsettling. "You have helped me to see this dreadful ordeal in an entirely different light," she explained, dropping her gaze in an uncharacteristic moment of shyness. "It's still tragic, yes, but at least now it's beginning to make sense."

Stephanos smiled gently. "The Lord never rebukes us for asking questions, Tabitha. He simply reminds us to take our questions before Him. He alone can provide the answers we seek."

"I suppose I must return to the house," Tabitha sighed, surprised by her own reluctance. She realized she could have easily shared this bench with Stephanos for hours, discussing exciting spiritual truths. How strange the ways of God! Wasn't it only a few short months ago she struggled to harness her envy toward this powerful man? And now, it would seem the Lord was blessing their growing friendship!

"I should do the same," Stephanos agreed reluctantly, interrupting Tabitha's pleasant train of thought. "I'm sure Mary has a nice stack of paperwork waiting for me on my desk."

"And, unfortunately, the chores have never been known to do themselves," Tabitha teased, rising gracefully from the bench.

Stephanos rose as well, reaching out to steady Tabitha's arm as she reached a standing position. Their eyes met for the briefest moment, and Tabitha's heart lurched in response. Somehow, it felt natural—his strong hand upholding her, his dark eyes fastened upon her, brimming with tenderness and warmth.

Clearing their throats in obvious discomfort, they laughed nervously as Stephanos withdrew his hand. Uttering very hasty goodbyes, they hurried away to tend to their various tasks. Moments later, as she opened the heavy double doors leading into the house, Tabitha found herself wondering what in the world had just happened.

Was she simply imagining the strange new undercurrents swirling about her and the handsome, fiery Hellenist? Passing into the frescoed vestibule and pulling the doors shut behind her, Tabitha leaned her back against the cool bronze surface, her heart pounding in the most disturbing way. Taking a deep breath, she chided herself yet again. She was behaving like a silly woman! Surely there was nothing going on between her and Stephanos.

Surely, surely not!

CHAPTER 32

Mary

"My lady!"

Mary glanced over her shoulder, alarmed by the hint of panic in the typically composed tone of her staid overseer. "Tobias, is something wrong?"

Hastening toward his mistress, Tobias paused respectfully before her, wringing his hands anxiously. "I do apologize for the intrusion, what with the believers assembling for worship and such," he amended, his dark eyes shifting nervously.

"What is it, Tobias?" Mary asked, striving for calm. Everything about her overseer indicated that trouble was at hand.

"I regret to inform you that there's a bit of an…ah, um…a *misunderstanding* transpiring at the gate. I thought you should know."

"A misunderstanding?"

"It's Zev, my lady. He has refused to permit a certain Pharisee to join us, and I fear the fellow isn't taking too kindly to our guard's curt dismissal."

A certain Pharisee? Closing her eyes, Mary drew a calming breath, praying for patience and guidance. Ever since opening her doors to the apostles and the growing church, Zev had become rather confrontational. Though the aggressive sentry had never been particularly easy to work with, he was swiftly becoming downright belligerent. And though Mary assumed he was simply zealous to protect the household he had guarded for nearly a decade, she was rather uncertain about how to reason with him. She was beginning to fear that his open hostility might intimidate truth-seekers venturing to her home, possibly even causing them to turn back. She supposed she should assign Zev's position of doorkeeper to another guard, designating a new post for the antagonistic sentry, yet allowing him to maintain his role as captain of her guard. But up to this point, she hadn't dared. Zev, dangerously proud by nature, would be terribly offended!

"Thank you, Tobias," Mary said, smiling warmly to reassure him. "I will speak with Zev now. I'm sure everything will be fine."

"I should go with you."

Touched by his concern, she waved his worry aside. "No, you go ahead and join the believers upstairs. I will be with you shortly."

"Are you certain, my lady?" Tobias studied her carefully, his neatly oiled mustache twitching slightly, his obsidian eyes shadowed beneath an elegant turban.

"I am certain. Thank you, Tobias."

Reluctantly, the overseer departed, climbing the stairs with an air of solemnity.

Turning on her heels, Mary left the reception

hall, passing through the frescoed vestibule and hastening toward the outer court, where trouble surely awaited her.

***

Pushing open heavy double doors, angry shouts met Mary's ears the moment she set foot within the outer court. Quickening her pace, she passed the bubbling stone fountain, hurrying beneath the impressive arched entrance leading to the main gate.

Zev stood with spear in hand, his broad shoulders thrown back in challenge, barring the open gate with his powerful body. Several other guards had joined him, undoubtedly confused about all the fuss, but clearly siding with the captain of the guard. Zev's entire body tensed when Mary placed a gentle hand upon his shoulder. Jerking his attention toward her, Zev looked at her with flaming eyes, his expression fierce. "My lady, return to the villa. *Now.* This situation is under control."

Mary could have argued otherwise. Instead, she inquired calmly, "What's going on, Zev?"

Rebuffed, Zev turned his attention back to the dark-robed intruder before him. "This scoundrel has asked to join your gathering—*over my dead body*," he hissed menacingly, slamming the rod of his spear against the flagstones.

"That can be arranged, you insolent fool," the Pharisee in question nearly spat, drawing aside his *tallith* and facing the guard head on. "Need I remind you about my powerful connections, Zev?" Grinning maliciously, the Pharisee folded strong arms across his broad chest, his entire being daring the doorkeeper to defy him.

In that dreadful moment, Mary's heart constricted in instant recognition. Even before the Pharisee had lowered his *tallith*, she had known to whom that pretentious voice belonged. "Saul of Tarsus," she said coolly, drawing alongside the rattled doorkeeper. "Don't tell me you've had a change of heart?"

Saul's dark eyes flashed, his lips tipping in sarcasm. "In the words of your eloquent doorkeeper, 'Over my dead body.'"

"Well, I certainly hope it doesn't come to that," Mary crooned sweetly, a hint of mischief sparkling in her gray eyes. "Tell me, why the sudden interest in our meetings?"

"Must I explain myself to you, woman?"

"If you wish to set foot in my house, you do," she replied, her tone tinged with icy sweetness.

"You're wasting your time, my lady," Zev hissed, his eyes locked upon Saul's arrogant form. "Allow me to send this wolf away, lest he devour your helpless little sheep."

Ignoring the disgruntled doorkeeper, Mary turned to Saul. "You come alone?"

"All the money in the world could not persuade my colleagues to set foot within these blasphemous borders."

"Unlikely," Mary countered, her eyes dancing merrily. "Your colleagues' love for riches is rivaled only by their lust for power."

Saul glared at her, his eyes flashing angry fire. "Will you let me in, or simply continue spouting cursed insults?"

"Tell me why you have come."

"Perhaps I'm merely curious."

"Is that all?"

"All *you* need to know."

Folding her arms, Mary studied the rigid Pharisee, silently seeking the Lord's guidance. To permit Saul within their gathering might prove dangerous to every believer present. But to turn him away? What if—by some miracle—the Spirit had drawn him? Mary certainly didn't wish to quench the Holy Spirit.

"My lady, don't be foolish," Zev snarled, breaking every unspoken protocol between master and servant. "Don't let him in."

"I thought *anyone* was welcomed by your Christ?" Saul countered, his dark eyes narrowing in bitter challenge.

"Do I look like the Christ to you?" Zev jeered, his face mere inches from Saul's. "*He* may welcome all, but I certainly will not!"

The answer hit Mary like a ton of bricks, though it certainly wasn't the answer she had expected. "No, Zev, he's right."

Zev looked at her then, his jaw clenching in barely contained fury. Saul, too, stared at Mary as if she'd lost her mind, baffled by her sudden capitulation.

"Before He returned to Heaven, Jesus told a parable about a dragnet that was cast into the sea. It gathered every kind of fish, and once the net was full, the fishermen took it to shore, sorting the good fish from the bad. While the fishermen kept the good fish, the bad were thrown away."

Zev stared at Mary incredulously, clearly questioning her sanity.

"Jesus assured us that it will be like that when He returns. We are simply commanded to be fishers of men, *all* men. It is the Holy Spirit who will perform the work in them, and Christ Himself will sort the good from the bad."

"What exactly are you implying, my lady?" Saul taunted coldly, his tone dripping with biting sarcasm. "That I'm a bad fish?"

"That has yet to be decided," Mary said firmly, ignoring Zev's obvious consternation. "On Judgment Day, you will stand before God, and He will decide. But until that day comes, I can only pray for you, Saul, welcoming you into our fellowship with open arms."

"Duly noted," Saul mused sardonically, casting a triumphant look toward the captain of the guard. "I'll keep that in mind."

Looking as if he might self-implode, Zev slowly stepped aside, reluctantly allowing Saul to pass through the gate and into the outer court.

Once the pompous Pharisee was beyond earshot, Mary turned to two other nearby guards. "Daniel, Jacob, please join us in the Upper Room this evening."

Understanding their lady's concern, the two young men hurried away without question, eager to resume their post. Mary watched them leave, plagued by misgivings. *Oh, God, have I done the right thing?* She certainly hoped so.

"That was a foolish decision, my lady."

Flabbergasted by Zev's inexcusable boldness, Mary met his stony gaze head on. "The wisdom of God is not like the wisdom of this world," she said with great conviction.

"Regardless, I cannot shield you from your own recklessness."

Mary stared at Zev rather blankly, blown away by his animosity.

"You'd best pray your Christ will protect this entire household, my lady. One thoughtless act on your part could easily lead to our demise."

Chilled to the very core by the hostility of the stony-faced guard, Mary was struck by his words— *your Christ*.

Her Christ, not *his*.

But hadn't Zev accepted Jesus Christ as Lord and Savior? Suddenly, Mary realized she had simply taken that assumption for granted. Not once had she thought to ask Zev about his religious convictions or lack thereof.

"Zev, do you believe that Jesus is the Son of God?" she managed weakly, heart pounding heavily in her chest.

Pursing his lips, the guard looked away, exasperated.

Heart breaking, Mary reached for his arm. "Oh, Zev..."

Jerking away from her touch, Zev turned his face from her, his message clear. "Look, you have your own convictions, and I have mine. Leave it at that."

Suddenly, Zev's deplorable behavior of the past year began to make sense. He resented her decision to follow Christ, believing she had placed the entire household in jeopardy by doing so. Shuddering slightly, Mary turned away, prepared to join the believers upstairs. Pausing at the gate, she said quietly, "I should have spoken about this with you long before now."

Zev looked at her then, his chiseled features both harsh and uncompromising in the silver moonlight.

"Forgive me, Zev." With tears in her eyes, Mary passed beneath the wide stone arch, silently beseeching the Lord to soften her sentry's stony heart.

CHAPTER 33

Tabitha

Tabitha's heart dropped to her feet the moment Saul of Tarsus strode into the Upper Room, as if he owned the place. Others noticed him too, although Tabitha wasn't the least bit surprised. The young Pharisee carried himself with the air of a prince, his elaborate robes trailing behind him, his entire being emanating restless intensity that fairly crackled in the air about him. Though somewhat slight in stature, his impressively clad, robust form fully compensated for that perceived deficiency. Confidence exuded from his every pore, rendering it nearly impossible *not* to notice his powerful presence.

"Stephanos," Tabitha gasped, grasping his arm in shock. "Look."

Standing beside Tabitha near the back of the large chamber, Stephanos followed her gaze. The moment his dark eyes landed upon Saul, Stephanos' swarthy features split with a broad smile. "Well, praise God."

Tabitha shot him a sideways glance, stunned.

"*Praise God?*" she exclaimed, indignant. "What is he doing here?"

"Perhaps he is seeking the truth," Stephanos exulted, shaking his head in awe. "Is it too difficult to believe the Lord can answer our prayers for him?"

"Our prayers for him?" Tabitha repeated dully, somewhat perplexed. Blushing, she didn't dare admit she'd never bothered to pray for Saul. Though she attempted to convince herself that she simply hadn't desired to waste her time praying for a man incapable of reform, she recognized there was a far deeper issue at hand—she resented Saul's interference; therefore, she simply refused to pray for him. Sighing, she acknowledged her glaring shortcoming, refusing to make excuses for herself. Her attitude simply had to change, and that only by the power of the Holy Spirit.

"Please excuse me, dear sister," Stephanos whispered near her ear, interrupting her silent confession and sending strange little shivers up and down her spine. "I shall go speak with him."

Incredulous, Tabitha watched as Stephanos crossed the room, pausing before the regal Pharisee standing behind the last row of wooden benches. Other believers cast nervous glances in Saul's direction, though none dared to approach him. Clearly, they were wondering how on earth he had evaded the guards, thus gaining entrance.

Instinctively, Tabitha wished a few of the burlier apostles were in residence that evening, but the former Zealot and all the brawny fishermen—men capable of holding their own—were engaged in other church meetings scattered across Jerusalem that night. It was Matthew, the former tax collector, who would speak this evening, and Tabitha doubted Matthew's quiet, intellectual presence would prove intimidating to a man like Saul.

"Brother Saul!" Stephanos greeted enthusiastically, slapping the young man heartily on the back. "Have you joined our ranks at last?"

From the back of the room, Tabitha couldn't hear Saul's response, but the somewhat comical expression crossing the Pharisee's dark features was enough to convince her that Stephanos was sorely mistaken about Saul's intent.

Someone must tell Mary, Tabitha realized suddenly, preparing to carry out the unpleasant task herself. She certainly hoped Saul wouldn't make a scene. After all, Zev would thoroughly enjoy removing the pompous scholar by force.

On second thought, Tabitha thought mischievously, watching as Saul raised suspicious eyes toward Stephanos, *that might prove terribly amusing...*

Turning on her heel, Tabitha nearly plowed headfirst into her mistress. "My lady!" Busily brooding, Tabitha hadn't noticed her lady emerging at the top of the large staircase.

Mary reached out to steady the troubled maidservant, smiling wanly. "I see our guest has caused a bit of a stir."

Our guest? Tabitha stared at Mary in disbelief. "Surely you did not invite him—"

"Quite frankly, it never occurred to me to do such a thing," Mary replied, warily watching the exchange between Stephanos and Saul. "He arrived by his own accord, demanding entrance."

"And you permitted it?" Tabitha gasped, stunned.

"Perhaps the Spirit is at work," Mary mused, watching as Saul's features tightened in obvious anger. Clearly, he disagreed with whatever Stephanos was saying to him. "Remember, Jesus said no one can come to Him unless drawn by the Father. It is possible the Spirit of God directed Saul's arrival tonight."

"I imagine his own two feet had something to do with it, as well," Tabitha huffed, shaking her head in dismay. "Not to mention the burning hatred that drives him."

"Saul may not even be aware of the Spirit's leading at this time," Mary said, watching him intently. "But I believe there is a reason he's here tonight."

"May I ask *why*, my lady?" Tabitha dared, her indignation rising steadily.

"Because God has commanded me to pray for him every day, without ceasing."

Tabitha's mouth dropped open. "And you *do*?"

"Of course, I do."

Folding slender arms across her chest, Tabitha bit back her own opinion, though she was sorely tempted to air it.

"Perhaps God will perform a mighty work in Saul's heart. It isn't beyond His power, you know."

Dubious, Tabitha nodded in reluctant agreement.

"A man like Saul—utterly consumed with fire and passion and burning zeal—can be used by God to gain incredible victories for His kingdom," Mary expounded softly. "Right now, Saul's zeal is misguided. But the Lord knows how to gain a man's attention, Tabitha, and I believe we must continue to pray for Saul."

Listening respectfully to her mistress's entreaty,

Tabitha secretly remained skeptical. More times than she cared to recount, she had witnessed Saul at the Temple or in the Synagogue of the Freedmen, engaged in passionate, heated debate. Though the young Pharisee was zealous for the Law and the traditions of the elders, he was far more zealous about being *right*. He lived and breathed to crush his opponents in fiery debate, utterly obliterating anyone who dared to cross him.

"Trust the Lord, dear one. Nothing can happen without His permission or consent—not even the arrival of a sworn enemy like Saul." Squeezing Tabitha's shoulder, Mary departed to greet the guests milling about the Upper Room before the prayer service commenced. Sighing, Tabitha watched her go before returning her attention to the charismatic young man standing before a rigid, red-faced Saul, no doubt testifying of the risen Lord. It was blatant-ly obvious Saul held Stephanos in utter contempt, and that frightened Tabitha more than she dared admit. Saul was a powerful man, with even *more* powerful connections.

Tabitha shuddered to think of the havoc Saul could inflict upon the church should he choose to set his mind upon it.

***

Mary

Matthew's message was clear and concise, drawing multiple *amen*s from a rapt audience. Even so, Mary found it difficult to concentrate on his sermon, for Saul glowered throughout the entire delivery, even refusing to be seated among the brethren. Instead, he stood rigidly behind the last row of wooden benches, his dark brows drawn fiercely together, his countenance grim.

Mary suppressed a huge sigh of relief when Matthew's sermon eventually drew to a close. The apostle's discomfort within Saul's glowering presence had been evident throughout his careful delivery, and yet Matthew had bravely carried on with his message, emphasizing many truths the Savior had taught the disciples during His time on earth.

Standing near the wide stairwell to bid her departing guests farewell, Mary wasn't terribly surprised when Saul ignored the others and moved toward her, his stride reminding her somewhat of a shadowy predator even as his long robes swished behind him in the dignified manner of the Pharisees.

"I trust you enjoyed Matthew's instruction this evening?" Mary said with a mischievous smile. However, Saul's dark expression convinced her that he certainly hadn't experienced a change of heart.

"I understand the man who delivered this evening's instruction was formerly a tax collector," Saul observed coldly, ignoring several guests nodding cordially toward Mary as they descended the marble steps.

"Indeed," Mary replied, smiling sincerely. "Matthew is living proof that our God can reach anyone, regardless of his or her past."

"His very presence has defiled your home," Saul pronounced darkly.

"Matthew has been redeemed by the precious blood of Christ," Mary replied calmly, unperturbed. "His sins are forgiven, Saul."

"You never cease to amaze me," Saul observed, shaking his head in wonderment. "How you can simply stand there, smiling so very sweetly while uttering unthinkable blasphemies, is truly shocking."

"And how can you be so certain I speak blasphemies?" Mary dared, her cool composure further frustrating the bristling Pharisee. "Have you weighed our claims against the Law and the Prophets, as you've most certainly been trained to do?"

Saul bristled anew, though Mary hadn't missed the look of confusion passing over his taut features before he carefully concealed his displeasure. She couldn't have possibly known that his beloved mentor, Gamaliel, had already posed the same question, nearly word for word. Clearly, her straightforward inquiry disturbed him more than he cared to admit.

"Your theology was disproved within five minutes of that worthless tax collector's dull instruction," Saul argued combatively, drawing the attention of several nearby guests. "According to that bloody tax collector, your *Christ* declared He did not come to destroy the Law or the Prophets. I believe this was a direct quotation—*till Heaven and earth pass away, one jot or one tittle will by no means pass away from the law till all is fulfilled.*"

"Ah, you were paying attention," Mary observed, her eyes dancing.

"And yet that is a blatant corruption of the truth," Saul continued, shaking an impassioned fist. "Your so-called Christ made a mockery of the Laws of Adonai, thumbing His nose at God's commands at His every turn."

Maintaining her peace, Mary debated calmly, "How so?"

"It is said He healed a man with a withered hand—on the *Sabbath*!"

"How is that a violation of God's Law?" Mary responded, praying silently as she engaged the hardened Pharisee in debate. "If a man's animal falls into a pit on the Sabbath, is he not permitted to render aid? How much more does God expect us to help our brothers and sisters in need, even if their plight is made known on the Sabbath? In the sight of God, of how much more value is a man than a sheep?"

"If that healing was even legitimate, it could have waited for a more appropriate time."

"And had that been *your* withered hand, dear brother, would you have uttered the same wish? To wait for a more appropriate time?"

"If you refuse to accept reason in this instance," Saul said coldly, sidestepping Mary's pointed question, "then how do you explain the incident when your alleged Messiah commanded a man to carry his mat on the Sabbath Day?"

"Ah, you are referencing the man healed at Bethesda," Mary acknowledged knowingly. "Tell me, where in the Scriptures are we forbidden to pick up a mat on the Sabbath Day?"

"It is the oral tradition—divine inspiration from the righteous lips of our fathers!"

"From our fathers, yes, but not by the mouth of God," Mary countered quietly. "The revered sages and scholars of the Law did possess great wisdom, Saul, but we mustn't bow to their man-made doctrines at the expense of the Word of God."

"The fathers would turn over in their graves to hear a foolish woman speak such blatant blasphemies."

"Jesus came to *fulfill* the Law and to *destroy* the works of the devil, Saul."

"I could blow your pathetic and groundless arguments right out of the water," Saul said, his flashing eyes narrowing to form two tiny slits. "But I refuse to waste another valuable moment debating with one foolish woman entirely ignorant of the Scriptures."

Mary could have argued with the pompous young scholar's unfair assumption by effortlessly reciting dozens of Psalms or by quoting the Levitical Law by heart. Instead, she simply nodded her gentle understanding, recognizing that only God could change Saul's heart.

"You should know," Saul said, leaning in so closely Mary could smell the spices upon his breath, "this little utopia you have created is about to come crashing down around your ears. The religious leaders have taken notice of your conduct, and they are not happy."

"First," Mary said evenly, "*I* have created nothing here. This is all the Holy Spirit's doing. I am but a willing vessel in the hands of God, and this house is an offering. Nor am I in any position of authority in the church, as God has directed the apostles to lead His growing flock. And lastly," she said, uncowed by the Pharisee's hostile front, "we belong to God. Our future belongs to Him, and we needn't fear *those who kill the body but cannot touch the soul.*"

"Ah," Saul mused, stroking his neatly cropped beard in a manner indicating he was relishing her impending doom. "We shall see if you cling to such noble convictions when your delicate life hangs in the balance. Word travels fast in Jerusalem, or hadn't you noticed? We know about the suspicious deaths of two of Jerusalem's finest citizens. I demand to know who dared approve an execution apart from trial by Sanhedrin?"

"Despite the fact that you are in no position to demand *anything* in this house," Mary responded without missing a beat, "the execution was by the hand of God. Not one of us laid a hand upon the guilty parties, and we have myriad witnesses to prove it. I imagine that explanation should suffice, given the fact that the Law requires only two or three witnesses."

Saul studied her coldly, crossing his arms in cool disbelief. "Only time will tell, brave soul. Only time will tell." Adjusting his flowing robes in a dignified fashion, Saul lifted his brows, offering a bemused smile before stepping past her and descending the marble stairs.

***

Tabitha

"I worry for her," Tabitha said quietly, watching as Saul stepped haughtily around Mary, descending the broad steps with a pretentious air. Completely undaunted, Mary simply turned her attention to several approaching women, stretching her arms out to them and greeting them warmly. She was a remarkable woman, a true pillar of the faith.

"We are *all* in the hands of God, Tabitha," Stephanos assured her, interrupting her thoughts. "We must always remember the words of the mighty prophet Isaiah—*No weapon formed against you shall prosper, and every tongue which rises against you in judgment you shall condemn.* Even on those occasions when it appears we have been defeated, our God is still working on our behalf, working all things together for our ultimate good. We must trust in that promise, even when the enemy comes against us in blazing wrath and fury."

Closing her eyes, Tabitha released a long, tremorous sigh. *Oh Lord, I believe; help my unbelief!* How she longed to cling to the precious promises of God, embracing His will with her entire being, forever banishing the gnawing fears tearing at her heart.

CHAPTER 34

Tabitha

The first day of the seventh month, called *Tishri*, ushered in the Feast of Trumpets, and with it, great joy and merriment. On the first day of the great feast, trumpets sounded in the Temple from dawn until dusk, inviting the inhabitants of Jerusalem to ready themselves for the single most sacred day of the Jewish year—the awesome Day of Atonement, which would commence upon the tenth day. The holy days adjoining the two sacred feasts were religiously observed as the sacred Days of Awe, in which God's chosen people reflected upon their sin and their dire need for repentance. In hindsight, Tabitha understood that the animal sacrifices of these esteemed feasts had been instituted by God to foreshadow the perfect, sinless sacrifice of His precious Son. Only by His blood could one be truly cleansed.

As the sound of mighty trumpets wafted through the still morning air, Tabitha swept the outer courtyard, somewhat awed by the powerful blasts proceeding from the Temple Mount on the opposite end of the holy city. Smiling to herself, she remembered the apostles believed that the mighty trumpet call of God would herald Jesus' imminent return. Perhaps that awesome day would sound something like this!

When the iron gate creaked open behind her, Tabitha turned to see Candace passing beneath the stone arch, baby Rufus balanced on one curvy hip.

"Greetings, dear sister!" Candace said, raising her soft voice to be heard above the din of blaring trumpets.

Pleased, Tabitha propped her broom against a stone wall and hurried to greet the graceful young woman. After a meaningful embrace, Tabitha leaned back, stroking Rufus' small back. Shyly, he turned his head, burying his face in his mother's soft shoulder.

Laughing softly, Candace smoothed back the baby's curly black hair, shaking her head in amusement. "My, my. Aren't we shy today," she observed, smiling knowingly at Tabitha.

"Shall I inform my lady of your arrival?" Tabitha asked, always pleased to welcome a sister in Christ.

"You needn't disturb her," Candace insisted, shifting baby Rufus' weight upon her hip. "I simply stopped by to deliver a message from my husband."

"Ah, how *is* Simon? And your dear son, Alexander?" Tabitha pressed, ushering the young woman into the frescoed vestibule of the magnificent home.

Candace followed Tabitha into the reception hall. "They are doing well," she nearly shouted, her dulcet voice ringing through the marble hall. Smiling sheepishly, she laughed, "Forgive me, Tabitha. I've grown accustomed to shouting above the sound of the trumpets today. I suppose I needn't raise my voice within this house." Candace's smooth, dark cheeks grew rosy as she laughed again, a bit bashfully this time.

Joining in Candace's mirth, Tabitha chuckled merrily, reaching for baby Rufus. "May I?" she asked, always ready to cuddle the sweet child.

"Of course," Candace gladly consented, placing the infant in Tabitha's eager arms.

"My, you've grown since last I saw you," Tabitha crooned, bouncing the baby on her hip. Grinning broadly to reveal two very small, nubby front teeth, Rufus hid his face in her shoulder, giggling contentedly.

Taking a slow step back, Candace tilted her head to one side, watching the lovely maidservant in fascination. "My, you're a natural."

"A natural?" Tabitha glanced up, confused. When baby Rufus took her hand, gumming contentedly at her fingers, she did not refuse him but simply laughed—a soft, silvery sound that echoed pleasantly through the vast hall.

"You will be an excellent mother someday," Candace observed, her dark eyes sparkling in both fun and admiration.

"A *mother*?" Tabitha exclaimed, startled. "Oh my!"

"You object?"

"Well, of course not," Tabitha faltered, her cheeks flaming with color. "It's just that I...well..."

"You imagine motherhood is a good, long ways in the future?" Candace pressed gently.

"Yes!" Tabitha declared, her color further deepening. "*If* the Lord desires for me to wed, and *if* He chooses to bless me with children…"

"I said the same," Candace teased, her expression playful. "Right before I met my Simon."

"Speaking of Simon, you said you bear a message from him?" Tabitha asked quickly, gladly returning to the subject at hand.

"Yes, indeed," Candace smiled, intrigued by Tabitha's response. Her smooth, dulcet tone every bit as soothing as her calming presence, Candace explained, "Many of the brethren of our small assembly have begun collecting food, clothing, and funds to lay at the apostles' feet. Simon hopes to deliver the donations soon after the Day of Atonement, yet before the Feast of Tabernacles commences."

"Your husband is a wise man," Tabitha chuckled, bending to kiss Rufus' soft cheek, "avoiding the quagmire before the floodgates open and thousands of pilgrims pour into Jerusalem to commemorate the Feast of Tabernacles!"

"Indeed," Candace agreed with a smile. As all Jewish men were required by law to return to Jerusalem during the Passover, Pentecost, and the Feast of Tabernacles, Jerusalem's streets became overwhelmingly congested during those festival seasons, her borders swollen with an endless deluge of religious pilgrims. Those spilling beyond the walled city crammed endless rows of tents just outside the towering stone walls, illuminating Jerusalem's borders with burning torchlight night after night.

"Word has spread about the followers' generosity here in the Upper City," Candace continued, reaching out to tickle her son's tiny chin. "The residents of our neighborhood desire to participate as well.

After all, *it is more blessed to give than to receive.*"

Tabitha shook her head in awe. Candace and her husband, Simon, hosted a church gathering in their own modest house in the Lower City, where the poorest of Jerusalem resided. It was truly touching to witness those who had so much less concerned for those even less fortunate than they. "I shall pass that along to my lady, who in turn will alert the apostles," Tabitha assured her, moved by the believers' eager generosity.

Before Candace could respond, the bronze double doors beyond the vestibule creaked open, slamming shut again with a resounding thud.

Tabitha and Candace looked to each other in question just as Stephanos rounded the corner, his arms burdened with ledgers. Offering an easy smile, he nodded toward both women.

"Good morning, dear sisters," he said, his strong voice echoing in the marble hall. "Candace, please send my greetings to your husband, Simon, and your son, Alexander."

"Of course." Candace nodded with a gracious smile.

Lingering briefly in the entryway, Stephanos' dark eyes fell upon Tabitha as she bounced little Rufus on her hip, cooing words of love and taking his tiny fingers in her own. Lifting her gaze, Tabitha noticed his dark eyes, filled with warmth and...*something else*, something she couldn't quite identify...resting upon her. Could it be tenderness? Longing? Or simply her own wild imagination at work?

Sensing the startled question in Tabitha's eyes, Stephanos swiftly averted his gaze. "Regrettably,

I must see to these ledgers in the *bibliotheca*," he explained somewhat stiffly, taking purposeful strides as he passed by the two women. "*Shalom*, dear sisters, and good day."

"*Shalom*," Candace repeated quietly, her soft brown eyes flitting toward her dear friend, Tabitha. The golden-haired maidservant appeared frozen in place, Rufus' small hand clasped tightly in her own, her hazel-green eyes wide, her lips slightly parted in surprise and…disappointment, perhaps?

Closing the distance between herself and the pretty, ruffled maidservant, Candace said softly, "He's a bit too attractive for his own good, wouldn't you agree?"

Flustered, Tabitha blushed prettily, her color further deepening as Candace chuckled her understanding.

"So my suspicions *are* correct," Candace assessed warmly, attempting to meet Tabitha's gaze even as the maid averted her eyes in humiliation. "How long have you felt this way about him, dear one?"

"Lower your voice, I beg you," Tabitha hissed, even though Stephanos couldn't possibly overhear their whispered conversation in the sequestered *bibliotheca* at the opposite end of the sprawling villa.

"Come, sit with me," Candace suggested, taking a seat on one of the many straight-backed chairs lining the far wall. Gazing up at the flustered maidservant, she gently patted the seat beside her.

Glancing hurriedly about the hall to ensure that the coast was clear, Tabitha hurried over to the stiff row of chairs, obediently taking the seat beside Candace. Carefully lifting baby Rufus, she turned him around in her lap so that he was facing her. Gurgling playfully, he reached for a large chunk of her golden hair, attempting to stuff it in his mouth.

"So?" Candace prompted, her dark eyes filled with understanding. "Shall we discuss it?"

"I've spoken of this to no one," Tabitha said quietly, fearful to do so even now. "Not even Mary knows."

"My dear friend, I guarantee you Mary knew long before *you* even recognized it for yourself," Candace laughed, and Tabitha realized her friend was probably right. Mary was an incredibly observant woman, almost always one step ahead of everyone else.

"It isn't proper or seemly for a woman to chase a man," Tabitha whispered, her cheeks flaming with color. "Besides, I'm not even entirely sure how I feel about Stephanos. One moment, I'm certain I have deep feelings for him. But the next, I feel so exasperated with him I wish to smack him upside the head."

"And you're certain you're not already married to him?" Candace teased, her brown eyes dancing. "I've heard many a wife state that same declaration."

"It doesn't matter, anyway," Tabitha sighed, smoothing back Rufus' adorable ringlets. "For months, I was convinced Stephanos had taken an interest in me. But now? I'm certain he's changed his mind."

"The way he looked at you just now certainly doesn't indicate a change of heart," Candace observed quietly, a knowing smile tipping graceful lips.

"Perhaps he considers me an amusing distraction," Tabitha admitted. "But certainly nothing more. If so, he would have made his intentions known by now. I desire to honor God, Candace, so I refuse to chase after him like a silly, shallow woman. The Lord designed men to woo and pursue their brides as Christ pursued and claimed *His* beloved bride, the church. So if Stephanos has lost interest in me, then I certainly will not bare my heart before him nor go chasing after him."

"You are a wise woman, Tabitha," Candace said, offering the troubled maid's hand a gentle squeeze. "But I believe your assumptions about Stephanos are incorrect. I am certain he will make his intentions known—in God's perfect timing, of course—if marriage is His will for the two of you."

Marriage! Tabitha's heart sprang into her throat at the mere thought of it. Coloring deeply, she attempted to calm her tumultuous emotions, for the prospect of a union was indeed a daunting consideration. After all, she was a headstrong, decisive young woman—a work in progress, to be sure! Was she truly prepared to set aside her independence to become a devoted helpmate? Was she even qualified to do so? Stephanos was a powerful man of God. Already, rumors rippled through the city as the fiery Hellenist was reputed to perform miraculous signs and wonders alongside the apostles. Although Stephanos was far too humble to boast of such awesome feats, Tabitha was beginning to wonder if the rumors were true. Was this man—whom she was beginning to care so deeply about—truly a prophet and a miracle-worker as many brashly speculated? If so, what kind of a woman would be required to walk beside him, to support and encourage him in his mission?

Sensing the direction of her friend's troubled thoughts, Candace squeezed Tabitha's hand once more. "I'm so glad you shared this with me, dear sister. Times like these are when we believers are privileged to unite in prayer, beseeching God to work out His perfect will in our lives. And you can be sure of this—I will be praying for you every single day, that God will establish your steps, guiding every aspect of your life in accordance with His will."

Pushing against her with two chubby legs, Rufus gurgled happily, as if in agreement. The women laughed, amused by the baby's antics. Shyly raising slanted eyes to meet Candace's sincere gaze, Tabitha knew one thing with absolute certainty—Candace would, in fact, keep her promise, remembering Tabitha and Stephanos in daily prayer.

Already, she felt better about her future—a future looming ominously before her, so daunting, so full of unanswerable questions. Though Tabitha seriously doubted that she—a lowly, orphaned servant with virtually nothing to offer a powerful man of God—would be privileged to wed, the simple reminder that her future was sheltered safely within the Savior's nail-scarred hands filled her entire being with a deep sense of peace.

CHAPTER 35

Mary

Standing sedately upon the graceful balcony overlooking the outer court, Mary watched as excited staff members ushered believers into her home. Most wore expressions of sincere joy, washed in an unexplainable sense of peace, gladly anticipating an evening of worship and fellowship with the brethren. Gradually, the structure of these services had begun taking shape, with one of the apostles opening each meeting with a simple, earnest prayer. During this time of prayer, Mary considered how the apostles must ache for Jesus' reassuring presence. Often, tears streamed down the apostles' faces as they sought the Savior in prayer, recalling Jesus' tender friendship and healing touch. How they all missed His physical presence among them! And yet how good He was to send the Holy Spirit in His stead, to lead and to guide, to strengthen and empower. Where would they be without the mighty presence of the Spirit of God?

Typically, after asking the Lord to bless their time of prayer, study, and fellowship, one of the apostles would then address the assembly, reading large passages of Scripture. Next, he would expound upon the teachings of Jesus, vividly recounting His parables and reviewing the lessons He had taught them. Mary was always deeply refreshed by this instruction, for the Holy Spirit never failed to shed light upon practical ways in which she might incorporate these teachings in her daily life, deepening her walk with God, strengthening her faith, and providing ample opportunities for her to exercise obedience.

At the end of each service, the assembly knelt in both prayer and thanksgiving, presenting their petitions and requests to God. Careful not to overlook any request, whether great or small, the followers presented these requests before God, united in both thought and purpose. Not only did the believers pray during the service, but as instructed by the apostles, they remembered to pray about the requests throughout each busy day. It was truly affirming, knowing a great cloud of witnesses laid one's petitions before God throughout each day. Mary had never known fellowship so sweet, so edifying. And as the Holy Spirit moved throughout the gatherings, strengthening each believer, the followers continued to grow in both might and power like a united, unstoppable force. It was truly wondrous to behold!

Finally, at the close of each service, the believers lifted their voices in song, praising God in psalms, hymns, and spiritual songs as instructed by their Lord. After each meeting, the believers were truly refreshed, further equipped to spread the Good

News. And Mary knew the same could be said about dozens of other homes scattered throughout Judea and Galilee, where thriving churches continued to assemble each day.

In addition to church gatherings, most followers of Jerusalem continued to meet at the Temple for morning and evening prayers. Many even attended afternoon prayers alongside the apostles each day. After prayers, the believers often gathered at Solomon's Porch, where they shared the glory of the gospel with anyone willing to listen. The Good News was confirmed for thousands upon thousands as the apostles performed signs, wonders, and healings by the power of the Holy Spirit. Despite these glorious miracles, Mary had noticed a great rise in hostility steadily increasing against the Way. Heart constricting, she wondered how much longer they would be permitted to worship at the Temple.

Clenching the railing with both hands, Mary closed her eyes, attempting to prepare her heart for worship. Her efforts proved futile, however; dozens of urgent considerations vied for her attention. Sadly, she thought of Zev, her zealous doorkeeper and captain of the guard. Her heart broke anew each time she remembered his stout refusal of Christ's love. Many times, she'd considered posting him within the Upper Room during services, desperately hoping his stony heart might be softened by the gospel so neatly presented at each meeting. Sighing, Mary dismissed the idea for the umpteenth time. After all, she knew the stubborn guard well. If Zev felt *forced* into anything, he would simply become even more antagonistic and resentful, further closing his heart to the message of the gospel. No, if Zev was brought to the saving knowledge of Christ, it would be by the power of the Holy Spirit—not by manipulative works of her flesh. Mary reminded herself of this, *yet again*.

Then there was the mounting attraction between two people she dearly loved and treasured—Tabitha and Stephanos. Mary knew it was only a matter of time before Stephanos appealed to her, seeking the hand of her maidservant. On one hand, Mary was thrilled for the young couple. They were a perfect match. Stephanos' brazen and fiery nature demanded a woman of grit and substance, a woman unafraid to stand beside him, battling the forces of evil. And Tabitha fit the bill. And yet, on the other hand, Mary knew she would most certainly lose her dear Tabitha should she wed her beloved Stephanos. The thought troubled Mary more than she cared to admit, for she had grown to love the young woman like a daughter.

Opening her eyes, Mary's gaze swept over the courtyard below, observing the steady stream of guests passing beneath her balcony and entering the house via massive double doors. Eyes narrowing, she studied the shrouded form of a newcomer, a reclusive woman in her mid-thirties donning a pauper's tattered garments.

And now there's this...Mary thought, squinting as the mysterious figure passed beneath her balcony, vanishing from sight. The stranger hadn't attended a church meeting in several months. Even so, Mary recognized her instantly. Something about the mysterious woman set off warning bells in Mary's practical mind, for the stranger seemed to be a bizarre study of contradictions. Though the tall, unfamiliar woman dressed in soiled rags, she carried herself with a regal, queenly bearing that instantly snagged Mary's attention. Not only that, but carefully preened, slender eyebrows, smooth, flawless skin, and neatly manicured fingernails sorely contradicted her peasant's attire.

Something about that woman simply didn't add up, and Mary fully intended to discover what was amiss.

***

Tabitha

Pausing before the opened double doors leading onto the balcony, Tabitha tilted her head, studying the still form of her mistress. The young widow stood overlooking the courtyard below, her delicately embroidered garments fluttering gently in the cool evening breeze. Dramatically framed by the flaming hues of the sunset, Mary's lovely profile appeared exquisitely regal as dark ringlets framed her bronzed face. A thick, waist-length braid peeked from beneath her gauzy, scarlet-hued head covering, bespeaking both elegance and practicality.

As guests continued to pour into the Upper Room, Tabitha knew Mary's tranquil escape would soon be overrun. When the mysterious figure of a woman dressed in rags emerged at the top of the stairs, Tabitha's observant eyes quickly absorbed the discrepancies in the woman's careful presentation.

Something didn't add up.

Slipping quietly onto the balcony, Tabitha joined her mistress, folding her hands upon the railing.

"Is everything all right, my lady?" she whispered in concern, her eyes traveling over the guests milling about the courtyard below. "You appear troubled."

"Troubled?" Mary repeated, turning her regal head to study her maid. "Deep in thought, perhaps. But not troubled."

Tabitha sighed, relieved, as they turned to observe the guests pouring into the Upper Room just beyond the open double doors of the elegant balcony. Instinctively, their eyes landed upon the mysterious newcomer, who, clearly attempting to be invisible, settled herself unassumingly upon a bench near the back of the large chamber.

"That woman," Tabitha said under her breath, her eyes flashing protectively. "She's not who she claims to be. You know that, don't you?"

Mary studied the woman with great sympathy. Clearly, she was immensely uncomfortable in the believers' presence. "And who does she claim to be?"

"Not once has she identified herself," Tabitha admitted, crossing her arms in indignation. "But she certainly presents herself as a pauper."

Mary nodded in agreement. "That, she does."

"But have you observed her closely?" Tabitha pressed insistently. "She rarely speaks, but when she does, her voice is ridiculously cultured. And her hands! Her hands are smoother than oil, her fair complexion untouched by the sun."

"I have noticed that, as well," Mary admitted, her heart going out to the woman for some reason unbeknownst to her.

"I guarantee you that woman hasn't worked a day in her life," Tabitha nearly snorted. "So why does she pretend to be something she's not?"

Mary had asked herself the same question, to no avail. "Perhaps she is a wealthy or influential woman seeking answers, and yet she fears association with the Way might place her household in jeopardy."

"She's going to have to get over that if she decides to join us."

"It's merely an assumption, Tabitha. I could be wrong."

"And if she has been planted in our midst by the Sanhedrin—or, *worse*—by the Romans? Then what?" Tabitha asked boldly, fiercely protective of those she loved. "My lady, perhaps you should send her away—at least until she decides to reveal the truth about her identity."

Sighing, Mary returned her attention to the contradictory stranger. The woman in question sat with perfect posture, her spine rigid, her hands folded elegantly in her lap. Her eyes remained shyly downcast, as if to discourage overzealous guests from engaging her in conversation. "I cannot send her away," Mary said softly, compassion gripping her. "Who am I to decide who is worthy of the gospel?"

Taking a deep breath, Tabitha attempted to mask her mounting frustration. She understood Mary's desire to reach the lost, but shouldn't one draw the line at some point? What of the others' safety?

"I believe the Holy Spirit guides those who attend, even if they first arrive with ulterior motives," Mary continued, nodding graciously toward several guests who noticed their hostess on the balcony. "All we can do is present the Truth to them, Tabitha, living by example. We must trust our God to take care of the rest."

Stifling a frustrated sigh, Tabitha forced a slow

nod of agreement. She wondered why she had even bothered discussing this with Mary. After all, *this* was the woman who had fearlessly welcomed that dreadful Pharisee, Saul—their sworn enemy—into her home!

"Have you noticed," Tabitha dared, pressing the issue once more, "that she attends only during festival seasons? Then she disappears for months at a time?"

"I've wondered about that," Mary agreed. "Perhaps she is from Galilee or some outlying region. She may even travel here to Jerusalem with her husband for the feasts. That would explain why she attends only during the festival seasons, would it not?"

Tabitha nodded. It was certainly a feasible conclusion.

"I simply worry for you, my lady," Tabitha admitted, lowering her eyes in humble acquiescence. "You know I love you, and these believers are my family. I fear for them."

"You must remember that we belong to God, dear one. And no matter what happens in this life, we have the next to look forward to."

"Do you believe her presence will result in disaster?" Tabitha asked, further alarmed.

"As of now, we have no reason to assume that," Mary assured her. "I'm simply saying we mustn't lose sight of what's truly important—evangelism, salvation, eternity with God. Jesus conquered death so we needn't fear loss of any kind. Knowing this, we can wholeheartedly engage in the Lord's work, without holding back."

Tabitha acknowledged the truth of Mary's words with a subtle nod. She agreed, though she certainly intended to keep an eye on that questionable new-comer.

"And, beloved," Mary pressed gently, capturing Tabitha's attention once again, "we must always remember that any loss our Lord permits is for our ultimate good. Suffering of any sort—whether great or small—reminds us that this world is not our home."

When Tabitha remained pensively silent, Mary held out a hand to her, smiling invitingly. "Now, shall we go welcome our guests?"

Ruefully following her mistress into the cheerful glow of the Upper Room, Tabitha prayed for the Lord's wisdom and protection. With dangerous tensions mounting against the believers from all sides, they needed the Holy Spirit's guidance now more than ever.

CHAPTER 36

Tabitha

"She claims that she travels to Jerusalem with her husband for the feasts, but I'm certain she's a *Gentile*," Tabitha told Candace as they sat upon the earthen floor of Simon and Candace's modest limestone dwelling in the Lower City, discussing the enigmatic stranger of the previous night. "So why attempt such a treacherous journey if they are Gentiles and needn't observe the feast days?"

"Perhaps her husband is Jewish," Candace suggested, gently adjusting baby Rufus in her arms as he slept. "Or perhaps she and her husband have converted to Judaism."

Tabitha shook her head, unconvinced. "Something isn't right, Candace. I'm sure of it."

"Don't go borrowing trouble now," Candace gently advised, reaching out to touch Tabitha's arm. "We know absolutely nothing about her."

"That's what concerns me!" Tabitha declared more hotly than she intended. "Who *is* she? Why does she shroud herself in secrecy, posing as someone she's not?"

"It's no secret both Jews and Romans are becoming increasingly hostile toward the Way," Candace explained. "Perhaps she simply desires to reach a solid conclusion before aligning herself with the church of God."

"Mary thinks that may be so," Tabitha admitted, still unconvinced.

Scanning the gathering of believers assembled within Candace's modest Lower City dwelling after prayer meeting, Tabitha's chest tightened in fierce protectiveness. She loved these people. She loved the Way. She had no desire to allow wicked men—or women—to destroy her cherished brethren.

Sighing resignedly, her gaze traveled across the one-room house, landing upon her mistress, seated across the room on the floor with her long legs tucked comfortably beneath her, two small children piled on her lap, chattering happily as they tugged at her thick, long braid or placed tiny hands upon her sculpted face. Tabitha was amazed by Mary's ease in this unassuming stone dwelling so unlike her magnificent Upper City mansion. Unlike the opulent villa across town, this home was a simple limestone structure coated in a smooth layer of stucco. The square-shaped house sat amidst a small, unpaved courtyard encircled by rough stone walls. A steep flight of stone steps led to the flat-topped roof, functioning as a multi-purpose area for storage space and an open-air second floor of sorts. Inside, the house was dimly lit with flickering oil lamps. The furniture was minimal, and several wooden chests doubled as tables and benches. A symmetrical structure consisting of a single room, there were no adjoining rooms or bedchambers to be found. Yet Mary appeared completely oblivious to these drastically diametrical arrangements. It would seem the young widow was every bit as comfortable in this precinct as she was in her own lavish neighborhood.

Tabitha admired Mary's eagerness to attend meetings at the various house-churches dotting Jerusalem's streets and alleys. Clearly, her intent was to unite rather than divide the brethren. It would have been easy for the various gatherings to form inhospitable cliques at each of their own home bases, with the wealthy, middle class, and poorer followers remaining in their own familiar comfort zones. Instead, the believers traveled from house to house, welcoming one another with joy and gladness.

Though Tabitha had grown rather accustomed to the church in Mary's home, surrounded by beauty and elegance, she knew most of the churches throughout Galilee and Judea were far more like this humble gathering assembled in the house of Simon the Cyrene, and his lovely wife, Candace. Tabitha was glad the believers continued to grow together as a loving unit, rather than forming tight-knit groups in their own home churches.

"This woman we're speaking of," Tabitha remarked, drawing Candace's attention from her sleeping son. "Has she visited the church here in your home?"

"Never," Candace responded, adjusting Rufus' worn blanket. "Why do you ask?"

"See!" Tabitha exclaimed. "She dresses in rags

and claims to serve a wealthy man. But wouldn't a woman of her station be far more comfortable in a humble setting, rather than in an Upper City mansion?" Catching the rueful smile flickering across Candace's serene face, Tabitha mentally kicked herself. *Will I ever learn to* think *before spouting off the first thought that comes to mind?* "Oh, Candace, I meant no disrespect," she groaned, ashamed. "You truly have a lovely home—"

"There's no need to apologize, dear one," Candace interrupted graciously. "God has gifted all of us in different ways, placing each of us in the circumstance He knows to be best for us. To some, He grants wealth and influence, knowing they will utilize it as a tool to further His kingdom. To others, He assigns humbler circumstances. The Scriptures are brimming with tales of those who have more, and those who have less—both of whom accomplished mighty feats through the power of the Holy Spirit. Why should I be discontent on the path which God has lovingly placed me? I may not reside within the walls of a magnificent palace, but God has richly provided not only enough, but *even more* than we need. He is faithful."

Tabitha nodded slowly, admiring Candace's wisdom and humility. "It also seems that God assigns different circumstances throughout the various seasons in a believer's life," Tabitha reflected thoughtfully. "Consider King David, for example. He spent his early years as a forgotten shepherd boy. Then he became a fugitive, lacking the most basic necessities—even food and shelter, at times. Later, God granted him the kingship."

"And the Lord used him mightily during *every* season of his life," Candace added with a warm smile, "through his affliction, persecution, and, eventually, great affluence."

"Perhaps I should cease obsessing about that strange newcomer's masked intent," Tabitha admitted, resignedly folding her hands in her lap. "Mary says the Holy Spirit draws everyone who attends, even if their motives aren't in the right place, at first."

"Mary is a wise woman."

Sighing, Tabitha wondered why she found it so difficult to relinquish her cares into the capable hands of God. Surely He could handle her predicaments—great or small—far better than she! But rather than trusting God, she fixated upon her concerns, turning them over and over in her mind, as if attempting to wrestle them to the ground, choking them into submission. If only it was that simple!

But it is *simple,* she reminded herself, closing her eyes and basking in the peace of the quiet gathering. All around her, soft conversation floated upon the air as believers conversed. Soon, everyone would gather their belongings and return to their homes for the evening. *Jesus commanded us not to worry. I mustn't disregard His clear command. He is in control, and He knows what He's doing. It's as simple as that.*

"Tabitha, has this mysterious woman disclosed her name?" Candace asked quietly, interrupting Tabitha's turbulent train of thought.

Lips tipping ruefully, Tabitha replied, "I introduced myself to her last night, attempting to glean more information about her. But I think she saw right through me. She has perceptive eyes like my mistress."

"And?" Candace prompted, curious.

"She calls herself *Sarah*, although I'm certain that is not her true name."

"Hmm...*Sarah*," Candace mused, her dark eyes narrowing as if attempting to grasp a vague, distant memory. "A lovely name, though it is rarely heard now."

"These days, our people call all their women *Mary* or *Salome*," Tabitha teased, and Candace smiled appreciatively at Tabitha's reference to *our* people. Though Candace had been born and raised on an entirely different continent, far from the Promised Land, she and her husband, Simon, had embraced the faith of God's chosen people even before the coming of Christ. The Messiah's sacrifice simply confirmed their staunch belief in the God of Abraham.

"Perhaps there is a reason she chose that particular name to represent herself," Candace murmured, deep in thought.

"What do you mean?" Tabitha asked blankly. "Most likely, she assumed the first Hebrew name that came to mind. Like I said, I believe she is a Gentile posing as a Jew."

"But if that is so, then why shouldn't she choose a more common name? Like Mary or Salome?" Candace teased.

Tabitha shrugged in concession. Candace had a good point.

"Correct me if I'm wrong, but I believe the name *Sarah* means *princess*, yes? An even better translation might be *noblewoman*, would it not?"

Tabitha nodded slowly, stunned, suddenly grasping Candace's brilliant assumption.

Noblewoman. Princess.

Perhaps the mysterious visitor had unwittingly provided them with the first clue about her identity.

***

A hush fell over Judea on the solemn Day of Atonement, ushering in a national day of both mourning and fasting. Tabitha was saddened by the confusion of her people, for many of them had rejected their Messiah, the Holy One of Israel. Rather than embracing the tender mercies of a loving Savior, the Jews put their trust in fearsome blood sacrifices pronounced by a capricious high priest. But Tabitha knew all the sin offerings in the world could not purge her people of their sin. Only faith in Christ's perfect sacrifice made one truly clean.

The celebrated Feast of Tabernacles arrived five days later, inviting yet another week of feasting and festivities, culminating in the great and holy day of assembly on the eighth and final day of the national feast.

When the feverishly frenzied month of *Tishri* finally faded into the quiet and uneventful autumnal month of *Cheshvan*, Tabitha breathed a deep sigh of relief. She had savored every moment of joy and feasting with her brethren, glorying in the miracles the Holy Spirit had enabled the apostles to perform at Solomon's Porch in the sight of all the people. Daily, their numbers grew as men and women accepted the truth about the Messiah, inspired by awesome miracles and powerful teaching.

But now, nearly two weeks later, Tabitha basked in the tranquility of a quiet, ordinary night.

Passing through the inner courtyard, now cast in fiery hues from burning torchlight, Tabitha planned to tidy Mary's magnificent *bibliotheca* in preparation for the following day. Most of the servants had already taken to their beds, for the hour was late. But Tabitha was still far too energized from weeks of celebration to settle down. Rather than wasting time lying abed, longing for sleep that wouldn't come, she decided to make herself useful.

Passing beneath the office library's impressively pillared entryway, Tabitha froze, jolted by the unexpected sound of quiet weeping.

Glancing around the dimly lit chamber, Tabitha's eyes rested upon a huddled form seated in the mammoth chair behind the equally mammoth desk stationed before a massive row of wooden shelves.

Tabitha's heart sprang into her throat at the sight of her ever-composed mistress, crumpled in her throne-like chair, weeping inconsolably.

"My lady!" Rushing to her side, Tabitha knelt by Mary's chair, taking her cold hands in her own. "What has happened? Are you hurt?"

Mary grew deathly still. Instantly quieting, she turned wet, red-rimmed eyes toward her concerned maid. "Tabitha, forgive me," she managed, her typically dulcet voice quivering slightly. "I thought I was alone."

"My lady, are you all right?" Tabitha persisted, reluctantly releasing Mary's hands.

Sighing, Mary cupped both cheeks, swiping away her tears. Forcing a brave, wobbly smile, she turned to face Tabitha—still kneeling before her—more fully. "With God's help, I try to be strong, Tabitha. For my son, for the brethren, for the unbelievers watching to see what I'll do next..."

"My lady, you are truly the strongest woman I know," Tabitha assured her, hoping Mary didn't consider her one to criticize a rare, fleeting moment of weakness.

"There are times when I am assaulted by painful memories, times when I least expect it," Mary explained apologetically, "and I am caught unawares. I'm sure you understand what that's like."

Tabitha did. "You miss your husband, Mark."

"Just as you must miss your father and mother."

I do, Tabitha thought, swallowing hard. *Every single day.*

"Sometimes," Mary continued a bit shakily, "amidst the most mundane of tasks, a bittersweet memory will hit me like a stone wall. The sound of his voice. The gentleness of his touch. The warmth and strength of his embrace. And, despite my very best efforts, I fall apart."

Tabitha had known a few of those moments as well, especially when her bereavement was raw and fresh. "I apologize for intruding upon this private moment, my lady. It was thoughtless of me."

"How could you have known?" Mary assured her, lightly touching the top of Tabitha's modestly covered head. "Besides, I'm sure your arrival was God-ordained."

Tabitha stared at her, confused. "How so?"

"Self-pity is a dangerous thing. To wallow in it is a temptation quite difficult to resist. Your arrival cut that temptation short," Mary confessed wanly.

"Thank you for that, dear one."

"May I ask what prompted your sadness tonight, my lady?"

Shaking her head, Mary responded with a flourish of her graceful hand, "I suppose I simply wish Mark could see this—*all* of this. The miracles. The signs and wonders. The thriving, growing church. Tabitha, he would be amazed."

Yes, Tabitha thought, shaking her head in agreement. *Yes, I suppose he would.* As would her parents, had they lived to witness the Savior's mission.

"I must admit," Mary said softly, tenderly running her hands over her late husband's open ledgers, "there are times when I am tempted to succumb to self-pity and discouragement. But then I am reminded of the way God has walked beside me, carrying me through the hardest of times. The night Mark was taken, I was certain I wouldn't make it through *one night*. And yet God has carried me faithfully nearly *two years* since! It's truly amazing—to see your greatest fear realized, and yet to overcome it by the power of the Holy Spirit."

"Your example has inspired so many, my lady, including myself," Tabitha said honestly. "These are wicked days, and many others will experience loss. But when they look to you, they will know it *is* possible to overcome."

"When they look to *God*," Mary clarified, squeezing Tabitha's shoulder. "Without Him, I am the weakest of women. Without Him, I would have long since crumbled and fallen apart."

Still kneeling beside Mary's chair, Tabitha placed her hands firmly on her knees, rocking back on her heels and pondering the events of that fateful night when Mark had breathed his last. It was such a blur now, nearly two years later. That night, she had desperately roamed Jerusalem's streets for what seemed like hours, combing the dark alleys and empty shop avenues for a physician. When she finally found one, he was certainly the last person she had expected—a young Gentile with warm brown eyes and a heart for the truth.

She couldn't help but wonder if he had discovered it.

As if sensing Tabitha's train of thought, Mary said, "Do you remember that young doctor—the one called Luke? He was able to begin his practice in Antioch with the money Mark had set aside for medical work. He has a tender heart toward anyone in pain, physically or emotionally."

"I didn't realize you kept in touch," Tabitha said, surprised.

"By letter, of course. Stephanos handles all our correspondence."

At the casual mentioning of the handsome evangelist, Tabitha's cheeks colored slightly. She hoped Mary was too deep in thought to notice.

"It's a shame Luke hasn't accepted Christ as Savior," Mary went on sadly. "He is still intrigued by our ways, but he seems to believe that ours is a Judean God, disinterested in the Gentiles."

Tabitha understood Luke's hesitation. How many Jews had she encountered on Jerusalem's streets who detested Gentiles, calling them filthy dogs and pigs? Certain Pharisees even avoided Gentiles passing by on the road, fearful they would be defiled if even the shadow of an "unclean" person fell upon them. A bit nettled, Tabitha couldn't help but assume Saul of Tarsus was among that haughty class.

"Well, I suppose we've traveled down Memory Lane long enough for one night," Mary sighed wistfully, preparing to rise from her chair.

Tabitha rose along with her, a niggling question on the tip of her tongue. Dare she voice it aloud? "My lady," Tabitha winced, speaking boldly before dissuading herself, "may I ask you a very personal question?"

Mary had risen from her chair. Noting the sober expression upon her maidservant's taut features, she chuckled and teased lightly, "You sound quite serious. Should I be seated again?"

Standing before her lady, Tabitha twisted her hands nervously. "This should only take a moment," Tabitha assured her, glancing nervously about the large chamber. She wanted to be certain they were still alone. "Knowing what you know *now*," she dared, her tone little more than a haunted whisper, "do you regret marrying your husband, Mark?"

A series of expressions passed over Mary's face—shock, sadness, understanding. Reaching out to tuck a stray curl behind Tabitha's ear, Mary responded gently, as a mother might, "Not for a second, dear one. I would do it all over again—in a heartbeat—even knowing how it would end. Every moment I shared with Mark—every tender moment, every shared secret, every trial and every victory—has a very special place in my heart. Loving Mark was one of the greatest privileges God has ever granted me, and I thank Him for it with every ounce of my being."

For some reason unbeknownst to her, tears sprang to Tabitha's eyes, unbidden. Unlike most women she knew, Tabitha didn't cry easily. But something about the way Mary spoke—with such great love and unwavering conviction—struck a chord deep within her soul. Would she, Tabitha, ever possess the courage to love another with such uninhibited veracity?

Intently studying her troubled maidservant, Mary thought she understood. Taking Tabitha's hand in her own, she said softly, "Beloved, do not let fear of what may never come rob you of your greatest blessing."

Embarrassed, Tabitha lowered her gaze. "I don't know what you mean."

"I think you do," Mary replied, tipping her servant's chin with one delicate finger, studying her veiled expression. "You lost both your parents, Tabitha. Years later, you lost Mark as well—a man you loved as deeply as a father. And now there's another man—a man you've not only grown to love, but to respect and admire deeply—a man whose mission you may be called to share."

Crossing her arms anxiously, Tabitha looked away. It was as if Mary could see into her very soul. Must she lay bare her secret anxieties and deepest fears?

"The secret, dear one," Mary continued, her luminous gray eyes lighting with hope, "is to treasure every moment God grants us with those we love. And if we are separated in death, then we must choose to relish the reunion—that glorious day when we will be raised to eternal life in Christ! For then, nothing will ever separate us again. It's a living hope, Tabitha, and not even death can destroy it."

"A woman needn't be married to fulfill God's

purpose in her life," Tabitha pointed out, more to distract than to prove a point.

Smiling knowingly, Mary nodded her agreement. "As you can imagine, that fact is a great comfort to me. When I lost Mark, I felt as if my purpose had been laid to rest with him. But it hadn't. God calls some to marriage, others to singleness, and still others to widowhood. The beauty of it all is that He knows what is best for each of His beloved daughters. But it's up to us to embrace His calling, accepting His will with joy."

"My lady!"

Tabitha's color deepened at the sound of Tobias' voice in the entryway. How long had he been standing there listening?

"Tobias," Mary breathed, surprised. "Is everything all right?"

Mustache twitching nervously, Tobias avoided her gaze. "I certainly do hope so, my lady," he muttered, wringing his hands anxiously.

Suppressing a mischievous chuckle with the back of her hand, Tabitha realized the reason behind Tobias' obvious angst. Donning his simple bedclothes and devoid of his characteristic and familiar turban, Tobias had clearly already bedded down for the night before the untimely interruption. Obviously, he resented being summoned from his cozy bedroll.

"A rather imposing stranger has just arrived at the gate," Tobias continued breathlessly. "He demands an audience with you."

"An audience? With me?" Mary repeated, perplexed. "Tobias, it is the middle of the night!"

"I'm relieved *someone* has noticed that obvious fact," Tobias muttered irritably, his bedclothes fluttering about him in his chagrin.

"Has this man disclosed the nature of his visit?"

"Not a word about it, my lady."

"His timing is thoughtless and inappropriate," Mary remarked frankly, disturbed by the visitor's manner. "Please send him my regrets and inform him that I will gladly receive his company upon the morrow."

"I do apologize, my lady," Tobias said, clearly peeved, "but that's exactly what we told him."

By *we*, Tabitha assumed Tobias must be referring to himself and Zev.

"And?" Mary prompted, perplexed.

"He refuses to be dissuaded. He says it is urgent that he speak with you, that the lives of many men may be forfeit should you refuse an with audience him."

Mary and Tabitha exchanged looks of deep concern. There was something threatening, even ominous, about the stranger's warning. Offering a silent prayer, Mary petitioned the Lord once again. *Gracious Father, what shall I do?*

The answer came to her, swift and clear.

Straightening behind the massive desk, Mary lifted her chin, evenly meeting her overseer's gaze. "I will see him now. You may send him in."

CHAPTER 37

Mary

"Mary of Jerusalem! I must admit, I am delighted to meet you. You have become quite a legend throughout Judea."

Rising to her feet, Mary acknowledged her guest—a devastatingly handsome man with neatly groomed hair dark as a raven's wing, chiseled, clean-shaven features, and a broad yet slightly mischievous smile. Somewhat apprehensive, Mary was grateful for the massive desk serving as a barrier between them.

"Please, do be seated," the dashing young man insisted, lowering himself onto one of the straight-backed chairs before Mary's large desk and folding his well-shaped hands as if settling in for a nice, long chat with a trusted friend. "You needn't rise solely on my account."

Tabitha, standing stiffly at her mistress's elbow, prepared to leave.

"Tabitha, please," Mary instructed, exchanging a

knowing look with the young maid, "remain with us."

"Yes, my lady." Tabitha understood her mistress's silent plea. The young man seated across the desk was terribly attractive, exuding both confidence and masculine grace. Clearly, Mary considered it inappropriate to sequester herself within the *bibliotheca*, alone with a mysterious man, especially at this ridiculous hour. Tabitha would gladly remain with her, a witness to the strange events about to transpire.

"Pardon the late hour, my lady, but I simply could not risk being seen," the young man apologized, an enigmatic smile tipping his lips in rueful acknowledgment.

"And why is that?" Allowing herself a more thorough perusal of the man's striking features, Mary instantly recalled where she had encountered him before. Now intrigued and reservedly cautious, she wondered about the nature of this meeting. But rather than divulging her revelation, she decided to hold her tongue. Better to see if the man spoke the truth about his identity.

"I'll get straight to the point," the man announced, his dark eyes flashing in...what? Excitement? Anticipation? Mary wasn't sure.

"Yes, please do," Mary prompted, picking up a stylus and tapping it thoughtfully upon her desk.

"My name is Alexander, and I work for our most gracious and noble high priest, the venerable Joseph Caiaphas."

The sardonic edge to his tone was unmistakable, and Mary's curiosity was further piqued. Glancing over her shoulder, Mary exchanged knowing looks with Tabitha. The young man had spoken truth about his occupation—clearly a questionable one to any follower of the Way, given his close association with a high priest determined to crush the fledgling church.

Admiring his brass, Mary folded her arms upon the desk, leaning forward. "You were one of the stenographers at the apostles' trial that day in the Royal Stoa."

"Guilty. *I'm* guilty, that is. Not Peter and John. Their innocence is evident to anyone with decent eyes in his head."

Alexander knew the apostles by name? Mary raised a brow in question.

"You may wonder how the favored servant of your greatest nemesis is on a first-name basis with your men. I've spoken with them on multiple occasions—under cover of darkness, of course. I'm sure they will vouch for me. I'm especially cozy with your niece's husband, the one called Simon Peter. There's a bit of amusing history between us."

"How so?" Mary prodded, making a mental note to consult the apostle about the truth of Alexander's statement.

"He cut off my cousin's ear, actually." Alexander grinned in amusement, leaning back in his chair. "It was rather gruesome."

The pieces began falling into place for Mary. "The night of Jesus' arrest?"

"Exactly. My cousin also served the high priest at the time. But, please, you needn't lecture Simon Peter about the unfortunate incident. His brash act resulted in my own salvation, if you can believe it."

Mary stared at Alexander, her lips parted in awe. "Because you witnessed the Savior heal your cousin's severed ear?"

"Right again. You're good at this," Alexander grinned.

Exchanging yet another curious look with Tabitha, Mary returned her attention to Alexander. Still leaning comfortably back in his chair, he crossed solid arms over his broad chest. He watched her with brow lifted, clearly gauging her reaction.

What exactly *was* her reaction? She wasn't entirely sure what to make of this brash and daring young stranger.

"You wish to know the nature and purpose of this meeting," Alexander stated simply, as if reading her thoughts.

"Yes," Mary answered honestly. "I do."

"So here it is. When my cousin, Malchus, left Caiaphas' employ, I assumed his position as the favored manservant of the high priest. Trust me—it's not what I desired. I had just proposed to the woman of my dreams and planned to whisk her away to some remote location—preferably by the sea—to live the remainder of our days delighting in our newfound faith and in each other's company. But—as I'm sure you've noticed—the Lord's plans often contradict our own."

Considering the course her own life had taken, Mary readily nodded her agreement. She certainly never could have imagined her life as it was now—widowed, with her house functioning as the homebase for a persecuted and hunted faith, overseeing dozens of thriving businesses, raising her son without her husband's reassuring presence. No, her life was far different than she had envisioned it, and yet she was perfectly at peace—safe within the will of her loving Father.

"Mere hours after pronouncing my wedding vows, I was summoned by the high priest. His guards saw me confronting Simon Peter in the courtyard the night of Jesus' arrest. Naturally, they assumed I was against the disciples. When Caiaphas offered a higher position, I knew God was directing my path, somehow. To remain in that lion's den was the last thing on this earth I wanted, and yet the moment I accepted the position—in turn, accepting the will of God—I knew a very real peace."

Mary nodded, blown away by the bold young man's testimony. Silently, she prayed that his words could be trusted, asking the Lord to show her if she was deceived. "And now?" she asked quietly, tilting her head to one side. "Has the Lord shown you why you must remain with the high priest?"

"Absolutely, at least in part. Will we ever truly know the marvelously intricate complexities of His plan?"

Mary's lips tipped in a knowing smile.

"I believe God has placed me *on the inside*. No one within the palatial mansion—excepting my believing wife, of course—knows of my 'defection.' As a stenographer, I am present during most meetings of the Council, including public and private trials. I have access to all the records, penning some of them myself. I can alert the followers about potential strikes against them, keeping you informed about the Sanhedrin's plans. Can you see how having a set of eyes and ears within the priestly mansion might prove exceptionally advantageous to the Way?"

Glancing at Tabitha, Mary saw the girl was intrigued. "It sounds dangerous," Mary observed, considering Alexander's new wife.

"Less dangerous than refusing the will of God," Alexander quipped, leaning forward in his chair. Resting both elbows on his knees, he folded his strong hands. "I know what I'm getting into, as does my wife, Mara. We are at the Lord's disposal, and thus, at your own."

"How did you know to come here?" Mary asked, another test. After all, there were dozens of other home churches he could have chosen.

"A reliable source informed me this was the church's home base."

"Which source?"

"Simon, the wealthy merchant prince, also a believer. Speak with him yourself. He will vouch for me."

Mary nodded her understanding. She would surely trust Simon's judgment. He had also begun hosting a church in his own elegant villa, faithfully donating large funds to relieve the poor. He was a kind, generous man, full of the Holy Spirit.

"My cousin, Malchus, and his lovely wife, Melina, work for Simon," Alexander supplied, interrupting Mary's train of thought.

"I see," Mary responded, praying silently about whether to accept Alexander's proposal. True, the inside information should prove terribly helpful. But what of the well-being of this young manservant and his new bride? If she accepted his offer, they would be placing themselves in a terribly dangerous position. And should they be found out, their lives would most certainly be forfeit.

As if sensing the direction of the widow's battling thoughts, Alexander rose from his chair. Placing a strong hand upon Mary's desk, he lowered his proud head to meet her gaze, the intensity of his own burning like two fiery coals. "Listen, a time may come when my wife and I are called to stand boldly for Christ, *before* Caiaphas, *before* the Sanhedrin. When—or *if*—that day comes, we will not deny the name of Christ. But for now, I truly believe the Lord has placed us in an incredibly unique position, one that may prove invaluable to the growing church of God."

Mary studied him intently, her heart pounding in her chest. *Lord, what is Your desire?*

"Mary, will you work with us?"

"My lady," Tabitha dared, her hands folded carefully before her, "it is indeed a clever plan."

The answer came, and with it, a thrilling reassurance. Flashing a rueful smile, Mary extended her arm across the desk. "I look forward to working with you, Alexander."

Taking her hand in a firm grip, Alexander grinned broadly. "Ready to shake things up a bit?"

"I believe we already have," Mary teased, accepting his firm handshake. "Now, what can you tell us about Caiaphas and the Sanhedrin?"

Lowering himself back into the straight-backed chair, Alexander folded strong arms across his chest, his mouth curving in sardonic amusement.

"What with the signs and wonders, the healings, the miracles, and the numbers increasing by the thousands, Caiaphas has worked himself into an absolute frenzy."

"And?" Mary prodded, leaning forward conspiratorially.

"*And*...I can tell you that they're running scared," Alexander surmised, a broad grin conveying his deep pleasure. "So, by all means, keep up the good work."

CHAPTER 38

Mary

"Surely you are not suggesting that we refrain from preaching the gospel!"

"You know I would never suggest such a thing," Mary said calmly, biting back an impatient sigh. She recognized that look on Simon Peter's face—unflinching determination backed by a dogged will. He stared back at her, his dark eyes flashing in challenge.

"You have one clandestine meeting with this brazen young upstart, and already you have offered him the helm?" Peter exclaimed bitterly. "Have you also asked him to draw up plans, outlining our mission and doling out assignments?"

"Simon," Anaia, his docile wife, scolded gently, reaching for his arm. "My aunt has served Christ and His followers faithfully. The least we can do is listen to what she has to say."

Silently thanking God for her niece's calming presence, Mary raised level eyes to Simon Peter. "Alexander believes the Sadducees will rise up against the apostles. They want to silence the Twelve, once for all. They plan to arrest you—"

"On what grounds?" Peter demanded. "What is their charge?"

"Disregarding a direct order from the Sanhedrin," Mary supplied quietly. "You continue to preach in the name of Jesus."

"And I will continue to do so until I draw my final breath!"

"Which may occur far sooner than we desire if you refuse to heed Mary's counsel," Anaia broke in firmly. "Please, Simon, lower your hackles and *listen* to what she has to say."

"You mean listen to whatever this pompous *Alexander* has to say," Peter huffed, a twitching muscle in his otherwise firm jawline betraying his resentment.

"Alexander is a believer now, my husband," Anaia reminded him gently. "One of us. He isn't our enemy."

Tentatively, Mary watched as her niece quieted Peter's perturbed spirit. She thought she understood Peter's hesitation. After all, he and Alexander hadn't exactly gotten off to a great start. Mary had later learned that it was Alexander who questioned Peter so vehemently in Caiaphas' courtyard the night of Jesus' arrest, instigating Peter's third denial of Christ. Mary was certain even the fleeting mention of Alexander's name was enough to fill his mind with shameful recollections he longed to forget.

Releasing a long, frustrated sigh, Peter crossed broad arms over his chest, turning his attention to Mary. "I recognize it is good to have a connection inside the palatial mansion. I'm just not entirely certain we can trust the source."

"I have spoken with the powerful merchant prince called Simon—a trustworthy believer and a host of another Jerusalem church. He has vouched for Alexander."

Running his hand through unruly dark hair, Peter sighed in reluctant concession. "What exactly is he saying?"

Closing her eyes, Mary released a silent prayer of thanks. He was ready to listen now. "Come," she said, holding out her hand to them. "We can discuss this in the *triclinium,* where you will surely be more comfortable—"

"The hour is late," Peter interrupted, clearly struggling to curb forward emotions. "Let's discuss this quickly, here and now."

"All right, then," Mary replied, willing to remain standing in the vast reception hall if it would set Peter's mind at ease. "Last night, I met with this Alexander, the manservant of the high priest. Caiaphas has called yet another emergency meeting of the Council. The Sadducees plan to arrest you and the others if you speak the name of Jesus again."

"And you think it would be wise to refrain from preaching?"

"Absolutely not," Mary replied firmly. "I believe you should seek *God's will* in this matter. He has given each of the apostles a divine assignment, Simon Peter. As you've already reminded the religious leaders, you answer to God—not to them."

Shuffling sandaled feet upon the cold marble floor, Peter sighed. "We planned to instruct the people at Solomon's Porch tomorrow after morning prayers. What now?"

"The Holy Spirit will direct you, Peter," Mary responded without missing a beat. "If He wills for you and the others to preach tomorrow, He will show you."

"And if not?"

"He will show you that, as well."

"How so?" Peter asked, somewhat bleakly.

Exchanging troubled looks with Anaia, Mary's heart went out to Peter. The bold young apostle was running himself ragged instructing the brethren, preaching to the masses, overseeing the treasury, providing for the needy, and traveling from church to church, strengthening the brethren. The work was never-ending, debilitating. Extreme exhaustion was evident upon Peter's taut features.

"Oftentimes," Mary responded slowly, "when I am unsure about a decision, I simply take it to the Lord in prayer. He is then faithful to fill my entire being with peace regarding the decision in question. If His answer is *yes*, then I move forward, filled with a peace that surpasses my own understanding. But if His answer is *no*, then my peace evaporates and my spirit becomes unsettled, ill at ease. Do you understand what I am saying?"

Nodding slowly, Peter massaged his temples with nimble fingers. "I will pray about this with the apostles. And if the Lord commands us to return to the Temple and face the Sanhedrin's wrath tomorrow, so be it."

The color drained from Anaia's face, and yet she stood staunchly beside her husband, ready to support him despite her own doubts and misgivings.

"I will be praying, too," Mary assured them, recognizing their intense inner struggle.

"We will send word," Peter said, turning toward the arched opening leading into the vestibule, "when the Holy Spirit makes it plain."

"And if God calls you to Solomon's Porch," Mary said firmly, her eyes traveling first to Anaia, then to Simon Peter, "I will be there to stand beside you. No matter what happens."

Nodding his head solemnly, Peter turned and disappeared into the vestibule, his anxious wife trailing closely behind him, her lips moving in silent prayer.

***

Mary received word from Simon Peter before sunup the following day. With trembling fingers, she unrolled the slight scroll delivered by a solemn messenger. The inscription upon the scroll was clear and concise, bearing three simple words. Three simple words loaded with power and purpose.

We go forth.

Lowering the scroll, Mary bowed her head in prayer, bracing herself for what lay ahead.

***

Mary stood near the front of a massive throng of believers tightly packed beneath the inviting shade of Solomon's Porch at the Temple compound. Nervously intertwining slender fingers in her trailing shawl, she listened attentively to Simon Peter's impassioned preaching even as she prayed silently for the apostles' safety and divine protection. Tension crackled heavily in the air, a nearly tangible force so strong Mary could almost taste it.

Even so, throngs of believers and new converts pressed in tightly about the twelve apostles, forming a powerful human barrier between the wanted men and their oppressors. Mary watched, amazed, as the apostles took turns addressing the crowd, their faces shining with radiant, otherworldly light, their postures relaxed, their features bathed in peace. Clearly, a night spent together in prayer had bolstered their spirits, emboldening them to stand against the dark forces so intent upon crushing the Way.

Allowing her gaze to travel over the enormous group assembled at Solomon's Porch, Mary noted bands of men and women lingering on the edge of the crowd. Some looked genuinely intrigued, while others were clearly offended by the message preached. Still others appeared torn, drawn by the apostles' powerful teachings, yet haunted by the rigid traditions of their forefathers.

Would the Sadducees dare come against the apostles amidst this enormous crowd? To do so would surely incite tremendous revolt! Closing her eyes tightly, Mary prayed the religious leaders would see reason in this instance. A riot might prove deadly to the entire nation, granting their Roman oppressors the perfect excuse to brutally crush the faint sliver of religious freedom they currently enjoyed.

Fleetingly, Mary wished her dear maidservant and friend, Tabitha, was present. But Tabitha was occupied at the Synagogue of the Freedmen, distributing her handmade garments with Candace.

Perhaps I should have informed Tabitha about the apostles' preaching this morning, Mary thought, torn. *Had I told her, she would be standing right here beside me now.* But Mary hadn't wished to disrupt Tabitha's ministry of love. The widows and orphans of the impoverished precinct sorely depended on the maidservant's friendship and generosity. Besides, Mary hadn't any reason to simply assume this day would bring trouble. After all, the apostles had been preaching for nearly an hour now, uninterrupted, untouched by trouble of any kind. Perhaps Adonai had seen fit to foil the Sadducees' wicked plans, as He had done so often throughout Christ's earthly ministry. But if danger should arise, Mary didn't wish to place her beloved maidservant directly in harm's way. Calming her own turbulent thoughts, Mary considered her energetic son, John Mark, sequestered safely at her villa with his tutor, under strict orders not to leave the premises for any reason. Should a violent uprising erupt in the streets, Mary didn't want her son anywhere near the Temple district.

"You there! You who call yourselves apostles!"

Mary froze, her entire body going cold. Turning her head, her heart skipped a beat as her eyes swept over a vast arsenal of approaching Temple guards, their terrible metal-topped hats clinking along with their uniforms, their deadly spears glistening in the early morning sunlight.

Instinctively, Mary took Anaia's hand. The young woman stood beside her, the color draining from her face as the guards reached the edge of the crowd.

"Make way!" a fierce-looking guard shouted, his stance resonating with unchallenged authority. Mary vaguely recognized him as the captain of the Temple guard, a burly man with chiseled features, black hair tied at the nape of his neck, and cold, merciless eyes. "Make way by the order of the high priest!"

Riddled with confusion, the crowd parted hesitantly, making way for the long row of uniformed temple guards.

Mary watched in horror as the armed men violently pushed their way through the crowd, eventually reaching the front where the apostles stood, waiting calmly and unperturbed. Half-expecting—and somewhat *hoping*—the crowd would revolt, Mary was perplexed by the gathering's timid compliance. Why weren't they threatening or fighting against the temple guards' unjust orders?

The captain had reached the apostles first, pausing pointedly before Simon Peter. The guard eyed him coldly, not bothering to mask his disdain. "You are all under arrest, to be questioned by the Sanhedrin."

"You're arresting them?" A man hidden in the crowd shouted, dismayed. "On what charge?"

"Disorderly conduct, disturbing the peace, and disregarding a direct order from the Sanhedrin," the captain sneered, roughly jerking Peter around and binding his hands behind his back.

"You and your uniformed cronies are the only ones disrupting the peace here," another man shouted, incensed.

"Silence!" the captain bellowed, his sun-bronzed features mottled with rage. "Unless you all wish to be taken into custody along with them."

When the second protestor recklessly rushed at the captain, the brutal guard drew a hidden dagger, slamming the butt end into the man's temple and sending him sprawling across the pavement. "Anyone else wish to challenge the direct orders of the high priest?" the captain dared, his cold black eyes scanning the crowd in challenge.

The gathering quieted in both fear and apprehension, holding their collective breath as more temple guards closed in, surrounding the apostles and unlawfully binding their hands behind their backs.

Mary watched, a pang searing her heart, as her brothers were bound. Even Simon the Zealot turned of his own accord, allowing a temple guard to bind his wrists. The former Zealot was a human powerhouse, highly skilled in the art of war, trained in every imaginable form of combat and self-defense. He could have easily incapacitated half the Temple guards surrounding them, and yet he restrained himself, clearly determined to accept the will of God. Yet his intense inner struggle was evident upon his taut features.

"Get them out of here," the captain snarled, giving Peter a hard shove toward the parted crowd. Another guard reached for Peter, continuing to push him through the angry throng. The captain's armed underlings followed suit, shoving the apostles' headlong through the gaping crowd.

Mary turned sympathetically toward Anaia. Tears traced two slender lines down her niece's pale cheeks. The young woman's lips were moving rapidly in silent prayer, her eyes locked upon her bound husband as he was pushed roughly through the crowd. The throng was growing dangerously restless, enraged by the unfair treatment bestowed upon the apostles as the guards shoved them down the center of the parted crowd. Sensing the tension, the officers hastened their pace, clearly eager to escape the people's wrath.

Now halfway through the gathering, Peter paused before his wife, his dark eyes searching hers, conveying his deep love and unwavering devotion to her.

Weeping softly, Anaia reached out, cupping his bearded face in one hand. "God be with you, Simon," she whispered as Peter's guard, discomfited by the touching scene, propelled him forward. "Move on," the guard snarled gruffly, daring a glance over his shoulder as they passed. Mary wondered if the guard's conscience was pricked by the small yet unbending form of Peter's young bride.

As the apostles were ushered past the crowd, the assembly became increasingly violent. Fists began waving adamantly in the air, accompanied by fierce shouts and demands. Jostled roughly by the ensuing madness, Mary reached for Anaia's arm to steady her. The clamor was fast becoming deafening.

"What should we do now, Mary?" Anaia had to shout above the uproar, her eyes growing round at the mounting danger.

Closing her eyes tightly, Mary wished she knew. She hadn't the faintest idea where the apostles were being taken, and she knew better than to follow after the armed guards.

"Mary, Anaia!" Stephanos pushed his way through the revolting crowd, reaching out to steady both women. "Are you all right?"

"We must do something!" Anaia said vehemently, blinking back tears.

"We must pray," Stephanos said firmly, his dark eyes scanning the rigorous crowd. "Please, let me escort you both to safety so we can seek the Lord's guidance in this matter."

At that moment, a tall, somewhat plain woman slammed into Mary, nearly knocking her off her feet. Had Stephanos not been there to steady her, Mary was certain she would have been sent reeling headlong into the roaring crowd. Stunned, Mary stared incredulously at the careless woman, expecting an explanation.

Instead of an explanation, however, the heavily cloaked woman ignored Mary's presence entirely. Brown eyes fixed straight ahead as if casually observing the mayhem, the woman shouted above the din, "Don't look this way nor act as if you know me," she ordered tersely, clearly addressing Mary, Anaia, and Stephanos while attempting to blend with the crowd. "The apostles will be held in the common prison overnight while the Sanhedrin regroups, preparing to convene. They will be tried upon the morrow."

It took all the willpower Mary possessed not to stare at this woman, stunned and openmouthed. Instantly, the pieces fell into place. This must be Mara, Alexander's new bride. The woman had risked her life to meet them here, divulging the apostles' whereabouts. Overwhelmed with gratitude, Mary fought the urge to turn and embrace her daring sister in Christ.

Without another word, Mara slipped her hooded cloak over her head, turned sharply on her heels, and vanished amidst the jostling crowd.

CHAPTER 39

Tabitha

Startled, Tabitha glanced up when Mary, Anaia, and Stephanos burst into the quiet Upper City villa with determined, purposeful strides.

"My lady!" Tabitha exclaimed, concerned by their clouded expressions. "I expected you back long before now. Candace and I finished distributing garments earlier than usual—"

"There was a bit of trouble at Solomon's Porch," Mary said briskly, accepting the pitcher and basin Tabitha hurriedly brought to her. Setting it upon a marble-topped table near the entry, Mary smiled warmly as Rhoda slipped into the reception hall, eager to be of service.

"May I wash your feet and the feet of your guests, my lady?" young Rhoda asked shyly, a towel draped dutifully over one arm.

"That would be lovely, Rhoda. You may do so while we discuss a plan of action," Mary said, fondly patting the top of the girl's covered head. Despite their current plight, Mary gracefully lowered herself onto one of the straight-backed chairs lining a frescoed wall, gesturing for Anaia and Stephanos to do the same.

Intently watching her mistress, Tabitha surmised that something was terribly wrong. Despite Mary's calm, cool demeanor, observant Tabitha noted the firm set of her jaw, the fierce glitter of her gray eyes. Knowing her mistress well, Tabitha sensed the young widow was already strategizing between moments of silent prayer.

"Please, do be seated," Mary encouraged her guests once more, sensing Anaia's tension and Stephanos' unease. Tabitha wondered if Mary had accepted Rhoda's kind offer simply to distract Anaia momentarily while she and Stephanos drew up plans.

Anaia seated herself woodenly beside Mary, too numb to argue. Stephanos, obviously eager to establish a plan without delay, appeared a bit discomfited by the traditional, though lavish, gesture.

"Please see to our guests first, Rhoda," Mary instructed kindly, and Rhoda knelt diligently before an ashen-faced Anaia. Tabitha couldn't help but smile at Rhoda's sweet innocence, for most servants were trained to serve the male guests first. But tenderhearted Rhoda naturally gravitated toward the woman in distress, the one most in need of a compassionate touch.

"My lady," Tabitha asked, accepting a second pitcher and basin delivered by another prompt maidservant, "tell me what has happened." Tabitha then realized she needn't have voiced the question, for one look at Anaia's tear-stained face told her everything she needed to know. "Oh no. They've been arrested, haven't they?"

"This is what we know," Mary said, watching approvingly as Rhoda removed Anaia's worn sandals and gently washed her aching, dust-covered feet. "Caiaphas ordered the arrest of all twelve apostles. They were taken while preaching at Solomon's Porch this morning—"

"My lady, if I may be so bold as to interrupt, may I assist Rhoda? Time may be of the utmost importance."

"Thank you, Tabitha," Mary consented appreciatively. "An excellent idea."

Kneeling before her mistress with the heavy pitcher and basin, Tabitha was caught off guard when Mary waved a delicate hand. "Please tend to our guest first, dear one. Rhoda may assist me after she finishes helping Anaia."

Blinking in surprise, Tabitha stared at her mistress in near panic, her cheeks blooming with rosy color. *Her?* Wash *Stephanos'* feet? Though it was customary for maidservants to wash the feet of guests, some Jewish men refused the gesture offered by a female servant unless she was a member of his own staff. Foot washing was considered the lowliest of tasks when carried out by servants. Yet, on the contrary, it was considered quite honorable for a wife to tend to the aching feet of her husband after he returned home from a long day's work. Further mortified by that thought, Tabitha wondered what Stephanos must be thinking.

Immediately sensing Tabitha's discomfort, Stephanos held up both hands. "You needn't concern yourself, dear sister," he said quickly. "Allow me to wash my own—"

"Nonsense," Mary interrupted, and Tabitha wondered if she merely imagined the mischievous flicker in Mary's gray eyes. "Tabitha, you don't mind, do you?"

Had the circumstances been different, Tabitha might have laughed aloud at Mary's polite inquiry. After all, few—if *any*—aristocratic women asked their staff if they *minded* carrying out their assignments! No, servants were simply expected to *perform*—swiftly, obediently, without question. Though Tabitha respected her lady's considerate nature, she did *not* appreciate being asked to wash the feet of this ridiculously attractive man. Surely her trembling hands would splash water all over the place and she'd make an absolute fool of herself!

"Mary, this truly isn't necessary," Stephanos argued, sensing Tabitha's reluctance. "If we intend to return—"

"No," Tabitha interrupted, a bit more tersely than she had intended. Boldly meeting Stephanos' gaze, Tabitha straightened defiantly, galvanized into action by his expression. Clearly, Stephanos considered her too timid to carry out this task! Well, she'd show him otherwise! She wasn't a bit intimidated by him, after all. At least, that's what she tried to tell herself as she steadied her nervous hands.

Rolling up her long sleeves, Tabitha knelt before Stephanos, her bright eyes flashing. With trembling fingers, she removed his dusty sandals, setting them off to the side and gingerly lifting one foot, then placing it in the basin. His olive-toned skin felt warm beneath her cool fingertips. Steeling herself, she attempted to steady her hands once more. She certainly had no intention of revealing her nervousness to him!

"Stephanos," Mary said as Rhoda finished assisting Anaia and bent to untie the straps of Mary's elegant sandals. "What action must be taken at this point?"

"Prayer first," Stephanos responded readily, offering Tabitha a rueful smile that knotted up her insides.

"And then what?" Mary asked, guarding her tone in front of Anaia, who remained seated limply on the chair, her strained features ashen. "Shall we invite the believers to gather and pray for the apostles' release?"

"Were you intending to host the prayer meeting here?" Stephanos asked, clearly a bit distracted by the lovely young woman washing his feet.

"That's certainly what I had intended," Mary responded. "Unless you have an alternate suggestion."

"What if we rally at the common prison?" Stephanos pressed.

Tabitha raised her eyes in alarm. Mary, too, looked surprised by his suggestion.

"The common prison," Anaia murmured, her eyes filling with fresh tears. "Mary, why would the high priest send them there?"

The solemn look exchanged between Mary and Stephanos wasn't lost on Tabitha. In fact, she was somewhat certain she already knew why the Sanhedrin had ordered it so. Unlike the quiet holding cell burrowed deep beneath the house of the high priest, the common prison constituted the city's public jail, built specifically to house the most dangerous criminals, the most notorious offenders. Undoubtedly, their brethren now shared a foul-smelling stone cage with violent cutthroats and thieves.

Daring another glance at Stephanos, Tabitha saw that he had no desire to further alarm Peter's young wife. "I suppose," he said softly, "the Sanhedrin intends to send us a loud, clear message by detaining them in such a way."

"A message?" Anaia managed shakily. "What do you mean?"

"Clearly, the Sanhedrin considers members of the Way to be little more than common criminals, and therefore, we shall be treated as such."

"Not only that," Mary added, her eyes flashing in her resolve, "but they intend to humiliate and demoralize us. We cannot let them succeed."

"No," Stephanos agreed, the strength of his tone somewhat bolstering Anaia's spirits. "We absolutely cannot." When Tabitha lifted her gaze, she found his own resting upon her, his dark eyes betraying his amusement. His expression sent Tabitha's heart racing once again.

Tearing her gaze from the handsome Hellenist's, Tabitha silently chided herself in annoyance, attempting to slow her racing heart. After all, there were far more important things to consider right now! The lives of her brethren were at stake, and yet here she was, completely distracted by a man! Well, no more. She must focus upon the matter at hand!

Lifting Stephanos' clean foot from the basin, Tabitha patted it dry with a soft towel. She had always detested foot washing, and yet, her Savior had instructed them to delight in the most menial of tasks—even foot washing—while serving others with a pure heart. Though Tabitha had always been repulsed by handling sweaty, dirt-encrusted feet, she realized that Stephanos' were not entirely unpleasant. Strong and well-shaped, his feet were deeply tanned rather like his toned, muscled calves. Attempting to squelch the unwanted color mounting in her cheeks, Tabitha quickly reached for his sandals, hastily sliding them onto his feet and neatly tying the straps. Relieved to have completed her task, Tabitha lifted the now empty vessel and basin, ready to empty the basin's dirty contents in the slop bucket.

"Thank you, dear one," Stephanos addressed Tabitha appreciatively, his entire being radiating with purpose as he rose from his chair and stood before Mary. "You are wondering why I have suggested meeting at the common prison," he continued, directing his speech toward the lady of the house. "The first time Peter and John were arrested, the believers stood together as a mighty unit, demonstrating unwavering devotion toward our brethren. I believe we must do the same now. It's no secret the Sanhedrin is afraid to incite a revolt."

"Then perhaps we ought to give them something to worry about," Tabitha spoke up, passing her pitcher and basin to Rhoda, who had just finished washing her lady's feet. Scampering from the room, Rhoda slipped beneath an arched doorframe to dispose of the basin's contents.

"Something to worry about…" Stephanos mused, arching a dark, mischievous brow. "Such as a tremendous show of support for our brethren? A monumental gathering outside the common prison, perhaps?"

"It could work," Mary responded, rising from her

chair. "I think we should split up, taking separate ways and gathering as many believers as we can find. Let's plan to meet on the road outside the prison within the hour. There, we shall pray until dark. We can reconvene at the Temple tomorrow morning when the trial is set to commence."

Tabitha agreed with the plan but couldn't dismiss the surge of annoyance coursing through her hot veins. Why had Stephanos allowed her to wash his feet if he'd known they would be promptly returning to the dusty streets? She opened her mouth to voice her obstinate query, but promptly closed it again. Had not her beloved mistress been present, Tabitha would have been sorely tempted to demand an explanation of him!

"The Lord's brother, James, may still be at the Temple with Philip," Stephanos surmised, interrupting Tabitha's rebellious thoughts. "I'll start there. They will help us rally more believers."

"And I'll ask Candace and her husband, Simon, to do the same," Tabitha said quickly, dismissing her annoyance with a bit of effort.

Mary turned to her niece then, her expression full of sympathy. The poor young woman had nearly wilted in her chair. "Oh, beloved," Mary said softly, helping the tearful bride to her feet. "Come along with me, dear one. You needn't be alone right now."

Anaia nodded, failing miserably as she attempted a lopsided smile.

"We have a plan then," Stephanos declared, eager as always to confront a problem head-on. "Let's move."

CHAPTER 40

Mary

The late afternoon air crackled with tension as the sun, a smoldering ball of flame, steadily descended upon its sheltered bed just beyond the western hills. A mighty throng had gathered outside the common prison, lining the paved street for what seemed to be miles on end. A gentle hum rose from the gathering as hundreds of believers petitioned the Lord in prayer on behalf of the imprisoned apostles. Some lifted their voices and their hands in worship, singing hymns of faith and praise. Others simply stood their ground, the intensity of their gazes bespeaking their firm resolve.

Her gaze sweeping over the ponderous crowd, Mary silently thanked the Lord for His provision. He had provided a great cloud of witnesses united in both thought and purpose to band together during this trying time. Surely this vast sea of devoted followers publicly demonstrating their unyielding loyalty toward Christ's specially appointed apostles would deter the Sadducees from their mad course!

Even so, Mary committed the entire situation into the Lord's hands, knowing He was fully capable of protecting the apostles. He needn't their assistance to accomplish the impossible. Nevertheless, Mary thanked the Lord for allowing them to participate in His plan.

Drawing Anaia close, Mary studied her niece with a practiced eye. "Are you all right, dear one?"

"It seems as if this day will never end," Anaia admitted, swiping at a stubborn tear. "I just want my husband safely home again."

"Amen," Mary agreed gently. "May it be so."

"How are you holding up?" Stephanos asked Anaia sincerely as he joined the two women near the front of the gathering.

"God is with me," Anaia responded, grasping at her shawl as if it was a lifeline. Her fingers twisted nervously within the soft folds as she drew the fabric more tightly about her shivering form.

"He is, indeed," Stephanos said softly.

"They have doubled the guard," Mary informed Stephanos, observing several rows of visibly anxious guards lining the heavily walled outpost.

"It would seem our presence has proven a bit unsettling." Stephanos grinned broadly, enjoying the guards' obvious discomfort.

"Have you seen Tabitha and John Mark?" Mary asked uncertainly. She would have preferred them to stay together rather than wandering off and dispersing among the crowd.

"John Mark joined Tabitha a few moments ago. They are with a large group of children near the back of the throng, entertaining them with stories and songs," Stephanos replied, his eyes betraying his admiration. "I think John Mark is assisting her, making the children laugh. She is so good with them."

"She is, indeed," Mary affirmed, her eyes twinkling knowingly. "She will make an excellent mother someday. Wouldn't you agree?"

Surprisingly, Stephanos didn't shy away from her gaze. His dark eyes betrayed the depths of his feelings as he responded meaningfully, "She will, indeed."

Mary concealed a knowing smile. Perhaps Stephanos would be seeking an audience with her sooner than expected. She wondered what her boisterous maidservant would have to say about the fiery evangelist's obvious aspirations.

A soft gasp from her niece drew Mary's attention to the neatly paved road before them. An entourage of Pharisees approached in the gathering dusk, their crisp black and white garments fluttering in the cool breeze. Mary watched as they passed the army of believers, their every move calculated and carried out to impress. Hands clasped piously before them, they traveled in a slow, steady cadence, their proud heads held high, their expressions aloof.

"What are they doing here?" Anaia breathed, her dulcet tone laced with disgust.

"That's a very good question," Mary murmured, tilting her head as she studied the solemn, steadily approaching entourage. There were five of them, but one held himself apart from the rest, leading the sober band with an arrogant, princely air.

"What is the meaning of this gathering?"

Snapping her head in the opposite direction, Mary bit back a snide comment as a familiar Roman soldier crossed the road, his armor clanking in time to his angry steps.

"Ah," Stephanos grinned, offering his hand. "Lucius, isn't it? We meet again."

"You have no right to be here."

Stephanos clicked his tongue chidingly. "My good man, must we really go over this again? As I'm sure you can see, we've been quite careful to keep all toes out of the road. As you must recall, you gave us strict orders to do so last time."

"I thought you were stationed at the house of Caiaphas," Mary dared, wondering why this irritating officer continued to pop up when least desired or expected.

"Caiaphas has ordered his most trusted officers to guard the prisoners, not that it's any of your business," Lucius smirked, his free hand resting somewhat casually upon the hilt of his gladius. "Now, I must command this gathering to disband. You are causing a disturbance."

"You call *this* a disturbance?" Stephanos countered, waving a hand to encompass the peaceable multitude. "We are a peaceful gathering!"

"Your presence is unsettling, and you must leave."

"Come now," Stephanos grinned, his tone cajoling. "Your men have trained to clash with barbarians in the heat of battle. Don't tell me they're concerned about a few lamblike men, women, and children!"

"If you know what's good for you, then you'll scatter like the foul rats you are!" Lucius sneered, his battle-hardened face mere inches away from Stephanos'.

Mary stepped forward then, surprising even herself with her boldness. "This is public property, sir, and you don't own the road. We will stand firm and pray as long as our brothers remain in chains."

Lucius' color deepened in fury. Jabbing a finger in

Mary's face, he barked, "Now listen, here—"

"*You!*"

The soldier's attention was temporarily diverted when the leading Pharisee barreled toward them, one finger pointed accusingly toward the bold young widow. Lucius drew back, measuring the religious man who dared interrupt their dispute. Lucius' expression betrayed the fact that he had noted the Pharisee's stony features and imposing build. Unlike most of his peers, this Pharisee was no soft, timid scholar. His fierce gaze and stocky bearing denoted that of a warrior, one boasting raw strength coupled with dangerous intelligence.

"Saul, how nice of you to join us," Mary cooed, undaunted by the smoldering presence of either man.

"What are you doing here?" Saul demanded, his dark eyes bordering rabidity. Mary wondered if he would begin foaming at the mouth.

"I could ask you the same," she replied calmly.

"I have far more right to be here than you do!"

"My, there's no need to be confrontational," Mary chided, clicking her tongue with an impish smile.

"Officer, I demand that you remove this woman and her wretched followers by force!" Saul demanded imperiously.

"You have no right to demand anything of me!" Lucius nearly spat, his ire instantly redirected by Saul's pompous tone.

The Pharisee's dark eyes settled upon Mary, conveying a very clear message. Mary smiled sweetly in return, which merely fanned the flames of Saul's enmity. "I should have known you'd be the one leading the rally," Saul hissed, his tone dangerously low.

"What do you want, Pharisee?" Lucius snapped,

his wrath now fully directed at the imperious Saul.

"My colleagues and I seek to question the criminals," Saul stated, still attempting to pin Mary in place with his cold gaze, but with little success.

"Out of the question," Lucius snarled, his knuckles whitening as he gripped his deadly looking spear. "Now move on."

"Are *you* commanding *me*?" Saul demanded in arrogant disbelief.

"Defy me, Pharisee, and see just how serious I am," Lucius snarled, turning sharply on his heel to join the other guards.

Seething, Saul watched the hardened soldier cross the street, joining his comrades on the other side. Directing his attention back to the lovely young widow before him, Saul's entire countenance darkened. Leaning in so closely that Mary could smell the cloying scent of leeks and garlic upon his breath, he hissed, "I will ruin you."

Protectively, Stephanos stepped forward, but Mary placed a calming hand upon his chest, stilling his protest. Her mouth tipped knowingly as she flashed Saul an unperturbed half-smile. "You can do nothing without our Lord's permission."

"Ah, I wouldn't be so sure of that." Adjusting his regal garments, Saul turned sharply on his heel and departed along with his religious brethren.

***

When the sun finally slipped beneath the western hills, darkness descended steadily upon Jerusalem, shrouding the city in darkness as heavy as the fear tugging at the believers' hearts. Still, thousands upon thousands of brilliant stars winked and glistened overhead, rather like the faint glimmer of hope burning in the souls of every man, woman, and child present. No one doubted that God was at work, despite the dire situation.

"The men believe we should turn in for the night," Stephanos informed Mary after speaking with several others. "The little ones are exhausted."

"They have been very courageous, these dear little ones," Mary said, smiling faintly. "Are you going to address the gathering?"

"The Lord's brother has asked me to do so," Stephanos admitted humbly, his gaze flitting over to Anaia and Tabitha now standing at Mary's elbow.

"James is a wise man. You are the perfect speaker to address the assembly," Mary assured him, touching his arm. "Will you let everyone know they are free to join me at the villa to continue in prayer throughout the night?"

"Mary, you should really get some rest—"

"I'll be fine," Mary assured him, smiling warmly.

Hesitantly, Stephanos nodded and took his place before the crowd. The gathering was so immense that his words would have to be passed along to those on the fringes and outskirts of the assembly, but the believers had long since perfected the art of communication within their ranks.

"My dear brothers and sisters," Stephanos announced, clapping his hands to get their attention.

Instantly, the crowd grew silent.

"It is time to turn in for the evening. We plan to reconvene at the Temple at dawn. For those of you called to pray throughout the night, please feel free to join us at the house of Mary. There, we shall remain vigilant in prayer for our brothers in chains."

The gathering uttered soft murmurs of approval, nodding their heads in understanding.

"But before we depart, I'd like to remind you of the promises of our great God, penned by the prophet Isaiah," Stephanos said, his mighty voice ringing out over the throng. Even several soldiers looked their way, their gazes dark and pensive. "*I, even I, am He who comforts you. Who are you that you should be afraid of a man who will die, and of the son of a man who will be made like grass?*"

Closing her eyes, Mary uttered a soft *amen* along with the rest.

"*You forget the Lord your Maker,*" Stephanos continued, his voice packed with power and strength of purpose as he quoted the sacred texts, "*Who stretched out the heavens and laid the foundations of the earth; you have feared continually every day because of the fury of the oppressor, when he has prepared to destroy.* But my dear brothers and sisters," Stephanos continued, his handsome features ablaze with the glory of God, "why should we fear mortal man? Never forget we serve a powerful God!"

"Amen!"

"He is far greater than those who are against us!"

"Amen. Praise God!"

"And what has our God promised? He said, '*I am the Lord your God, who divided the sea whose waves roared—the Lord of hosts is His name. And I have put My words in your mouth; I have covered you with the shadow of My hand.*'" Pausing to smile fondly at his beloved brethren, Stephanos repeated in wonder, "He has covered us with the shadow of His hand. Praise our God. We are safe, dear ones, nestled in the palm of His mighty hand."

Sidling alongside his mother, John Mark smiled warmly up at her, though Mary noted—with a bit of alarm—that her handsome son was nearly as tall as her. Lovingly placing her hands upon his broad shoulders as John Mark stood before her, Mary closed her eyes, savoring the promises in Stephanos' powerful speech. Truly, she and her loved ones were safe in the hands of her Creator. Mary knew that didn't necessarily guarantee freedom from hardship, for they lived in a sinful, fallen world. But one thing she knew with absolute certainty—the Lord would preserve His own, ushering them into the glorious hope of eternal life. Jesus had shown her the Way, enabling her to truly understand the psalmist's awesome proclamation: *In God I have put my trust; I will not be afraid. What can man to do me?*

Feeble men may have power over this physical body, Mary thought, comforted to her very core. *But the enemy cannot not touch our souls.*

CHAPTER 41

Tabitha

In the flickering lamplight of the Upper Room, Tabitha knelt in prayer, her folded hands resting upon the wooden bench before her. The room was filled with believers, all of them praying fervently. As Stephanos stood before the group, leading them in prayer, Tabitha couldn't help but sheepishly lift her gaze, watching him in awe. Stephanos spoke to the Lord as easily and intimately as if Jesus stood directly in front of him.

Jolted by a pang of guilt, Tabitha swiftly lowered her gaze. She should be entirely focused on praying for the apostles—not snatching discreet, hidden glances at the handsome evangelist leading the prayer vigil! Repenting silently, Tabitha asked the Lord to purify her heart, to steady her thoughts upon Him. Sighing deeply, she absorbed Stephanos' heartfelt prayer, her own heart stirred by his humble strength.

"Righteous Father," Stephanos prayed, lifting his

hands in fervent prayer, "You have given us precious promises, and we believe them. You have said, '*He who dwells in the secret place of the Most High shall abide under the shadow of the Almighty.*' We believe this, Lord. Redeem our brothers. Deliver them from bondage. In the name of Your precious Son, Jesus, who shed His blood for us, we ask and pray. Amen."

The Upper Room resounded with meaningful *amen*s, nearly shaking the paneled walls encompassing them.

Tabitha glanced up when Mary slid onto the bench beside her. Despite her evident weariness, Mary's entire being resonated with a calming sense of peace.

"How is Anaia?" Tabitha whispered, lightly touching her mistress's arm.

"Asleep, at last," Mary responded softly, greatly relieved. "I finally convinced her to retire in the guest room nearest my own."

"She must be exhausted," Tabitha sympathized, thankful the Lord had provided the frightened bride a peaceful respite.

"And what shall we say of the Lord?" Stephanos exclaimed, drawing both Mary and Tabitha's attention from their whispered conference as he raised a fist in triumph.

The Upper Room fairly shook with the believers' roaring response. "*I will say of the Lord, 'He is my refuge and my fortress; my God, in Him, I will trust!*'"

"Surely He shall deliver us from the snare of the fowler, just as He has promised!" Stephanos cried out.

"Amen!" Tabitha heard her own voice, along with

Mary's, joining dozens of others.

"*He shall cover you with His feathers,*" Stephanos continued. "And where shall we take refuge?"

"Beneath His wings!"

"*His truth shall be your shield and buckler!*" Stephanos proclaimed, his declaration nearly shaking the rafters. "*You shall not be afraid of the terror by night!*"

"Hallelujah! Praise God."

"Oh, righteous Father," Stephanos petitioned, kneeling in fervent intercession. "Grant Your mighty angels charge over our dear brethren to keep them in all their ways, to bear them up just as You have promised."

A shiver of anticipation skittered up Tabitha's spine. Had she simply imagined it, or had the chamber visibly brightened amidst the evangelist's heartfelt plea?

***

Simon Peter

Trapped with the apostles and hordes of unsavory characters within a foul holding cell, Simon Peter raised his head, a passage from Scripture resounding so loudly in his mind, he wondered if someone hadn't whispered it in his ear.

For He shall give His angels charge over you, to keep you in all your ways. In their hands they shall bear you up...

The surrounding criminals slept fitfully, but the apostles remained tentatively awake. Peter's eyes traveled across the faces of his startled brethren, now blinking in confusion.

Did they feel it, too?

For He shall give His angels charge over you...

A blinding light exploded in the cell, so brilliant, so dazzling, that the apostles were forced to shield their eyes from its all-consuming glow.

***

Tabitha

Stephanos paused mid-address when an unexpected ruckus erupted just beyond the Upper Room. Apprehensive, the believers propelled themselves to their feet, exchanging looks of question along with hints of concern. The sound of pounding feet bounding up the broad, marble steps resonated in the still air of the cheerfully lit chamber.

Tabitha looked to Mary, a question in her eyes. "Were you expecting more guests, my lady?" she asked doubtfully. "At this late hour?"

"It would seem so," Mary replied, her tone reservedly cautious.

"Could it be trouble?" Tabitha dared, her heart hammering in her chest. Had the Sanhedrin ordered *their* arrest as well, sending armed guards to apprehend them?

Tabitha's questions were cut short when all twelve apostles burst into the Upper Room, their eyes afire with excitement, broad grins stretched across their winsome faces. Simon Peter was leading the way.

Drawing a hand to her heart, Tabitha heard her own sharp, sudden intake of breath. Her ears rang as the previously quiet chamber erupted with gasps of surprise, along with shouts of joyful exclamation.

"The apostles have been released!"

"Our prayers are answered!"

"Hallelujah! Praise God!"

Mary immediately went to them, embracing her niece's husband in sheer relief. Tabitha stood watching the joyful reunion at a distance, her heart overflowing with gratitude. Slowly raising her eyes heavenward, she thanked the Lord for His goodness.

"Surprised?" Simon Peter grinned once Mary released him. "At least *this* group is happy to see us."

"Well, of course we are!" Mary laughed, her eyes bright and welcoming.

"I'm afraid that's far more than we can say about your chief guard—that doorkeeper of yours," Peter remarked. "I didn't think he was going to let us in."

Tabitha glimpsed her mistress's clouded expression and wished Peter had kept his observation to himself. And yet, to do so would be entirely unlike him. Peter's impulsivity rivaled her own. But she knew how Zev's refusal of the Way tore at her lady's heart. Oh, why must that impossible man be so stubborn? Was he utterly blind to reason?

"Simon! My Simon!" Anaia burst into the Upper Room then, laughing and crying as she threw her arms around her husband's neck. Swooping his wife off her feet, Peter held her close. When her small bare feet touched the ground again, she clung to his arm as if fearful to release him for even a moment. "I knew I heard your voice, Simon! I was so worried for you, so afraid for your safety—"

"We are safe, love," Simon Peter assured her, brushing her long dark hair behind her ear. "We are safe."

Smiling faintly, Tabitha watched the enthusiastic interaction between the apostles and the brethren, her heart brimming with gratitude. She couldn't even fathom the relief Anaia must be experiencing, having her husband safely home again. She had seen firsthand the agony the poor woman had endured during her husband's brief incarceration.

"Praise God."

Startled by his sudden nearness, Tabitha caught her breath as Stephanos drew alongside her, observing the happy scene along with her, obviously deeply moved. His chiseled profile appeared softer in the warm lamplight, his typically flashing eyes uncharacteristically wistful as he watched Peter consoling his anxious wife. Fleetingly, Tabitha wondered what it would be like to be loved by Stephanos, this brilliant evangelist so full of zeal and purpose. How did he truly feel about her? There were moments when his tender gaze nearly stole her breath away, moments when she felt certain he must care for her. But then she would engage in the same familiar mental argument, the one she now wearied of repeating. After all, if Stephanos desired a future with her, then surely he would have acted by now! Folding her arms and lifting her chin, Tabitha told herself she didn't care. Besides, she was far better off this way. Their oppressors sought to destroy every single follower of the Way, and Tabitha couldn't imagine the burden of worrying over a husband's safety in this cruel, uncertain world. Surely Anaia could vouch for that after a day like this one!

With great effort, Tabitha pulled her attention away from the attractive man beside her, directing it toward the apostles instead. She was desperately eager for an explanation regarding their unexpected appearance. And clearly, the followers now struggled to suppress their curiosity, as well. Clustering about the twelve apostles like a sea of buzzing bees swarming a hive, they released a volley of animated questions, filling the entire chamber with lively chatter.

Peter was telling the story, his eyes glowing in excitement, his hands moving rapidly in animated gestures. "And there we were, locked away in that cold stone cell, surrounded by criminals. Out of nowhere, a blinding light illuminated the entire cell, and a fierce angel of God stood before us. It was an awesome sight to behold."

"I will never forget that moment as long as I live," the Apostle John added, his eyes glistening with tears of gratitude and amazement. Several of the apostles murmured their agreement as Peter plunged forth with his dramatic narrative.

An angel? Astounded, Tabitha exchanged looks of wonderment with Stephanos as gasps of awe rippled through the entire gathering. A volley of lively questions was hurled toward the apostles once more. Tabitha noticed Mary still standing beside her niece and nephew by marriage, her lips curved in a soft, knowing smile. Yet again, Tabitha marveled at Mary's quiet strength. The woman remained a constant embodiment of peace, regardless of the feverish excitement rising in the chamber.

"What did the angel look like?"

"Were you afraid?"

"Were the criminals released along with you?"

"It was incredible," Peter admitted, smiling down at his pretty wife still clinging to his arm. "The prisoners slept through the entire thing. Even the rigid guards were oblivious to the blinding light and the angel's fearsome presence. The angel opened the gates for us at every checkpoint, and we walked right past every armed guard on the premises. They never saw a thing."

"I imagine they'll be in for a rude awakening when they eventually notice our absence," John declared, grinning broadly as his brother James slapped him loudly on the back.

"Oh, I imagine so," Peter agreed, a hint of mischief in his tone.

"Perhaps this will put a stop to all the persecution," Stephanos' good friend, Philip, suggested, standing near James, John, and the Lord's brother. "The Sanhedrin cannot deny this miracle."

"I disagree," Stephanos spoke up for the first time, his striking features exceedingly solemn.

Tabitha glanced at him sideways, somewhat peeved by his tidings of doom. Why couldn't he keep his annoying practicality to himself, rather than dousing the joy of the moment?

"If they can so easily deny our Lord's irrefutable resurrection, what's to keep them from denying *this*, as well?" Stephanos soberly explained. "I believe we must be on guard. This miracle will only further incite their wrath."

Miffed, Tabitha wished Stephanos had kept his depressing opinion to himself, even if it *was* true. Why dampen the wonder and joy of this miraculous moment? She was further piqued when joyful expressions grew instantly sober as the believers pondered this very real possibility.

"What must we do?" Anaia spoke at last, clearly

troubled.

"We must return," Peter responded without missing a beat. Crossing strong arms in front of his chest, Peter allowed his fiery gaze to sweep across those in the Upper Room, almost daring anyone to question his resolve.

"Return?" Anaia repeated, puzzled. "Return where?"

"To the Temple."

Anaia's former pallor returned full force, her wide eyes betraying her fear as the apostles were immediately bombarded with questions, just as they had expected to be.

"But why return to the Temple? To attend your own trial?"

"What if you're apprehended again?"

"The Sanhedrin isn't going to like this."

"Frankly, I don't care what the Sanhedrin likes or doesn't like," Peter interjected impatiently. "We must return. We don't have a choice."

"But why not?" This from gentle Philip, deeply concerned for his brethren.

Intrigued, Tabitha watched as the apostles exchanged knowing glances. Their postures visibly straightened as they drew courage from the miracle they had so recently experienced. Squaring broad shoulders, Peter turned to address the perplexed gathering. "When the angel released us from prison, he commanded us to return to the Temple to preach the gospel. It wasn't a suggestion. It was a direct order, and we intend to obey it."

"Well, it seems like a convenient arrangement— the Sanhedrin orders your arrest, then an angel sets you free," Philip grinned. "How many times do you think the high priest will lock you up before he catches on?"

Everyone laughed at Philip's lighthearted attempt to ease the tension in the room. Tabitha couldn't help but smile at the ridiculous concept. What she wouldn't give to witness the high priest's expression when he learned of the apostles' release!

"And if you're arrested again?" Anaia dared, clearly less convinced than Philip. "Or worse?"

"Then God will provide the strength to endure," Peter said firmly, squeezing her hand. "Jesus warned us this would happen, love," he added gently, intertwining his strong fingers with hers. "We must stand firm. God will be with us."

"He will never leave us or forsake us," John added quietly.

Closing her eyes, Tabitha attempted to draw strength from Peter and John's exhortation. Even so, she couldn't help but worry for those she loved so dearly. What if the Sanhedrin prevailed against them? What if the apostles were taken from them? She released a slow, shaky sigh...and then caught her breath in awe.

Unexpectedly, a strong, masculine hand sought hers. Warm fingers closed tightly about her own, willing her strength, support, and—dare she even think it—*love*?

Shocked to her very core, Tabitha opened her eyes, her gaze traveling toward her own captured hand. The hand now clasping hers was deeply tanned and beautifully formed, strong enough to bear up, yet gentle enough to tenderly caress.

Fighting to maintain her composure, Tabitha's heart pounded so frantically she was certain the entire gathering could hear it. Shyly lifting her gaze, her luminous hazel-green eyes met Stephanos', so filled with promise she could hardly breathe.

"Be still, beloved," he whispered, offering her his peace, his quiet strength. "God is our refuge and our fortress. He will not fail us—not in life, not in death. Eternity is ours because He lives."

Encouraged by his faith and receiving his quiet strength, Tabitha was amazed by the peace and joy coursing through her entire being, and not only because Stephanos had calmed her raging fears...

At long last, this daring man of God had made his intentions known!

CHAPTER 42

Mary

"Still burning the midnight oil, I see."

Glancing up from the parchment scrolls scattered across her desk, Mary smiled wanly, her gaze lifting toward the handsome evangelist propped against one of the large pillars at the entrance of the *bibliotheca*. "What with all the excitement tonight, sleep has evaded me," Mary admitted, carefully rolling up her scrolls before folding her hands patiently atop the wooden desk. "I keep thinking about the apostles and their courage. They intend to return to the Temple at first light, just as the angel commanded them. I have been praying for them without ceasing."

"As have I," Stephanos said with great feeling, crossing the mammoth office library and closing the yawning gap between them. Pausing before a gilded, straight-backed chair, he offered Mary a consoling smile.

"I offered you a guest room hoping you would finally get some rest," Mary observed ruefully, her lips tipping with good humor. "But it would seem something else is on your mind."

"I suppose it is," Stephanos admitted, lowering himself into the chair opposite Mary's desk. "Since sleep has evaded both of us, I believe the Lord may have presented the opportunity to discuss something that's been on my mind for quite some time now."

Tipping her head to one side, Mary folded her hands beneath her chin, intently studying the attractive young man before her. She had always admired Stephanos, for he possessed a passionate love for God, a burning zeal to serve Him wholeheartedly. Despite the fact that Stephanos was charismatic, intelligent, talented, and ridiculously good-looking, he remained ever humble, never considering himself "above" anyone else. His desire to further God's kingdom was evident, for he spent nearly every day frequenting popular synagogues and gathering places, boldly and unapologetically sharing the gospel with anyone willing to listen. Not only did he fearlessly preach the gospel amidst great opposition, he mentored dozens of new believers, setting a godly example for them in both word and action.

Now, for the first time since she'd met him, Mary noticed that Stephanos appeared visibly nervous. Even so, he plunged ahead, his eyes clear, his tone steady. "Mary, may I have a word with you?"

Mary nodded her gentle encouragement, both thrilling and mourning inwardly. Already, she knew what this was about. She had been expecting it for quite some time now. A smile teased the corners of her lips as she adjusted the flickering oil lamp on her desk.

"Go on, dear Stephanos. I am listening."

***

Tabitha

The rising sun teased the gold-washed peaks of the eastern hills as Tabitha stood alongside Candace and her husband Simon at Solomon's Porch, listening with rapt attention as the apostles addressed the rapidly growing gathering assembled beneath the magnificent, double-columned portico. The apostles' very public arrest of the previous day had been no secret, so naturally their audience demanded an explanation for this shocking, unforeseen appearance. This in turn provided the apostles a natural opportunity to testify about their miraculous, God-ordained release.

Tabitha smiled broadly as Simon Peter recounted their glorious encounter of the previous night—an astonishing rescue by a formidable angel of God. The great crowd of listeners was awestruck, unable to argue with the apostles' shocking testimony. After all, they had witnessed the violent arrest themselves, and they knew the Sanhedrin had not yet convened, much less secured the men's release. The apostles couldn't have possibly escaped the heavily guarded prison without the supernatural aid of God Himself. Now, many kneeled in repentance, weeping and begging the apostles to lead them in prayer. And all the while, the vast crowd grew and grew until men, women, and children spilled beyond the covered portico, straining forward, and craning their necks to hear the message preached.

"It does my heart good to see so many receiving Christ as their Savior," Candace observed, her brown eyes glistening with a soft sheen of tears.

Tabitha nodded, her heart nearly bursting with joy and gratitude. Not only had the Lord delivered her brethren from prison, He was now blessing their testimony and drawing hundreds more to Himself. Not only that, but the sweet memory of Stephanos taking her hand last night was still fresh in her mind. Try as she might, she couldn't suppress a happy smile at the recollection. Her color heightened as she considered the possibilities the future held for them.

"Now wait a minute," Candace declared, wheeling around to face Tabitha head on. "Simon, do you see that smile on her face?"

Tabitha's dreamy smile froze in place, her blissful reverie shattered.

"All right, Tabitha, what are you *not* telling us?" Candace demanded, taking her friend by the shoulders.

Blushing, Tabitha waved Candace's curiosity aside. "Haven't you ever seen me smile before?"

"Now what kind of question is that?" Candace teased, her eyes shining with joyful suspicion. "Of course, we've seen you smile before. But never like *that!*"

"I must admit, you do look radiant this morning, dear one," Simon agreed, drawing his wife a bit closer. "I think Candace is right."

"Well, of course, I'm right," Candace teased. "Now, confess. What is it you're not telling us?"

"There's nothing to confess," Tabitha insisted, mortified. But her conscience pricked, so she quickly amended, "Well, not really, anyway."

"It's about that good-looking evangelist, isn't it?" Candace grinned, squealing like a young girl. "I knew something was going on between the two of you. I've been praying ever since we spoke about it."

"Which evangelist?" Simon interrupted, clearly out of the loop.

"I know I'm right," Candace plowed ahead, playfully tweaking her friend's arm. "So don't bother trying to deny it, my friend."

Color deepening, Tabitha frantically scanned the growing multitude, desperately praying that Stephanos was completely out of earshot. Fortunately, she saw no sign of him. He must be near the front of the large gathering. Mary was somewhere among the crowd, as well, standing staunchly with her niece. Perhaps Stephanos had joined the two of them. But most likely, he was with his friend, Philip, or with James, the Lord's brother.

Drawing her attention back to Candace, Tabitha couldn't help but smile as her typically composed friend teased and cajoled. The young woman had appeared somewhat bereft upon her arrival at Solomon's Porch that morning, having entrusted her young sons to a relative's care in case danger arose at the Temple compound. Tabitha was glad Candace now had something to occupy her mind, even if the present topic was rather discomfiting.

"Well?" Candace prodded, abashedly recovering her peaceful demeanor when several nearby listeners glanced at them askance. "Just look at me now," she chuckled, shaking her graceful head. "Carrying on like a squealing girl! See what you've done to me, Tabitha?"

Tabitha laughed, warmed to her core by her friend's sincere enthusiasm. "As of yet, there is little to report. But I think our prayers have been answered, Candace. Last night, I was given reason to believe so."

"I want to hear all about it!"

When Tabitha's slanted eyes flickered self-consciously toward Simon, Candace nodded, discerning the reason for Tabitha's hesitation. The young maiden was reluctant to speak of such an intimate subject before another man.

"Ah, I understand." Candace chuckled knowingly, reaching out to squeeze Tabitha's hand. "Later, then. But don't you dare forget!"

***

Alexander

The crackling tension within the magnificent Royal Stoa was so thick Alexander was quite certain one could have easily sliced it with a knife. Self-important members of the Sanhedrin were already seated upon their designated gilded chairs, their stiff religious garb further exaggerating their pompous and overstated appearance. At the very center of the enormous semi-circular pattern of straight-backed chairs lining the central apse sat the high priest in his gold-plated, throne-like chair, situated majestically upon an elevated golden dais framed by velvety, blood-red tapestries.

Strategically seated at his makeshift wooden desk

before the Council just opposite his fellow stenographer, Alexander feigned readying his tablet and writing instruments while discreetly deciphering the body language and expressions of each member of the Council. His master, Caiaphas, appeared as formidable as ever, eager to inflict punishment upon the troublesome sect now threatening his power and position. Seated at his right and left hand, the *Nasi* and the *Av Bet Din* presented a fascinating study in contrasts. While the famously lenient *Nasi* appeared thoughtfully concerned, the rigid *Av Bet Din* leaned forward in his chair, his dark eyes gleaming dangerously, clearly relishing the apostles' inevitable demise. Caiaphas' notorious father-in-law and former high priest, Annas, was also present with several of his sons. The aging man sat rigidly in his chair, his eyes smoldering with diabolical hatred. Despite his declining health, Annas remained as dangerous and volatile as ever, his dreadful presence daring anyone to challenge him and suffer the consequences.

In stark contrast to the majority of the Council, Nicodemus and Joseph of Arimathea carried themselves with sober confidence, their postures straight and their shoulders held high even as they remained seated in their designated places. Alexander admired the brass of both men, for they clung to their faith in Christ despite fierce opposition. Joseph, a fiery man with a bold and daring temperament, forbade anyone to challenge his convictions with a mere flash of his blazing dark eyes. Nicodemus, on the other hand, carried himself in a meek, humble manner, gently reasoning with his fellow councilmen. Alexander assumed the Great Sanhedrin had not yet eliminated either man, considering Nicodemus far too gentle to pose a threat, and Joseph of Arimathea far too formidable. The fact that both men were among the wealthiest and most powerful figures of Judea also provided sufficient reason to make even the Great Sanhedrin think twice before taking action against them. *No, they far prefer pouncing upon hapless unknowns, Alexander* thought, suppressing a sardonic curve of his lips. *Those too helpless, too poor, too insignificant to create any dangerous repercussions upon their groundless demise.*

For all the grand pomp, ceremony, and splendor of the high priest and the Great Sanhedrin, Alexander knew most of them were spineless cowards, quick to pounce upon the meek and defenseless. Shamelessly, they straddled the fence erected between government and religion, groveling before steel-fisted Romans, catering to the whims of a godless empire to maintain illusions of power and control.

Forcing his thoughts back to the present, Alexander's gaze casually swept the three rows of twenty-three religious scholars seated rigidly on the cool, mosaic tiles before the convening Council. His keen eyes swiftly detected Saul, a steadily rising archnemesis of the Way. Alexander had encountered the pompous young Pharisee only once in the house of Caiaphas, and that was one too many times, in his opinion. Lips tipping somewhat ruefully, Alexander couldn't help but compare Saul to himself before he had received Christ as his Savior. In a strange way, Saul was something like a religious version of whom Alexander had once been—arrogant, maddeningly antagonizing, brimming with pride, relishing the discomfort of others. Fully aware of his own charisma and strikingly good looks, Alexander had once considered himself a gift of the gods to women—until he came face to face with the one true God, discovering his own glaring failures and shortcomings. Though Saul was no ladies' man, he certainly thought highly of himself, considering himself far above most piteous mortals.

Dismissing his brooding thoughts, Alexander readied himself for the impending trial, praying silently for the apostles' safety. Reaching for his stylus of choice, he tapped it a bit impatiently upon his desk, earning a menacing glare from the high priest. Instantly regretting that decision, Alexander dipped his head in an overdone gesture of submission, laughing inwardly as he did so. If Joseph Caiaphas only knew that his privileged manservant had infiltrated his innermost ranks!

As the time dragged by, the thunderous silence filling the marble hall possessed a deeper and more ominous quality as the high priest—tense and drawn—awaited the prisoners' appearance. Alexander was certain the same question resounded loudly within the mind of every man present.

What on earth was taking so long?

The sound of pounding, hobnailed sandals eating up the distance between the lengthy hall and the central apse where the Sanhedrin now convened filled the entire stoa, resonating throughout the grand chamber and bouncing off the marble walls, swiftly drawing Joseph Caiaphas to his elegantly sandaled feet. Alexander watched with great interest as an entourage of officers burst into view, breathless and visibly unsettled. Alexander's spine stiffened as Lucius—a despicable cretin in his own estimation—emerged at the forefront, his strained features uncharacteristically pale, his typically iron grip trembling slightly as he clutched the hilt of his gladius.

"Well?" Caiaphas demanded, his luxurious robes sweeping about the dais while he paced in fierce agitation. "Where are my prisoners, soldier?"

"The prisoners have...uh, well..."

"Speak up, for heaven's sake!"

"They've disappeared, sir."

Caiaphas' entire body went rigid as the basilica erupted with gasps and hushed conversation passed between members of the Council. "What do you mean, *disappeared?*" the high priest demanded, his cold gray eyes narrowing in outrage.

It took every ounce of self-control Alexander possessed to refrain from leaning forward in his chair. Instead, he donned the emotionless expression of a household servant, chronicling the events on his tablet with a practiced air of boredom.

"The prison was securely shut, my lord," Lucius responded, clearing his throat in discomfort. "Armed guards remained stationed at every gate, every door, every checkpoint. But once we reached the prisoners' cell, they had vanished without a trace."

Biting back a grin of triumph, Alexander gleefully recalled Lucius' concealed panic the morning he had failed to keep the resurrected Lord inside His tomb, despite drastic security measures and a slew of armed mercenaries on loan from Pontius Pilate. It would seem the Roman soldier was having no better luck keeping the apostles inside their cell! Perhaps Lucius was now recalling that unfortunate little mark on his service record, as well. Suppressing his amusement, Alexander wondered if the thick-headed soldier was tiring of this endless game of cat and mouse...

Ignoring the taut-faced soldier standing at attention before him, Caiaphas exchanged a meaningful look with the captain of the Temple, who, moments prior, had been leaning indolently upon a nearby pillar. Now, the fierce officer straightened to his full height, his swarthy countenance blazing as he clutched a deadly looking spear. But before Caiaphas or the captain of the Temple could further question Lucius and his entourage, a disgruntled Temple guard burst onto the scene, his chest heaving, his leather garments drenched in sweat as he steadied himself with the thick rod of his spear.

"My lord!" he rasped with an awkward, exaggerated bow in the general direction of the high priest.

"I demand to know the cause for the untimely interruption of this sacred assembly," Caiaphas ground out through gritted teeth, his swiftly darkening countenance fearsome to behold.

Visibly shaken, the Temple guard straightened as best he could, swiping at the beads of perspiration dotting his brow. "It's the men we arrested yesterday, my lord—the very ones whom you imprisoned!"

"What of them?" Caiaphas spat out roughly, his gray eyes flashing dangerous fire.

"My lord, the apostles are *here*, instructing the people at Solomon's Porch!"

Alexander hid a knowing grin as Joseph Caiaphas nearly strangled.

"WHAT?!" Slamming around to face the unfortunate temple guard, the high priest's cry of indignation echoed sharply throughout the vast chamber, reverberating off the imposing marble walls.

CHAPTER 43

Mary

"Make way! Make way by order of the high priest!"

Releasing a silent plea for divine intervention, Mary felt rather than saw Anaia stiffen beside her. Reaching for her niece's hand, Mary winced as Anaia's fingernails dug into her palm.

"Oh, Mary, not again," Anaia moaned as the redoubtable captain of the Temple guard roughly shoved his way through the throng, coming face to face with the immovable Apostle Peter. Stationed at the front of the crowd, Mary was riveted by the scene. For there stood Simon Peter, a powerful unbending force, facing off the captain of the Temple guard, undoubtedly a worthy opponent. And though the captain of the guard possessed every possible worldly advantage—brute force, deadly weapons, and an entire fleet of skilled Temple officers at his disposal, not to mention the support of the indomitable Great Sanhedrin—it was the staunch form of Simon Peter, a simple fisherman, which appeared the most formidable. Instinctively, Mary knew it was because the otherwise insignificant Galilean was powered by the very Spirit of God. And if God be for him, who could possibly be against him? Clasping her hands before her, Mary's lips moved in silent prayer even as her eyes absorbed every detail of the unfolding drama.

Gasps of surprise and cries of frustration rippled through the crowd as a league of armed temple guards pushed insistently through the gathering, marching straight down the middle of the crowd. Donning formidable uniforms, their weapons sharpened and gleaming, they created an imposing sight, indeed. Even so, one look at the twelve apostles convinced the uneasy crowd that these bold men were completely unfazed by the guards' pompous and unnecessary show of strength.

As the fierce guards encircled the Twelve, the crowd grew dangerously unruly, emboldened by the apostles' calm demeanors and their miraculous release of the previous night.

"What are you, blind? Can't you see the hand of God upon these men?"

"Exactly how many times do you plan to arrest them, officers?"

"Don't you know when you've been bested?"

The crowd rocked and swayed, shouting violently and shaking their fists, clearly on the verge of revolt. Sensing the danger of a mob of such massive proportions, the captain of the guard held up a commanding hand. "Enough! As you can see, we have done these men no harm."

"And that's no credit to you," a man hidden among the crowd shouted in accusation. "You couldn't even keep them in their cell!"

The captain's dark features became mottled with fury as the crowd roared with laughter. Even so, Caiaphas would have his head if his own recklessness instigated a riot. By some miracle, the captain held his peace.

Heart pounding in her chest, Mary watched in amazement as the captain, ignoring the throng, addressed Simon Peter instead. "The high priest requests an audience with you and your men," he said, his tone dangerously low, his black eyes daring Peter to object.

"*Requests?*" Peter repeated in amusement, cocking his head to one side in mock question. "Since when has the high priest issued a polite request to any of us?"

Mary heard Anaia catch her breath at her husband's candid observation as a muscle jerked in the captain's hardened jawline. Drawing a calming breath, he said coldly, "Shall I inform the high priest that you have rejected his invitation?"

Exchanging a knowing look with his fellow apostles, Peter met the captain's fiery gaze head on. "Absolutely not," he replied casually, eliciting great interest from the crowd. "You may tell the high priest that we shall acquiesce to his *request*. After all..." Peter paused, his dark eyes glinting with mischief. "It's always nice to be asked."

***

Tabitha

Tabitha watched in amazement as the Temple guards led the apostles past the crowd without even a hint of violence. The grim-faced officers hadn't even bothered to bind the apostles' hands this time. The Twelve allowed the guards to usher them away, strolling calmly, casually, of their own accord.

"What has changed?" Tabitha dared, turning questioning eyes toward Simon and Candace. "The guards treated them like human beings!" Recalling Philip's hopeful suggestion, she wondered if perhaps he had been right. Perhaps the Council, fearing supernatural repercussions, had finally decided to back off.

"Caiaphas is shrewd," Simon responded grimly, shattering Tabitha's hopeful reverie. "Should he arrest the apostles after so great a miracle, the people would most certainly revolt."

Silently, Tabitha thanked God so many believers had rallied in support of their brethren. What if they had dismissed that still small voice within prompting them to courageously stand beside the afflicted? How different the outcome might have been!

"We must continue to pray for their safety," Simon added grimly, interrupting Tabitha's train of thought.

"But they were apprehended without violence," Candace pointed out, perplexed. "Is that not reason to rejoice?"

Simon's gentle eyes conveyed his deep concern. A quiet man by nature, he seldom spoke. But when he did, his words rang true. "Joseph Caiaphas is a serpent in priestly robes, and our brothers have humiliated him before the entire nation."

"Simon," Candace said softly, her lovely dark eyes betraying her concern. "What are you saying?"

"Of this we can be sure," Simon said grimly, the

eyes of both women resting upon his careworn features. "The high priest will find a way to vent his wrath, to inflict his revenge."

***

Alexander

"Did we not strictly command you *not* to teach in the name of your wretched, so-called Christ?" Caiaphas' voice rang out over the marble hall, his gray eyes filled with the turbulence of a dangerous, raging sea.

Alexander's stylus flew across his tablet as the apostles stood staunchly before the Council, unperturbed even as the high priest glowered down at them from his "throne" upon the dais. Snatching a quick glance between his notes, Alexander observed the stern, uncompromising manner of the high priest, the somewhat cautious expressions upon the faces of the elders, and the unveiled astonishment of Gamaliel, the president of the Sanhedrin. Seated before the Council, the religious scholars watched in rapt attention, clearly amazed by the Twelve, though their sense of self-preservation required them to mask their great interest. The one exception among the fascinated scholars was Saul, whose stiff form radiated both tension and scarcely harnessed rage, his dark eyes glittering in fury. Alexander was quite certain the young Pharisee would have gladly torn the apostles apart, limb from limb, with his bare hands had he been granted the privilege to do so.

"You have filled Jerusalem with your wretched doctrine," Caiaphas spat, stretching forth one arm as if to encompass the entire city, the billowing sleeves of his elaborate robes swishing majestically as he did so. "And now you intend to bring the blood of this dead Man upon us!"

Instantly, Alexander recalled another time, another place. Jesus had stood upon the platform with Pontius Pilate and a fierce revolutionary named Barabbas, His bruised and bloodied form unrecognizable after many savage beatings. Pilate had repeatedly declared the Savior's innocence, and yet the Jews had refused to accept his verdict. Amidst the savage roar of the bloodthirsty mob, Pilate had once more proclaimed Jesus' innocence, symbolically washing his hands of the entire ordeal: *"As for me, I am innocent of the blood of this Man."* And Joseph Caiaphas had led the hellish cry of the rabid, blood-lusting mob: *"His blood be upon us and our children!"*

Driven by burning hatred, the high priest had brought innocent blood upon his own head—by his own free will. He needn't any help from the apostles to do so.

Alexander's mouth formed a thin, grim line as he recalled the diabolical events of that fearsome day— the day the armies of Heaven clashed against the forces of evil in a cosmic battle for the souls of men. The day Jesus Christ willingly laid down His life for the sake of all mankind. By His tortuous death on the cross, all who embraced His merciful sacrifice were freed from the power of death. And the keys of death and destruction were snatched from the devil's cruel grasp, further inciting his malevolent rage. On that fateful day, the earth quaked and the elements raged as the enemy of God unleashed his burning torment upon the Lord's Anointed and all who embraced His name.

Turning his attention back to his tablet, Alexander drew a steadying breath. If only they had known that day was just the beginning. The war against the saints had only just begun, and the devil raged against them like a roaring lion, determined to devour anyone in his path.

Shaken by dark recollections, Alexander bowed his head, convinced a wave of persecution unlike anything they had ever seen was just around the corner.

God, grant us strength. Heaven knows we're going to need it.

CHAPTER 44

Mary

As the hours dragged by, Mary noticed Anaia's mounting tension. Even so, the brave young bride participated with her fellow believers as they busied themselves at Solomon's Porch, praying for the apostles and instructing new believers.

"I've received word."

Mary turned to face a beaming Stephanos, his handsome features alight with a broad grin. "What have you learned?" she asked, her heart racing.

Swerving around to face the evangelist, Anaia's entire countenance brightened with hope. "Please tell me they are all right."

Anaia flinched when Stephanos unexpectedly clapped his hands loudly together, garnering the attention of those remaining at Solomon's Porch. "Everyone! Everyone, may I have your attention, please?"

Surprisingly, the crowd quieted, eagerly awaiting Stephanos' pronouncement.

Raising his fists in triumph, Stephanos shouted boldly, "The apostles will be released!"

Anaia nearly wilted in relief, falling into Mary's open arms as the crowd erupted with joyous cheers and heartfelt applause. Mary held her niece close, far more relieved than she cared to admit. *Thank You, gracious Father,* she prayed. *You have delivered us once again.*

Drawing strength from her staunch aunt, Anaia pulled away, turning toward Stephanos once more. "When will they be freed?"

"Soon, I would imagine. It would seem one of the most respected Pharisees dissuaded the others from detaining them."

"Which Pharisee?" Mary asked, intrigued. "Joseph? Or Nicodemus, perhaps?"

"I'm sure we'll find out soon enough," Stephanos responded with an easy smile. "For now, we can rejoice over yet another victory."

"I should send word to the staff," Mary decided, recognizing the apostles would most likely be tired and hungry after facing the Great Sanhedrin. "I shall ask Tabitha to return to the villa to alert the staff and make all the arrangements."

***

Tabitha

Hastening toward the Upper City villa, Tabitha crossed the magnificent viaduct spanning the Tyropoeon Valley, descending near the ancient Hasmonean Palace. As her destination awaited her at the far opposite end of the Upper City, Tabitha quickened her pace, taking a secluded back alley rather than the congested main thoroughfare. The apostles had endured a challenging day, and she intended to have Mary's house in order with the baths prepared, the guest rooms readied, and steaming hot meals awaiting them upon their arrival. Speed was of the utmost importance, and she hadn't time to push through throngs of people, nor wait for heavily laden wagons, carriages, or lumbering manservants bearing rich men's litters to pass before her.

The intense afternoon heat soaked through Tabitha's clothing, despite the shade provided by the dim, heavily shadowed alley she now traveled. Fanning her face with one end of her shawl, Tabitha shook her head in annoyance before jerking the pesky covering entirely off her head. After all, who was going to see her in this secluded alleyway far removed from the bustling city streets? She would discreetly replace her shawl once she reached the open avenue on the other side.

Sighing in contentment, Tabitha resumed her hurried pace, enjoying the cool breeze upon her face as her thick mane of honey-gold curls spilled down her back and billowed around her shoulders. What a blessed relief from the afternoon heat! Winter was nearly upon them, and yet the sun continued to blaze as if completely uninformed about the changing seasons. Tabitha hoped the early winter month of *Kislev* would usher in much cooler weather along with the feverishly patriotic Feast of Dedication.

"Hey there, sweetheart. Why the hurry?"

Tabitha froze at the sound of an accented male voice drawling directly behind her, mentally kicking herself for her carelessness. She knew better than to travel these secluded alleyways alone! How could she have been so foolish?

Turning slowly on her heel, Tabitha's blood grew cold as a dashing Roman soldier approached her—the bold, blue-eyed Briton she had glimpsed at the market with Mary. She'd seen him about the city several times since that uncomfortable encounter. Each time, he had studied her boldly, brazenly, without apology.

As he did so now, approaching her with a roguish grin broadening his rugged jawline. "You're a sight for sore eyes. What's your name, gorgeous?"

Instinctively, Tabitha drew her shawl over her head. Poised like a doe ready to take flight, she quickly scanned her surroundings. Wedged between an unforgiving stone wall and a long row of interconnected structures, shielded overhead by open awnings, there was little hope of escape. Had she any tools of self-defense readily available? Her eyes landed upon a heavy, upturned urn near the back of a stone structure, but that was certainly no match for a powerful man equipped with a sword and gladius. Her best chance was to run like the wind, screaming while doing so. The moment she broke free of the darkened alley, she would most certainly encounter numerous passersby capable of rendering aid. But would they interfere if confronted by the Roman soldier?

Why, oh why, had she chosen to travel alone? She had known better. Candace and Simon would have gladly accompanied her had she bothered to inform them of her plans. But no, she had been in such a confounded hurry to reach Mary's house that she had taken leave of her senses.

She hoped it would not cost her life or her innocence.

Gracious Father, forgive me for foolishly placing myself in harm's way. Please, deliver me. Heart racing, Tabitha could hear her own steady pulse pounding loudly in her ears. The soldier's uniform *clink-clink-clinked* in cadence to his eager steps as he drew closer, his grin broadening as he avariciously eyed his prize.

"Darling, how many times must I remind you to travel the main thoroughfare?"

Relief coursed through Tabitha's entire being when the familiar voice of her beloved Stephanos filled her sharpened senses. She saw the soldier stiffen before her, his cold blue eyes narrowing, as the brassy evangelist approached her from behind, having entered the opposite end of the alley.

"I thought I'd never find you," Stephanos lectured fondly, drawing alongside a trembling Tabitha. Pulling her close, Stephanos met the soldier's gaze and extended his hand. "I cannot thank you enough for locating my betrothed, officer," he said sincerely, throwing the soldier into a fit of confusion.

The Roman's inner struggle was obvious as he mentally weighed his options. On the one hand, he could accept this Jew's gratitude for "locating" his missing bride and simply move on, avoiding any charges that would most certainly be brought against him should he defile another man's wife, Jewish or not. Or he could fight for the prize he desired—the lovely blonde maiden now clinging to the arm of her groom.

The soldier measured Stephanos evenly, assessing his grit and ability. The Jew was tall and well-built with a swarthy complexion, flashing eyes, and a fiery persona...surely one to be reckoned with. Though the armed Roman clearly had the upper hand, his better judgment won over his desire. His eyes flickered over Tabitha briefly as he responded coldly, "Be on your way, Jew."

"Good day to you, officer," Stephanos responded cheerfully, taking Tabitha's arm and gently guiding her down the alleyway. When they emerged at the other end, Tabitha squinted against the shocking sunshine greeting them like a blinding beacon. Overwhelmed with relief at the sight of heavily traveled marble avenues, Tabitha turned to Stephanos and fell into his arms, far too relieved to care about the curious pedestrians eyeing them smugly as they passed.

"Oh, Stephanos," she breathed, shuddering slightly. "Thank God you found me. How did you know?"

Stephanos held her, bending to plant a kiss atop her covered head. "You left the compound alone, and I grew concerned."

With her head pressed against his sturdy chest, Tabitha realized she could hear the steady beat of his heart. Her own pulse quickened, recognizing their nearness for the first time. Drawing back in embarrassment, she lifted her face toward him. "Thank you for coming to my rescue, Stephanos." She could hardly believe he had faced an armed Roman on her behalf!

"Gladly, but let's not make a habit of that, shall we?" he responded easily, playfully tweaking her shoulder.

"I've never been more relieved to see another human being in my entire life," Tabitha admitted.

"And you resolved the entire issue without violence. Thank you, Stephanos. Had you not arrived, I don't know what might have happened."

"I'd prefer not to think about that."

"Yes, I wouldn't have wanted to hurt him," Tabitha remarked honestly.

Looking at her in shock, Stephanos burst into hearty laughter.

Tabitha glared at him in annoyance. "You don't think I could have defended myself?" she huffed, her irritation evident.

"Tabitha, he was *armed*!"

"You forget I survived on the streets for months as a child," she reminded him, proudly lifting her chin.

"Ah, that you did," Stephanos grinned, pausing amidst the broad, palm-lined street. "And I'm so thankful that you did, beloved."

Coloring self-consciously, Tabitha looked away, disturbed by the powerful feelings this handsome young man aroused in her. One moment, she was livid with frustration toward him. And the next, she found herself desiring to melt into his strong arms. What was wrong with her, anyway? Dismissing her contrary emotions, she attempted to reclaim her irritation with him. After all, that was a far safer emotion.

But Stephanos reached for her shoulders then, shattering her reserve as he drew her close to him. His hands glided lightly down her arms before taking her hands in his. "There's something you should know. I spoke the truth back there in the alleyway, Tabitha."

Raising her eyes in confusion, Tabitha searched

his handsome face. "The truth?"

"Yes." Stephanos' dark eyes softened, becoming so tender she felt frozen in place. Any hint of irritation she had previously felt evaporated instantly. "I hadn't wished to tell you yet," Stephanos explained. "Not here, not now. But I wouldn't have you consider me a dishonest man."

"Stephanos, I could never—"

"I spoke with Mary, and she has given us her blessing. You truly *are* my betrothed, Tabitha. And I am indeed your bridegroom—if you'll have me."

Tabitha's entire world reeled in an instant. She, Tabitha, his *betrothed*? And Stephanos, *her* bridegroom?

"So..." Stephanos smiled broadly, his striking features transformed with joy and anticipation. "Will you have me?"

Heart constricting in her chest, Tabitha looked down and saw that Stephanos still held her hands captive. For a moment, she struggled to breathe. Desire mingling with fear coursed through her entire being. What would it be like to love this man, to share his home and bear his children? What would it be like to give herself entirely to him? Fleetingly, she thought of Anaia and the agony the poor woman had recently endured as her husband was repeatedly hunted down by the high priest and the Great Sanhedrin. Did she, Tabitha, have the strength to endure such grievous trials?

Lifting her gaze, she locked eyes with the fiery evangelist she had slowly, surely, grown to love. And in that moment, she knew. To deny her love for Stephanos was hopelessly futile. It was far too late to protect her heart now. It already belonged to him.

Turning her attention to her beloved, Tabitha realized his expression had slowly morphed from joyous excitement to hopeful expectance, and now his countenance reflected his deep concern. Gently lifting her chin, he looked deeply into her eyes. "I love you, Tabitha. I love your heart for God, your passion to serve, your godly perseverance. I love your eyes, the curve of your smile, your silvery laughter. Honestly, I never thought I would marry. But when our gracious God brought us together, I knew I could no longer fight against it. I want to *marry* you, Tabitha. I want to hold you, to treasure you, to comfort you and rejoice with you, facing the joys and challenges of this life together as one flesh. So I am asking, humbly, once again. Will you have me?"

Pierced to the heart by Stephanos' profession of love for her, Tabitha lifted her hand, tracing the firm curve of his strong jawline. Eyes gleaming with a soft sheen of tears, she managed a wobbly smile. "I thought you'd never ask."

Laughing in sheer relief, Stephanos took her hand and kissed it.

CHAPTER 45

Tabitha

Everything was prepared and the villa was in perfect order when the apostles arrived that evening, but Tabitha was completely unprepared for the sight that met her eyes upon their late arrival.

The Twelve filed into the cheery villa with the assistance of their fellow brethren, leaning heavily upon them for support. Bodies bruised and swollen, their torn and bloodied clothing bespoke the brutality they had endured.

Stifling a gasp, Tabitha rushed for Mary, who was steadying a weeping Anaia. The poor woman stumbled alongside her husband, who, like the other apostles, was clearly faint from trauma and loss of blood. "My lady! What has happened?"

"The Sanhedrin ordered their punishment—thirty-nine lashes for their 'disobedience,' before releasing them," Mary said, her gray eyes flashing angry fire despite her composed demeanor.

"No!" Tabitha gasped. "And the people allowed

it?"

"The people didn't know," Mary responded tiredly, helping Anaia ease her husband onto a chair. Peter groaned as the chair brushed against torn, inflamed flesh. "It was done secretly, quietly. The Sanhedrin feared an uprising should their actions be made known."

"We waited for hours," Anaia wept bitterly, kneeling beside her grimacing husband. "We didn't know what had happened or where they had been taken."

Watching in horror as the injured men were gently lowered onto chairs, Tabitha's heart was pierced by their groans of anguish. Thirty-nine lashes... it wasn't entirely uncommon for a man to perish during the cruel method of torturous "punishment". Though the whip of the Jews was far less barbaric than that of the Romans' frightful instrument of punishment, to be scourged was an excruciating ordeal. Some perished days or weeks later, their open wounds festering with deadly infections. Others suffered for weeks or months on end as bone-deep cuts reopened at their slightest movement, refusing to heal. Forcing herself to assess the damage, Tabitha saw that the backs of the apostles' robes were in tatters, still seeping with fresh blood. Even the back of their shirtsleeves had suffered the sting of the whip. Tabitha realized they all needed medical attention. Immediately. They would also require new garments, as theirs were now stained and shredded beyond repair. It would seem the warm baths and steaming hot meals would have to wait.

Springing into action as she had seen her mistress do on countless occasions, Tabitha said quickly, "I'll alert the staff about the change of plans. First, we must tend to these wounds. We will need salve, warm water, and bandages."

"Thank you, Tabitha," Mary said, her eyes conveying her deep appreciation. Kneeling in front of Simon Peter, she touched his knee. "How are you holding up, beloved?"

Peter managed a grimacing smile. "We're grateful," he responded faintly.

"Grateful you survived?"

"Grateful to be counted worthy to suffer shame for His name," Peter managed, wincing as Anaia opened the back of his tunic to get a better look at his oozing stripes. "Grateful I did not deny Him amidst bitter torture. It was my greatest fear—the fear of denying Him again—but He supplied the strength." The sheen of tears sparkling in his dark eyes brought tears to Mary's own as he managed brokenly, "Praise our God."

As Tabitha directed dozens of servants into the reception hall, bearing pitchers of warm water, salve, and bandages, Mary watched as the women who had returned with them swung into action, taking up the medical supplies and tending the painful wounds.

Rising to her feet, Mary prepared to join the women in their cause. Tabitha drew alongside her, shaking her head in righteous anger. "I can't believe the Sanhedrin would do this. Will they be all right, my lady?"

"We must pray, Tabitha," Mary answered honestly. "If infection sets in..." her voice trailed off, for she was loathe to voice the dreadful possibilities. "If only we had a doctor among us—"

"A doctor, you say?"

Both Mary and Tabitha's heads came up as a familiar, smiling young man emerged from the vestibule, a large leather satchel in hand.

"It would seem your God really does answer prayers."

"Doctor Luke!" Mary shook her head in utter disbelief as relief flooded her entire being. "How did you know we were in need?"

"Actually, I didn't." Luke grinned, setting down his bag. "But it would seem my timing is impeccable."

"The *Lord's* timing is impeccable," Mary responded, exchanging a knowing look with Tabitha, "And your fortunate timing, dear Luke, is undeniable proof. Thank you, sir, for heeding His call."

"Quite frankly, I had no idea I was doing so," Luke admitted, smiling wanly. "Even so, I'm happy to help." Rolling up the fitted sleeves of his tunic, the kind doctor lifted his bag and cheerfully set to work, immediately setting the exhausted, pain-ravaged apostles at ease with his calm manner and willing smile.

***

"He's really something, isn't he?"

Tabitha smiled faintly as Stephanos drew alongside her, watching in fascination as the kindly doctor picked up his satchel, following Mary and Tobias for a quick debriefing in the *bibliotheca*. The apostles had been treated, their wounds carefully cleansed and properly bound. After bedding them down for the night, Luke had given each of them strict instructions about how they were to conduct themselves throughout the healing process—no sudden movements, no physical exertion, and "no argument," he had added, his brown eyes twinkling with mischief. He'd explained that he would need to remove the bandages often to cleanse and reexamine the wounds to safeguard against infection. Within a few weeks, they should be good as new.

Impatient to carry on with their preaching, the apostles naturally balked against his instructions. But Luke calmly reminded them that they would be convalesced far longer should they infect or reopen their angry wounds.

Turning to survey the lovely young woman, his betrothed, standing beside him in the reception hall, Stephanos' features softened. "You look dead on your feet, beloved. Come, rest a moment."

Smiling to herself, Tabitha allowed Stephanos to guide her to a chair and gently lower her into it. Seating himself beside her, he took her hand in his. Tabitha wondered if she would ever get used to having someone fuss over her so. It was an entirely new experience for one accustomed to taking care of herself.

"The doctor's arrival was a gift from God," Tabitha remarked, her heart racing as Stephanos' warm grip tightened. "Had he not arrived tonight, the apostles' recovery would be uncertain, at best."

"God's timing is always perfect," Stephanos agreed. "I still correspond with the good doctor quite frequently by letter, and I knew he intended to visit your lady once he arrived for the Feast of Dedication. He wished to thank Mary in person for funding his practice. But I certainly did not expect him to arrive so soon."

"Isn't the Lord amazing?" Tabitha breathed, shaking her head in amazement. "When the Holy Spirit prompted Mary to fund Luke's practice, she hadn't the slightest idea that God would use her generosity to draw Luke back to us the moment he was needed most. It truly *is* more blessed to give than to receive."

"Sometimes, we forget that God's commandments are *for our good*. We balk when He requires us to tithe, to part with our cherished earnings, or to give to those in need. But ultimately, it's for our good that He requires it. Had Mary refused to obey the Holy Spirit's prompting, Luke most certainly would not have been here to tend our brothers' wounds. And any doctor we might stumble upon here in Judea would surely refuse to treat the apostles, fearing the Sanhedrin's wrath."

"I suppose that principle applies in every area of our lives," Tabitha mused, reveling in the great wisdom of this godly man the Lord had so graciously brought into her life. "Obedience to God results in our ultimate good, as well as the good of others."

"Amen to that," Stephanos agreed, a smile in his eyes.

Tabitha's cheeks warmed as the two of them shared a meaningful expression. She was discovering that they had much in common. Both were consumed with zeal for the Lord and a desire to reach the lost, though Tabitha had to admit that Stephanos was even more passionate and far bolder than she. At times, she was convinced he was totally fearless. Several times, she had witnessed him standing up to Saul in the synagogue, boldly declaring the Way of life, utterly unperturbed by Saul's dark expressions or shocking threats.

Biting her lower lip, Tabitha closed her eyes, attempting to suppress frightful images of the apostles' agonized expressions, their oozing stripes, their bloodstained, tattered garments... and their uncompromising determination to return to the Temple to preach the gospel yet again. Their punishments severely increased with each "offense" committed against the Sanhedrin. Tabitha didn't even want to consider what might happen to them next. Would they, too, eventually be crucified as their Lord had been?

Clasping Tabitha's free hand, Stephanos lowered his head so that he was eye-level with his beloved. "What troubles you, dear one?"

"I wish I had more faith," Tabitha admitted, looking away in shame as her eyes filled with a soft sheen of tears.

"Beloved, I have seen your faith in action."

"At times, yes. But then there are other days—days like *this*—when I am filled with fear and doubt." Lifting teary eyes to her betrothed, Tabitha whispered hoarsely, "You preach as boldly as any of the apostles, performing signs and wonders by the power of the Holy Spirit, just as they do. What if the Sanhedrin comes after you, as well?"

Eyes softening in tender understanding, Stephanos smiled gently. "How did our Lord instruct us pertaining to *worry*, beloved?"

"*Do not worry about tomorrow*," Tabitha recited rather mechanically, little comforted.

"That's right," Stephanos said with a knowing smile. "We cannot possibly know what the future holds, but we do know that our God holds each of us in the palm of His mighty hand. His will prevails with each of His children. If He calls us to hardship of any kind, then He grants us strength to bear it."

"But how..." Tabitha dared, her coloring deepening as she ventured shyly, "how could I possibly bear losing you, Stephanos?"

Tenderly cupping her face with a strong hand, Stephanos said with great conviction, "You can do all things through Christ, beloved. God does not call us without first equipping us. Whatever trials or hardships may come, God knows what He is doing. He knows what is best. Believing this, we must entrust both our lives and our loved ones to Him, treasuring every sacred moment He gives. Why cloud the wonder and beauty of today with the doubts and fears of tomorrow? If we live our lives anxiously about what may come, then we forfeit the precious gift God has given us in this present moment, the moment we now share."

Closing her eyes tightly, Tabitha nodded her understanding as her tears traced two slender lines down both cheeks. Drawing strength from Stephanos' grasp and leaning into his touch, she willed to do as he proposed. She refused to relinquish the blessings of today by stewing about the *what ifs* of tomorrow. Instead, she would savor this present moment—the strength and tenderness of her beloved's voice, the warmth of his touch, the promise in his eyes, and the unshakable knowledge that her God was faithful. Deep in her heart, Tabitha knew He could be trusted—yesterday, today, and forever.

CHAPTER 46

Mary

Slipping cautiously out the back door used by the kitchen staff, Mary lifted her face heavenward, basking in the balmy night air. The cool nighttime breezes whispered softly about her frame, soothing her hot face and teasing her elegant garments. She desperately needed this moment of solitude, this moment of communion with God.

It had been an incredibly long, trying day. And yet the Lord had showered His people with tender mercies, sparing the lives of the apostles and providing the help of a benevolent doctor the moment help was needed. She had enjoyed her meeting with Luke and Tobias despite her intense weariness. Even with his impressive credentials, extensive knowledge, and superior education, the physician from Antioch was a compassionate, humble man. She had glimpsed the burning curiosity in his brown eyes while he cleansed and wrapped the apostles' wounds. Watching him work, she could almost read his thoughts: *What is it about the faith of these men that emboldens them to stand against impenetrable odds and excruciating torture? Is there really something to it, or are they simply misguided?*

Mary was quite certain the gracious physician would eventually recognize the truth. He had heard it—at least a dozen times this evening—while tending each of the apostles' wounds. And each time, he had smiled patiently, nodding and asking questions—mercifully distracting his patients from their burning pain rather than from any genuine interest on his part, Mary thought sadly.

Even so, she hoped that would eventually change. Already, Luke displayed an avid interest in the God of Hebrew Scripture. Perhaps he would also become curious about the Messiah foretold in the sacred texts. Of one thing Mary was certain—the Lord had brought this selfless young man into their lives for a reason. And she would pray for him unceasingly until he could be counted among the faithful followers of Christ. *Don't let the enemy claim this one, Lord. He has a heart for You.*

Slipping quietly out the back gate so she wouldn't alert the servants, Mary followed the massive stone wall encircling her courtly villa. She didn't wish to be disturbed, for she needed this time alone to sort through her thoughts, to prepare for what most certainly lay ahead. Once her heart was at peace, she would take to her bed as the others most certainly had.

Strolling quietly, leisurely, alongside the outer wall, Mary focused her thoughts upon the quietude of the present moment. It was truly a lovely night, reminiscent of those cherished evenings she had once strolled hand-in-hand with her beloved husband, Mark. Together, they had reveled in the glory of God's creation, rejoicing in the night song of happily chirping crickets and the rolling evening breezes whispering through the foliage. Tonight, just like countless nights before, thousands of twinkling stars splashed across the velvety night sky like a glorious canopy of diamonds. The moon rose high above the sleeping city, washing the broad marble avenues in brilliant silver light. The towering palms lining the high stone walls stood like mighty sentries, their verdant fronds rustling in the gentle breezes. She could hear the sputtering torches within the confines of the villa's elegantly walled outer courtyard, just beyond the stone barrier where she now stood.

Mary started to round another corner but immediately thought better of it. Should she do so, she would stumble upon the villa's entrance. And there, she would most certainly encounter Zev guarding the gate. And she didn't wish to be interrogated about why she wandered alone in the moonlight. The burly guard would undoubtedly lecture and scold like a protective father. Suppressing a smile of amusement, she was about to turn back when a strong hand grasped her arm, cold fingers closing upon her prickling flesh.

Drawing in a sharp intake of breath, Mary's heart pounded frantically in her chest as she spun around to face an unknown presence in the gathering darkness.

"Shhh! It's all right, Mary. It is I."

Squinting in the dim moonlight, Mary's eyes widened in sudden recollection. "Rabbi Gamaliel?"

"Yes, yes," the older man drew his ceremonial robe about him as if attempting to hide within the billowing folds. "I must speak with you, Mary of Jerusalem. It is urgent."

Heart still pounding like a war drum, Mary allowed the respected Pharisee to draw her further into the shadows, her curiosity piqued despite her caution. "My lord, would it not be wiser to arrange a meeting in broad daylight?"

"Please, Mary, call me Gamaliel. I am *my lorded* all day long in the courts and in the synagogues. And unlike your kindly gesture, such sentiments are widely insincere."

Puzzled, Mary studied the dignified president of the Great Sanhedrin, still donning his traditional black and white robes. Why had he risked so much to come here? Surely the Council would go ballistic if they learned of this clandestine meeting!

"I do hope your men have found pleasant respite in your lovely home."

Mary stiffened, instantly on guard. "You will forgive me if I am hesitant to disclose the apostles' whereabouts."

"I understand," Gamaliel assured her, lightly touching her arm as a father might console a nervous child. It was an unusual gesture of kindness and respect, for most strict Jewish men refused to touch a woman unless she was a relative, not wishing to render themselves unclean if the woman happened to be deemed so. "Truly, I do. Should I find myself in your position, I would remain guarded as well."

"May I ask the purpose of this secret meeting, my lor—" catching her blunder, Mary quickly amended, "I beg your pardon. Gamaliel?" It felt odd addressing the revered *Nasi* by his given name.

"Here I stand, riddled with confusion," the respected Pharisee confessed, spreading his hands ceremoniously. "Your men—they stand boldly before the Sanhedrin, professing Jesus of Nazareth to be the Christ. Repeatedly, they have been warned against so doing, and yet they persist."

"When the commandments of God contradict the orders of men, we must choose to obey God instead," Mary responded without missing a beat, wondering if her arrest would swiftly follow.

"So they have said...several times," Gamaliel acknowledged, a hint of amusement upon his prolific features. "And yet even as they stated such bold declarations, their tone bore no malice, no disrespect toward the Sanhedrin."

Mary simply waited for Gamaliel to continue, hoping there was safety in silence. Was this brilliant scholar attempting to trap her with her own words? If so, why had he approached her under cover of darkness without witnesses to attest to his accusations?

"Your apostles possess the pluck and courage of seasoned warriors, yet they lack the flagrant rebellion so characteristic of both Zealots and revolutionaries. It appears to me a great contradiction."

"The apostles are not Zealots, nor are they revolutionaries," Mary said quietly, attempting to decipher the Pharisee's weathered features in the moonlight. "They are ambassadors for the truth."

"I must confess," Gamaliel admitted, stroking his neatly groomed beard as if deep in troubled thought, "I have diligently pondered their cause, only to find myself facing a vast sea of endless contradictions."

"But does our teaching contradict the inspired Word of God, or rather the age-old traditions and doctrines established by men?" Mary pressed very gently.

Gamaliel released a humorless chuckle. "Therein lies the crucial question—and one that keeps me awake far into the lonely night hours."

Exulting inwardly at the Pharisee's shocking confession, Mary prayed that God would supply *His* perfect words as she addressed this humble teacher, for the Holy Spirit was clearly drawing him. Reaching the uncontested ruler of the Sanhedrin would be no small task, for Gamaliel remained hopelessly mired in centuries of rigid, religious tradition. *But nothing is impossible for You, Lord,* Mary prayed fervently. *Merciful Father, show him Your truth.*

"Has anyone seen to the apostles' wounds?" Gamaliel inquired candidly, surprising Mary by this sudden turn in conversation.

The silver moonlight was momentarily barred by a cloud, encompassing them in inky darkness. Mary couldn't help but wonder if Gamaliel's true motives for this clandestine encounter were hidden in darkness, as well.

"We do not wish to bring trouble upon any Judean physician," she answered guardedly, wondering if Gamaliel sought information about their allies within the city limits. Watching him closely as the moon became visible once again, vaguely illuminating the Pharisee's guileless features, Mary attempted to gauge his reaction. "But in His great mercy, the Lord has sent a doctor to help us—a Gentile who does not answer to the Sanhedrin."

"A *Gentile?*" Gamaliel's wizened brows lifted

in stunned surprised. Somewhat scandalized, he pressed earnestly, "And you believe our great Jehovah would send a *Gentile* to the home of a respected Jewish citizen?" It was an honest inquiry rather than a condemnation.

"I do," Mary responded with great conviction. "And thank you, sir, for the compliment," she added with a hint of mirth, "although I must admit I am no longer held in such high regard among our religious and academic community."

"This Gentile, is he a proselyte?"

"Not yet, but I believe he soon will be."

Gamaliel shook his head in awe. "You really do intend to reach all the world with your gospel."

"As our Lord commanded," Mary reminded him with a warm smile.

"You should know," Gamaliel said, releasing a slow intake of breath, "I hadn't the slightest idea the Sanhedrin had scourged your men. The meeting had long since adjourned when I received word of the shocking incident from one of my students."

Mary studied him, somewhat skeptical.

"I had counseled the Sanhedrin to release them."

Mary stared at him blankly. "May I ask why?"

"By taking action against the apostles, the Council has merely promulgated the very message they wish to dismiss," Gamaliel responded without hesitation. "Turning the apostles into martyrs will only garner sympathy for the cause. Judea always has been—and always will be—a land of revolutionaries and violent uprisings. Our people revel in romanticized tales of glorified martyrs, often siding with the scapegoats."

Mary studied the aging Pharisee intently, sensing his thoughts encompassed far more than he had divulged. "Is this the only reason you sought to free them?"

"You are a very perceptive woman." Releasing another long sigh, Gamaliel shook his head in something akin to dismay. "This land, our people, are divided. Those who should stand united remain stubbornly divided. Here, we have Romans. We have Hebrews and Hellenists, Pharisees and Sadducees, Essenes, Gnostics, and the occult. We have prophets and scholars, Zealots and revolutionaries, each sect claiming sole knowledge of divine truth."

Mary listened respectfully, hoping her eyes conveyed the kindness and sympathy she felt toward this conflicted leader of Israel.

"As for me, I seek the truth, Mary—*divine* truth," Gamaliel confessed, lifting his gaze heavenward as if attempting to find life's answers etched in the swiftly moving clouds. "These are turbulent times in which we live. Our lives hang delicately in the balance as we remain at the mercy of a cruel and godless empire. Your men have caused quite a stir, Mary, and our religious rulers fear possible repercussions."

Mary said nothing, listening intently to Gamaliel's exposition. Nodding slowly, she indicated her own understanding, encouraging him to proceed.

"What the Sanhedrin does not yet understand is this: If the apostles' mighty deeds are the works of mere men, they will eventually come to nothing. But if it is the work of the Most High God, no power on earth can stop Him. No army nor council can overthrow Him."

"You are a wise man, seeking God's truth rather than clinging to popular opinion," Mary remarked.

She had always admired Gamaliel's logic and practicality, his desire to pursue truth rather than simply accepting convenient or self-gratifying doctrines.

"Above all, I do not wish to find myself fighting against the Almighty," Gamaliel revealed sagely. "It is no secret our people have a notoriously long history of doing that very thing."

"Rabbi Gamaliel," Mary said deferentially, "you are a learned man. You know Torah like the back of your own hand. If I may be so bold, I beseech you to study the sacred texts anew, weighing the apostles' teachings against the promises of Scripture."

"I have offered my students the very same counsel."

Mary lifted her slender brows in surprise. This was shocking news, indeed.

"Ah, but you must forgive the philosophical musings of this old scholar," Gamaliel apologized with a wry smile. "I have not come seeking answers pertaining to your gospel, though I must admit your doctrine both mystifies and fascinates me."

Mary studied Gamaliel closely, his form barely discernible in the waxing and waning moonlight.

"I appreciate the alliance forged by our respective families, and this is why I have come to warn you, Mary."

"To warn me?"

"Your association with this new sect has tainted your reputation, but I believe it is not beyond repair should you wisely distance yourself at this crucial point," Gamaliel said, his weathered features conveying his deep concern. "The Sanhedrin has determined to crush this sect beneath their heels. Quite frankly, I fear for you."

"I appreciate your concern, Rabbi Gamaliel," Mary said sincerely. "But I cannot forsake the Way. You are correct in your assessment—this *is* a crucial point in the founding of the faith, and I shall not retreat. In the will of God, there is safety."

"With all due respect, Mary, you don't know what the Sanhedrin is capable of. Consider what is at stake. Consider your businesses, your livelihood." Lowering his tone, Gamaliel leaned in even closer. "Consider your son."

"Is that a threat?"

Mary's heart constricted as Zev's gruff demand pierced the still night air. Stepping protectively alongside his mistress, he lifted his burning torch, casting Gamaliel's careworn features in writhing shadows. A dark scowl split Zev's features, his strong hand resting tensely upon the hilt of his dagger, issuing a clear warning.

Mortified, Mary reached for Zev's arm. His muscles tensed beneath her gentle touch. "Please, Zev, I assure you everything is all right."

"Please accept my humble apology," Gamaliel addressed the zealous guard with both patience and understanding, though Mary knew it was well within his rights to order the man's arrest for such blatant impudence against a religious leader. "I meant no disrespect—"

"I must order you to vacate the premises immediately," Zev growled, his dark eyes flashing angry fire.

"Zev!" Mary gasped, dismayed. Zev's wrathful display was certainly no way to win a reluctant convert. "Don't you know who this is?"

"I may not be religious, but I don't live under a

rock," Zev snarled, lifting his smoldering torch to get a better look at the aging Pharisee. "Of course, I know; and I don't give two mites about who he is. He could be the great emperor himself, for all I care. My role is to protect this household from *any* threat, however lofty or self-important."

Utterly mortified, Mary turned beseeching eyes toward Gamaliel. "Rabbi, please forgive this shocking display. My guard is merely concerned for my welfare—"

"As am I," Gamaliel said quietly, humbly. Drawing his *tallith* closer about his frame as if seeking solace from its traditional folds, Gamaliel turned away. "I bid you a good night, Mary of Jerusalem. May the God of our fathers be with you."

"I bid the same to you, Rabbi Gamaliel," Mary said with great feeling, her heart going out to the well-meaning Pharisee. "May our righteous Father grant you peace."

CHAPTER 47

Mary

"You shouldn't be out here alone. It isn't safe."

Wincing, Mary prepared herself for the stinging lecture that was surely to come. After all, Zev had stumbled upon her secret conference with a possible enemy of the Way. To make matters worse, the perceived offense had transpired under the worst possible circumstances—hidden in darkness, far removed from the watchful eyes of protective household guards. Now, her steely captain's penetrating gaze rested upon her, her features cast in the bronze light of his steadily burning torch.

"I am curious as to whether you intentionally and repeatedly place yourself in harm's way for the mere thrill of it or to test the limits of my patience."

Mary dared to meet Zev's stony gaze, feeling somewhat like a reprimanded child. "It is said our patience grows when tested," she reminded him, her eyes betraying a hint of mischief.

Zev was not amused. "Have you absolutely no

regard for your own safety?"

"Zev," Mary implored, reaching out to touch his muscled forearm. "How often must I remind you that I am in God's hands?"

"Your so-called Christ couldn't even save Himself from the Sanhedrin's wrath. So why should He shield *you* from it?"

"Had He saved Himself, we would all be lost," Mary gently pointed out. "Don't you see? Jesus willingly sacrificed Himself to make atonement for our sins—"

Zev held up an uncompromising hand. "Enough, Mary. *Enough.*"

Stunned by his insolence and the bold use of her given name, Mary halted mid-sentence, cautiously searching Zev's uncompromising expression.

"You speak of a dead Man as if He had any power at all to save you," Zev nearly spat, his dark eyes glittering in disdain.

"Jesus is alive, Zev," Mary declared, her features glowing with deep conviction. "You know this. He appeared to us in this very house—"

"He appeared to you, perhaps, and to the Twelve. But not to me."

"And you believe I would lie to you?" Mary asked, her soft eyes searching his.

Pierced by her grievous expression, Zev looked away, running a nervous hand through his dark, closely cropped hair. "Not intentionally," he admitted, roughly clearing his throat in discomfort. "But you were distraught when word reached us about that Man's grisly death. You could have been easily deceived in such a state—"

"Over five hundred people witnessed the resurrected Lord," Mary put in stoutly. "Were all of them deceived, as well?"

"I did not come here to argue with you," Zev said gruffly, ignoring the look she gave him. "I simply do not understand why you place such great faith in this crucified Prophet, so certain He will protect you. Do you see *Him* standing here now, looking out for you, risking His life on your behalf?"

Mary opened her mouth to protest, but Zev plowed on ahead of her.

"That's because He *isn't*, Mary. And yet the man who has faithfully done so for nearly a decade stands before you now. But do you see *me*, Mary? Do you see the sacrifices I've made, the opportunities I've rejected just to be near you? Just to look out for you?"

Just to be near you? Mary raised questioning eyes toward her fierce sentry. In one unguarded moment, raw emotion had flickered across Zev's stony features, his dark eyes conveying the depths of his feelings as if silently pleading with her to understand, pleading with her to assure him she would be more careful for her own sake...and for his. Blown away by Zev's confession and his open admonishment, Mary simply stared at the powerful guard, speechless and utterly astonished.

And for the first time since embracing the Way, Mary realized that Zev's animosity toward the faith was deeply rooted in an emotion she had never expected her dauntless guard to possess—the cold, debilitating *fear* of losing someone he secretly held dear. Just how dear, Mary did not wish to ponder. It was far too uncomfortable, far too disturbing to think about.

Clearly angry he had revealed so much, Zev's features tightened once more, banishing any mingling traces of tender protectiveness. Mary could almost feel the gaping chasm widening between them as, once again, she became the mistress—he the indifferent, hired watchman, emotions carefully concealed. Without another word, Zev turned sharply on his heel and left, leaving Mary to stand alone in the gathering darkness.

***

Descending the dark stone staircase and emerging within the cool storage vaults burrowed deep beneath the house, Mary thanked the quiet manservant who had lighted the torches for them before he scurried back up the first and second flight of steps. Turning her attention to Peter and John just a few short steps behind her, she listened quietly as they discussed a problem that had arisen within church. Apparently, deep tensions had developed between the more traditional Jewish converts, dubbed the Hebrews, and the far less conservative Jews and proselytes called Hellenists. It wasn't too surprising that issues had arisen undetected. After all, the apostles were stretched completely thin spreading the gospel, preaching at the Temple and in the synagogues, attending meetings at the various home churches scattered throughout Judea, managing church donations and funds, and distributing food and clothing to the poor. Burdened with endless responsibilities and the care of thousands upon thousands of new believers, it was simply impossible for the Twelve to monitor or investigate every little quibble or qualm that cropped up. Yet despite the enormous demands placed upon the weary men, converts still managed to find fault with the apostles' tireless efforts. The Hellenists stoutly insisted that their widows and orphans were being overlooked in the daily distribution of food and clothing. It seemed many of the Hellenists were convinced that the Hebrews were receiving special treatment.

Mary was certain the accusation was unjust. Being a Hellenist herself, she knew the apostles were impartial in their ministry to both widows and orphans, regardless of their background. Even so, the problem must be addressed. Mary knew that sweeping the issue under a rug certainly wouldn't make it go away. She was saddened that the believers had already begun to quibble among themselves. What of their godly witness to the watching world?

Passing beneath the stone entryway, Mary ushered Peter and John into the largest vault room. The apostles remained deep in conversation, scarcely aware of her presence. She felt rather intrusive waiting quietly, absorbing their every word. But Peter had stoutly insisted she accompany them anytime they deposited funds deep within the vaults. She supposed he desired additional accountability, and she respected him for it. The disciples' former treasurer, Judas Iscariot, had embezzled an exorbitant amount of funds prior to his ruthless betrayal and subsequent suicide. No doubt scarred by Judas' toxic greed, Simon Peter didn't wish to be placed in a position of temptation or false accusation.

Gracefully lowering herself upon a nearby trunk, Mary folded her hands in her lap, respectfully allowing Peter and John to carry on their heated conversation as they tucked away recent donations for future use. She wished with all her heart that the two young men were merely paranoid about the current predicament, but she knew that wasn't the case. Just last week, Tabitha had returned home from the Synagogue of the Freedmen, frustrated and disheartened. The Hellenists attending the meeting had openly addressed Stephanos before a sea of Jewish nonbelievers, demanding retribution for the unfair treatment they were supposedly receiving. Fuming, Tabitha reported that Saul of Tarsus had gloatingly observed the shameful ordeal, snidely commenting about the believers' "false and hypocritical claims of unity". Saddened, Mary released a short sigh. Had the believers so quickly forgotten the Spirit of God within them?

"I simply do not understand it," John was saying, opening a large trunk and carefully counting the coins he dropped inside. "Everything was going so well. The believers were willingly sharing all they had, constantly looking out for the needs of their brethren. What has changed, and why so suddenly?"

"Perhaps it was simply too good to be true," Peter huffed, producing a small booklet and scratching in the amount John had just doled out. "I think the honeymoon stage is over."

John said nothing, but the dejected set of his broad shoulders indicated he didn't disagree with Peter's sad assessment.

"Gentlemen," Mary interrupted, pained to see them so disheartened. "If I may be so bold, may I bring something to your attention?"

"You know you are always welcome to speak with us," Peter reminded her, dropping wearily upon another large chest, his dark eyes somewhat vacant.

"Do you recall the story about Moses and his father-in-law, Jethro?" Mary ventured a bit reluctantly. "Well, of course you do. You know the Word far better than I."

Peter and John exchanged curious glances, unsure about where the conversation was headed.

"Go on," John prodded, clearly willing to hear out any suggestion.

"I can't help but notice the similarities between your current situation and the predicament Moses faced in the wilderness after God delivered His people from Egypt. This was shortly after Adonai confirmed His covenant with our ancestors, just as Christ has confirmed the new covenant with us. Moses was utterly exhausted attempting to meet the needs of all the people. He ran himself ragged attempting to appease everyone, and still, countless needs went unmet."

Peter and John exchanged another fleeting glance, their eyes narrowing in thoughtful recognition. "So Moses' father-in-law, Jethro, spoke to Moses," Peter mused, stroking his beard in consideration.

"Yes," Mary affirmed, her eyes glowing as full realization struck. "Perhaps Jethro's wise advice applies to you, as well. As Moses once was, the apostles are stretched entirely thin overseeing a job far too great for any man. But the Lord had a solution for Moses, just as He must have a solution for you."

"I remember the story well," John declared, recognition lighting his haggard features. "Jethro said to Moses, '*The thing that you do is not good. Both you and these people who are with you will surely wear yourselves out. For this thing is too much for you; you are not able to perform it by yourself.*'"

"Just as we are unable to meet all the needs ourselves," Peter commented wryly. "I had forgotten
about Moses' dilemma."

"At least we're in good company," John quipped,
flashing his boyish grin.

Mary smiled warmly, thankful to see their hope
returning. Rising from the chest, she waited patiently, allowing the apostles to make the necessary
decisions regarding Jethro's ancient counsel. She
had no desire to intrude upon the leadership role
God had assigned to them.

"So Jethro counseled Moses to select able men,
men of truth who feared God and hated covetous-
ness, to assist him in his responsibilities toward the
people," Peter mused.

"Exactly," John agreed, his excitement showing.
"And Jethro reminded Moses, '*So it will be easier for
you, for they will bear the burden with you.*'"

"And he went on to say, '*If you do this thing, and
God so commands you, then you will be able to endure, and all this people will also go to their place in
peace,*'" Peter said, shaking his head in sheer relief.

"Are you thinking what I'm thinking?" John
grinned, extending a hand to help Peter to his feet.

"We need to assemble the Twelve," Peter finished
for him, his energy visibly returning. "Let's pray over
this and seek the Lord about this matter, as Moses
did." Taking Mary by the shoulders, he planted a
firm kiss upon her cheek. "Thank you, Mary," he
exclaimed, his eyes betraying his mounting excitement. "I believe the Holy Spirit has spoken through
you, providing the answers we were far too weary
to see for ourselves!"

Warmed to her very core, Mary's smile conveyed

her great relief as she watched the youthful apostles bounding back up the flight of stone steps. Clasping her hands, she uttered a prayer of silent thanks, her heart swelling with gratitude toward God. For she, like Jethro of old, had been granted the unspeakable privilege of suggesting a worthy alternative.

CHAPTER 48

Tabitha

"So I heard it's official."

Situated behind her mother's old loom, a wide smile teased Tabitha's shining features as Candace slipped into her friend's simple chamber containing several wide looms, a wooden table boasting her tools of the trade, and large woven baskets brimming with materials for sewing and weaving. Here, hundreds of practical yet lovely pieces took shape beneath Tabitha's skillful hands. Mary had gifted the use of this chamber to Tabitha after discovering what an incredibly gifted seamstress the girl was shortly after her arrival. As a newcomer to Mary's palatial and somewhat intimidating villa, the young Tabitha had become habited to laying out her bedroll in the simple chamber each night—rather than bedding down in the maidservants' sleeping quarters—and slumbering near her mother's old loom. At first, she had felt closer to her departed mother sleeping beside the woman's most cherished possession. Compassionate Mary had gone to great lengths to locate the impressive piece of machinery after welcoming an orphaned Tabitha into her home. But Tabitha had soon discovered she appreciated the solitude apart from the servants' sleeping quarters and had claimed the formerly neglected space as her own.

It was a simple, square-shaped chamber located near the back of the magnificent villa, clearly constructed as a workroom of sorts. Though Tabitha boasted few worldly possessions, she had scattered colorful woven rugs upon the stone floor, giving the workspace a homier atmosphere.

"Candace!" Tabitha grinned, ignoring her friend's prying comment. "Where are your sweet boys? I seldom see them these days."

"Rhoda is entertaining them in the courtyard," Candace supplied, refusing to be distracted from her initial inquiry.

"She is so good with children," Tabitha observed fondly, remembering Rhoda's tears when the girl had been informed of Tabitha's engagement. With tears of her own, Tabitha had assured Rhoda that she would visit as often as possible, preferably several times a week. The people within Mary's villa were *family*, and she couldn't imagine life without them. Nor did she wish to.

Leaning casually against the doorjamb, Candace crossed slender arms and arched a brow in question. "Well? Do you intend to drive me mad with curiosity?" she teased.

Laughing musically, Tabitha ran her fingers along the edge of the smooth fibers she intended to weave into durable garments for the many poor. "I assume you are speaking of my betrothal to Stephanos?"

"Then it *is* official!"

"The paperwork has been drawn up and my lady has spoken to a priest, an old family friend, about initiating the ceremony."

Releasing a gasp of delight, Candace swooped into the room, gathering up her friend in a warm embrace. "I rejoice for you, my sister!"

Blinking back tears of happiness, Tabitha returned Candace's embrace. "I can scarcely believe it myself."

Releasing her blushing friend, Candace gracefully lowering herself upon a plush cushion across from Tabitha's loom. Resting her hands lightly upon her knees, Candace was clearly settling in for a nice, long chat. "You must be so proud of him, beloved."

Tabitha knew Candace was referencing Stephanos' new responsibilities within the church. He, along with his good friend, Philip, and five additional Spirit-filled men had been appointed to oversee the distribution of food, clothing, and other vital necessities within the church, freeing the apostles to carry on their ministry of prayer, instruction, and preaching. As a result, the infant church continued to thrive as needs were met by capable men guided by the Holy Spirit's leading. And Tabitha had already observed noticeable spiritual growth among believers as the apostles were now free to train them up in the ways of God. Quibbling ceased and petty differences were overlooked as the followers strove to abide by the apostles' teachings by showing preference to one another and seeking the welfare of others above their own.

"I *am* proud of him," Tabitha admitted shyly,

clasping her hands in her lap. "Stephanos has been assigned to minister in the district within the City of David just south of the Temple Mount. He has established his beloved Synagogue of the Freedman as a home base, of sorts. There, he carries on his teaching and preaching."

"He is a powerful speaker," Candace observed.

"The Lord has gifted him mightily," Tabitha agreed, her eyes shining. "Last week, he addressed a group of disgruntled Hellenists, the ones so certain they had received unfair treatment. Stephanos reminded them that their constant bickering was damaging their witness, since we are Christ's representatives on earth. 'Rather than looking to your own interests,' he advised, 'remain focused on meeting the needs of others'. He explained that this is our calling in Christ. I was a bit on edge, concerned the people might take offense. Instead, they wept in heartfelt repentance."

"Praise God," Candace breathed, shaking her head in amazement. "It is wonderful to see the believers rallying together, happily contributing toward the needs of others."

"It is," Tabitha agreed excitedly. "Stephanos has recruited me to make blankets and clothing for distribution in his district. It is thrilling to see how everyone has a specific role to play in the body of Christ, and each part is important. Some donate funds, while others contribute food or clothing. And many believers have happily volunteered to help distribute these goods to the orphans and widows within the deacons' various districts—that's what the seven men are now called, *deacons*," Tabitha explained.

"Ah, a worthy term to describe the seven chosen for the task," Candace surmised with a knowing smile, "assuming it has been derived from the Greek word *diakonos*, meaning *servant* or *minister*, of course."

"They are certainly passionate about serving others," Tabitha commented thoughtfully. "The deacons' ministry has helped me understand why the church is called the *body of Christ*, Candace. Since Jesus is no longer physically walking among us, He has assigned His church to go to the places He would go, to minister to the people to whom He would minister, to meet the needs that He would meet. We truly are His hands, His feet, His *body*. And He has graciously given us the Holy Spirit to guide us in this divine endeavor."

"Amen," Candace agreed softly. "And you say Stephanos has recruited you to supply blankets, garments, and such? That's the perfect role for a skilled seamstress such as yourself."

"I was a bit reluctant to do it at first," Tabitha admitted, nervously biting her lower lip. "I have always overseen my own ministry, distributing clothing at the times and locations of my choosing. Now, I will be under the deacons' authority."

"I see," Candace acknowledged with a knowing smile. "But you agreed to work with Stephanos anyway?"

"I thought it might be good practice," Tabitha acknowledged wryly. "Once we wed, Stephanos will become the head of our household. I suppose I must learn to work alongside him and respect his authority now."

Candace released a laugh of amusement. "I shall

enjoy watching you learn the art of submission, dear sister."

"It should be entertaining for everyone," Tabitha admitted with a good-natured laugh. "Thank God I am marrying a patient man!"

"And when will you marry him?"

Tabitha felt her own color deepen. "You know as well as I, Candace, that the bride never knows the day or the hour her bridegroom will return for her!"

Candace smiled mischievously. "I imagine you now have a far better understanding of what Christ meant when He referred to the church as His bride."

"I do," Tabitha admitted, blushing even more deeply. "Sometimes, I feel as if I'll burst waiting for him to come for me, to take me to the home he has prepared for us, to give myself entirely to him, to abide with him forever. It is no wonder Jesus has referenced Himself as the Bridegroom and the church as His bride. We must await His return with the same eager longing and expectation a bride experiences while waiting for her bridegroom to return for her."

"And we must always be ready for Jesus' coming," Candace added, her eyes sparkling with joyful anticipation. "As you said, we cannot know the day or the hour of the bridegroom's return. Just as the trumpet call announces the impending arrival of the bridegroom, so will the coming of the Son of Man be. His arrival will commence with the blast of a mighty trumpet, and we, the bride of Christ, mustn't be caught unawares."

"Amen to that," Tabitha agreed, reveling in the sheer wonder of it all. Once she had finally surrendered her fears into the capable hands of Christ, the true Lover of her soul and the ultimate Bridegroom, she was truly astounded by the depths of her love for the powerful and fiery evangelist. Deep down, she knew the Lord had been gently drawing them together for quite some time, as if softly whispering to her heart, *I want to bless you beyond your wildest imagination, beloved, if you will only lift willing hands to accept it.*

Smiling softly, Tabitha thanked her righteous Father for granting her the courage to do so.

CHAPTER 49

Tabitha

"He is exceptional, dear sister," Candace whispered softly toward Tabitha, shifting baby Rufus' weight on her slender hip. "Lives are being transformed before our eyes."

Tabitha watched, spellbound, as her handsome betrothed addressed a large gathering assembled below the great stone steps of the Synagogue of the Freedmen. Patiently, Stephanos expounded upon the prophecies pointing toward Jesus as Israel's long-awaited Messiah. His speech was both powerful and profound. Already, several men and women had knelt in repentance, accepting Jesus as their Lord and Savior.

It was a glorious autumn morning, and Tabitha was quite certain she could have stood in the warm sunshine listening to her beloved Stephanos all day long. The fact that she was now his to claim still filled her heart with wonder. She couldn't help but consider...would today be the day he came for her?

The prospect filled her entire being with excitement, so much excitement, in fact, that she trembled at the thought. She knew Stephanos was preparing a place for them, a modest house located somewhere in the Lower City near his beloved Synagogue of the Freedmen. She could hardly wait to hang the curtains she had lovingly sewn, to scatter the colorful rugs she had so carefully woven, to make the place their own.

"Tabitha, do you know what is happening?"

Drawn from her blissful reverie, Tabitha turned toward Candace. The woman wore a troubled expression, her dark eyes trained upon Stephanos.

Disturbed, Tabitha followed her friend's troubled gaze. Stephanos had paused amidst his powerful delivery, addressing a small, unassuming man now hastily retreating from the gathering. "You, my brother," Stephanos called out warmly, snagging the deserter's attention before he could escape. "You have faith to be made well!"

Tabitha and Candace exchanged questioning looks as murmurs of curiosity rippled through the vast crowd. In Tabitha's opinion, the man Stephanos had addressed appeared to be perfectly well. He was short of stature and narrow in build, with a balding pate and large, sorrowful eyes. But even the observant, watchful Tabitha detected no sign of sickness or disease.

What had prompted Stephanos to address him so?

Unsure about what to expect, Candace drew Baby Rufus a bit closer, squeezing the hand of her oldest son, Alexander, still standing obediently at her elbow. Sensing Candace's concern, Tabitha draped an arm over Alexander's small shoulders, pulling him close.

"Sir, what is your name?" Stephanos called over the crowd, his eyes resting compassionately upon the man's hesitant face.

"I shouldn't be here," the man responded, his voice faltering in contrition. "I came because I have no hope."

"There is hope for you in Christ, my brother," Stephanos said, stretching forth his hand. "Please, return to us."

Exchanging another look with Candace, Tabitha wondered at the stranger's obvious regret. He was clearly overcome with guilt about something. Shifting a bit uncomfortably, Tabitha watched the unfolding narrative with mounting apprehension.

The man shook his head brokenly. "The words of your Messiah have pierced my heart," the man wept, drawing up his tunic to cover his nose and mouth. "He said, '*Just as you want men to do to you, you also do to them likewise.*' I have not considered others in my haste to find hope, to find answers, for myself. May your Christ forgive me." Several listeners standing near the man drew back, uneasy. What was he talking about? Their instincts warned them that something wasn't quite right.

"The Holy Spirit has revealed your torment, my brother," Stephanos said, reaching out his hand again. "It is no accident you joined us today. God has a purpose. Please, come."

Tabitha watched as the agitated stranger anxiously scanned the crowd, now openly gawking at him. Nearly smothering himself with his own tunic, he reluctantly approached Stephanos, mounting the broad stone steps and standing beside the evangelist at the top.

"What is happening?" Candace whispered, concerned for her two sons.

"I'm not sure," Tabitha whispered back, watching her betrothed with avid curiosity. "But the Holy Spirit must be at work."

"I repeat," Stephanos said, his voice rising in both volume and power. "You have faith to be made well."

"I am unworthy." Weeping, the balding man shook his head, still covering his nose and mouth.

"We are *all* unworthy," Stephanos said with a knowing smile. "If we were deserving, then our Lord wouldn't have had to die for us, providing the final atonement for our sins."

The man appeared less than comforted.

"Please, be seated on this top step and remove your sandals," Stephanos instructed, placing an encouraging hand upon his trembling shoulder.

"You should not touch me!" the man cried, jerking away in fear.

Stephanos understood. "My Savior will protect me," he assured the man. "What is your name?"

"Raphael," he managed, his voice quivering.

"Ah, how fitting." Stephanos smiled heavenward, as if acknowledging the unrivaled perfection of God's plan. "Raphael, meaning *God has healed*."

Raphael gazed up at Stephanos bleakly. "If only that were so."

"You said you were pierced to the heart by my Savior's teaching, Raphael. Why is that?"

"His words ring true. Standing amidst this gathering, I felt as if He was right here beside me, speaking directly to my heart."

"Amen," Stephanos acknowledged quietly. "Raphael, do you believe in Jesus Christ, the Son of the Living God?"

"I do," Raphael responded with great conviction, his eyes welling with tears.

"And do you believe He has the power to heal your affliction?"

Stephanos' powerful query was followed by a thunderous pause. The entire gathering held its collective breath as the frail, balding man seated at the evangelist's feet contemplated the shocking question.

Catching her breath, Tabitha reached for Candace's arm. The air crackled with tension.

Raising solemn eyes toward Stephanos, Raphael spoke with great conviction. "I do."

"Please remove your sandals and lift your feet, Raphael."

Releasing the wrinkled tunic he had drawn over his nose and mouth, Raphael bent at the waist to perform the evangelist's bidding. Unstrapping his sandals with trembling fingers, Raphael laboriously removed his sandals. Lifting the hem of his garment, he raised his bare feet before the crowd.

The air was filled with gasps of horror and cries of fierce wrath as Raphael revealed the soles of his feet, riddled with discolored leprous ulcers.

Drawing a hand over her mouth in surprise, Tabitha's heart went out to the poor man, for he bore the marks of the earliest stages of the deadly illness called leprosy. People diagnosed with the disease were required to self-quarantine far from cities and villages, leading desolate, pain-ridden lives until their rotting, disease-ravaged bodies finally succumbed to the dreadful infection. She suddenly understood what Raphael had meant when he said he hadn't considered others in his haste to find hope. Now he had exposed the entire crowd to the lethal contagion.

"Unclean! Unclean!" people shouted, drawing back in shock and outrage. "How dare you expose us to your foul disease! You fool!"

Both frightened and saddened, Tabitha and Candace attempted to shield young Rufus and Alexander—not only from the fatal infection but also from the crowd's rising fury, which was equally contagious. Craning her neck to see above the crowd, Tabitha saw Raphael still seated on the stone steps, tears tracing slender lines down his dirt-smudged cheeks as the gathering continued to rage against him.

"Please!" Stephanos shouted above the din. Addressing the rattled crowd, he chastised them firmly, "Where is your faith? Do not quench the Holy Spirit at work."

The crowd quieted reluctantly, their consciences stinging from Stephanos' quiet rebuke. Tabitha held her breath along with the rest of them, burning with curiosity. Her heart constricted as she considered her beloved's close proximity to the diseased man. *Oh God, please, protect my dear Stephanos. Shield him from disease.*

Stephanos stood before Raphael, his entire being radiating with power and purpose. Turning toward the humiliated man slumped on the steps, Stephanos placed a firm hand on Raphael's shoulder. "In the name of the Father, the Son, and the Holy Spirit, I say unto you, *be healed!*" His command rang out like a mighty waterfall, billowing over the gathering like powerful ocean waves.

The crowd strained forward as one, blinking in sheer unbelief. The telltale lesions devouring the flesh upon the soles of Raphael's feet had vanished in an instant.

Tabitha heard Candace's sharp intake of breath, along with gasps and excited whispers rippling through the crowd. By the might and power of the Holy Spirit, yet another captive soul had been set free!

"Praise God!" Stephanos declared as dozens of men and women dropped to their knees, lifting their hands in worship.

Bounding to his feet, Raphael embraced Stephanos, weeping in heartfelt gratitude. Stephanos simply held him, patting his back as a father might console a sobbing child.

Tears had sprung to Tabitha's eyes as well, for she was blessed beyond imagination watching the Holy Spirit at work in the man she loved so deeply. Swiping at her tears, she felt certain that nothing on earth could possibly diminish the joy and peace coursing through her entire being...until her gaze flickered toward a subtle movement in the darkened, arched stone entry of the synagogue. There, Saul of Tarsus perched like a bird of prey beneath the intricate stonework, his jaw firmly set, his fiery gaze fixed upon Stephanos.

Tabitha's entire being went cold, for murder glittered in the dark eyes of the seething Pharisee. She couldn't help but wonder if it was only a matter of time before he unleashed his rage against him.

CHAPTER 50

Tabitha

Fingering the soft fabric of the simple but elegant gown she had lovingly designed, Tabitha smiled faintly, considering the many preparations she had made for her future wedding day. Being the favored maidservant of an affluent mistress, Tabitha had attended dozens of extravagant wedding banquets. Many such feasts lasted for days, sometimes even a full week, during which hundreds of richly dressed guests attended, often donning the elegant outer garment provided by the master of ceremonies. Attendees would lounge upon plush couches, enjoying rich wine and sumptuous fare while being entertained by professional musicians and storytellers. There was always singing and dancing, clapping and cheering, and good-natured pandemonium as hundreds of guests offered the wedded couple gifts and well-wishes.

Smiling again, Tabitha acknowledged that her wedding would be quite different. Whereas many brides donned exquisite finery, their wrists, arms, ears, and throats adorned with stacks of glistening gold, silver, and jewels, Tabitha would wear a simple, snowy white gown for her bridegroom. Though it was far from elaborate, Tabitha was reminded of freshly fallen snow every time her gaze fell lovingly upon it. In this gown, she would present herself to her husband as a pure woman before God, a woman who had saved herself entirely for him. She had carefully stitched a matching white veil, the gauzy fabric both enchanting and whimsical in its elegant simplicity. She knew that Stephanos admired her looks, but it was her increasing inner strength, her commitment to God and her desire to do right, that truly delighted him. She hoped her simple, spotless gown would bring to mind the church's holy calling rather than simply drawing attention to her physical beauty.

Mary had generously offered the Upper Room to host a lavish wedding banquet, but Tabitha had requested to use the lovely stone courtyard instead. She desired a simple ceremony, surrounded by the few people to whom she was the closest. There, amidst the vibrant greenery and softly splashing fountain, she would exchange sacred vows with the man she loved. A simple wedding feast would follow, as the servants had agreed to set up a lovely table beneath a dusky sky after the ceremony.

"I see you are prepared for the arrival of your bridegroom."

Glancing over her shoulder, Tabitha saw Mary standing in the doorway, her regal head tilted as she studied her dear maid.

"I do hope so." Tabitha laughed nervously, lowering her gown with a twinge of embarrassment. What must Mary think of her, watching her fawn over her own wedding gown like a giddy young lass? Draping it carefully over a wooden table, Tabitha turned to face her beloved mistress.

"It is indeed a lovely gown," Mary observed, moseying into Tabitha's quarters with a mysterious smile. "At first, I balked when you requested a simple wedding. I longed to give you nothing but the best, beloved. And yet I can see why you desired to keep it this way."

"I have witnessed many anxious brides driving themselves and their entire families to distraction, insisting that everything must be *just so* for her wedding day," Tabitha divulged a bit ruefully. "As a result, everyone is so stressed, irritable, and exhausted it is simply impossible to savor the wonder of the sacred occasion when it eventually arrives. I truly believe there is beauty—and *peace*—in simplicity."

"You have always been wise beyond your years."

Warmed by her lady's sincerity, Tabitha reached for her hand. "I will miss sharing this home with you, my lady. You have always been so good to me, even before you knew me."

Mary's gray eyes flickered slightly, but she concealed her emotion with a practiced smile. "Your husband-to-be works in this house every day, dear one. I imagine you will find plenty of excuses to visit me. And if not, then I will track you down and drag you here myself," she teased, her eyes sparkling with mischief.

Tabitha laughed merrily.

Crossing the room, Mary lifted Tabitha's wedding gown, admiring her maidservant's meticulous handwork. "How you designed such a breathtaking piece with a minimal amount of simple fabric is beyond me. You are truly gifted, beloved."

"I didn't wish to waste an exorbitant amount of time or resources on a gown I plan to wear only once, when there are thousands of garments and blankets still to be made for the many, many poor," Tabitha explained, her hazel-green eyes searching Mary's. Did her elegant mistress understand her reasoning?

Mary smiled to herself, pleased. Her fiery Tabitha was fast becoming a thoughtful, selfless woman, deeply concerned about the needs of others. She was a worthy bride for Stephanos, a spirited young woman determined to embrace her calling within the body of Christ.

Stretching forth her arms, Mary said warmly, "I couldn't be more proud of you, dear one."

Blinking back tears, Tabitha went into the motherly arms of her lady. Clinging to the only mother she had known since childhood, Tabitha wondered if it was possible for one's heart to burst with love and gratitude.

Reluctantly releasing her dear maid, Mary held her at arm's length, a knowing smile teasing her lips.

Tabitha's slanted eyes narrowed in suspicion, intrigued by her lady's enigmatic smile. "My lady," she grinned, raising slender brows in question. "Why, may I ask, are you smiling like that?"

Eyes dancing, Mary responded lightly, "There is excitement in the air this morning, is there not?"

As if on cue, a shrill trumpet blast rent the air, shattering the serenity of the quiet morning, and sending Tabitha's heart pounding on overdrive. Raising shocked eyes to her mistress, Tabitha's lips parted in surprise.

"Well, well," Mary pronounced knowingly, her entire expression alight with joy, "it would seem your bridegroom approaches, dear one. We'd best summon Rhoda. It is time to prepare you for your husband."

***

The ceremony was everything Tabitha could have possibly hoped for, and so much more. Surrounded by her brothers and sisters in Christ, Tabitha was presented before a beaming Stephanos. Standing before her in his best garments, Tabitha was certain the bold evangelist appeared even more handsome and confident than she had ever seen him.

Amazed the Lord had brought them together, Tabitha decided that her husband-to-be, with his raven black hair, flashing eyes, and olive skin, was the most desirable of men. Stephanos was impassioned, ambitious, full of life and purpose. But most importantly, his love for God was unshakable and profound. Tabitha knew she could trust Stephanos with her heart without fear of mistreatment, because her betrothed chose to honor God in all his actions. She had known many unfortunate women who had fallen prey to attractive men, deceived by their flattery and good looks, only to later discover the evil residing in them. Tabitha thanked God that He had directed her toward a man who truly loved Him, and in return, would cherish her as Christ so loved the church, His bride, sacrificing Himself for her.

Standing before the glistening fountain, their closest friends clustered excitedly about them, Tabitha and Stephanos pronounced their sacred vows, their hearts joined in love for God and for each other. Tabitha's heart lurched when the elaborately dressed priest instructed Stephanos to lift her veil.

Heart pounding and cheeks growing warm, Tabitha lowered her gaze as Stephanos' strong fingers clasped the delicate seam of the snowy veil. Gently, reverently, he lifted the gauzy veil, carefully smoothing it back over her head before reaching down to take his young bride's hands in his.

Shyly lifting her gaze, Tabitha was overwhelmed the moment her eyes met the powerful gaze of her beloved. The tenderness, the longing, the steadfast love and assurance of his gaze left her nearly breathless. Clinging to his powerful hands like a lifeline, Tabitha knew she would cherish this sacred moment for the rest of her life.

***

Mary

Steeling herself against the comfort of tears, Mary watched as the kindly little priest guided Tabitha and Stephanos in the pronouncement of their marriage vows. Tabitha was a vision in her simple gown, her honey-colored tresses spilling down her back and shoulders in a cascade of stunning ringlets, her hazel-green eyes shining with love and happiness. Despite the obvious lack of grandeur, there was something pure, wholesome, and honest about Tabitha's humble yet lovely appearance. Stephanos, too, was a sight to behold. Broad shoulders thrown back, head held high, he clasped the hands of his young bride, his eyes shining with all the love and promise in the world.

Sensing his mother's silent suffering, John Mark firmly took Mary's hand in his. Glancing at her handsome, fourteen-year-old son in surprise, Mary couldn't help but wonder when she would watch him pledge his love and loyalty to a blushing bride of his own...probably far too soon! How swiftly time flew by! Dismissing the worrisome thought, Mary offered her son a genuine smile, then directed her attention back to the glowing bride and groom standing before the great stone fountain in the outer court.

The young couple was surrounded by a cloud of beaming witnesses—among them Simon Peter and his gentle wife, Anaia, James, and John ,the sons of thunder, along with the Lord's thoughtful brother, James. Stephanos' best friend, Philip, was also in attendance, grinning broadly, along with Simon and Candace, and their two young sons. Rhoda stood dutifully at the edge of the gathering, her soft brown eyes glistening with a sheen of tears as her beloved Tabitha pledged her love and devotion to an adoring husband. Tobias was also present, his oiled mustache twitching in approval.

Uneasy, Mary's gaze strayed in the direction of the massive wrought iron gate, where Zev undoubtedly guarded the entrance with the other sentries. She wondered what he thought about the ensuing ceremony. Had the burly guard ever been married?

Doubtful, she thought, imagining the cynical sentry probably smirked upon the sacred institution. Her stomach clenched in discomfort when she recalled Zev's unintentional confession the night he stumbled upon her secret conference with Gamaliel. She was still unsure about what to do with him. Briefly, she had considered releasing him from her employ, but feared such an act would forever harden him against the Way.

Sighing wistfully, Mary returned her attention to the happy couple as the Levite presiding over the ceremony joyously pronounced them husband and wife in the sight of God.

Those assembled in the courtyard exploded in exuberant exultation, clapping, cheering, and shouting blessings and exhortations to the beaming newlyweds as Stephanos drew his glowing young bride to his side, planting a firm kiss upon her delicate temple.

Heart nearly bursting within her, Mary clapped elegant hands along with the rest of the gathering. *Praise be to God,* she thought with a happy little smile. *Precious Lord, these times are so uncertain. May this dear couple never relinquish this blissful sense of wonder nor forsake their trust in You. No matter what may come.*

***

Tabitha

It was a joyous procession that accompanied Stephanos as he led his beautiful bride to the place he had prepared for her—the cozy little stone house they would share.

After many heartfelt well-wishes, Simon Peter's emotional prayer committing both the house and the newlyweds into the Lord's hands, and half a dozen embraces from Mary, Candace, and young Rhoda, the happy gathering dispersed, each returning to their own homes.

Standing in the small outer court encircling both the front and one side of the modest, box-shaped house located snugly within the Lower City, Tabitha recognized that the one-room structure was absolutely nothing like the lavish mansion in which she had previously resided. Even so, to her, the house was perfect.

Grasping her hand, Stephanos smiled down at her, tenderly tucking a stray curl behind her ear. "Are you ready to see your new home, my bride?"

Warmed from the top of her head to the tip of her toes, Tabitha squeezed his hand. "I can hardly wait, my husband."

Blushing deeply as Stephanos guided her toward the entry, Tabitha paused, her heart fluttering nervously within her chest as Stephanos pushed open the wooden door. With a grand sweep of his arm, he ushered her inside.

Catching her breath, Tabitha passed beneath the simple doorway, her bright eyes absorbing every detail of her new home. The one-room structure reminded her of Candace's humble dwelling. Though sparsely furnished, it was homey and inviting. Unlike the sprawling mosaic floors of Mary's familiar villa, the ground was simply hard-packed earth. And rather than beautifully frescoed walls, this structure boasted a rough façade of neatly applied stucco. Warm sunlight streamed in from a square-shaped cut-out in the roof and several small, intricately latticed windows.

Despite the drastic change in environment, Tabitha was certain she couldn't possibly be happier. It was obvious her bridegroom had thoughtfully prepared this simple home for them. Neat wooden shelves were lined with pottery, cooking utensils, and tools. Flickering oil lamps placed strategically throughout the house filled the place with a warm, cheerful glow. A simple but delightful feast had been spread upon the only table in the house, and Tabitha was thankful she had eaten sparingly during the wedding banquet. In reality, she had been far too eager for this moment to indulge in the rich delicacies prepared by Mary's professional chefs. Blushing, Tabitha observed a delicate tapestry serving as a simple partition, neatly dividing a makeshift bedchamber from the rest of the small house. She was particularly impressed with the garlands of fresh flowers hanging from the walls and the delicate, sweet-smelling petals strung about the floor. Turning around, Tabitha saw that Stephanos remained rooted in the doorway, anxiously awaiting her reaction.

Warmed to the core by his desire for her affirmation, Tabitha went to him. "I could not ask for a lovelier home," she breathed, taking his hand.

Stephanos' striking features instantly relaxed, his expression bathed in relief. "I must admit, it is a far cry from the home to which you are accustomed," he confessed a bit ruefully.

"It is absolutely perfect," Tabitha declared, shaking her head in awe. "Stephanos, it feels like home already—not only because it is beautiful, but because *you* are here with me."

Stephanos' eyes flickered with emotion. Gently closing the door behind him, he turned to face his young bride, his eyes gleaming with mischief. "Were you surprised by my arrival this morning?"

"More than you know," Tabitha laughed, surprised at how natural it felt to be alone with this man. "Most weddings do not commence until at least a year after the betrothal."

"I'm thankful you were ready for me," Stephanos smiled, tipping her chin, studying the face he loved. "I was counseled against waiting the full year to wed, despite the traditions associated with the act of betrothal. Though I felt impressed to act now, I feared my eagerness to marry you might be solely based on my desire for you," Stephanos admitted, admiring the warmth springing into Tabitha's glowing cheeks. "But when I brought my concern before the apostles, they were in agreement. These are uncertain times, and God has given us a very distinct mission. Together, we can unite, Tabitha, to accomplish His good purpose. We are moved by the Holy Spirit now, and though the Spirit will never speak contrary to the unchanging Word of God, there will be times when His leading may contradict the traditions of men."

"In this case, I'm relieved," Tabitha confessed with a shy smile. "I am so glad you came for me, my husband." *My husband!* What a thrill to address this remarkable man as such! Exulting inwardly, Tabitha allowed Stephanos to draw her close, so close she could smell his spice-scented breath. She was amazed by the intensity of her desire for him, overwhelmed by the joy she experienced in his presence. *Thank You, Father, for the gift of marriage. What a wondrous thing it is!*

Cupping Tabitha's face in one strong hand, Stephanos looked into her eyes, his own burning with intensity. "I wish I could tell you how I've longed for you, my bride. The nights I have lain awake thinking of your eyes, your smile, longing for your touch...I praise God for blessing me beyond my wildest dreams, granting me the unspeakable privilege of taking you as my wife."

Trembling, Tabitha drew her arms about Stephanos' neck, nearly having to stand on tiptoe to do so. But she didn't care. She adored his nearness, the feel of his arms around her waist, the warmth of his gentle touch. She reveled in the wonder of this moment, the joy of becoming one with this man the Lord had chosen for her.

Running a hand through Tabitha's lush curls, Stephanos gave her a secret smile, leaning so close his lips brushed against her ear. "*Like a lily among thorns, so is my love among the daughters.*"

Instantly recognizing the quote from Solomon's love-soaked song, Tabitha shivered in delightful anticipation, warmed by her husband's heartfelt praise. Melting into his strong arms, she exulted in the wonder and whimsy of God's incredible plan for husband and wife, the sacred institution called marriage.

CHAPTER 51

Saul of Tarsus

The night was unusually dark, the hour late—far too late to disrupt the rabbi's evening. But that unwelcome fact did little to deter the dark-robed Pharisee as he pounded down a dimly lit chamber, emerging moments later within a large office library. The room appeared somewhat eerie and mystical in the flickering lamplight. Rows upon rows of ancient shelves crammed with records and parchment scrolls indicated the vast importance of the quiet, unassuming chamber.

Glancing up from the documents scattered about his large cedar desk, Gamaliel slowly raised his head, offering the rigid young Pharisee a weary smile. "Saul, my ever-zealous student," he remarked somewhat dryly. "To what may I attribute the pleasure of your company at this late hour?"

"I apologize for the disturbance, Rabbi," Saul conceded gruffly. "But I must speak with you. It is urgent."

Calmly, the venerable *Nasi* folded weathered hands upon his desk, waiting in thoughtful silence.

"You should know that the so-called apostles have disregarded the Sanhedrin's ruling...*yet again*," Saul stated coldly, his confidence waning slightly as a hint of exasperation crept into the eyes of his teacher. "They continue to preach and to heal in the name of their foul Prophet."

"Another healing, then?" Gamaliel mused, thoughtfully stroking his well-kept gray beard. "Of what sort?"

"A leper, sire," Saul conceded, rage coursing through his entire being at the recollection. "The miserable cretin exposed an entire gathering to his disease. But rather than delivering him to the authorities, one of the leaders of that repulsive sect laid hands on him and healed him, rewarding his despicable negligence."

"Thank you for bringing this to my attention," Gamaliel said politely, clearly distracted as he shuffled through his papers. "Though I cannot say I am surprised the apostles carry on."

Saul waited, irritated by Gamaliel's apparent apathy. "And?" he demanded expectantly, leaning as far as he dared over the elder's desk.

Gamaliel studied his impatient student, leaning back in his chair. "You know the Sanhedrin's ruling as well as I."

"But these men have defied your orders!"

"Surely you expected them to do so," Gamaliel pointed out rather blandly.

"Just as I expected the Sanhedrin to punish their dereliction! They have willfully violated a direct command!"

Gamaliel waved aside Saul's heated outburst. "Have I not repeatedly stated that making martyrs of these men will only promote their cause?"

"I disagree," Saul declared vehemently.

Gamaliel was neither offended nor threatened by Saul's aggression. "That is well within your rights," he replied calmly, further raising the young man's ire.

Pausing long enough to compose himself, Saul resumed his agitated pacing before the large cedar desk, reminding Gamaliel of a restless, prowling beast. Turning to face his instructor head-on, he said coldly, "You truly believe this entire movement will crumble like the walls of Jericho if we sit back and do nothing?"

"I do," Gamaliel responded sagely. "*If* it is not Adonai's doing."

"With all due respect, Rabbi, how can you even entertain such a thought? Have you so soon forgotten the reason our order was born?"

"Of course not," Gamaliel supplied, his voice and eyes distant. "Over time, the order of the Pharisees evolved to protect the Law, to preserve it from corruption."

"At any cost," Saul hissed, planting both hands firmly upon the desk as he leaned in. "Our ancestors became passive, compromising the laws of God. They did nothing to obliterate the pagan, worldly influences permeating our nation. As a result, they became tainted with sin and they were punished, taken captive, and scattered among heathen lands! We cannot afford to lower our guard as they did, Rabbi. Not for one moment."

"And you believe the almighty God who parted

the Red Sea and toppled the imposing walls of Jericho needs *our* help making His involvement—or lack thereof—known regarding this movement called the Way?" Gamaliel asked in his easy manner, his sharp eyes observing his pupil's agitated movements.

"Of course not," Saul nearly spat, running an impatient hand over his prayer shawl. "Neither does He command us to stand idle as a blasphemous cult abolishes centuries of sound tradition."

"And if these traditions can be so easily abolished," Gamaliel ventured calmly, "can we truly call them *sound*, dear student?"

Saul could not believe what he was hearing. "Hundreds more have joined this rising sect—just since our last meeting! Do you wish corruption upon our entire nation?"

Dismissing Saul's brazen disrespect, Gamaliel leaned forward in his chair, folding aging hands upon the desk. "Saul, you will recall my parable about the fish."

Forcing himself to draw a calming breath, Saul returned his teacher's earnest gaze. "Your fish analogies are famous throughout Judea and Galilee. How could I forget?"

Reaching for a handy stylus and tapping it thoughtfully upon his desk, Gamaliel's weathered features appeared enigmatic, cast in dancing shadows. "When you studied Torah with me, we discussed several different kinds of students, each of them represented by different types of fish. Now you will remember that we discussed students resembling a *ritually impure fish*—one who studies avidly, one who has memorized all he needs to know, and yet has no understanding. We have also discussed a *ritually pure fish*—represented by a privileged one, one who has learned his lessons and understood them. Even so, he does nothing to incorporate such teachings on a daily, practical basis."

Bored, Saul attempted to feign interest despite his mounting indignation.

"We also have fish teeming in the Jordan River, do we not? I liken them unto a student who has learned everything at his teacher's knee, and yet does not know how to respond—what to *do with it*, if you will. And then there are boundless fish within the borders of the Mediterranean Sea. We will call them the wise fish, the ones who have not only learned everything, but know how to respond to such teachings. Not only do they hear the sacred words, but they also live by them. This, indeed, is a rare kind of fish."

Saul's eyes narrowed, his suspicion mounting. What, exactly, was Gamaliel implying?

"Though we have four vastly different kinds of fish, only one rare type knows what to do with all the fancy learning in his head. Only one knows how to rightly interpret and apply the written Word."

Saul waited, his pulse pounding loudly in his own ears.

"Now I must ask the crucial question," Gamaliel said quietly, his eyes reflecting a deep, aching sadness. "Which fish are you, my zealous student?"

A black rage unlike anything Saul had ever experienced coursed through him, filling his entire body with a burning heat, fanning the flames of his hatred and wrath. It was then that the face of a beautiful woman filled his vision with such shocking clarity he was utterly shaken. In that rage-saturated instant, Saul was mentally transported to another night, another place—to the house of Mary when the believers met to worship their so-called Christ.

He remembered standing at the gate that night. The sneering lout guarding the gate had denied him entrance. But Mary had intervened, shocking everyone—including him.

"Before He returned to Heaven, Jesus told a parable about a dragnet that was cast into the sea," Mary had explained, her mesmerizing gray eyes begging Saul to understand. *"It gathered every kind of fish, and once the net was full, the fishermen took it to shore, sorting the good fish from the bad. While the fishermen kept the good fish, the bad were thrown away."*

Saul had merely sneered at her, amused by her self-righteous preaching. What right had she—an unskilled, uneducated woman—to instruct *him*?

But Mary had plunged ahead, undaunted by his condescending manner. *"Jesus assured us that it will be like that when He returns. We are simply commanded to be fishers of men, all men. It is the Holy Spirit who will perform the work in them, and Christ Himself will sort the good from the bad."*

"What exactly are you implying, my lady?" Saul had taunted her, his tone dripping with deadly venom. *"That I'm a bad fish?"*

"That has yet to be decided," Mary had responded with conviction rather than condemnation. Even so, Saul had despised her with every ounce of his being. *"On Judgment Day, you will stand before God, and He will decide. But until that day comes, I can only pray for you, Saul, welcoming you into our fellow-*

ship with open arms."

On Judgment Day, you will stand before God, and He will decide.

Consumed in the red haze of his own wrath, Saul shook his head vehemently, forcing himself back to the present moment. He was almost startled to find himself still standing before Gamaliel's desk in the quiet study. Annoyed, he saw that his childhood instructor was watching him intently, clearly sensing the young man's inner struggle.

"Saul..." Gamaliel rose, extending a hand to him, almost beseeching him.

Fuming inwardly, Saul ignored the peaceful gesture, turning sharply on his heel. Stealing down the familiar, torchlit corridor by which he had come, he was plagued by dark thoughts, enraged by the apathy of his boyhood idol. For despite Gamaliel's great knowledge, impressive credentials, and esteemed title, the rabbi was becoming an ignorant pacifist, convinced that a growing threat would simply take care of itself. Nearly plowing over a surprised maidservant as he rounded a sharp corner, Saul snarled a stinging rebuke over his shoulder before slipping out a private side door and bursting into the crisp night air.

Drawing a dark cape over his prayer shawl, Saul broke into a steady run, his sandaled feet pounding heavily upon the flagstones below, his heart beating like ancient war drums, fueled by his steadily mounting rage. Unlike his aging mentor, Saul determined not to be counted among those doing absolutely *nothing* to defend the age-old religion his forefathers had lived and died to protect.

Those foolish enough to embrace the Way would

suffer for their insolence. And Mary of Jerusalem would pay for her infidelity, preferably with her life and everything she held dear.

Let's see if your Christ can save you, Saul fumed, pausing, breathless, in the middle of a darkened, empty street. In the distance, the magnificent Temple compound loomed before him on the easternmost edge of the great city, the glorious, gold-crowned structure glistening in the smoldering light of a thousand burning torches. Lured by its beauty, drawn by ages of pride and tradition, a fierce protectiveness welled up within the ruthless Pharisee as he gazed upon the crowning gem of the holy city, rivaling even the most resplendent structures of Imperial Rome.

In that fateful moment, a decision was made that would forever change the course of Saul's life—and the lives of many others. Gazing upon the pride of an entire nation and goaded by malevolent forces he could not possibly comprehend, Saul swore a silent oath to crush the fledgling church, to destroy the witless fools who dared embrace the Way.

I'm going to make an example of you, Mary of Jerusalem—of you and your pathetic band of hapless miscreants. A malefic smile touched the corners of Saul's hardened mouth. *An example this watching world will never, ever forget.*

CHAPTER 52

Mary

Standing at her bedroom window, Mary watched in awe as the flaming sun rose majestically above a sleepy Jerusalem, bathing the marble city in a glorious flood of glistening golden light. Below, early risers set about their day, bustling along broad avenues and cheerfully going about their business. Others remained within dark, shuttered houses, slumbering away the earliest and most crucial hours of the day.

Tugging her shawl a bit closer around her slender shoulders, Mary pondered the obvious lesson buried within the details of daily life. As with the breath-taking ascension of the dawn, Christ's light had been freely bestowed upon all men. Some, like the exuberant pedestrians traversing the paved streets below, embraced the light, having waited anxiously for its appearance. Bathed in the glorious light of the gospel, they determined to utilize the precious gift they had been given, knowing that sunset would inevitably come. Others, like those who remained shuttered within their dark houses, existed in a state of oblivious slumber. They hadn't sought the light, nor did they embrace it upon its glorious arrival.

Mary shivered, drawing her shawl closer still. There was a chill in the air, ushered in by the final wintry month of *Adar*. Even so, the bright and rising sun graciously extended its warm fingers, wrapping Mary in a faint blanket of warm golden rays. Closing her eyes, she basked in the soothing rays, reminded of the great God of creation and His loving provision for mankind.

It is fitting, Mary thought, smiling to herself as her gaze swept across a pastel-colored horizon encircled by a wreath of distance hills. *The final month is now upon us, and a brand-new year shall soon begin.* For so, too, had a wondrous season in her own life drawn to a gentle close. It had been a breathtaking and awe-inspiring time, filled with signs and wonders, power and miracles, finding the Way of life everlasting. Yet somehow, Mary was quite certain that even greater things were yet to be. A new and exciting chapter was about to unfold, not only in her own life, but for the entire body of Christ.

Delighted, Mary stretched forth her hand as a dove lighted upon a branch near her window. Raising eyes toward Heaven, she thanked her righteous Father for the indescribable gift of His precious Holy Spirit. It had pained her, yes, when Christ returned to His Father in Heaven. But Jesus had promised His followers it would be better for Him to do so. When Christ had walked the earth as a man, He had suffered human limitations. Due to human constraints,

Jesus was required to be in one place at one time. But now the Holy Spirit resided within every believer upon the face of the earth. What an unspeakable privilege to know that the blessed Spirit of God resided within oneself!

Wonderful Father, she prayed, lifting her hands in worship. *What marvels You have wrought! You have faithfully grounded this infant church. See how it flourishes upon the solid foundation which You have established—the Rock upon which it was built, faith in Your precious Son! By His sacrifice, we are cleansed and ushered into Your holy presence. How great You are! How merciful!*

Shaking her head in awe, Mary's entire being tingled with joyous anticipation. She could hardly wait to see what God would do next. But until then, she would remain firmly planted in His will, daily walking in obedience, safe beneath the shadow of His wings. God had proven Himself faithful time and time again. And He had a plan for His beloved church, a plan so remarkable, so inconceivable, that Mary knew her finite, human mind could never fully comprehend it. But by His grace, the believers would stand together, united in thought, prayer, and purpose, proclaiming the message of the cross.

Fueled by the power of the Holy Spirit, the church of God had exploded into an unstoppable force, one that would ignite the entire world, setting it ablaze by the power of the gospel of Christ.

True, the enemy rages against us, Mary thought, watching as the dove spread its tiny wings and took flight, soaring across an emerald sky like a beacon of hope for all to see. *And the enemy shall continue to rage against us, knowing he has little time. Even so, the people of God must stand firm.*

Smiling softly, Mary praised Almighty God for the grace He had lavished upon them, for the strength, faith, and patience He had provided to stand against the wiles of the wicked one.

Yes, indeed, Mary thought, excited to embark upon the journey of a brand-new day and soon, a brand-new year. *We belong to You, Lord, regardless of what may come.* With all her heart, Mary knew she could trust an unknown and uncertain future in the hands of a knowing, loving God. And of this, she was absolutely certain—by His grace, God's people would stand firm.

To the very end.

A LOOK AT BOOK FIVE:
SEEKING THE TRUTH

Experience the power and tension of the early church in this compelling tale of faith and conflict.

As Tabitha and Stephanos, still revelling in wedded bliss, navigate an explosive new message of the gospel that is dividing Jerusalem's inhabitants—and forcing everyone to take sides—danger looms further when a fiery implication of repentance and salvation reignites the blazing wrath of religious leaders, including Saul of Tarsus.

Meanwhile, Candace is stunned by the shocking appearance of her long-lost sister, Kelila. And while Candace rejoices in the opportunity to share the love of Christ with Kelila, she can't help but suspect that her sister is harbouring troubling secrets.

Across Jerusalem, Mary faces her own challenges. Persevering against the enemies of the fledgling church—some of which are openly hostile while others are secretly hidden within Mary's own ranks—Mary must remain relentless on her mission to cultivate the growing church and stand firm in the face of adversity and hovering threats of persecution and death.

Seeking the Truth is a breathtaking tale of courageous followers learning to fully trust in Christ amidst mounting fears and personal trials.

AVAILABLE AUGUST 2023

ABOUT THE AUTHOR

Rachael C. Duncan is a passionate follower of Christ. Her goal is to reach as many people as possible for the sake of Christ and His kingdom. She believes that God has gifted each of His children with different gifts to be used to strengthen the body of Christ and fulfill the Great Commission. (Matt. 28:19-20; 1 Cor. 12)

Rachael was blessed to be raised in a strong Christian home, and she accepted Jesus Christ as her Lord and Savior at a very early age. Since then, she has determined to live her life in accordance to His Word and to share the love of Christ through the gift of writing.

Rachael has been passionate about writing since she was a small child. She especially loved writing plays and short stories. At the age of fourteen, she wrote her first play, which was performed as a dinner theatre production by a local school.

She has been actively involved in both women's and children's ministries for over a decade. Currently, she enjoys teaching a weekly girls' Bible study, writing plays for a local homeschool group, and participating in local ministry outreaches for women and children.

Rachael currently resides in Texas with her husband and their first "child"—a playful rescue puppy named Riley! In addition to her writing, she is an enthusiastic "keeper of the home" and "helpmeet" as well as being actively involved in ministering to the women and children God has placed in her life. (Titus 2:3-5; Gen. 2:20-23)